THE MISTRE

'Welcome, once again, to Al
wonder. But be forewarned:
tive writer's fictions are not

A

'Witty, gorgeously written, stuffed with verbal trickeries, metaphor, conceits, sly allusions, sleights of hand and all the verbal feints and counterfeints at the disposal of the writer.'

Elizabeth Buchan, *Metro*

'Alison Fell wields glittering 18th century pastiche prose like a deadly letter-opener in a lady's purse.'

Helen Stevenson, *Independent*

'Stylish and witty . . . generous in its response to Swift's text and the liberties it takes.'

Tom Keymer, *Times Literary Supplement*

'A polemic that puts the treat back in treatise.'

Donny O'Rourke, *The Mix*

'The plot is bursting with eccentric, colourful characters and Swiftian landscapes.'

Sharon Barnes, *Examiner*

'The story is beautifully narrated, its pitting of desire against chauvinism is enthralling.'

Stella Clarke, *Weekend Australian*

'. . . holds up a mirror to the conundrum of women's modern day relationships with men, while casting a long glance backward.'

Barbara Erskine, *Express*

THE PILLOW BOY OF THE LADY ONOGORO

'It is rare to come across a book that offers quite so many pleasures, all very different . . . which in its own eloquence makes its point with wisdom, wit and a charming lightness of touch.'   Mary Scott, *New Statesman*

'. . . a clever concubine who certainly isn't going to take the men's rules lying down.'   Gill Pyrah, *Cosmopolitan*

'. . . a great pleasure to read, a postmodern take on a pre-modern culture in which past and present, verse and prose, fuse into a harmonious whole.'
                Gregory Feeley, *Philadelphia Inquirer*

'Alison Fell invests an age-old subject with both contemporary relevance and wit.'   Susannah Frankel

'The book's eroticism is re-enforced by its underlying hu-mour.'   *The Big Issue*

'Fell is a poet, and this novel is enriched by her feeling for resonant images.'   Lucy Hughes-Hallett, *Sunday Times*

'The Pillow Boy is a book for true romantics and the content is, of course, sexually explicit but written with impeccable good taste.'   June Campbell

'A paean to the seeking and intertwining of textual and sexual pleasures.'   Aamer Hussein, *Literary Review*

'Not for the coy.'   Lisa Clarke, *The Punter*

'. . . sinuous grace, mixing feminism with unforgettable adult fairy tales.'   *She*

'. . . lascivious, poetic prose . . .'   Everywoman

'She has the touch of a butterfly.'
                Anne Woolfe, *Literary Review*

TRICKS OF THE LIGHT

'The descriptions of grief and trauma are real and beautifully expressed.'   *Good Housekeeping*

'. . . a fantastic achievement – beautifully written, painful to read, but utterly convincing in its defiant portrait of love triumphing overdeath.'   Andy Croft, *Morning Star*

DREAMS, LIKE HERETICS

'These are poems painted, as it were, with a brave palette. Their promise lies in that they are beyond description; gorgeous illuminations of private moments of love and fear.'
Kathleen Jamie, *Scotsman*

'Remarkable for its unashamed passion and literary power.'
Michele Roberts, *Independent on Sunday*

MER DE GLACE

Three times now I've read this book, and each time I have found in it more and more that matters.'
Sheila Harrison, *Alpine Journal*

'A brave, intelligent novel.'   Jenifer Shute, *Boston Weekly*

'. . . elusively beautiful and haunting . . . about climbing mountains, writing and being in love.'
Zoë Fairbairns, *Everywoman*

'. . . acute perception, a well-paced story rich in symbol, image and natural detail.'
Dermot Sommers, *Climbers Club Journal*

Alison Fell is a Scottish writer who lives in London. Her poetry collection *Kisses for Mayakovsky* was winner of the Alice Hunt Bartlett Award, and her alpine novel *Mer de Glace* won the Boardman Tasker Memorial Award. Her novel *The Mistress of Lilliput* won unanimous acclaim, and with her picaresque novel *The Pillow Boy of the Lady Onogoro* has been translated into many languages. She has been a Writing Fellow at the University of East Anglia, and a Royal Literary Fund Writing Fellow at University College, London and The Courtauld Institute. She is currently Senior Teaching Fellow on the MA Creative Writing Programme at Southampton University. *The Element -inth in Greek* is her eighth novel.

the
element
-inth in Greek

ALISON FELL

SANDSTONEPRESS
HIGHLAND | SCOTLAND

First published in Great Britain by
Sandstone Press Ltd
PO Box 5725
One High Street
Dingwall
Ross-shire
IV15 9WJ
Scotland.

www.sandstonepress.com

The publisher acknowledges subsidy from
Creative Scotland towards publication of this volume.

ISBN: 978-1-908737-02-1
ISBN e: 978-1-908737-03-8

Cover design by River Design, Edinburgh.
Typeset by Iolaire Typesetting, Newtonmore.
Printed and bound by TOTEM, Poland..

For the archivists

Acknowledgements

I'm very grateful to the Arts and Humanities Research.Council for awarding me the three year Research Fellowship which funded all the research for this book, and most of the writing, and to Middlesex University for hosting the Fellowship. My thanks also go to the Royal Literary Fund for financial assistance.

I'd also like to express my gratitude to Tom Palaima, Professor of Classics at the University of Texas, Austin, for his generosity in sharing all the Kober materials in the PASP archive, and to Sue Trombley, for showing me Alice Kober's "cigarette carton" files of Linear B signs. Thanks also to Sue Sherratt of the Department of Antiquities at the Ashmolean Museum, and to Patricia Graf, great-niece of Alice Kober, for doing everything she could to further my research. Sanna Aro-Valjus of Abo University, Finland, generously sent me the correspondence she'd unearthed between Kober and Johannes Sundwall, and also translated some of the Kober letters which were written in a rather archaic German.

I'd also like to acknowledge the assistance given by the University of Pennsylvania Museum, the Guggenheim Foundation, the American School of Classical Studies at Athens, Brooklyn College, Hunter College, the Linguistic Society of America, and the North East Region Federal Archive, NYC.

Tony Delamothe of the British Medical Journal supplied a fund of information about forensic matters, and geneticist Anoushka Dave was unfailingly patient in trying to convey the basics of her field. Thanks also go to Vicky Evdokias, for additional information about the Greek police force, and to Warrant Officer Evagelos Garganourakis of the Heraklion Tourist Police, who also assured me that no police officer by the name of Yiannis Stephanoudakis was currently serving in Crete.

No.	Sign	Value	No.	Sign	Value	No.	Sign	Value
01		da	30		ni	59		ta
02		ro	31		sa	60		ru
03		pa	32		qo	61		o
04		te	33		ra_3	62		pte
05		to	34			63		
06		na	35			64		
07		di	36		jo	65		ju
08		a	37		ti	66		ta_2
09		se	38		e	67		ki
10		u	39		pi	68		ro_2
11		po	40		wi	69		tu
12		so	41		si	70		ko
13		me	42		wo	71		dwe
14		do	43		ai	72		pe
15		mo	44		ke	73		mi
16		pa_2	45		de	74		ze
17		za	46		je	75		we
18			47			76		ra_2
19			48		nwa	77		ka
20		zo	49			78		qe
21		qi	50		pu	79		zu
22			51		du	80		ma
23		mu	52		no	81		ku
24		ne	53		ri	82		
25		a_2	54		wa	83		
26		ru	55		nu	84		
27		re	56		pa_3	85		
28		i	57		ja	86		
29		pu_2	58		su	87		

Chart of eighty-seven Linear B signs, with numerical
equivalents and phonetic values.

1

In Oxford's Ashmolean Museum there is a portrait of Sir Arthur Evans, the discoverer – or, some cynics might say, the inventor – of the Minoan civilisation of ancient Crete. The portrait is dated 1906, and shows Evans tieless, in a floating white shirt and a baggy linen suit with an orchid in the buttonhole. Cupped in his hand is a small clay tablet, visibly scratched with the characters of the script he had discovered at the site of Knossos, and had named Linear Class B. Although his expression is modest, even inward-looking, the artist has posed Evans in front of a palace fresco, throned him, in effect, as though he were King Minos himself.

Evans had coined the term Linear B to distinguish the script – dated from about 1450 BCE – from similar-looking but distinct characters found on archaeologically older tablets which had been excavated at Phaestos in the south of the island. This Linear Class A script, dated from 1750 BCE, also appeared on devotional objects, such as libation vases and stone altar tables. To an even earlier, pictographic script, dated from 2100 BCE and chiefly engraved on seal-stones, Evans gave the name Cretan Hieroglyphic. He was to spend the next 35 years of his life trying to decipher the unknown inscriptions.

At his death in 1941, Evans left the drawings, sign-lists and photographs of the inscriptions in the care of his colleague Sir John Myres, Emeritus Professor of Ancient History at Oxford, charging him with the task of organising and publishing the material in a comprehensive editio princeps. Of around 3000 inscriptions – many of which had been drawn from autopsy, often poorly, by Evans himself, and never checked by other trained eyes – only some 300 had been published. Sir John Myres was hardly an epigrapher; he was also a man in his 70s, of uncertain health. The task Evans had bequeathed to him was a gargantuan one.

The Myres archive is housed in a small study-room in the basement of the Department of Antiquities, tucked away behind the glass cases which contain the Minoan collections – the ceramic snake-goddesses and bull-vaulting acrobats uncovered by Evans in his excavations of the so-called Palace of Minos site at Knossos. Hidden among the shelves of files that line the walls of the archive, a single dusty box-file contains the letters Myres received from Alice Elizabeth Kober, lowly Classics lecturer at Brooklyn College, New York. Letters full of longing.

In 1906, the same year that the portrait of Sir Arthur Evans was painted, Alice Kober was born in Manhattan to poor Hungarian immigrants. She attended Hunter College High School, and graduated with honours from Hunter College in 1928. She took her PhD at Columbia while teaching at Hunter College, and in 1932 joined the Classics faculty of the newly-opened Brooklyn College. On graduating, her tutor recalled, Kober had announced confidently that the unsolved mystery of Minoan writing was to be her life's work, and the publication in 1935 of some of the first Linear B texts – in Evans' Palace of Minos Vol IV – must have further galvanised her energies, for thereafter she devoted her research time entirely to the enigmatic scripts.

Previous attempts at decipherment Kober dismissed – often scathingly – as unscientific in method and fantastical in result. Logic, simplicity, and the demonstration of proof – those were the signposts Kober believed would lead the way to a secure decipherment.

'Even a tentative phonetic pattern,' *she wrote to Myres,* 'based on internal evidence – not on guesswork, or the supposition that I was a Minoan in another incarnation, or have a spirit-guide who speaks Minoan – will help.'

And so – systematically, and with a single-mindedness that the 21st century reader may find hard to credit – Kober set about the studies she believed would best equip her for the task. The list is exhaustive, not to say exhausting. Although she was already teaching a back-breaking timetable of Classics courses at Brooklyn College, Kober knuckled down to the study of Chemistry, Physics and Astronomy, for their scientific method, and Mathematics for its use in statistics. She tackled Field Archaeology in New Mexico in 1936, and in 1939 at the American School of Classical Studies in Athens. She studied advanced Sanskrit at Yale, travelling weekly to New Haven for the purpose; meanwhile, at the Linguistic Institute, she was taking courses in Hittite, Old Persian, Tocharian, Old Irish, Semitic grammar, Sumerian, Chinese and Basque. Her object in doing so was to familiarise herself with the structure of as many unrelated languages as possible, in the hope that light might thereby be thrown on the interpretation of Minoan.

In December 1946, in a clear sloping hand, on super-thin post-war paper, Kober wrote to Sir John Myres:

'I must confess, strong as the statement sounds, that I would gladly go to the ends of the earth if there were a chance of seeing a new Linear Class B inscription when I got there.'

The irony is, however, that there was material closer at hand. In 1939 Carl Blegen had uncovered the first Linear B tablets to be found outside Crete, at Pylos on the Greek mainland. Once documented, the tablets were hidden in a bank vault in Athens to wait out the war. In the summer of 1940 Alison Frantz's photographs of the inscriptions were smuggled out of Greece on the last American ship to leave the Mediterranean, and were deposited at the University of Cincinatti, where Blegen was a Professor. In 1946, on hearing that she had received a Guggenheim Fellowship, Alice Kober had written immediately to Carl Blegen, asking to be allowed to study the unpublished scripts. Professor Blegen, however, replied that 'It would be impossible to grant such permission.'

One might be forgiven for wanting to know why. The excavator of the Palace of Nestor at Pylos was an archae-ological superstar; by comparison, Kober was a mere upstart.

Blegen's response is perhaps a measure of the rivalry and protectionism that prevailed among scholars in the epigraphy field at the time.

If American generosity had failed Kober on this occasion, British generosity did not. By return of post Myres assured her that he would be glad to help in any way, and invited her to come to Oxford at the earliest opportunity to see the inscriptions for herself. After Blegen's curt refusal, it was an offer she had not allowed herself to expect, and one that she could not refuse.

Clearly the concept of leisure did not rank too highly in Alice Kober's scheme of things. In March 1947, about to embark at last on the longed-for trip to England, she wrote excitedly to Myres that the seven day voyage 'should give me just about enough time to grasp the basics of Egyptian'.

No deck quoits for Kober, then – no poolside tanning or cocktails at the Captain's table. Her remark was apparently made in all earnestness, and while one has to admire such selfless dedication to the task at hand, with hindsight what is poignant is the glimpse it affords us of a young woman who was to sacrifice everything – marriage, children, personal life, even, in the end, her health and strength – to the pursuit of an intellectual goal.

4

2

The cool hours before the sun strikes her bedroom window are usually the most productive. Around 10.00am, bleary-eyed from the laptop screen, reading-glasses still dangling from the cord around her neck, Ingrid smokes on the balcony, watching the slow stirring of the village below.

Beyond a patch of waste-ground where chickens scratch among melon-flowers, a scattering of stark white houses follows the shoreline. The sea is morning-perfect, smooth as cut butter. In its supple newness, millenia melt away.

She remembers a classroom, dust in the air, chalked symbols on the blackboard. Miss MacMillan, her skirt nipped at the waist by an elastic belt with a snake clasp, her hair held back from her forehead by two tortoiseshell combs. Her back was straight, her neck long, her shoulders hieratic.

C. A. T.

The symbols frightened her, because they were mysterious, and she wasn't the sort of child who liked mysteries. Up till then she'd been a good girl, a clever girl, always the first to provide the right answer. Miss MacMillan was her goddess; she ached with the need to please her.

Miss MacMillan stood by the blackboard, tapping the signs with her pointer. Sounds came from her pretty mouth. Separate sounds that meant nothing, with chasms in between.

Kuh, which was as threatening as a kick.

Aah, which was what her father made her do when he shone a light down her throat.

Tuh, like the tsk sound at the start of a scolding.

Miss MacMillan tapped the letters again, more quickly

5

now, so that the three sounds got closer together, the darkness between them decreasing.

Kuh- Aah -Tuh. She appealed to the class, her eyebrows raised in expectation.

And then, quite suddenly, like the sun, an animal entered the room, graceful, four-footed, and entire. A split second passed before she realised that it wasn't an actual animal, that it didn't purr or wind its tail round Miss MacMillan's nyloned ankles. Instead, it was a phantom thing, an idea of itself that walked only in her mind.

She remembers the moment as if it were yesterday. The bright pall of chalk-dust hanging in a sunbeam. The synthesis – its shocking, spacious delight.

Philology: how sound falls in love with script. But if you didn't know what sounds the script stood for, let alone what language it represented? The thought dizzies her – although clearly it hadn't dizzied Alice Elizabeth Kober.

It's late already – late for Ingrid, that is, if not for the other, bona fide holidaymakers. In the kitchen – cramped, basic, like the rest of the one-bed apartment – she organises breakfast and carries it back out to the balcony. Greek yoghurt and grapes, topped with the strong dark honey you can buy downstairs in the Minimarket, with branches of thyme suspended in the jar.

Tomorrow, Knossos. The pursuit of the prehistoric. The pilgrimage Alice Kober never made, the one Ingrid must make for her, lending the dead her living eyes. A daunting responsibility, all the more so because she knows her gaze can never measure up to Alice's – in terms of clarity, of sheer pig-headed purpose.

Hard to imagine Alice time-wasting, for instance, dawdling on a balcony, gaping at the sea and the sky. Not to mention licking honey off a spoon – honey she can't help noticing is the exact colour of sun through eyelids – and wondering what could be done with it, in a culinary sense. How you could drizzle it over the kind of eye-wateringly powerful *cassis* sorbet she and

Tim had eaten on that holiday in the Luberon. Or make a honey ice-cream, perhaps, flavour it with cardamom. Serve it with a *coulis* of blackcurrants – for there always has to be a third term, something bitter and dark to offset the sweetness. (One thing she's never been able to comprehend is how Greek cooks manage not only to ruin the perfectly good produce available to them, but also to ignore that crucial chthonic third.)

Focussing her intelligence on the tip of her tongue, she lets it rest there for a moment before traversing the lateral buds. Contrasts, colourations, comparisons. The exercise a kind of stratagem, perhaps – a sneaky way of marking herself off from Alice. Alice the bluestocking. Alice of the 'frigid logic', as Michael Ventris had scathingly put it.

Poor Alice, dead at 43, while Ingrid, at the same age, is very much alive.

History has neglected Alice, and Ingrid's intention is to bring her, belatedly, into the public eye, to take up the cudgels for her and settle the scores. Ingrid knows where her loyalties lie, or at least where they ought to lie. And however brief her life had been, Kober's achievements certainly merited a solid biography, let alone a monograph that even now – thanks to a predictable fit of jitters at the publishers – threatens to end up as a mere essay in an edited collection.

Women in Archaeology, shrunk to fit. *Plus ça change*, thinks Ingrid.

On her first student trip to Athens, she had fallen in love, not only with the brilliant white marble of the Parthenon, but also with the entire building-site of the city, where every park and yard was littered with fragments of pediments, metopes, fluted columns. Shards of alabaster, transparent as the rim of an ear. She had to stop herself bending down every few minutes to squirrel another specimen into her rucksack.

For those magpie habits she supposes she had her father to thank. Her tall, stooped father, who was not nimble, who had, perhaps, never been young. The amateur geologist with his hammer and hand-lens and haversack. Supporting himself

7

on his walking-stick, he'd follow doggedly behind as Ingrid scrambled up gullies and pounced on likely-looking outcrops. Sunday walks were field-trips on which they chipped, sized and sampled: Cairngorm granite, oolite, spangled schist. It was the white deposits Ingrid prized above all others – the calcites, rock crystal, pearly gypsum. Even in dark weather their lustre caught and held the light.

Although nothing had ever been said, she sensed that her father was as relieved as she was to escape from the squat sandstone house where her mother drank gin *sans* tonic behind white net curtains. There was a brass nameplate on the gatepost: *Dr. W.A. Laurie M.D. F.C.R.S.*, and a steep gravel drive up which patients dragged their feet to the twice-daily surgeries.

While other girls at school collected Barbie dolls or Banarama records, her own bedroom shelves were crammed with labelled finds. Black basalt, garnets, the rare green-veined marble of Glentilt. She remembers these as happy times – tomboy days, when she still glittered like quartz in her father's eye. Until puberty came along, as puberty will, and shattered the cosy sense of conspiracy.

Whenever she tries to trace the events of adolescence in any ordered way, she draws a blank. What she does remember is the onset of strategic thinking. How hard she tried to conceal every cut or bruise or bellyache, in order to avoid her father's surgery with its chilly stethoscope, its atmosphere of pained distaste.

Wherever Thor's hammer strikes the ground, no plants grow.

Witness the bare earth under the holly-tree, or was it the hawthorn? She can't remember now – the Norse legends belong to a substratum of childhood, long since overlaid by the myths of Classical Greece.

Down below, Panomeli is waking. First Demosthenes emerges from his garden gate and flip-flops across the road to open up the Minimarket. Then Androula the keeper of sunbeds limps shorewards in shoes that have outgrown her, stopping now and again to wait for the little boy who toddles in her wake. The sunbeds overnight under a bamboo shelter on the narrow strip of beach. Every morning old Androula sets them out in pairs, one umbrella to each pair, with difficulty.

The Minimarket bears the Union Jack marque of the tour company. A small storeroom annexe doubles as the Flagstaff office, where you can meet the Rep. between the hours of 12 and 2, should you wish to sign up for an over-priced excursion, borrow a book from the shelf of dog-eared Stephen Kings and Danielle Steels, or even, for a small fee, access your email.

Snobbishness aside, the package holiday has obvious advantages for the anxious traveller. Flights, transfers, accommodation are all taken care of. That much shepherding she can handle, if it staves off the capricious travel gods of Greece.

To the west, hidden from view by an olive-clad headland, the holiday apartments of Katomeli – which boasts a 2 kilometre stretch of imported sand, disco-bars, and a new strip of coast road down which shuttle-buses sizzle from the airport – wear the logos of Dutch, German and Italian operators. Here in the old village of Panomeli, however, England claims the monopoly, and middle-aged England at that. Cheerful, irreproachable couples from Manchester and Middlesborough, with the sole exception of the honeymooners in the apartment above hers.

The Wilson-Wilsons are an oddly symbiotic pair in their mid-twenties, with skin as white as candle-wax. She assumes they're newlyweds only because a small scree of confetti, missed by the maid's broom, lurks on the bottom tread of the shared outside staircase.

On the beach they squeeze oh so strictly under the shade of their sun-umbrella, yet somehow manage not to touch one another. A prohibition which – judging by the marked absence, overhead, of voluptuary noises – extends to the hours of the night.

Yesterday the Wilson-Wilson boy had staged a rebellion. Humping his lilo out of the shade of the connubial umbrella, he placed it decisively a few metres away, in the full glare of the sun. And there he lay, face down, scowling out across the bay. The erotic voltage humming from him. Sunglasses or not, you could tell that the whole beach was staring. Even middle-aged England knew what it means when a young man lies face down on a lilo, sulking at the sea.

She remembers a summer day in Dunelg, the air full of dandelion clocks and the white seed-fluff of rose-bay willow-herb.She'd come up from the Firth in her new red bathing suit, 13 or 14 maybe – a perfect scallop shell clutched in her fist, and so full of herself there was no rule on earth that could hem her in. Slithering through the gap in the hawthorn hedge, she crossed the hot tarmac of the road and crunched up the gravel drive.

The waiting room was at the front of the house, in what had originally been the dining room, and adjoined the new Surgery extension at the side. There were hard upright chairs, a trolley which held out of date copies of the *Scottish Field*, and a vase of flowers on the mantelpiece when her mother remembered. In the corner near the Surgery door, a grandfather clock ticked away the meek, echoey minutes.

There was a dragging feeling at the bottom of her stomach which made her badly want the lavatory. It was forbidden to use the front door in Surgery hours, but if she just scooted straight through the hall and up the stairs surely no one was going to notice.

In the front porch stood a brass stand for her father's walking-sticks, where patients could leave their umbrellas on rainy days. Her hair, still soaking wet, shed drips across the tiled floor.

The door of the waiting room was usually kept closed. Too late she saw that someone, presumably because of the heat, had propped it open

Her father was standing at the door of the Surgery, holding it open to see out old Mrs. Michie and her walking-frame. It was the look he gave Ingrid over his glasses that made the waiting patients draw in their breaths.

'Mr. Duff, please,' he said, after an icy pause.

She clutched the rolled-up towel to her chest, understanding how the sight of her hurt his eyes, also that she'd known all along, but had somehow managed to forget, just how much it would provoke him. She'd fled up the stairs then, locked herself in the toilet, and when she wiped between her legs there was blood, like a blight on her.

He father had grounded her for a week. Not that he'd actually locked her in her room; it was Ingrid herself who'd done that.

At one point she heard quarrelling downstairs, she heard the word *hormones*. Her mother came wheedling at the door, but Ingrid didn't reply. Twice daily, trays were deposited on the landing, and removed hours later, untouched. For several days she refused to eat a thing – a feat which strikes her now as fairly impressive. It was enough to sit cross-legged on the bed, cutting off hanks of hair with her penknife. The handle was mother-of-pearl, translucent and smooth to the touch. Crazy Ingrid, holding the blade of the knife to the pale inside of her forearm, stroking it against her skin.

As the room subsided into stillness, resistance solidified in her mind. True power lay in negation: from their shelves the stones in their dead weight agreed with her.

On the balcony railing her bathing suit has dried overnight. As she steps into the one-piece she remembers the tautness of the trunks across the Wilson-Wilson boy's buttocks, and how his girl-bride simply turned her back on him, blotting out his anger, his desire. After a silence which, in her memory at least, lasted a good hour, the girl laid her Harry Potter aside, donned a sarong, and sauntered off along the beach towards the Totem Bar. When she returned ten minutes later, eating a pink ice-cream shaped like a torpedo, the face he turned on her was thunderous, the hurt too plain now to be even faintly amusing.

'What about me, then?' he demanded, in a voice loud

enough for everyone to hear, but his young wife merely shrugged, throwing him a vindictive little smile.

Ingrid had the impression that the whole beach was quietly, collectively, seething. Not that anyone said a word, of course. Like good Brits, they just went on minding their own business.

She parks her breakfast bowl in the sink, stashes her laptop in the bottom of the wardrobe, and stuffs her beach-towel, Alice Kober file, and Hutchinson's *Prehistoric Crete* into her tote bag.

But still, she thinks: a single solitary ice-cream. And she didn't even offer him a lick.

3

Where the cobbled street peters into sand-strewn concrete and meets the beach-track, an old rabbit-hutch has been wedged in the cornerstones of the wall. Every morning Androula brings produce to display behind the wire-netting door: a few aubergines, potatoes, fresh eggs in a white tin bowl. The prices – approximate, for there are no weighing scales – are scrawled in felt-tip on a piece of cardboard. For money there is a cracked cup, used infrequently, since the English visitors prefer the unambiguous labels of the Mini-market, or the glossy greengroceries of Katomeli. And those who do stop to look, and occasionally to buy – the woman in the red bathing suit being a case in point – are so afraid of appearing dishonest that they pay double or triple the price. This evokes in Androula a certain amount of scorn, as well as a suspicion that this prodigality masks a guilty urge to grab her goods and pay her nothing.

From the hayfield above the beach Androula keeps an eye on the new arrivals while she gathers *horta* for Asterios' lunch. Today she'll make *hortopitta* with green beans, mash potatoes and garlic together for a *skordalia*. And there is slicing sausage in the refrigerator, some fresh peaches.

On the lower sector of the slope the hay has been cut, and at the top the gradient rises steeply to meet the terrace wall of the Shoestring Bar, but at the mid-level the grass is long and full of sweet peppermint, poppies, and the succulent wild leaves of the *horta*. From the Bar come smells of baking lamb and the intermittent throb of music, not Greek but English, American. Spiraki, who has been helping her to harvest the greens, is hot and bored now, wanting ice-cream, swiping at butterflies.

Leaning on her stick, Androula bends to pull another handful. The sun beats down on her back, heavy as the curses she once measured her beauty by. *Kathara mou* from the women passing her in the street, their eyes on her legs, her breasts, her rope of shining hair. *Kathara mou, My curse on you for all eternity.* And her heart would swell with pride while her hips, oiled by the women's envy, would swing the more provocatively.

When she straightens up the heat drums in her right ear, signalling the pressure in her blood. The woman in the red bathing suit is swimming out beyond the other bathers. Her overarm stroke is easy and lazy; on every fourth stroke her wet head surfaces and her invisible mouth drinks in the air. Under the surface her feet kick a milky wake across the turquoise sea. The Sheely Valentai. This is what they call them now, these women without family, belonging to no one. Women with dyed hair who wear the bright revealing clothes of the young. Women who come to Greece to look for men.

This morning the Sheely Valentai was late. For once she did not have her money ready when Androula did her rounds of the sunbeds. Instead she lay flat out, sunbathing bare-breasted as they all did, and when Androula's shadow fell across her she covered herself quickly with a towel and sat up to rummage in her beach bag for her purse. Unable to distinguish the denominations of the notes, she removed her sunglasses, and for the first time Androula saw her eyes: pale grey like moonstone, made brilliant by a thin black rim around the iris. *Ftou ftou ftou,* she said to herself, to ward off the dangerous gaze. In her mind she made the sign of the cross before the ikon in the parlour alcove, the one she mists thrice daily with holy water. *Panayitsa mou*, deliver us from evil. Conjuring up the comforting grape-dark of the Panayia's eyes.

'*Oriste*' said the Sheely Valentai at last, plucking out a 5 euro note and handing it over. From the shelter of Androula's skirts Spiraki peered out, wide-eyed.

'*Bos te lene?*' the woman asked him in her foreign accent, with her foreign smile.

The *mikraki* cringed back, glancing up fearfully at Androula. '*Yia yia?*' he whimpered.

'*Po po po!*' she'd scolded, even though he was trembling, tears welling up in his eyes, because a child must learn to be respectful towards his elders.

Distracted by the memory, Androula throws the last handful of leaves into the basket and wipes her forehead with her scarf. She thinks of the little *lexico* that lay beside the woman's sunbed, worming its way ever deeper into the fine white sand. The Greek words at the top of the cover and the English ones lower down, already half-submerged. Had the Sheely Valentai understood *yia yia*? She had given no sign of it, lounging there splay-legged with her boyish muscles and her salt-snarled hair. And if she did understand, thinks Androula in a moment of defiance, she had only herself to blame. Up close anyone could see she was no spring chicken, so what did she expect a little one to think?

From the terrace above comes the clink of glasses, a fusillade of foreign laughter. Spiraki is picking poppies without his sunhat, which lolls on the ground near Androula's feet. When she calls to him he toddles towards her through the long grass, holding the flowers above his head.

Androula is enchanted. 'For me?' She claps the sunhat on his head and straightens the brim. '*Panapounes?* For your *Thitsa* Droula?' She flirts her hand out to receive the bouquet.

'*Ochi!*' Spiraki grasps the stems tightly, withholding the flowers. His bottom lip juts. His eyes flicker towards the beach, where the woman is emerging from the sea, wading thigh-deep through the shallows. The poppies are that most brilliant of reds, like wet silk, redder even than the bathing suit.

'*Yia yia!*' he accuses, hurling the flowers away from him.

They scatter across the heads of the high grass and hang there limply by their stems. He gives Androula a wicked, testing look.

'*Ela, mikraki mou!*' she tuts, shaking her head at him, for who can divine the mind of a child. 'Come, *Thitsa* Droula will get you an ice-cream.'

'*Yia yia!*' he roars, triumphant now, thrashing at the poppies with his little fists, beating them down.

4

A youth, brown hair, 1 metre 80. At first Yiannis had assumed he was North African, because of the skin tone, until the pathologist established that the discolouration was a result of the manner of death.

He lay under an olive tree with his arms stretched above his head, as if trying to embrace the trunk. It was, Yiannis thought as he approached, an attitude of abandon. A man asleep after coitus – or rather, a boy. A fat boy at that. When he and Christos came closer neither looked at the other but both had seen. The erection, the size of the glans. This before they registered the stillness.

From the undergrowth came the lazy buzzing of a bee. There was a scent of peppermint flowers and also of some-thing else, something not death or decay, but sweeter. A whiff of the pastry-shop. As if the youth had been stuffing his face in the *zacharoplasteion*.

Although Yiannis had seen enough of death to know that he would not find a pulse, he laid the back of his fingers briefly against the exposed throat. His fingers came away sticky. He saw then that the body was not fat at all, but grossly swollen. The honey seemed to ooze from every pore. Behind him Christos let out a high hee-hawing laugh.

'Like a fucking baklava, sir!'

Christos was only 20, from Thessaloniki, seconded to the island for the lager-lout season. Yiannis radioed headquarters, turning away while the rookie vomited into the peppermint flowers.

What appeared to be small black olives, fallen prematurely, littered the ground around the body. Then one of them quivered and crawled. A queasy sweat broke out on Yiannis's brow. He saw the puncture-marks, in hundreds. He jumped up and stamped his boot down hard on the fugitive insect.

Bees, for Christ's sake. They were fucking bees.

He told Christos to make a preliminary search of the area while they waited for the ambulance. Somewhere there would be clothing. Bathing trunks at least, or a towel, wallet, cellphone.

He wiped his fingers on a handkerchief and, retreating to a safe distance, hunkered down on a tree-stump to smoke. On the yellow earth ants ran to and fro, telegraphing one another, fanning out excitedly around his feet. Soon the fan would form itself into a column which would advance in disciplined fashion on the honeyed corpse. Yiannis flicked his lighter and held the flame to the bum of a glossy big general. He watched the back legs shrivel. His hand was shaking.

Christos was blundering about in the undergrowth, cursing at nettles. The sea was invisible through the dense mass of trees but Yiannis, hearing the disco blare of a boat, forced himself to picture it: a tall tiered castle packed with Aussies and beercans, hugging the coast, leaking music and detritus.

Christos emerged from the undergrowth, zipping up his fly. 'Can't see a thing, sir. So do we know whose land it is?' At the corner of his mouth a spot of sick clung to an incipient moustache. Yiannis looked at it with distaste.

'Stavlakis. Old boy, lives up top, by Agia Stephanou.'

The trees were ill-kept, and on the north-facing slope the olives were small and poor. Here and there rotting nets lay in snarls. The terrace walls, washed down by winter rains into yellow gullies, had been left unrepaired, for Stavlakis was alone now, his sons and daughters emigrants to London, Munich, Melbourne.

The alarm had been raised not by the old boy but by an English couple hiking round the headland, who had run back to the Totem Bar to telephone. The Harknesses. When Yiannis got there they were flushed with sunburn and fright, the husband gulping down a Metaxa at 9.30 in the morning. White strap-marks criss-crossed the woman's red shoulders. A busty Rep. from Flagstaff strove to instil calm, dipping napkins into ice water and applying them to the back of the woman's neck. Her name, he remembered, was Lynda. The look she'd turned on him both begged and blamed. This he'd found unfair, if understandable. Horrors happened which even with the best will in the world the police could not prevent, but it didn't take a Socrates to work out that this kind of incident could scupper a whole season.

When he looked at his watch he was surprised to see how little time had passed since then. It was as if death's stillness had acted contrarily on him, accelerating the inner clockwork of his hours. In the corner of his eye the corpse in shadow was a windfall, a swollen plum. Tapping a brusque finger to his upper lip, he pointed at Christos. '*Elaré, pedaki-mou.* Clean yourself up before Forensics get here.'

'Time of death, between 4 and 6am.' The doctor's tone nursed some age-old Homeric grudge. 'Approximately,' he snapped, as if Yiannis really needed to be told. Yiannis was reminded of the day he'd arrived back in Greece, ten years ago now. In the Immigration queue, his head stunned into emptiness by the long white hours of the flight, he'd wondered what on earth the Passport Officials were scowling at. Then he realised that this confusion was a measure of just how long he'd been away – long enough to forget that, in the mindset of the Greek male, a smile signified weakness, submission. The male face was supposed to impress, to impose its authority, not to charm.

So it was dawn, thought Yiannis: the dew-damp dawn of summer. A perfect hour. People could have been about. *Yia yias* struggling up the hill to the church. Service workers heading for the hotels of Katomeli. Bakers, midwives, squid-fishers pottering about on the crystal sea.

The scene had been photographed and taped off, pending a more thorough examination. The paramedics had zipped the sheeted body into a bag and stretchered it down the slope and along the beach-front track to the ambulance, which was parked outside the Totem Bar.

The *Iatrodikastis* had stripped off his white jumpsuit and bundled it into the boot of his car; now he crouched by the standpipe outside the Bar, splashing water over his face and hands, cursing at the heat. Water ran down his bare arms and puddled in the sunlit road.

Yiannis fetched two cans of Pepsi from the cold cabinet inside the Bar and handed one to Christos. On the terrace Aphrodite – a good three dress sizes up from the original, but otherwise not entirely misnamed, in his opinion – and her sister Fotini, who had been pretending to wipe down the tables, hovered mutely. Little Fotini had crumpled a corner of her apron across her mouth; while her big sister was simply, hugely, staring.

He held the cold metal can against his cheek, thinking of the stickiness of the honey, the way the stains had seeped darkly through the sheet. For the moment the fat boy's body was hidden, and sweltered in the heat like the rest of them, but not, he knew, for long; soon it would rest in the enviable cool of the Mortuary.

He told Christos to drive them back to the station, to take the lad's mind off the item in the ambulance. They bumped along the rutted road behind it, in a silent, anti-climactic procession: lights, yes, but it was a damn sight too late for sirens. There were maize-fields on either side of the road, olive groves; laundry airing on the vine-shaded terraces of smallholdings. The Pantelides' donkey, untethered from its ethnic tourist cart, munched on thistles in their yard.

Just then old Asterios came roaring round the corner on his *papaki*, his gnarled brown knees jutting at a reckless angle. A cockerel that had been manning the roadside leapt for cover. Asterios still kept his newspaper kiosk in Katomeli's main square, but at his age, four top-speed commutes a day was surely pushing it. He waved to Yiannis and wobbled, swerving into the middle of the road.

For a second memory plied its shrieking brake in Yiannis' stomach, as the old man corrected, missing them by a whisker. So close, you could almost smell the ouzo on his breath.

'*Ai gamisou!*' Yiannis turned to shake his fist at the wake of dust. 'He'll prang that thing one day. We'll be scraping him off an olive tree!'

'Bit of a *mangas*, eh?' Again Christos unleashed his pent-up dismaying laugh. His eyes were shocked and bright.

Yiannis patted his top pocket for cigarettes and went to shake one out for Christos. He found himself looking at an empty packet he'd picked up near the bottom of the path. He'd been on automatic by then, clocking it less as evidence, more as careless loutish litter. Davidoffs. The ads were everywhere these days. *The More You Know.* A ladies' sort of smoke, upmarket from Assos, but that wasn't saying much. He placed the packet carefully in the glove compartment.

The ambulance picked up speed on the coast road, heading for Heraklion. They left it at the intersection and turned right into town. In Solomos Square, several streets back from the ceaseless commerce of the beachfront, civic Katomeli drowsed in the lunchtime heat. Yiannis told Christos to drop him off at the Station, maybe drive around for a bit, get some wind back in his sails. His report could wait an hour or two, given the circumstances.

Inside the Station ceiling-fans stirred the decrepit air. Sotiris, the Watch Sergeant, smoked at the front desk. Panayotis' door was closed but he wasn't at lunch; through the wrinkled glass panel Yiannis glimpsed the tall black *kalimafki* of a cleric.

'What's with the *Archigos*?'

'He's holed up with the Patriarch. Remember that Gazi business last year, when the Jehovah's Witnesses were trying to muscle in?' Sotiris leaned across the counter to whisper. 'They're taking it all the way to Strasbourg.'

Yiannis passed through the barrier and checked his pigeon-hole. 'Persistent buggers, the Jehovahs. But you have to hand it to them. Every last one was offed in the war, did you know that? No other church totally refused to cuddle up to the Nazis.'

'Is that so?' said Sotiris, scenting a political discussion and shifting quickly into neutral.

Although he was pushing forty, Yiannis still thought of him as Young Sotiris. Younger than Yiannis, certainly, but then so was everyone else in the station, including Panayotis. He could still remember how they'd teased the kid when he first joined up: the goatherd's son from the Lasithi, long-armed, short-legged, his boots still stinking of goat-shit. Years in the force had dulled the wild gleam of his grin and turned him into a wary, deferential man. Some, of course, would say sensible. Not the type, at any rate, to fuck off mid-career like Yiannis and jeopardise his chances of promotion. Sotiris might not be a fast-tracker, but at least there were no shadows on his service record.

On the other hand, thought Yiannis, nor were there any shining lights.

Ruefulness was a habit he must have picked up with the language, like the shrug of acceptance, the self-deprecating Aussie grin. Impatient with his un-Greek ironies, he went to his desk and sat down to type his report. But first he phoned his lunch order through to the *Delfini*. They knew his needs there, catered for the tastes of a man with no sense of taste to speak of. Cucumber, apple, their sharpest ewe's-milk cheese. Crisp textures and definite tastes, nothing bland or mushy.

He took out the Davidoff packet and placed it on the blotter. It was probably contaminated,, but worth bagging just in case. He noticed writing on the side of the pack, in black ink. Roman capitals. He poked the packet with a pencil, swivelling it round.

AKA. Also known as – in English, at least. Then a name. KALLIS.

'Hey Sotiri. Ever heard of a Kallis? K.a.l.l.i.s.?'

'Not in these parts. Could be a mainland name. Or Pontian, maybe. Want me to check?'

Yiannis went over to study the screen. An odour of stale sweat hung around Tassos: ironically the accident which had robbed him of all sense of taste had sharpened his sense of smell.

The screen flagged a No Result.

'You could try Supplementaries?'

Yiannis snorted. The Supplementary lists hadn't been updated for three years, and in any case it was a slow business, scrolling through them.

'Thanks but no thanks. I'd be better off with the phone book.' He went to the shelf and flicked through the Ks. Nothing.

He went back to his desk, rang Gaylene Evnochides in Heraklion, and left a message. Gaylene was a girlfriend of his sister's; she was also Flagstaff's Head Rep on Crete. English, but married to a Greek who ran a dress shop called Dragonesse on Kalokairinou, Gaylene had a management style which was cool but appeasing – a combination that worked equally well with both nationalities. If he wanted to talk to the Flagstaff clients he was going to need her on board.

While he waited for his lunch to arrive he communed with Karen's photograph.

Ela, Yianni, ela! Her smile teased him from a time when they were both innocent of the knowledge of illness; her red hair burned in the Antipodean light. The only woman he'd ever known who could simultaneously tan and freckle.

Aka Kallis.

'Kallis' meant nothing; it could only be a name. Kall*os*, on the other hand, meant beauty.

Oh so many mornings, he thought, as the great darkness woke again inside him, *and ten thousand miles behind*.

Aka kallos, he told Karen's photograph: Also known as beauty.

When Yiannis got home Terpsikore was waiting at the gatepost to greet him: his *kore*, his lovely dancer. A real Cretan cat, sharp-featured, long-eared, with a narrow body and the tail of a snake. Her white coat was creamy in the afternoon sun, dappled by the shade of the fig leaves. She flowed like water down the wall and reconstituted herself at his feet.

Into his mind came an image of the two plump Persians D.I. Mattei kept in his Paris apartment in *Le Cercle Rouge*. Every night they waited for his return, each on its personal brocaded cushion, and every night Mattei whispered the same endearments, switched on the same table-lamps in the same order, set down the same dainty bowls on the spotless kitchen floor.

D.I. Mattei was fastidious, predatory, a man who never missed a trick. Yiannis remembered a wide-angle shot of winter trees, a phalanx of police fanning out across the misty furrows of a French field. Katomeli had its video-shops, but you had to go to Heraklion to get the real classics: Visconti, Antonioni, the Nouvelle Vague. The ultimate cool of Jean-Pierre Melville.

If D.I. Mattei was punctilious in every sphere, the Yves Montand character was his exact antithesis. Sanger the renegade, the washed-up cop. Boozy but still brilliant, his hangdog face a 50 year lesson in love and suffering. Sanger's apartment was a slum of empty *anis* bottles. When Sanger spoke of the 'occupants of the cupboard' you knew what he meant, because Jean-Pierre Melville let you in on his delirium, showed you the rats and roaches and lizards that crept out in the night and slithered under the bedclothes to have their wicked way with him.

If Yiannis hadn't actually been there, he knew it had been a close thing. After Karen's funeral his personal cupboard had a door that led to the underworld, and the key was alcohol. At nights he entered it eagerly, only to wake unsatisfied, until his *dipsa*, his thirst for her, was so great that it could no longer be slaked by the hours of darkness but grew to the size of the morning and the long day beyond.

At first he'd reported for work as usual, dull-witted and surly, his heart locked tight against the sympathy of his colleagues. Later he barricaded himself in the house and lay all day in the shuttered dark, drinking methodically, while friends and neighbours rattled like dry beans at the letterbox. How he'd hated them, for their utter irrelevance, and also for their ignorance. Why couldn't they comprehend that no living being could be the slightest bit of help?

When oblivion still didn't find him, he took to the road in search of it, tanked-up and tonning it down the Great Ocean Highway, burning up the miles for hour after hour, until he forgot what tongue he spoke, and what country he was in, and even which side of the road to drive on.

Only the accident, perhaps, could have forestalled the fate his will seemed set on.

He remembered the lights of a container truck, the swerve. His own Electra Glide in Blue across the gravel-dry craters of the moon. For a second his synapses registered the lit digits of the speedometer, like some implacable glyph of the Gods. And then there was nothing, neither moon nor sun, nor his love, nor even the bitter-sweet misery of abandonment.

In High School they'd been taught that *tragedia* was what happened when a man had one thing in mind for himself and the Gods another. Thus Homer, and the birth of the Hero. But Yiannis knew that he was no hero, and the Gods who had taken matters out of his hands were not, it seemed, death-dealers, but quite the opposite. Like his Aussie doctors, what was on their agenda was life, whether or not he had a taste for it, and there was nothing to do, in the end, but submit body and spirit to their wishes.

The cat had wound herself around his ankles. '*Ela, koritsi-mou*,' he murmured, bending to stroke her. The meeting with Flagstaff was set for 6pm. He would feed her early, take a shower, find a clean shirt. Stroll back to the station to pick up the car from Christos.

Terpsikore's high-pitched purr ceased abruptly. She sniffed at his shoes and stepped back, accusing him with her yellow eyes. Perhaps she had smelled the death on them. Or perhaps she had smelled the honey. With a small sneeze of protest she turned her back on him and stalked towards the door.

Shaved and sweet-smelling, Yiannis headed down the hill towards the town centre.

Pericles was in his favoured spot on the stoop of the grocer's, nodding his head over his worry-beads. Spying Yiannis across the street, he produced the usual straight-armed salute which Yiannis had decided long ago not to interpret as a comment on the fascist tendencies of the police force.

Pericles, he reflected, was a sad case. He'd been a postman all his life, a solid, reliable worker, until one Christmas when he had stolen all the gifts he was meant to deliver: wind-chimes, scented candles, Belgian chocolates, cowbells from the Bernese Oberland. Most of the haul had been lavished on his elderly mother; the rest he had stashed in his bedroom, which the old lady, being too frail to climb the stairs, no longer cleaned.

The first sign that something was amiss had come when a sack of mail was discovered in a water-trough – hundreds of postcards, all stamped and ready to fly off to Germany and Holland and New York; postcards in every language, their messages now dew-soaked and indecipherable.

When Yiannis, alerted by the Post Office, arrived at the house, he found shelves stacked with stinking merchandise: French cheeses, whole Scotch salmon, rotting paw-paws and mangoes. It was astonishing, really, the things people thought they could send through the post. Even more curious, though, was that Pericles had recorded each item in a series of ledger books, dutifully noting down its weight, its value, its provenance.

Pericles had been sentenced to 2 years, and released on parole after 18 months. But his job had gone, and the shock had proved too much for his mother, who died soon afterwards. In the years since then he had drifted around the neighbourhood, doing odd jobs when they were offered, smiling his eager smile, smoking on the stoops of several shopkeepers who had adopted him. Pericles had been a reliable postman in his day, and because the people of Katomeli remembered this, he was seldom scolded or maligned, and never lacked for an ouzo or a glass of raki.

Yiannis hailed him cheerfully and hurried on. Pericles might be a wierdo, but his wits were largely intact, and it was worth sounding him out from time to time, for his eyes were sharp and his tongue always ready to wag for a good plate of *kleftiko*.

Dora's place was a hundred metres farther down the hill, on the corner where Limonas Street met Vassilikou.

Xenes Glosses, announced the red neon sign above the street entrance: *Foreign Languages*. A growth industry, as Dora had correctly assessed some years ago. When her divorce had forced her to take money seriously, she'd given up her post at the High School and set herself up in business, teaching English and German to Cretans who aimed to make a career in tourism, and Greek to English and Germans, who aimed to make a life of it.

He glimpsed her dark-red head through the open window and stopped to lean on the high sill. She was in the office, watching TV with a group of students. Philippoussis was lumbering about the screen like a beetle-browed Hercules, fighting off match-points; Henman was the gadfly, tormenting him.

'An English tennis lesson?' said Yiannis in English.

'Ai Yianni! You scared me!' All in a fluster, Dora jumped up. She came to the window smoothing down her hair. 'Won't you come in? We are watching a re-run because it's raining at Wimbledon, of course. Won't you join us? It's quite an epic. The British are eating their Union Jacks to ribbons.'

'Chewing,' Yiannis corrected. Dora's English was fluent but not idiomatic. 'Sorry, I'm still on duty. Tomorrow still okay? I'm meeting Tassos and Irini at 8.'

The flicker of anxiety in Dora's eyes reminded him that he should have said 'we'.

27

'So you'll.?' Her lashes fluttered down demurely.

Yiannis was embarrassed for her. Nodding to a couple of students who were eyeing him with a mixture of curiosity and respect, he lowered his voice. 'Pick you up. Of course. At 7.30.'

On the screen there was a reprieve. The score flashed up two sets all. The students roared with delight. Philippoussis clenched his fist at the crowd and scowled majestically. 'Enjoy the match!' said Yiannis, making his escape.

He and Dora had been seeing each other casually for a couple of years: an adult arrangement, or so he'd supposed. Lately, though, Dora had shown signs of the kind of deference he neither expected nor enjoyed in a woman. She seemed wary, submissive. She seemed to be waiting.

His irritation mounted as he rounded the corner and passed the park, a desultory plot bordered by scrubby oleanders, where some children were playing on a roundabout. More than once Dora had mentioned 'talking about our relationship', but about that he had nothing to say, for some un-reconstructed prideful part of him insisted that he was not a man who had 'relationships', he was a man who had great loves. And Dora – sadly but certainly – was not one of those. But he could see no kind way to tell her that it was her friendship he required, her humour, and her energetic spite: all those attributes, in fact, which now seemed to be in decline, fading away into oblivion, like the unsaid words at the end of her sentences. It was possible, of course, that he was to blame for this diminishment, but all the same he couldn't help recoiling from those shadowy lacunae, so hopeful and so vulnerable, and from the hidden contract he detected there, which seemed to say that to complete Dora's sentences was to agree to complete her life.

5

At the east end of Panomeli's small beach the Shoestring Bar stands on a rise, with a spellbinding view out over the great gleaming pelt of the sea. Although the heat is building, a comfortable breeze ruffles the corners of the paper tablecloth. Above her head tamarisk branches whisk about, soft and fluffy as feather dusters.

Her red sarong is dry now, her bathing suit only slightly damp at the crotch. She lights a cigarette and opens Alice Kober's *Notes on some "Cattle" Tablets from Knossos* – the original typescript, xeroxed for her by the archivist at the Ashmolean. What she has to do is to tally the numbers Kober assigned to them in Scripta Minoa II with the system of numbering now in force at the Heraklion Museum. A laborious, finicky job, but one she hopes will up her chances of setting her eyes on the exact tablets, the ones Kober, for all her efforts, never managed to see.

The quotation marks around 'Cattle' showed Kober was still uncertain about what kind of livestock the logograms represented; not until after her death was it established that

the horned logogram ⌐ꝯ actually stood for 'sheep'.

Anchoring the article down with the ashtray, she brings out the Mycenaean glossary she downloaded from the Internet. You could download anything these days, even – amazingly – a standardised Linear B font, complete with keyboard code for operating it. The laborious hand-copying of the past is thoroughly obsolete. Alice, she imagines, would have been in seventh heaven.

Ingrid has never minded working while others take their ease. On the contrary, she loves the busy-bee feeling – so organic and secretive – that happens when you disengage from the collective, not to mention from the manic treadmill of Great Britain plc. It's no surprise to her if people are leaving in droves these days. Upping sticks, downsizing. Rearing llamas in Spain or olives in Tuscany.

It isn't as if she's immune from the national obsession herself.

A hill-village in the Luberon, perhaps. Alternatively, the Cyclades: some kind of shack by the sea with a wooden jetty to moor a boat, an outboard (10 horsepower would do), some vines, vegetables, and goats.

A lifestyle with livestock, you could say. As it happens she does know how to milk a goat, and although she can't make cheese, birth kids, or slaughter, these things can no doubt be learned. After all, according to Aunt Elsa Henderson, who has lately added genealogy to her list of hobbies, her Great-grandmother was a Highland crofter at Muirton of Ardblair. And the optimistic emigrants on the TV seem to set out with far fewer skills than she has. (What they do have, she reminds herself, is capital).

She has been gazing at the dazzle on the sea, and when she looks down at the glossary the page, in deep shadow, is an intense purple field. The syllabograms are ant-black, inscrutable. She stares unseeing at the triple logogram for 'sheep'.

a) sheep ⳨ b) ram ⳨ c) ewe ⳨

There's something too bland here, a gloss she can't quite bring herself to accept. That missing third term again. If b) and c) for ram and ewe seem fair enough, what's harder to swallow is a) sheep as general concept.

It's logical enough, she supposes, to the contemporary conceptual thinker – less so, however, if looked at from the point of view of the Minoans, whose thinking would surely have been ruled by agronomic imperatives. The herd, by necessity, would have been composed mainly of females and castrates, with a minority of males. As few as 2-4 per 100 animals in Ucko's estimate, if she remembers rightly.

30

So the herd, like the logograms, would have been trimodal.

While Kober had accepted that the variants indicated sex-distinction, she'd refused to commit herself on which variant was which. It's a pity, thinks Ingrid, that the phallocentric thinkers who came after her had lacked her perspicuity.

She checks the article again On every one of the livestock tablets featured, the irksome 'male' sign glowers out at her. On Alice's fb08, for instance, Heraklion Museum's H304:

At the time Kober was writing the numerical system, at least, had been established: 100 was denoted by the circle, O, 10 units by a horizontal stroke, and single units by a vertical. Kober had interpreted the numbers on the far right of the tablet as some kind of tax levied by the Palace administration on the total animals in a given herd – in this case, 100.

But a herd of 100 bulls is patently nonsensical, and as for sheep, what farmer in his right mind would keep a flock of 100 rams, with 100 pairs of horns, and 200 functioning cojones?

Ca' the yowes tae the knowes, thinks Ingrid. Even Robert Burns had a better grip on farming basics.

A voice hails her from below the terrace, and she looks over the railing and sees Lynda the Rep. toiling up the stone steps from the beach. Her outfit is formal and frumpy – a billowing mid-calf- length dress with mid-length sleeves, and black court shoes with mid-heels. The material of the dress is printed with tiny Union Jacks. Reaching the top of the steps, she rounds the parapet.

'Thought I might find you here!' Her face, for once, does not wear the bright harrying smile of the salesman; she looks, Ingrid thinks, perturbed.

Ingrid has nothing against Lynda except, perhaps, that Lynda makes her feel guilty. She is not, in Lynda's book, a good client. She has not gone on group outings, has missed the

31

Turtle-Watching trip, and the Greek Barbecue, and has failed to sign up for the Sunset Cruise with Bouzouki Music. Slipping the livestock tablet sheets into her folder, she pulls out a chair and invites Lynda to sit.

'No thanks,' says Lynda, fanning herself agitatedly with her red plastic wallet-file. 'Sorry to disturb you, but I'm just, like, rounding up the flock. We're meeting at 6, at the Minimarket.'

'Any particular reason?' Ingrid is surprised. Has she missed something?

Lynda looks at her. 'You haven't heard?' On her flushed face a small rosebud mouth works inscrutably at its worries. She puts her cellphone and file on the table and sits down. 'They found someone in the wood. Drugs overdose, it looks like.' She's breathless, her big flustered bosom rising and falling. 'The police need to check if anyone, you know, saw anything.'

'Good God, when was this?'

'This morning.' Lynda fusses a straight blonde streak of hair back from her face and clips it into a sequined kirby-grip. Ingrid feels sorry for her – it can't be much fun, after all, being the bearer of such uneaseful news

'Look, can't I get you a drink? A coke or something? You look like you've had quite a day of it.'

Lynda's eyes glaze over with tears. She shakes her head mutely, batting away the sympathy with a stricken flutter of the hand. Jumping up, she gathers her things and gazes around distractedly. 'You haven't seen the Shapcotts at all, have you? The gentleman with the daughter?'

The Shapcotts are Ingrid's neighbours, their balcony a mere half metre from her own. She confesses that she hasn't.

Briefly from their vantage point she and Lynda scan the beach, the bar, the blue water, but the Shapcotts are nowhere to be seen. Near the off-shore rock where small boats are tethered, the Wilson-Wilsons, in tandem, are paddling their lilo across the shallows.

'See you at six, then' says Lynda, her flag-dress billowing again as she turns to go. 'Sorry about this, Miss Laurie.'

6

By 6.15 most of the Flagstaff clients had arrived. Some had come straight from the beach, burdened with towels and tote bags, impatient for their showers and lotions and aperitifs. One couple, who were still dripping wet, lugged a large inflatable turtle. Sarongs were tied tight as tourniquets across ample breasts; flip-flops spilled sand on the freshly-washed patio outside the Minimarket. According to Yiannis' sister Irini, who had trained as a hairdresser in London, the British spent their long winters in grey and black, and this was why they chose such gaudy colours for the summer: turquoise with blue, orange with pink, mauve with indigo. Colours that didn't go well with the bleached hair of the women and the reddish flush of tans that resulted from too great a greediness for the sun, as if Mother Nature, who hated to be hurried, had imprinted her exasperation on their skin.

Yiannis had promised Gaylene Evnochides that the meeting would be strictly low key. The Harknesses, she said, were talking of leaving, and her boss in the London office was already fretting about compensation claims, so he could understand, couldn't he, that she didn't want the whole group to follow suit.

Lynda had arranged a semi-circle of chairs on the terrace, and Demosthenes' wife Maria handed round cartons of orange juice and bottles of mineral water. While Lynda, haltingly, did the honours, Yiannis tried to correlate the company with the printout Gaylene had provided.

The Wilson-Wilsons. This was not a misprint, apparently, but a young couple who neither smiled at him nor met his eye.

The turtle pair turned out to be a Mr. and Mrs. Gifford.

33

The jolly elderly Giffords, who were dressed like adolescents, were presumably Mr. G.'s parents.

Miss Dodge and Miss Ottakar looked settled and Sapphic, grazing contentedly on a saucer of pistachios.

Mr. Shapcott, a pursed-up, professional-looking type of middling years, sat with his teenage daughter Zoe, who wore her beauty like a brand.

Ingrid Laurie (Miss? Ms?) appeared to be the only single. There were no children in evidence, no doubt because school vacations didn't begin until the end of the month.

Yiannis nodded sympathetically at Bill and Elaine Harkness. If death had laid a sobering hand on the Harknesses, it had also lent them an air of celebrity. They were dressed with marked formality, he in a suit jacket, she in a black linen dress that skimmed her ankles. The solicitude that surrounded them was palpable. Yiannis sensed that if he didn't soft-pedal, he would risk the wrath of their co-tourists.

He began with an apology for the interruption to their evening, and went on to assure them it was merely a matter of routine, since at this stage no foul play was suspected. A white lie, but excusable.

Thirteen pairs of eyes – serious, citizenly – stared back at him. As always, he was conscious of the pressure of unasked questions: their eyes might be on him, but he suspected it was the corpse that their instincts strained to see. He tapped out his cigarette and turned on his smile.

'Nevertheless. I'll be grateful for any help you can give me. Anything unusual you saw or heard last night, or early this morning. Something that seemed trivial, perhaps, at the time.'

The Misses Dodge and Ottakar were nearest to Yiannis. 'Ladies?'

They shook their heads as one. 'We tend to sleep late, you see,' ventured Miss Dodge.

'On *holiday*,' Miss Ottakar corrected her, with a reproach-ful smile. 'But apart from the racket from the Totem Bar – which is rather too close for comfort, I have to say- I don't remember hearing a thing.'

34

Yiannis nodded and turned his gaze on the young Mr.Wilson-Wilson. 'And you, sir?'

The boy's lips appeared to be trying to form sounds, but froze in the process. Yiannis smiled in encouragement, to no avail.

'No,' said the wife, with great finality.

'Thank you,' said Yiannis, passing quickly on to the Harknesses. It had occurred to him that although the track to Katomeli followed the beach, the body had been found higher up, on a path that might once have led to a beehive or water-tank, but which now led nowhere in particular.

He put the question casually. Had they climbed up in the hope of a view, perhaps, or of a shortcut to the beach at Katomeli?

The answer came with an embarrassed shrug. 'Lainey – my wife – can't stand mosquitoes.'

'Mosquitoes?'

'In the bamboo along the shore.'

There was a murmur of agreement. 'It's a proper swamp round there.'

The Giffords nodded solemnly.

'Show them, Charlie.' The elderly mother, elfish in her baseball cap, thrust out an arm to show off her bites. Loose skin hung in crepey folds from her shoulder to her elbow.

Elaine Harkness glanced at her husband and blushed visibly. Yiannis saw that it was a lie, if a harmless one. An alfresco screw, he decided, was more likely. The dappled light, the illicit impulses of summer. The thought made him feel distinctly wistful. If only the heat still did for him what it seemed to do for the English.

The younger Mrs. Gifford – fit, fiftyish – wore a silver chain round her ankle. Her husband had pushed the turtle out of sight behind a potted palm, as a mark, presumably, of respect. The whole family had been in the Shoestring Bar till 2am, he told Yiannis, celebrating the parents' 50th Wedding Anniversary.

'My congratulations!' said Yiannis, smiling at the old folks.

'Later on we had a nightcap on our balcony and played a hand of two of poker. So we were a bit the worse for wear this morning, to be honest.'

Mr. Shapcott voiced something inaudible, and Mr. Gifford bristled. 'Sorry mate. Just a one off. Special occasion, like.'

Yiannis, who had been trying to keep his eyes off the Shapcotts, now allowed himself to stare at Zoe. True to her name, Zoe was life itself, in its first fresh bloom. From the shiny waterfall of her hair to the peachy skin of her legs, she was jailbait, but innocent with it. Although she was almost as tall as her father, there was no gawkiness in her. Mr. Shapcott, in fact, was the one who looked awkward, as if abashed by warring currents of protectiveness and desire. *Etsi ine o Zoe*, thought Yiannis. *Such is life*. Although he had no children himself, it was easy to imagine the jealous frenzies such a daughter might provoke even in the best of fathers.

Tucking her bare feet up into a half-lotus, Zoe swept her hair back from her face. The gaze she fixed on Yiannis was frank and trusting.

'I was awake at 6.00, but we didn't hear anything, did we, Daddy?' Her voice had the sweet clarity of a distant bell. Her brow contrived a perfect little frown. 'Well, apart from that blasted cockerel!'

'Ah yes!' said Yiannis, dazzled. His head nodded understandingly; of their own accord his lips stretched into a smile. It struck him that there was nothing Zoe could have said that would not have evoked the same response. 'I killed him,' for instance, or 'I cut him up and ate his liver.' He sensed that he wasn't alone in this. Men held their breath when Zoe spoke; their eyes were awed and clung to her. He was only one more eager cockerel among the legions who would from now on queue up to make fools of themselves over Zoe.

He focussed his attention reluctantly on the Laurie woman. His respect for Mr. Shapcott had increased.

'I woke late, for once.' Her voice was flat. She folded her arms and looked at him unsmilingly, as if resolved neither to charm, nor to be charmed. 'So I'm afraid I'm no use to you.'

36

The antagonism didn't entirely surprise him. To be seated next to Zoe was an unenviable fate for any woman, let alone one so, well, *implacable,* somehow. He had a vague impression of blondness: spiky blonde hair, blonde lashes, cool white-blonde hairs winking on brown forearms. There was a long scratch on her right shin, another on her ankle. He made a mental note that Ms. Laurie – she was definitely a *Ms*, he decided – had been rambling among thorns.

'I see. So you saw nothing?'

'That's right.'

Subjected to her pale censorious gaze, Yiannis felt exposed. His skin prickled, as if scenting a change in the weather. He folded Gaylene's list in four and flattened the edges with a fingernail, trying to suppress the knowledge that his susceptibility to Zoe had been closely, cynically observed.

20 metres away, the car radio crackled out a call sign. He clipped his pen into his top pocket and rose to his feet.

'Thank you for your time. You've been very helpful. Should you need to contact me for any reason, Lynda has my cellphone number. But now, if you'll excuse me.'

A ripple of activity spread through the group. Class dismissed. People stretched and sighed and picked up their beach bags. Yiannis said a brief goodbye to Lynda and strode off the terrace with relief, remembering only at the last minute to say his *Yassous*, and wish them all a very pleasant evening.

7

Pericles can't help noticing that his friend the Sergeant has barely eaten anything – some salted nuts, and a few potato-chips, washed down with Coca Cola – although the *kleftiko* is fragrant with thyme and garlic, the lamb falling off the bone at the tap of a spoon. Sergeant Yiannis has ordered wine, too, a half-litre of red in a squat tin jug. Pericles digs out the last of the marrow from the bone, wondering if he can bring himself to decline dessert – which would be polite, since his companion is paying, but the rice puddings in the cold cabinet look so delicious with their crisp burnt-sugar topping that it will be hard to resist them.

His friend the Sergeant is a man of few words. The television set blares from its high shelf in the corner, and from time to time he glances without interest at the basketball game which is happening in primary colours on the screen. Pericles is a little sorry for him. He looks so tired, smoking his cigarettes, waiting with his good manners until Pericles finishes his meal. Pericles eyes his epaulettes with admiration and a pang of envy, for he misses his own Postal Worker's uniform, its badge with the winged insignia of Hermes the messenger. Of all the losses in his life, this is perhaps the one he regrets the most.

When he was in Nea Poli jail a magpie had come to share his breakfast, a magic bird with a gleaming gold eye and a petrol sheen to its feathers. Every morning he would feed it crumbs of bread through the bars, and it would reward him with bright scraps of stolen silver. When he looks back on these months, sometimes he wishes that he could have his day in

Court again, so that he could tell the truth and nothing but the truth, as he has come to see it. That he was no more a thief than the bees are who gather nectar for the hive. That, like them, he was only stocking up, he was storing. His mother had taught him, as the war had taught her: that a well-stocked cupboard was what stood between you and catastrophe. She had also impressed on him the importance of book-keeping, so that when the Sergeant arrived with his sorrowful face Pericles could account for every single item: its weight, its worth, its dimensions, its provenance.

Now he stores away only what the shopkeepers will give him: dry goods that have passed their date, cornflakes and batteries, boxes of cube sugar, broad beans in battered tins. Saturday evenings after stock-taking are the best times for salvage. Some goods like fruits can also be gathered in the orchards and hedgerows, and ever since he moved down to his mother's bedroom the bare floor of his upstairs room has been kept free for windfall apples and pears, which must be turned and tended, and watched weekly for bruises and worms.

On weekend nights he draws his chair up to the kitchen table and enters each new item in a squared exercise book, like the one he used for arithmetic at school. He has always had neat handwriting and a head for figures, and it pleases him to fill in his columns, left to right, the first for type and brand name, the next for calorific content, and the next for bar code, and the last two for marked price and place of origin. Or, if the pickings have been poor, he may check the labelling system on his kitchen shelves, or sit in the lamplight and browse through the pages of his old ledgers.

When he thinks of his latest acquisitions, guilt flows over his mind like a mist. For these are items without a type, un-branded. The gemstone with its engraved surface, like a franking-stamp. The perforated clay thing which looks like a salt-cellar without a space inside for the salt. Items without price or provenance. Every day he stares at them, and then at his columns, whose blankness has begun to merge in his mind

39

with a growing vagueness about how he came by the objects in the first place.

With a flick of his finger the Sergeant summons a rice pudding, and Pericles strikes at the burnt crust with his spoon. As he eats he studies the menu, the day's prices. *Psari* at 10 euros the kilo, *horiatiki* at 1.50. The new menu is stiff and shiny and made up of three leaves, so that it sits on the table like an altarpiece. One leaf is in German, one in English, and one in Greek. *Brot*, he reads, *bread, psomi*.

'*Lipon*,' says the Sergeant at last, passing him a cigarette. 'So how's tricks, Pericles? Seen anything on your rounds this week, eh?'

Pericles frowns, considering. After a moment he shakes his head solemnly. 'No, sir. Just the runners.'

This morning they'd come again, playing their game, tossing a clay ball or pomegranate between them as they ran. Appearing suddenly and soft-footed, alighting silently, like the magpie, their oiled skin as darkly glossy as his wings.

'Joggers?'

Pericles thinks of their odd garb, their wasp-waisted leather belts, like the belts worn by weight-lifters.

'Foreigners,' he says, deciding that it was not Greek they had spoken to him. 'Two of them.' Remembering the silence around them, and how they came unaccompanied by headsets or music, he adds, 'Quiet. Their hair is long, like girls.'

The Sergeant quirks an eyebrow. He is smiling.

'Been fraternising with the Neo Chori lot, have we?'

'No sir, not the Germans.' Pericles frowns at the mention of the hippies. They have money to buy land and Toyotas and goats, but not a cent of it has ever come his way. 'These ones are kind. They give me things.'

'What kind of things, Pericles?'

Pericles shrugs. 'Just things.' A wave of irritation sweeps over him as he tries once again to classify the enigmatic objects in his mind. 'How do I know what kind.?'

He can read the exasperation on the Sergeant's face, and a kind of panic builds in him, for he has not only failed his friend the Sergeant, he has also failed himself. Because no matter how hard he tries, he can find no name for them, no rhyme or reason.

Sergeant Yiannis sucks on a cigarette and sighs out the smoke. Lifting his briefcase on to his lap, he pulls out a photograph and slides it across the table to Pericles.

'Either of your runners look like this?'

Pericles stares at the half-open eyelids, the frozen features. Emptiness flows from the photograph and hollows out his being. He thrusts it away from him, shaking his head in shock.

'This is a dead man, sir!'

'Okay, my friend,' the Sergeant says hastily, returning the photo to the briefcase. 'Okay, you can calm yourself down now.' He pours the last of the wine into Pericles' glass and snaps his fingers for the bill. When the waitress has whisked away their plates he lays two 5 euro notes in front of Pericles. 'These things they gave you, Pericles. I'd be interested to have a look at them.'

8

When researching immigration into the USA in the early years
of the 20th century, the first thing one learns is that names are
negotiable. Clearly no immigrant wanted to take the risk of
contradicting officialdom, opting instead to bow to the power
of the scribe, to say Yes Sir, and let him write down what
pleased him. On her birth certificate, for instance, Alice Kober
is listed as Adele – presumably by a registrar who lacked an
ear for foreign accents. Her father appears as Franz on the
1914 Naturalisation petition, as Francis in the New York City
Directory of 1930; by 1935, on his Death Certificate, he is
listed as Fred. His wife, Alice's mother, appears as Cattalina,
Katharina, and latterly Catherine.

Surnames, one discovers, are equally slippery. In New
York's Municipal Archive, and also in the North East Region
Federal Archive, the Soundex system with its grouped homo-
phones is an essential key to the labyrinth of indexes.

In the dim white bedroom, a mist of tangled sheets. It's almost
dusk. She takes off her reading glasses and arcs her arms
above her head, stretching.

Shutters creak open on the balcony above, and a light goes
on. She hears a woman's voice, muted, scolding. 'Mucky
socks,' it accuses, 'Shaving water.' The young Mrs. Wilson-
Wilson certainly has the knack of adding discord to a day.

The auras of the partnered, like the Single Supplement, are
an occupational hazard for the solo traveller. She finds herself
waiting for retaliation, for some sign of spunk from the hen-
pecked husband.

In New York the walls of her hotel room were too thin to
block out next door's noises. Nightly her neighbours engaged

in bouts of irritable sex. The woman giggled and squealed a lot, and in the mornings greeted the dawn with a girlish Wheeee of pleasure, as if to assure herself or her man that she was simply tickled to death to be having such a wild time in a cheap hotel in Midtown Manhattan. They were on a mini-break, she'd decided, from somewhere far away and bible-bound: Utah, perhaps, or Nebraska.

Downtown, a keen east wind razored across the Brooklyn Bridge. Outside City Hall she'd found nowhere to sit, nowhere to smoke, nowhere to think – only a tiny locked park with bare trees and a few skinny crocuses. April in London meant municipally easeful spaces – parks with lawns and lakes, petunia beds, magnolia trees bursting with starry blossom. Here, though, the message was all too clear: New York was a place to make money, or spend it.

Unkissed by the prince of profit, the public sector was the Cinderella of the city, ill-funded and ill-esteemed. The Fire Department seemed to be the sole bastion of civic pride and confidence. The Fire Station near her 51st Street hotel was spick and span; inside, heroic scarlet-and-chrome fire trucks stood in polished ranks, primed and ready for disasters.

The cavernous lobby of the Surrogate Court building was windowless, the walls and ceiling faced with ginger-coloured ormolu; on either side of the entrance a dusty bronze eagle crouched astride a globe. The security guards had trouble with 'Municipal' and 'Archive'; 'Hall of Records' was what swung it in the end. She passed through the magnetometer, stuck her new blue security pass on her lapel, and was directed to Room 103.

'Whadya wanna research?'

The desk-clerk had his hands on the place where hips might have been expected. He was potato-shaped, with low-slung trousers and a peeled red face which gleamed with sweat.

Ingrid replied in her best British Library whisper. 'Alice Kober, the classical scholar, died 1950.'

'The whaaaat?'

'Archaeologist?' she offered, thinking of the security guards. On the wall behind the desk a row of high windows, dimmed with grime, had been painted shut. An L shaped bank of microfilm scanners jutted into the room, while free-standing carousels occupied much of the remaining floor space. Two of the walls were lined with grey metal filing cabinets and, on a third, shelves of ledger books reached almost to the ceiling.

She filled out her slip and paid $5 for a scanner. The machines looked ancient, and most of them were occupied; coats and mufflers festooned the backs of the chairs. There was an old-fashioned iron coat-tree in the corner but no one was using it.

'Do you happen to have a sheet of instructions?'

'No,' the clerk barked, clinking the keys on his belt.

No ma'am would do nicely, she thought. 'And if I can't work it?'

The clerk eyed her wearily. 'Then I guess we might have to show you.'

New York lesson 1 – never look lost. Lesson 2 – forget hallowed silences. It's the right of all Americans to talk at the tops of their voices.

Unlike the Municipal Hall of Records, the North East Regional Archive on Varick Street was cool and quiet, oiled by Federal money, and if the security guards on the ground floor hadn't actually smiled at her, at least they'd greeted her credentials with civility. The procedures, too, were reassuring in their familiarity – coat and briefcase in locker, pencils not pens.

The librarian – his badge, surnameless, announced him as Gerry – was red-headed, soft-spoken, with long musician's fingers and a decorously slender wedding ring. Although he confessed he hadn't heard of Alice Kober, he was clearly up to speed on the issues – the invisibility of women in the historical record, and so forth.

Twelve floors below, the Hudson river roiled soundlessly beneath the same piers on which the immigrants of the

44

Old World had first set foot on the New. At Battery Point she'd queued in the pouring rain for the Ellis Island ferry, while itinerant Africans hawked cheap Chinese umbrellas. In the Security tent she'd placed coat, cardigan, boots and brief-case in a green plastic tray; poker-faced, she'd submitted to the electronic frisking.

'No one in the States jokes about security any more,' her friend Maxine had warned before she set off. 'Don't even think about it.'

In the Ellis Island Museum there were photographs of the queues of immigrants, three deep, stretching from the dock to the vast Baggage Room, up a flight of stone stairs to the second floor, and into the great arched hall of the Registry. All of them wore tags pinnned to their clothing, – ship's name, Manifest number – like goods marked down in a bargain basement.

Having already been scanned, cursorily, for obvious signs of illness, they would undergo the mental and physical health inspections, during which they would be examined for con-sumption, excema, scabies, imbecility, and have their eyelids turned inside out by the 'buttonhook' men, who checked for trachoma. Then, if they were deemed to be strong and without defect, and once it was established that they were neither anarchists, polygamists, convicts, nor idiots, the door of limitless opportunity would swing open to let them through.

This was the story known to every American – the heroic high point, perhaps, of its history. Certainly there had been xenophobia, there had been pressure on the immigrants to assimilate, to naturalise, to learn English. But on the ferry Ingrid had also sensed the idealism that still infected their descendants: a memory of welcome, perhaps, of being en-folded in a new and democratic embrace.

When the Passenger Record flashed up she shook her head at the screen. She printed it out and went to the desk to consult with Gerry.

Ship of Travel: *Statendam*

Port of Departure: *Rotterdam*
Manifest Line Number: *0001*
Date of Arrival: *May 29th, 1906.*

'I'm not sure this can be the right Franz Kober. 1906 seems too late.'

'You should check the Manifest on microfilm. It'll give you a lot more detail. 0001. That'll be, let's see.' He tapped a command on his keyboard. 'Cabinet T715. End of the row on the left.' He scribbled numbers on a slip of paper. 'Roll 717, page 56.'

The scanner room was lit only by the bluish light of one screen, in front of which sat an elderly Jewish woman. An aluminium walking stick leant against her chair. Her face in the wintry glow was harsh with puzzlement, its shadows sharp as a woodcut. Ingrid threaded the film on to the spool and fast-forwarded. At page 50 she stopped and scrolled slowly through to 56.

The entries were in copperplate, column after column of them cramming the screen. In the top left hand corner the names leapt out at her.

Kober, Franz
Kober, Katarina

Below – proof, if proof were needed – was *Gruber, Anna, 18, occupation: cook.*

Katharina's maiden name was Gruber. She had been travelling with her younger sister.

The entries flowed on across the page, the writing so neat and small, executed with such a steady hand. No fountain pens in those days – just bare nibs dipped in inkwells, blotting paper pressed down punctiliously on the page. She pictured the clerks in their pince-nez, labouring like drones from dawn till dusk, stone-blind, no doubt, at 40. She stared again at the arrival date. May 1906. Alice Kober had been born in the December of that year. Although absent from the register, she'd been present after all. The scholar-to-be of ancient writing systems had entered the country invisibly, had slipped like a little fish through the net of scribal surveillance.

Gerry put his head round the door to check on her.

'It's them, all right!'

'It is?' He came over, grinning at her excitement.

'The amazing thing is, Katharina was pregnant on the ship.'

'Yeah? When was your scholar born?'

'December 1906. So she was – what? Two, three months?'

Gerry crouched beside her chair, studying the screen. 'They could have been in a hurry to go before she showed. Could be why they sailed then.'

The first trimester. A risky time, surely, to undertake such a journey. Yet against all the odds, Alice had hung in there, had survived the long train journey from southern Hungary to Rotterdam, and the discomforts of the 10 day sea voyage.

Conceived in Hungary, born in New York. For a moment she felt ridiculously proud of Alice. Even as a foetus, she'd shown remarkable tenacity.

Coming up from the subway at Lexington Ingrid found the station awash, water sluicing down the stone steps from the street. She picked up a sushi takeaway at the Korean healthfood bar on the corner of 51st and Third, and emerged into a thunderous downpour. Passing the Fire Station she noticed soapsuds sailing along the gutter. They're doing their housework, she thought – washing their lovely fire-trucks. Until she saw that the suds seemed to be foaming miraculously from her own feet.

After the Ellis Island trip her favourite Goretex boots – olive green, Italian – had developed a salty tidemark around the toes. She'd squeezed shampoo on them, scrubbed them with a nailbrush, and set them to dry on the radiator. And now the ingrained shampoo had reached critical mass in the deluge. It was like something out of the Marx Brothers. Each squelching step she took set off a new bout of lather, leaving a trail of foam like the wake of some transatlantic liner.

Her plane to Austin was at 7am next morning. In the hotel lobby she signed off her bill and ordered a 5am cab to Newark from the Bell Captain, a dapper Italian with the habit of sang-froid, who called her Ma'am and studiously avoided looking at her shoes. She pressed the elevator button for the 7th floor, looking neither to left nor right, daring anyone to stare at her.

Even before she opened her door she could hear that her neighbours were in residence. Within minutes of entering she was aware of a qualitative change in the proceedings. She pulled off her sodden boots and sat on the bed, listening. There were no giggles at all this time, which implied less tickling. She thought she could hear slaps. The shriekers, if she wasn't mistaken, had turned into spankers.

On the wardrobe door her clothes hung ready for the morning – lighter clothes, in lighter colours, like a ghost of her summer self. Tomorrow she'd be deep in the heart of Texas; tonight would be the last night of serious annoyance.

She packed her holdall, set the alarm for 4am, and got into bed with a certain optimism. Spanking was more visceral than tickling; perhaps it would bring things to a head, or at least speed up the whole performance.

For a while she lay in darkness, urging the couple on in a fairly neighbourly way, even contemplating in passing a parallel with her own pursuit of equally elusive – if more intellectual – goals. But then her thoughts segued, predictably, into self-criticism, for time wasted, and meagre successes. If she'd found out so little about the Kobers wasn't it because her method wasn't up to scratch? With only six days in the Texas archive, she couldn't afford to wander up any more blind alleys. She'd have to take a more logical approach, work out her plan of action, stick to it.

Just as she was drifting off, the *Wheee!* rang out, and she sat up with a jerk and yelled 'God's truth!' at the wall. They'd blown it again: that gay girlish whistle was a sure-fire signal. This time she felt personally let down, their failure rankling all the more because, just for once, she'd let herself harbour hopes of success.

She punched her pillow and lay down again, wide awake and seething righteously, because nothing, after all, was as infuriating as sheer bloody incompetence.

The New York City Census for 1930 is handwritten, in tiny copperplate script. The page is divided into 30 columns which detail colour, ethnicity, country of origin, language spoken, even whether the family had ever lived on a farm. At 662 Southern Boulevard in the Bronx, Franz Kober is listed, and below him his wife Katarina, daughter Alice E., and son William J. William is listed as a student, Alice as a Latin teacher, having graduated from Hunter College just in time for the Stock Market crash and the great Depression. Franz's occupation is hard to decipher. It appears to be 'pressing' in the 'upholstery' industry.

The rent of the property was $55 a month, compared to the $36.50 paid by the Kelly family in No. 661, so one assumes that the Kober's apartment had at least two bedrooms. At No. 663 there was an Italian family with seven children, aged from 15 down to 3 – Noni, Ernestina, Vito, Amelia, Ella, Victoria, Nico. The Kobers' other neighbours were Poles, Palestinians, Russians; the block would have been cramped, each stairwell a cavern of noise – hardly a place that would foster a single private thought, let alone a first-class intellect. It was perhaps from sheer necessity that Alice Kober developed such formidable powers of concentration.

The Kobers' block was part of a huge development of 6 storey tenements, bordered by East 149th Street to the west, and Leggett Avenue to the east. Straddling Leggett Avenue was the hauntingly-named Casanova Street station on the old Harlem River El; in its shadow were workshops and businesses – a cabinetmakers, a piano factory.

Searching for the warp and woof of Alice's early life – although one suspects that this reticent, enigmatic woman, who in letters mentions hardly a single personal detail, would not want us to know – one conjures up a picture of coal-carts and pawnshops, of gas lamps lining the sidewalk, and the girdered structure of the El casting its spider-web pattern on the cobbled streets below. Above, the hulking apartment blocks with their water-tanks on the roof, their armature of fire-escapes, their pulleys festooned with sheets, blankets, petticoats.

In the 1933 New York City Directories, the Kober name appears at the same address, but this time the head of household is listed as Kober, Alice E., instructor Brooklyn College, Women's Division. As a male, Franz would have been listed as such even if unemployed, and the absence of his name seems to imply that he had left the family home during that period.

In fact the 1935 Death Index shows that Franz – who has now become Fred – died aged 62 on December 17, 1935, of carcinoma of the stomach, in St Francis' Hospital in the Bronx. The doctor attending noted that he had undergone no operations, had received no prior treatment, and had died on the day of admission. The address given on the Death Certificate is 2134 Third Avenue, in the area of upper Manhattan now known as El Barrio. That this address was supplied 'by the deceased' suggests that no member of his family was present when he was admitted.

Fran's occupation is recorded as 'superintendent', which suggests that he may have become a night watchman or janitor of a warehouse or factory – a far cry from the 'weaver' or 'upholsterer' of earlier listings. The Depression had thrown millions out of work, and no doubt an immigrant from Old Europe could come down in the New World as easily as he could go up. It is possible that the immigrants' dream of 'a land of equality, where the gentleman works works alongside the labourer, where every man is a mister, and every woman can wear a hat and gloves and walk about like a lady' – may have failed Franz Kober in the end, and even that illness, alcohol, or other factors led to the breakdown of the family.

It is tempting to speculate about the effect such an estrangement might have had on Alice Kober's sense of herself as a woman, and while we will probably never know the truth about his demise, it is notable that nowhere in Kober's correspondence do we find any reference to Franz, nor, when she died 15 years later, were her ashes interred in Ferncliff Cemetery beside those of her father.

Although it was cancer that killed both father and daughter, it is not known what kind of cancer Alice suffered from. We know that she chain-smoked, and certain American scholars have taken this as a sure indicator of cancer of the lung – not least because, in an era before computer data-bases, Kober

*filed her Linear B sign-lists in Fleetwood cigarette cartons,
Fleetwoods being her favourite brand. But one might also be
tempted to draw a parallel with the brilliant biochemist
Rosalind Franklin, another dedicated workaholic, whose
beautiful X-ray photographs of the crystalline structure of
DNA led to the discovery of the Double Helix, but who died
of ovarian cancer before she could share the Nobel Prize glory
enjoyed by Watson and Crick.*

*Like Kober, Franklin had worked at the top of a field that was
almost exclusively male, had played by male rules, and had been
forced to absorb, if not actually accept, male chauvinist prejudice. Neither woman married or had children, and since both
had seen their femininity used to undermine or belittle their
achievements, it would not be surprising if they had felt the need
to suppress something that was so clearly disadvantageous.
Here it might be worth bearing in mind that elements which are
denied or suppressed tend to erupt in some other, somatic form,
and in the absence of solid proof one cannot rule out the
possibility that Alice Kober, like Rosalind Franklin, was cut
down in her prime by a cancer that was gynaecological in origin.*

Upstairs the Wilson-Wilsons' glass door slides shut, privatis-
ing the one-sided quarrel.

Ingrid closes the file and keys shutdown. The speculation will
have to go, of course. The trouble is that bare statistics don't
make a life, and in the absence of proof – she would have killed
for a fragment of diary, a single personal letter – her mind piles
supposition on conjecture, racing around like a rat in a trap.
She'll let it stand for the moment, but it really won't do at all.

Outside on the balcony she lights a cigarette and smokes in the
darkness. A pall of quiet hangs over the village; even the music of
the Shoestring Bar seems muted. It occurs to her that the news
will have spread by now: perhaps they're all indoors, observing a
funeral seclusion, murmuring behind closed shutters.

Without the blessing of sunlight the darkening sea holds
a foretaste of winter. For a moment she can imagine the
November rains, the empty holiday apartments locked up, the
few remaining villagers booted and squelching.

It would be dreich, certainly. Every bit as dreich as Dunelg.

9

On Monday afternoon Yiannis drove over to the Mortuary Office, which was attached to the new hospital at Pepargni. He had spent the morning scrolling through Missing Persons reports, printing out any file that matched the victim. The pre 1998 material was held on microfiche in the basement of the Heraklion HQ, but luckily, in this case the age of the victim made it unlikely they'd have to go so far back.

The Press Release was due to go out in time for the evening bulletins; afterwards there would be call-in sheets to collate. Apart from the standard crazy calls, there would be fathers seeking sons, sisters seeking brothers, fiancées abandoned inexplicably on the very day of the wedding. Screening the calls was no easy task because, as he had learned, people in search of answers – *closure*, as the Americans called it – could convince themselves of almost anything. There was never a shortage of punters eager to claim a deceased, and sometimes it seemed to him as if any deceased would do.

Missing Persons had yielded a poor crop. There were two possibles: Demos Xenopontes, 18, a waiter, born Piraeus, and Hassan al Aswani, 20, from Cairo, a deckhand on Minoan Lines.

When he'd checked the Piraeus number he'd received profuse apologies from the Xenopontes mother. Demos, she'd confessed, had returned home in January, after a three-month loss of memory. A steel ladder had fallen on his head, so that he had forgotten his own name, and his boss's name, and even the name of his own mother. Poor Demos still couldn't tell her quite what he'd done in the interim, but she thought he might have worked on a construction site in the City of London, for he talked of a tower called Kanari Wharf, and an English pub with a parrot in it at Piccadilly Circus.

Yiannis made an effort to be stern. 'You do realise, Madam, that it's your duty to tell us. Otherwise, how can we ever close the file?'

'Ah, *signomi, Astinomos!*' she'd wailed. 'I was so happy to have my boy home, everything flew right out of my head!'

The Cairo number on the Aswani file had been disconnected. Yiannis called Minoan Lines and got through to a secretary with hay fever who told him between sneezing fits that the Human Resources Department had recently moved offices. Nevertheless she would try her very best, she assured him, to track down the documentation. Twenty minutes later she called back to say the details had been temporarily misplaced.

Yiannis, who'd heard such excuses a hundred times before, stuffed the Aswani file into a cardboard folder; it was more likely that the documentation was incomplete, or had never existed in the first place. Even for casual workers the bureaucracy was cumbersome, and as long as the big shipping companies had schedules to keep, the Mediterranean would always have its share of Sinbads.

The cedars of Pepargni loomed up ahead, torn black flags on the crest of the hill. Yiannis passed through the Hospital checkpoint and parked in the restricted car-park beside the bleached concrete annexe of the Mortuary. He sat in the car for a moment, finishing his cigarette, thinking of the fat boy in the basement, who had divested himself of everything that could have helped to identifiy him. Did he do so out of a wish to meet his Maker in a state of nature, or because he really and truly didn't want to be known?

Taking the lift down to the basement, he walked along the strip-lit corridor towards the autopsy suite. On his left were the solid steel doors of the refrigerated facility, where stone-cold corpses waited to be claimed. If after a year no one had come forward, they'd be cleared out to make way for the new arrivals, their remains decently disposed of. Their particulars kept on file for future reference.

Although not an insect buzzed or crawled in this hygienic underworld, he was aware of a constant low-frequency disturbance, no doubt from the refrigeration units, but unsettling all the same. To him the sucking noise made by the doors of the refrigerated safes was the sound of closure, of finality. He couldn't help thinking of the souls behind them, engaged in their hopeless struggle against silence, still trying to tell him things, to name names and places.

I am so and so of such and such. Remember me.

He took a face mask from the dispenser by the door, and slipped foot-protectors over his shoes. Through the glass porthole he glimpsed the victim laid out on a steel autopsy table. He was relieved to see that the Y- shaped incision on the torso had already been sutured: at least he'd be spared the ghoulish process of weighing and measuring the organs.

Although he'd hoped that Theo Papaspyrou, philosopher and fellow movie-buff, would be on shift, it was Kallenikos who turned from the table to greet him, stripping off his surgical gloves and pulling down his mask. Kallenikos was tall and thin, with a crescent-moon curve to his long face, and a stance to match, as though he were recoiling physically- less from the world of the dead, Yiannis fancied, than from the palpable warmth of the living.

He had parked himself as far from the body as he decently could, but Kallenikos beckoned him closer. 'He won't bite, Sergeant. He's the one who's been bitten, remember!' On his face was the defensive, sarcastic smile of the painfully shy.

Yiannis breathed shallowly behind his mask, wondering if any normal person could ever accustom himself to the all-pervading smell. 'I was just passing,' he mumbled. 'Thought I'd look in to check if there was any news.'

The corpse had lost its initial puffiness, and the skin colour had faded to a bluish pallor. The fingertips were stained with

54

ink. Yiannis could see now that he had been a very handsome boy indeed.

'The news is that there's not a lot, macroscopically speaking.' Kallenikos leaned over the table and laid a proprietory hand on the lifeless shoulder. He seemed to be addressing not Yiannis, but the corpse itself. 'Some signs of angio-oedema, but no pharyngeal or laryngeal oedema. So, death was a result of shock rather than asphyxia. Anaphylactic, I'd say, but I'll wait for Immunology on that. We can't be completely sure until the mast-cell tryptase tests come back.'

Yiannis nodded hastily; he would have asked Kallenikos to explain, but his stomach was expressing an extreme reluctance to prolong this interview with the dead. Saliva flowed into his mouth, and he swallowed hard.

'So the bee stings killed him?'

'As I said, subject to microscopic findings. You'll have the report by fax.'

'I'm obliged to you,' muttered Yiannis.

Escaping to the corridor, he dropped his mask and bootees into the disposal bin, and headed for the lab. Two of the young assistants were bending over a horizontal light-box, but Theo's small side office was empty, the blank computer-screen bustling with post-it notes. One of them fluttered to the floor when Yiannis entered.

Autopsia: to look for one's self

He stuck the note back on the monitor, along with a message asking Theo to ring him. Leaving the ziploc bag which contained the Davidoff packet on the desk, he closed the door gently and took the lift up to the ground floor. Once outside, he leaned against the wall for a moment, breathing in the warm and ordinary air, trying to banish from his mind the memory of the long white hand that had made a pet or a cat of a shoulder.

On his way to Police HQ on Dikeosinas Street Yiannis stopped off at the video-shop on Kalokairinou to pick up *The Good Thief,* which Theo had told him was a remake of Melville's *Bob le Flambeur,* with the excellent Nick Nolte as

Bob. A poster of the 1955 original had travelled with Yiannis to Australia and back, and since then had held pride of place on the wall of his living room: Fedoras and smoke, Colette Fleury in a transparent plastic raincoat, a beret glued to the back of her head.

If Bob the gambler drove a white Cadillac and kept a fruit machine in his wardrobe, in his dealings with the world, and particularly with women, Bob the man had an impeccable moral code.

The 800 million francs in the Deauville safe were the chance of a lifetime, tempting enough to drag Bob out of retirement; *'L'affaire de ma vie,'* he told his faithful ex Yvonne.

'Don't do it,' Yvonne warned, 'You'll get caught, and you're past the age when you can take it.'

The *Bar Narcisse*. Flasks of *pastis* and yellow *Ricard* ashtrays, Paris rain streaming down the plate-glass windows. 'I was born with the Ace of Diamonds in my hand,' Yiannis murmured, squinting out at Heraklion's bright blue day.

The Courts of Justice were housed in the same tall Venetian building as the Police Station. The Court was still in session, the clerk told him; his own case would be delayed. Assault and insulting behaviour over at Agios Nikolaos. The three English thugs had been cooling their heels in Nea Poli jail; all going well, they would be fined and dispatched post-haste to Her Majesty's Constabulary, and Yiannis could wash his hands of them.

He slipped in and took a seat in the back of the court, where a Roma case was still in progress.

The *Sokadre* lawyer – a balding, fiery-eyed man in his fifties – was demanding to read a statement, even though, as the Magistrate pointed out, five of his Roma clients were to be released immediately without charge, and the other four following payment of outstanding fines for traffic violations.

The Magistrate frowned at his watch. 'I would remind you that you have already won the legal argument, yet it seems you must also win the moral one. In which case, the Court would appreciate brevity.'

Quite so, thought Yiannis. The *Sokadre* lawyers were increasingly on the offensive, but in his opinion what they notably omitted to mention was that citizenship carried not only rights, but duties. The social contract wasn't a one-way street.

The lawyer had produced a sheaf of papers from his briefcase, which he now proceeded to read:

'We believe that the methods adopted by the police – sealing off the whole Roma settlement at Nea Alikarnassos, instead of systematic calls on individuals to present themselves – are illegal, as they constitute an insult to human decency.'

Dignity, thought Yiannis, surely he means dignity. The defendants – men whose ages ranged from 18 to 60 – scowled and shifted in the dock. Yiannis caught the eye of one of them, and looked away, discomfited. In no way did he condone the persecution of minorities, but could he honestly deny that he harboured fairly deep-rooted cultural suspicions? Like the Jehovah's Witnesses, the Roma were a closed community, and this inevitably attracted prejudice. There was no getting away from the fact that their allegiances were to clan, not country. Presumably they paid at least some of the taxes required of them, but beyond that, well, it was hard to see what they contributed to the society at large.

Ask not what your country can do for you, he thought, *but what you can do for your country*. In many ways Kennedy's idealistic appeal seemed more prescient now than it had fifty years ago.

'Those methods of the police also contribute to the embedding of a stereotype that portrays the Roma as "the usual suspects",' the lawyer continued, 'something that the Greek Ombudsman has pointed out in his letter to the General Police Directorate of Thessaloniki following the carrying out of similar raids on the community of the Roma of the Gallikos River. If I may quote from letter 1/868/00/2.'

The Magistrate was visibly irritated. 'No you may not! Unlike your grievances, the Court's time is not limitless. I believe you have already made your point.' As the Court rose to recess, two of the arresting officers, bully-boys Yiannis knew from Police Security, were blatantly smirking.

Outside the Court he snatched a cigarette before his case was called, and watched the Roma men being claimed by their womenfolk, who looked handsome and archaic in their long skirts and black flower-printed headscarves. Perhaps there would always be groups like those, he reflected: groups on the margins of modern civilisation, nomads from another age. Perhaps there were chasms that no one, with the best will in the world, could ever cross.

The *Sokadre* lawyer stood alone on the steps of the Court-house, a desultory figure with his briefcase and his lightweight city suit. Yiannis watched as his clients, who had abandoned the guy with barely a handshake, bundled into battered cars, honked horns, shouted triumphantly to their relatives. If *Sokadre* had called a press conference, the invitation had gone singularly unheeded.

Shortly after he got back to the station Theo rang back, his 40 a day cough rumbling down the line. Yiannis tucked the phone under his chin.

Serology, he wrote on his notepad, watching his cigarette burn down in the ashtray. Karen's photograph frowned disapprovingly through the smoke. He moved the ashtray away from her.

'We've got semen on the thighs, and I'd hazard vaginal fluid as well, although I'd want to do Lugal's iodine for epithelial cells to be sure, or as sure as you can be with vaginal. If I get the go-ahead, that is.'

'Shit!' said Yiannis, letting out his breath. '*Cherchez la femme,* then.'

'Looks that way.' Theo's voice was animated. 'Think raven-haired maiden, Yianni, think temptress. We've got some hairs, long, dark, some with roots, so DNA could work. But the tox screen's even better. Stomach contents are *pretty* interesting. Your victim liked his drugs organic. Seems he

58

hadn't eaten for 24 hours, apart from raw opium. The genuine article, straight fom the poppy. *Papaver somniferum*, if you want to know.'

'Really?' said Yiannis, who didn't.

'What's even more unusual is the other opiate. Comes from the narcissus bulb. Basically it's a poison, but the quantities weren't enough to kill him. There're also traces of some kind of home-brewed beer, made from fermented barley.'

'Quite a cocktail!' Yiannis had been decorating his note-book with test-tubes and bunsen-burners, his mind milling about in the school Science Lab. Unlike Yiannis, Theo the A student had relished the instability of chemical compounds, the bright unnatural lights and sudden explosions. 'It's gone to Narcotics?'

'Yep. Something new for them to chew on, as it were. But between you and me, my friend, if the victim was female, I'd immediately think Rohypnol. A rough and ready version, okay, but a similar chemical makeup. The effects would be roughly the same.'

Yiannis saw that the test-tubes he'd drawn looked more like condoms. He crossed them out hastily. 'Meaning?'

'Well we're not talking Ecstasy here. Compliance to the point of coma is what I'm suggesting.'

Yiannis didn't hide his incredulity. 'Girl meets boy, girl rapes boy? Somehow I can't see it.'

'Unconventional, I agree. Although speaking as an old married man, I can only speculate on what consenting singles get up to these days. I mean, you're the bachelor boy, Yianni, you tell me.'

Yiannis ignored the jibe. One of Theo's less attractive traits was a tendency to indulge his envy to the point of insensitivity. Although he had married quite recently and, it seemed, happily, Theo was terminally wistful about his lost freedoms. In *tavernas*, on the streets, his eyes worked overtime at their mournful appraisals. Sometimes his lips worked too, and if to remind him of what he was missing. Luckily for Theo, no sounds came out; even more luckily, Livia either didn't notice this nervous tic of his, or was wise enough to wait until it withered away of its own accord, like the State was supposed to do under socialism.

'So we could be looking at an accident. Some sort of *folie à deux*, maybe?'

'We *could*. Must have been a pretty persuasive girl, though, getting her date to roll around in the honey-pot. Unless the stuff came after the act, of course. Didn't they preserve Alexander the Great in honey to bring him back to Greece?'

Yiannis' mind flashed up an image of the corpse on the autopsy table. By the time he'd arrived the honey had been hosed away, and until now he'd managed to blot out the sensations attached to his first encounter with the body: the cloying smell of the thing, its baleful stickiness.

'What about prints?' he asked. DNA evidence – if it was available – was fine for corroboration, but in investigative terms it was nothing.

'Some latents. Pretty blurred though. The honey didn't help.'

'But you're enhancing?'

'Trying to. Another wierd thing, though, is the pollen. Shed-loads of it, relatively speaking. Massive deposits just about everywhere they swabbed. If it was up to me I'd send it straight to the University but I'm not the one who makes the call.' There was an edge of bitterness in his voice. Despite Theo's superior qualifications, it was Kallenikos who was Chief Medical Examiner.

'So we wait.'

'We wait. But if Kallenikos gives anaphylactic shock as cause of death, where's your case?'

My case? thought Yiannis. If and when the ponderous wheels of justice began to turn, his involvement would be strictly peripheral, and Theo knew it.

'Unless someone wants to try taking a bunch of bees to court.'

Yiannis laughed. 'Even for Vasilakis, that would be a first.'

'So how did you get on with Monica Vitti?'

For a moment he had no idea what Theo meant. 'Stromboli?' he said. Theo had lent him the DVD a week ago. 'I was going to watch it last night, but something came up.'

He thought of Pericles' sad kitchen, with its cobwebs worthy of a Grimm's fairy tale. The smell of the place had made him gag. He remembered sour milk, mouse-shit, and something worse, some undertone of extreme organic nastiness. If it wasn't for the fact that he'd personally attended the old mother's funeral years ago, he'd have said her corpse was still in residence, easing its way through the several unspeakable stages of putrefaction.

The 'things' were clearly archaeological, although Pericles swore he hadn't been aware of it, and Yiannis was inclined to believe him. He'd zipped them into a polythene bag for protection and locked them in his desk drawer until he could pin down someone at the Museum. His phone call had elicited more irritation than excitement. The Assistant Curator, when he finally got through to her, pointed out that they simply didn't have the space to house every minor find, not to mention the dire shortage of the sort of skilled staff required to catalogue them. She didn't actually *say* they were already bursting at the seams with all that old Minoan junk, but that was certainly the implication.

10

On the way back from Knossos Ingrid has almost an hour to wait in Heraklion before the last bus leaves for Panomeli.

Tucked into the eastern armpit of the Venetian Port, the bus station is a noisy, chaotic encampment of ticket kiosks in the shadow of the huge Minoan Line ferries. The newer buses wear horns. Her first thought on seeing them was, how witty of the Cretans, to turn a bus into a bull. Then she noticed the German maker's marque. The forward-thrusting 'horns' were extensions to hold wing-mirrors, presumably designed to make passing easier on narrow country roads. The neon destinations which flickered above the windscreens were an archaeologist's primer: Arkhanes, Mallia, Zakro.

She buys a *frappé* in a styrofoam cup and carries it to a bench on a grassy plot near the old Venetian Arsenal, where she sits smoking, watching the planes carve out their westerly sky-track above the harbour before banking sharp right at the yellow ziggurat of the Lato Hotel, and climbing away to the north. On the fourth floor of the hotel two uniformed chambermaids laugh as they stretch and fold a white sheet across a half-metre gap between balconies.

Images of Knossos dart back at her. Two swallows whistling around the frescos of Evans' reconstruction of the *Piano Nobile*. The extreme angle of the cobbled ramp which sloped down to the Theatral Area – a ramp made for running, for gaining the momentum needed to explode into somersaults over the bull's horns in the *tavrokatharpsia*.

The huge clay *pithoi*, jars that had held oil, wine, barley, chickpeas – row upon row of them, stored in a labyrinth of underground alleys. The Palace built around them like a comb round honey. Although she knew perfectly well that the site was pre-Hellenic, she was aware of a mounting stress within, of missing the pleasure of recognition. But why had she expected to find anything that was remotely Greek about Knossos? If there were reference points they lay, surely, to the east, in Anatolia or Jericho or Uruk. Even the intricacies of the plumbing suggested a devotion to water equalled only by the Arabs. The lustral baths, the open stone conduits with their elbow joints and T junctions, to channel clear fresh water to every corner of the compound, its constant flicker a blessing, 4,000 years ago, in the blazing heat of the Aegean summer.

Think deep time. Think Neolithic.

A wordless landscape – not quite a blank slate, but a blue slate pavement written on by the *strophe* and *antistrophe* of feet.

The dancing priestesses, bright-bodied like bees, their poppy-capsule heads exploding in a rain of seeds.

Poppy-cults with their opium apparatus. Women falling in love with bulls.

Pelicans balance unsteadily on the swaying masts of the yachts in the marina. It's hot, that oppressive 6 o'clock heat which crams itself into the narrow streets of old Heraklion. The crowds at Knossos, the Palace itself, have left her dazed and a little panicky, as if she's sinking back into the pre-literate, understanding nothing. Knowing far less about the Minoans than she did before she set eyes on the place. Her head is at bursting point. Schliemann and Troy, Evans and Knossos. If imagination, rather than science, had always guided the spade, how could you ever hope to find the thread of truth, the link that would connect the present in some real way with the past?

Once again she tries to put herself in Alice's shoes. Sensible shoes, to be sure. Which is, of course, unfair of her. But all the same, she thinks, soaking a tissue with water from her bottle and wetting her neck and brow, all the same – *as a woman.*

A three-legged dog limps across the intersection and dives into the shade under her bench. Splaying up its hindquarters, it bares its teeth and worries eagerly at its fleas. She edges to the far end of the bench, imagining ringworm, intestinal parasites: like the rest of Greece, the island is overrun by sorry strays.

One thing, though, is certain. Alice Kober would have been outraged by Knossos. The woman who so abhorred fictive thinking would have taken one look at Evans' wishful reconstructions and snapped, 'Show me the evidence!'

11

Asterios, they call him, because of his head, which is too big, and his jaw, which is oblong and juts like the open drawer of a cash till. Asterios the Minotaur.

What men call you, you become.

Here in his cave of darkness shaved ladies arch their bodies like bows on the magazine-covers. Foreigners come up from the beach sun-blinded and blink over his counter, unable to see him in the gloom of the *periptero*, and the sand carried on their feet covers the pavements, glittering like glass splinters. *Parakalo!* they cry, wanting cheap cigarettes in cartons of 200, cans of Sprite, sugar-free chewing-gum. No change, they say, *den eho psila*, these bare-bellied blondes with jewels in their navels, these skinny pale-eyed beauties.

There are those who pity the miserable fate of a man whose mind is encased in the body of a beast, but he, Asterios, pities the bull, for no one appreciates the pain and despair a beast must feel whose pure instincts are disrupted by the agitations of a man's mind. Give a bull grass, sweet water and a willing heifer and he is happy. But a man is never content. If no gadflies of worry exist he will invent them. If today the till is full he will lie awake worrying about tomorrow, for these ochre clouds on the far horizon may be augurs of a *meltemi* that will drive the tourists from the shore, and then the sunbeds will lie empty and wind-lashed as the storm whips up, and Androula will take no euros for a day or more. But he, Asterios, is the one who will brood on the lost takings, for always it is the man who bears responsibility, and if the money shrinks away he is the one who feels the hurt of it, just as the man who makes the profit feels the pride.

What is sent by the Gods cannot be railed against, but a man bears the weight of his own mistakes.

Whenever he passes the Pantelides field, he spits on it.

In the old days, before cellphones and apartments, when tourists still queued at the *periptero* to make their long distance calls, the field was his millstone. On the upper slopes the soil was so thin and flinty that olives could squeeze no sustenance from it, and vines blighted and blackened on the salt-tainted marsh of the seaward strip. His father had broken his heart on that land, and so would Asterios have broken his, if he'd had his way, but as soon as the old man was in his grave he swore to rid himself of every worthless acre.

In those days Pantelides went barefoot and rode side-saddle on his donkey, so when he said he would take the field off his hands and pay money for the privilege, Asterios laughed up his sleeve. Pantelides said he would grow maize on it, keep goats. Asterios nodded and slapped the old boy on the back and drank his raki and did not disabuse him.

Pantelides had red rheumy eyes and a stupid smile, but what Asterios did not know was that the smile concealed cunning, and the eyes saw what his own did not. The future, white marble and mortar: 4 storey blocks of holiday apartments, balconies with balustrades sculpted in the shape of sunrays, gardens with rose-beds encircling plaster Aphrodites, crazy-paving paths flanked by bulbous lights which gleamed from the ground like toadstools. From the Golden Sun Studios it is only half a kilometre to the new beach, half a kilometre to the bars and dance-clubs of Katomeli. The Golden Sun Studios have become Pantelides' goldmine.

Pantelides had planted no maize, yet after a year or so he had a long black Mercedes, and no need of goats. Then the new road came curving through the valley, and what had been useless marsh became prime land for which the government paid topdollar. Once Pantelides had built a villa for his son and daughter-in-law, he began to sell the remaining land in plots, and soon other houses were thrown up – summer villas with swimming pools for people from Athens, and more apartment blocks for the swelling tide of foreigners. Pegasus Rooms, Apollo Studios, Herakles Apartments.

Four times a day Asterios passes by on the Katomeli road and looks neither to the left nor the right, but all the same he spits on them, on the Golden Sun Studios, and on the house of old Pantelides, and on the villa of Spiros his son, who is not old and who according to Manoli Dimeros has big plans. Manoli too is a man with plans, and this is why he can scent them on the breath of others. Spiros Pantelides, he says, is angling to buy the olive groves of old Stavlakis, which stretch from the Panomeli road across the headland as far as the cove where Manoli's grandfather built the Taverna Medusa. Katomeli will spread her tentacles, Manoli says; one day the villas and the studios will reach right around Panomeli headland and grasp the old village by the throat, and any man who tries to stop them will be a fool, and badly stung.

At nights Manoli waits table at the Taverna, but in the mornings he works at his English, his business studies. The Medusa which is his inheritance will not be enough for him; instead, his dreams are of an ApartHotel on the crest of the headland, with a jetty for yachts, and mini-golf, and a diving school. For this he needs Stavlakis' land, and for this he visits Pepargni Hospital, where the old boy is having a hip replacement, although no plastic joint or metal pin will ever make him fit enough to tend these rotten trees of his. There is no doubt that Stavlakis will sell, says Manoli – the only question is whether he will sell to a Dimeros, or a Pantelides.

'Look what's happened to Katomeli, Asterios,' says Manoli. 'Now it's Panomeli's turn to be up and coming, you'd be a fool to stand aside. You did it once, and see where it got you. At your age you and Androula should be thinking about a little nest-egg.'

Asterios thinks of the nest egg he lost to Pantelides, a huge egg like an eagle's, and rightly his.

'I have a friend,' says Manoli, 'an English friend who knows how to build. Let him have a look at that meadow below your house, such a good aspect, and just sitting there doing nothing for you. Why grow thistles, Asterios, when you could be looking at 80,000 euros?'

12

Dusk is already falling when the horned bus sets her down at the Panomeli turning. The sky has deepened to cerulean and the first stars are out above the hill of Agia Stephanou.

Once past the straggling suburb of studio apartments she becomes conscious of the winding road ahead, flanked by darkening olive groves, and wishes, too late, that she'd got off in Katomeli's main square, where taxis queue in a rank beside the *periptero*. There has been a death in the vicinity, perhaps even a suspicious one, and here she is, strolling alone in the gloaming.

The outline of the headland looms up on her left; there should be a junction fairly soon, whose right fork leads to Panomeli. It might be sensible to feel alarmed, even to act on it. Flag down a passing car, or make a dash for a farmhouse and beg for rescue. Only the thought of making an idiot of herself deters her.

Focussing her mind on her quiet balcony and an ouzo with ice, she strides on manfully, shoulders back, wearing the thick skin women grow to cope with the night streets of North London. The road has little in common with the one she walked this morning. Darkness has stretched its distances. Bats scissor silently overhead, and spectral chickens scratch behind the hedges.

She sees a torch beam ahead, advancing jerkily, and hears the phlegmy laugh of Mrs Gifford. Two cigarette ends bob, friendly as fireflies.

The Giffords have been on the island for barely a week but already they're Cretophiles: ardent consumers, not only of the sun, the food, the wine, but also of local handicrafts and culture. They sally forth on all the Flagstaff excursions, returning with rugs, crocheted tablecloths, pots shaped like cockerels, CDs of bouzouki music, ceramic coasters in the form of the Phaestos Disc. On the beach they ask her advice on archaeology, and star the sites on their map – the must-sees, the maybes.

Startled to see her looming out of the twilight, the Giffords fuss protectively: they're heading off to a fish taverna they stumbled on the other night while walking round the head-land.

'So we're standing there on the sand,' Glenys explains, 'like a pair of wallies in our shorts and stuff.'

'Well you don't know, do you?' Ken chips in, 'It could have been a private party.'

'Then the old mother spots us, and before you know it she's dragged us in and plonked us down with the free wine and the glasses.'

Glenys Gifford's breath is gin-scented; she's wearing some-thing silky and cocktailish, with high-heeled silver slingbacks. 'Why don't you come along with us? The Greek dancers are brilliant.'

Ingrid looks doubtfully at her own rolled up combats, her lightweight hill boots, but Ken dismisses her objections.

'You're fine, love, don't worry about it,' he says, claiming the torch from his wife and lighting the way for the ladies.

The left fork of the road descends through the olive groves until the lights of Katomeli appear again through the trees as distant reflections in the bay. The torch beam illuminates a sign nailed lopsidedly to a tree trunk: Taverna Medusa, with a cartoon of a drunken octopus. There's a narrow insect-ridden path, and then the rear of a concrete building, strip-lights, kitchen clatter. The path squeezes like a poor relation round the side of the house and emerges on an aristocrat of terraces, where tables are arranged around a stone-flagged dancefloor which, if smaller than the theatral area of the Palace of King Minos, has the same aura of intent. Fairy lights are looped between the tamarisk trees. Beyond a low stone wall a cool moon is rising over the water.

Madame greets the Giffords as if they were *oikoyenia*, her own long-lost relations. Grey braids snake girlishly round her head, and her broad face is as wrinkled as a walnut. Flapping her hands in apology for the oppressive heat, she ushers them to a table by the wall.

'*Kala?*' she barks, gold fillings gleaming in her triumphant smile. When she opens her palms to the sky the faintest breath of wind rises, as if summoned, from the sea.

'*Poli kala,*' Ingrid agrees.

'*Efkaristo, efkaristo,*' chorus the Giffords.

Although half the tables are already occupied, no one is eating yet. People are still at the ouzo stage, nibbling at olives, at wedges of cucumber.

Glenys nudges Ingrid. 'There they are! Isn't she gorgeous?'

The dancers are sitting at a small side table beside the glass door to the interior – an almond-eyed girl of eighteen or so, a boy who could be her brother, and a burly, handsome older man: the paterfamilias, if looks are anything to go by. They're sipping red wine, quietly observing the guests who are thronging in now from a car park hidden in the trees. The two men wear white shirts with red sashes, and baggy *vrakes* tucked into white stockings. The girl's headgear – a black scarf bandaged tightly over a high cone of hair – resembles the Phrygian cap Ingrid's seen on some of the later sealstones. And certainly she has a look of the East, with her parchment-white skin and black eyes which tilt like those of the bare-breasted beauties on the frescoes; unlike them, though, she hides her body under a high-necked blouse and full embroidered skirt.

Ken Gifford sighs with pleasure, settling in. His big red arms are planted on the table and his sunburned face beams good-will to all and sundry, raising a chorus of *yassous* and *kalisperas* from the neighbouring diners: an extended family

71

whose conversation slides fluently from Greek to German and back again. Black heads and flaxen gold.

The Giffords, she learns, run a builders' merchants in Solihull. Started by Ken's father in the 50s, it's now a sizeable concern. Glenys tells her proudly that Ken can turn his hand to just about anything – tiling, roofing, bricklaying, plumbing in jacuzzis.

Ingrid can believe it. She imagines a house like a hacienda, with stuccoed walls and marble steps and terracotta arches. A house with the wow factor.

'I'm for the seafood platter, girls, how about you?' Ken raises a casual finger to the waiter, as if he had been coming here for years. '*Yassou* Manoli!'

Balancing a tray of drinks, the man nods and detours towards them. After the gracious greetings he frowns intently at Ken.

'We will speak later? As you see, I have much work now.'

'Right you are,' says Ken.

'You like to have ouzo?' Manoli is already swerving away. 'I will bring some.'

Glenys is watching Ken curiously. 'What're you up to now?'

Ken hums a few pensive bars of *Mamma mia*, and lifts a finger to his lips. 'All will be revealed,' he promises, with a broad wink at Ingrid

Desperate for her ouzo, she smiles back dutifully. Not just a clubbable man, then, but a man who loves surprises. She likes the way he and Glenys touch and tease one another; 30 years of marriage haven't neutered them, which, after the dire dynamic of the Wilson-Wilsons, comes as a relief. Neither one defers to the other, and as far as she can make out the easy-going Glenys doesn't have a controlling bone in her body.

Hen-pecked men infuriate Ingrid, but not as much as controlling women. Women, like her mother, who take a perverse pride in their expertise. After the abortion she'd made what

Ingrid assumed to be a last-ditch attempt at intimacy. The village had been snowed in that week; all the trains were suspended, and with the A9 closed off there was no escape to Edinburgh. Although it was only 4 in the afternoon her mother was already on her second gin, and gaining confidence with every gulp. Firelight glinted on the crystal tumbler which rested briefly on the arm of her chair before rising again, eager as a bee, to hover at her scarlet lips.

All men are selfish, Ingrid. You have to learn to handle them. It's quite a knack, believe you me.

As if it was a mother's duty to inculcate the rules of female *realpolitik*, as if Ingrid wasn't perfectly well aware that Greta couldn't handle a boiled egg by that time, never mind a man. Now, in old age, Greta Laurie née Henderson seemed to have found her natural element. In Buncranna House – cream-stuccoed amid spreading lawns, with a view over effulgent rhododendrons to the seaweed-swagged shore of the Firth – Greta was waited on hand and foot, and lived a life that was at last free of all responsibility.

After Ingrid's father died – an event that seemed to have remarkably little impact on Greta – she had gone into the Home without protest. He'd been looking peaky all winter, Elsa told Ingrid; she'd been concerned about him. He'd taken on a locum to cover the home visits, so that he could devote more time to caring for Greta; characteristically, he had brushed off Elsa's offers of help. He'd keeled over one day in the middle of morning Surgery. A massive heart attack. He'd never said a word to her about any warning symptoms, although, as a doctor, he must have been aware of them.

She has an image of her mother at the funeral: the blonde hair that had never greyed, but instead had moved through increments of platinum to pure white, coiffed and curled for the occasion. She sat in a wheelchair, a tartan rug tucked across her knees. (She could perfectly well have walked, Ingrid was sure, if she'd bothered to practise with the hated wheelie. *If you think I'm going to fall on my face in front of all these folks, she said, and that was the end of it.*)

Queenly in cultured pearls, she accepted condolences from

what looked like the entire population of the village – in which Dr Laurie had been held in high esteem, if not exactly in affection.

Elsa – heroically, Ingrid thought – had offered to take Greta in, but with her sister hardly out of earshot Greta vetoed the very notion.

She'd drive me mad, her with her great big feet and her golf-clubs, she snapped, although in Ingrid's honest opinion Elsa was the one who'd be driven mad by the arrangement.

Pitlochry, where Elsa was living at the time, was the final stumbling block.

What would I want to be stuck up there for? Greta demanded, although Ingrid couldn't see why being stuck in posh Pitlochry was a worse fate than being stuck in dreary Dunelg. At an age when sibling rivalry should have faded into oblivion, Greta's blue eyes burned with scorn.

Never could get herself a man, that's Elsa's trouble!

The seafood arrives on a mound of sodden rice, ringed with french fries and the obligatory slices of cucumber. The wine waiter – a younger, frostier version of Manoli – proposes a pricey foreign Chardonnay. Since it's clear that the affable Ken will agree to absolutely anything, Ingrid asks if they have, perhaps, a house wine, a wine from the locality.

'*Ne, veveos,*' the waiter says curtly, for she has disobeyed the unspoken diktat that the man of the party will do the ordering. When he returns with a carafe of ochre wine Ken tastes it and nods his approval. He pushes a napkin towards Ingrid.

'Write it down for me, will you? How you ask for it.'

In block capitals, she transliterates. *MIPOS ECHETE TO DIKOSAS KRASI.*

Ken reads it back with surprising fluency, and she commends him. 'You've definitely got an ear!'

Glenys groans. 'Oh my Lord, don't encourage him. He'll be dragging a barrel home on the plane next!'

On the horizon the tiny lights of a night ferry slide north towards the Cyclades. Bullfrogs are tuning up their bass section in an invisible ditch. Suddenly a spot comes on, and, without announcement, the dancers move to the centre of the floor.

At the outset the music is stately, restrained. Poised on one leg, the older man is a tree or a pillar winds or earthquakes might topple. His arms are branches, his hands fluttering like birds' wings, then flattening into beaks. His chest is drawn up, his level gaze challenges the audience. When the long leaning moment ends, the fingers snap, and the strong stockinged legs weave sideways as he skips easily into double-time and back again to match the changes in tempo.

The boy and girl are egging the older man on, and the audience joins in, clapping in time, crying *opa! opa!* at the high immaculate kicks.

When the dance ends in an uproar of applause Glenys rolls her eyes at Ingrid. Sweat shines in the sunburned crevice between her breasts

'Talk about refreshing the parts other blokes don't reach!' she hisses.

Ingrid agrees entirely. Virile isn't the word for it.

'Hey, steady on, girls!' says Ken in a pantomime of alarm, and it crosses her mind that what she's providing here is the audience, the necessary third term. Ingrid the obliging single-ton. For a moment she wonders ungenerously if the private Giffords sparkle quite as brightly as the public pair.

The boy and girl begin haltingly. Evidently it's a courtship dance, gawky and tremulous, as if they can no more surrender to the music – Turkish-inspired, mournful – than they can surrender to each other. Maybe the affair will end badly, in loss or punishment or rejection. Can the swain be trusted with the girl's innocence? Will he seduce and abandon her without a thought, or, through his mastery of the figures of the dance, prove beyond doubt his strength, his honour, his *timi*?

Ingrid sees old Madame shuffling out of the door, a small wicker basket held in front of her, a smile breaking on her face like a good omen. As the music shifts into a celebratory key, handfuls of rose-petals plucked from the basket are tossed into the air, to float down on the heads and shoulders of the young couple.

'All's well that ends well, eh?' says Ken. Napkin tucked in at his neck, he's attacking a chunk of octopus, flesh-pink and pimpled with suckers. He gestures towards her empty plate. 'Eat up, lass. Don't go all anorexic on us.'

She serves herself with prawns and gingerly with soggy rice, pondering the contrast between the strait-laced gestures of the girl – the arms kept pinioned at her sides, the high prim neckline, and the hair too, banned and hidden – and the rampant, thrusting moves of the older man, until a burst of laughter erupts from the tables.

The young dancers have press-ganged someone from the audience, whisking him indoors, and now he reappears between them, supported by a stick: a mock-grandfather with hair greyed by a dusting of kitchen flour, his back bent double with arthritis, his legs bowed and pathetically wobbling.

The music begins gradually, easing into the old boy. She distinctly sees it enter the arches of his feet and flow upwards. Accelerating, it unlocks the rickety knees, straightens out the curve of the spine; the pigeon chest swells up with it until the man's linen jacket is stretched taut across his ribcage, held by a single button. Music is the medicine, dance the syringe that delivers it.

Ingrid feels the tears rise in her throat. If she'd known her father was ill, if she'd been there, would his gait have quickened, his grip grown firmer on his walking stick, his chest swelled to contain a heart grown young again, and elastic?

'Get a load of the dancing policeman,' says Ken. 'Isn't that our Sergeant Yiannis?'

'It never is!' Glenys protests, peering.

'None other,' Ken insists. 'Bit of a suave git, isn't he?'

Ingrid recognises him now, the narrow face, the diligent dark eyes, the deep lines which slant from the nostrils to the corners of the mouth. The stick, redundant now, is hurled away contemptuously, and the rejuvenation is complete: he's skipping about, frisking like a young goat in a deafening chorus of bravos. A donkey brays in a nearby field, adding its voice to the applause.

She knows she is staring, the trance of the music heightening rather than blurring her senses, the imperative of the bouzouki line which never breaks but ripples along insistently like water. At the table where the Sergeant was sitting she glimpses Gaylene, the Head Rep., with a balding Greek whose chest, tanned almost black, wears a mat of wiry white hairs. A younger couple with gel-sculpted hair cry *Ela, ela Yianni*! A little girl stands on her chair, steadied by a small, auburn-haired woman in a burgundy dress. The woman is sharp-chinned, muscular, attractive. His wife and child? Ingrid feels an unsettling pang of jealousy.

She looks again at Sergeant Yiannis, her smile fixed, her hands clapping determinedly. She remembers that, under the disguising flour, his hair is a light brown, flecked with real grey only at the temples. He takes his bow and, with a shy laugh, applauds the audience.

As he turns to leave the dance-floor his eyes rest briefly on the table where she and the Giffords are sitting, and she wonders if she has imagined his minute, almost crafty nod of recognition.

Later, in the line of women, she grasps Glenys' hand, feeling the cool metal of rings. Madame herself has toured the tables, magisterial, scooping the females from their seats, pooh-poohing all demurrals. Three cross-steps to the right, three to the left, then a slow advance followed by a minor retreat, like a lapping of the tide. Ingrid keeps her eyes fixed on the lead dancer, wishing for a dark red dress that floats, and above all not to stumble or fail. The moon is high now, shining its silver on the wet strip of sand beyond the wall.

Gradually her inhibition fades, and she straightens her back and lets her feet follow the dips and rises, the laws of light and water. *Strophe* and *antistrophe*. The tiredness has fallen from her, as if the mind-weight of the *logos* has been snipped off and cast in pieces on the waves. Without it, her breasts strain against the thin fabric of her vest; her body, effortless, levitates above the foam.

The men have risen from their seats, intent now, slow-clapping gallantly in unison. Ken catches her eye and gives her a double thumbs-up sign; Manoli the waiter has joined him at the table, and they are smoking, watching but not watching, their heads close together, as if hatching a plot.

Ingrid doesn't allow herself a single glance at the Sergeant's table, but as the night air swirls around her she's filled with a sensation of being watched properly, of being seen. Absorbed in the fluency of the movements, she doesn't stop to ask *by whom*, for in her mind the unattributed gaze – so gratifying – has already transmuted from the individual to the collective, and the visibility it confers on her is archetypal, and takes her beyond herself, and, magically, quells her envy.

13

What is invisible to man, Callasso says, *is visible to the gods.*

When Greta Laurie *née* Henderson wakes from her nap she thinks that it was considerate of William to build a ballroom on to the house and keep it a secret, just to surprise her.

She always thought the stairs on the top landing went up to the loft where he kept his old Army trunk with its ancient tin hat and greatcoat. A cobwebby dark place you'd never bother to go in. She'd told him time and time again he should have a good clear-out up there – but to move the workmen in without telling her, to raise the ceiling high as a kirk's, to put in the sprung dancefloor and the French polish as well – well, who'd have thought he had it in him? A man who was never one to go spending money, so honestly, you could have knocked her down with a feather. He'd had mirrors installed from floor to ceiling, too, so that she could get her posture perfect, back like a ramrod, up on tiptoe always for the *pas-de-basque* or the travelling step or the slower stately Strathspey.

Greta arches her instep, observing it. Good feet, she's always had. Small and ladylike, but strong, flexible. She thinks of the Hunt balls everyone used to go to, they knew what Community meant in these days. The men in the kilt, the ladies in their white dresses with a tartan sash pinned to the shoulder with the lovely big cairngorm brooch. Even though William didn't dance himself, it didn't mean he ever grudged her.

The Australian nurse huffs in bum first, maneouvering the tray. Her name is Elaine, but the way she says it sounds like Eyeline. On the tray there's a plastic cup with a nozzle and a straw, which Greta takes as an affront: just because she has the odd dizzy turn doesn't mean they should treat her like one of the gaga girls in High Care. Once again she considers demanding a proper cup and saucer, not to mention her silver teapot Elsa brought in for her, but once again she thinks better of it. Eyeline is tough as nails, and right now she doesn't feel up to an argument.

She eyes the plate, the napkin, the two round white iced biscuits. Eyeline slips the terry-towelling bib over her head.

'There you are, dear.'

Greta is hungry, her stomach full of war-cries and wind. She picks up a biscuit and bites into it.

'Don't gobble, Greta, you'll only give yourself a pain.'

Greta breaks the biscuit into four pieces and nibbles like a mouse.

Wee sleekit coo'erin timrous beastie, wha's put a panic in thy breestie?

Meek as a mouse, she squints at Eyeline. It's no good telling the daft besom that she doesn't give herself the pain at all, it gives itself to her, generously, night after night. As soon as she lies down flat it gnaws at her bowels and there's no stopping it, not with any kind of pill known to man and certainly not to MacLaren, who's just a doctor, not a proper specialist, although all doctors are a useless bunch as far as she can see. This useless pain has a long concertina'd name MacLaren spelled out for her because the silly bugger couldn't spell out the cure.

Di-ver-tic-ul-it-is. I'm afraid it's very common in the elderly.

There's something familiar about the biscuit. The jam in the middle, the red glacé cherry on the top.

'German biscuits,' she says, remembering.

'Empire, dear. They're called Empire biscuits now.'

Greta shakes her head. When did they do that, and why? German biscuits was always the correct name, there's no need to go chopping and changing it.

'*Etscar gispits?*' she says sarcastically.

'No dear, Empire.'

Isn't that just what she said? Irritated, suddenly, by the

obtuseness of the biscuit, the cherry on the top that looks like a clown's nose, she repeats it.

'*Etscar gisfits!*'

Hands on hips, Eyeline stares at her. Her smile is supposed to be pleasant but her eyes are gimlets behind her glasses. Greta scowls back. With the foreign nurses you had to make allowances – especially the ones from the Far East with their dolls' faces and little hands so gentle at washing your hair, and the Africans like Belinda with the big behind who has a sort of pidgin as a language, and always makes her think of the baby doll she used to have called Belinda, only that Belinda wasn't a yard wide and black as the Earl o' Hell's waistcoat. But Eyeline's an Australian, for Pete's sake: she, at least, ought to understand the Queen's English.

14

Androula eases her legs out of bed and shunts her body across the mattress until the soles of her feet encounter the cool tiles of the floor. Dawn light shows through the slats in the shutters. She hoists herself up on her elbows, easing her toes into the waiting slippers, and sits on the edge of the bed until the floating room solidifies. Then she wraps her shawl around her shoulders and goes into the kitchen, where the coffee things in the sink indicate that her brother is already up and about. She rinses the grounds away, plugs in the new cordless kettle, and proceeds to the shrine in the parlour. Gathering her nightdress between her thighs, she kneels down stiffly on the striped woollen rug, fixes her eyes on the welcoming face of the *Panagia,* and begins to pray.

She prays for her brother Asterios, and for their mother and father, who lie five hundred metres higher up the hill in the cypress-shaded cemetery of Agia Stephanou, and for her cousin Angelika, grandmother of Spiraki, who has lain there for as many years, and for Angelika's daughter Sophia, may the Lord preserve her wits and make her a good mother to the poor *mikraki.*

She prays also for her fiancé Vagelis Pappos of Fortetsa village, who fell under the spell of the one-eyed Englishman and died a hero against the great city wall of Heraklion. At 20 Vagelis was assistant to the foreman at *sta pitharia*, the place of the jars, on the hillside of Kephala they now call Knossos – a good job for one so young, he said, with a good wage and the promise of training. On Sundays when he rode over to visit on his motorcycle, he would tell her excitedly of the digging and the finds, and of the fiestas thrown at the end of the season when the archaeologists went back to England and a whole kid was roasted and wine flowed till late into the night; later he talked, too, of their wedding, and how he would build them a house in Fortetsa village when the war ended.

Vagelis' family would not let Androula see his body. It wasn't a sight for a young girl, they said. But his mother gave her the tooled leather boots Vagelis had been so proud of, the boots that still sit in the bottom of her wardrobe, the boots she oils and tends each year on the day of his martyrdom. Good as new, the boots say to her, when she brings them out to stand, knee high and gleaming, on the sunlit terrace.

It's the English Androula blames for fomenting the rebellion. The English with their War Office and their shipments of rifles, and particularly the one-eyed Plebbery, *archigos* at the Villa, who spoke Cretan Greek, and dressed like a Cretan, and, according to Vagelis, also drank like one. Without Plebbery's instigation the menfolk might have kept their noses clean and waited under the protection of Our Lady for the war to blow over, as it would have done, for what had Crete known in its whole history but wars, invasions, occupations?

And I wouldn't have been left with only kisses and promises, thinks Androula, fixing her gaze on the *Panagia,* whose moist eyes glisten with tears for the misfortunes of all women.

None of this can she can confide in her brother Asterios, for whom the subject of *timi* is salt in an unhealed wound. She remembers the day, not long after Vagelis' death, when Asterios announced that he was going to the mountains to join the *andartes*. She can still hear her mother's shrieks, her wheedlings, and the curses hurled at her only son, who had betrayed her. Until Asterios ran weeping from the house, and was not seen for three days and a half. Later Androula learned that he had spent those nights on Mount Yuchtas, sleepless in a goatherd's bothy where wind hustled in at the empty windows and stirred the straw on the floor. This, her cousin Angelika had told her, Angelika whom everyone thought Asterios would marry.

He had stumbled back to the house that day, unshaven and smelling of raki. As soon as Androula saw the look in his eye she knew that he had changed. Then he fell on his knees in front of Mama, that greatest of arm-twisters, swearing that he would stay at home and do his duty, and he kept kneeling there until, relenting, she kissed his cheeks and gave him her blessing.

As the years passed, though, Androula saw that for her brother the sacrifice had been great. Asterios didn't marry Angelika; in fact he didn't marry anyone, even though Mama begged him to find a bride. She made sure there was no lack of candidates, too: a parade of dark-browed, capable girls who came with their parents to sit shyly in the parlour over coffee and cherry-cake. But although Asterios appeared compliant, his gruff monosyllables were enough to frighten any girl off, and no marriage contracts were forthcoming. It was as if, having submitted to his mother's wishes on that one critical occasion, he could never again allow his wishes and her own to coincide. Silently, stubbornly, Asterios resisted, until it was clear that, even at the cost of his own happiness, he would cut the tongue from his mouth rather than say yes to her.

Androula's happiness, in the meantime, was a subject entirely overlooked. Her parents – may they be forgiven – had little sympathy to spare for her lost prospects, and no energy left for canvassing the parents of marriageable sons so that their only daughter could have a choice of suitors. Cousin Angelika had married, though, and well, but not happily, and on Sophia's tenth birthday the heart that misery had weakened had finally failed her.

Androula's knees are beginning to ache, but because the living need her prayers as much as the dead, she makes a special plea for Sophia, who has managed to do just the opposite of her mother by marrying badly, but for love. Not that Andonis hasn't been good to her, but he is no businessman, and when his garage failed he took to driving container-trucks to the far corners of Europe. Postcards would arrive, and telephone calls, from Ancona or Trieste or Rotterdam. Poor Spiraki, who more than anything needed a father's hand, was left well-nigh fatherless, and Sophia, husbandless, had to knuckle down and work for her living by cleaning the apartments dirtied by the English.

Androula worries about the strange absent-mindedness that has overtaken Sophia. It's as if the effort of remembering which country Andonis is in has overloaded her mind's capacity, so that Androula feels she must call in every day to check that the poor girl hasn't lapsed into one of her dazes and forgotten which apartments to clean, or what the *mikraki* will and will not eat for breakfast.

Crossing herself three times, Androula rises unsteadily to her feet, pays her morning visit to the toilet, and washes her face and hands. In the kitchen she crumbles cake into a saucer of milk and sets it down by the hole under the sink, for the house-snake. Although she can't swear that she 's actually seen this protective animus, she has heard its cool rustle at siesta-time, and sees no reason not to believe, as her mother believed, that its presence has the power to prevent earth-quakes, or at the very least to divert them, so that they wreak their vengeance on other houses, other orchards. If Asterios scoffs at the old wife's tale Androula simply points to the empty saucer, although she doesn't add what he of all people ought to know – that good luck is hard to come by, so it does no harm to court it a little. As she straightens up, steadying herself against the sink, she feels that the house, at least, is grateful for her concern, and sits more solidly on its founda-tions, and breathes more easily.

Through the kitchen window she glimpses Asterios by the beehives at the bottom of the field. A car she recognises as the Dimeros boy's is parked where the track terminates in a dusty turning circle.

Filling a plastic container with seed, she goes out to feed the chickens and collect the eggs. From the terrace she can clearly see the yellow banner of Manoli's shirt. There is someone with him; even at this distance she can make out the ruddy skin of a foreigner. All three men are gazing up the hill towards the house. Asterios has stretched his arms wide, as if to indicate its width. His hands cut the air in slices, boxing in the field, the grey stumps of old vinestocks, the thistled ruts where maize once grew.

What on earth is Asterios up to? Manoli Dimeros is as sly as his father before him, and always has his beady eye on the money, but if Manoli thinks he can turn her brother into a tourist guide, to show off her own house as if it was history.

Androula's stick strikes sounds of protest from the flag-stones as she marches round the corner of the building. When she unlatches the wire-netting gate of the chicken run the birds scuttle at her, the cockerels bullying their way to the front as usual. The boss one, a greedy hectoring fellow, pecks savagely at one of the youngest hens and draws blood. Androula swipes at him but fails to make contact. Suddenly incensed, she up-ends her stick and hooks his neck in with the handle. She has been patient for far too long, and now the wretch will get what's coming to him. Quick as a flash, she hoists him up by the legs and shakes him out like a wet lettuce.

Upside down he is almost as tall as she, a heavy ungrateful bird she has fattened on her good seed, her apples and worms. She shakes him once more for good measure, laughing at the gaping affronted beak, the shit-spray of fear on the iridescent feathers.

'You're for the pot, my lad!' she cries, dragging him across the terrace. 'I've had just about enough of your shenanigans!'

15

Light fills the white room. The doors to the balcony are open, the muslin curtains billowing on the wind; outside Ingrid can see a blue rink of sky with hasty scudding clouds.

In her dream her amiable ex-husband Tim had announced that what she needed was a companion. Which is all very well for Tim, now smugly remarried to Amanda the original earth-mother. Not that she grudges him whatever happiness he enjoys with her, for Tim is not a bad man and, unlike Ingrid, Amanda is a born provider, a presider over Agas and board-games, playgroups and supper-parties; unlike Ingrid, Amanda is hard-wired for wifehood.

What does rankle, though, is the neutering word *companion*, which implies that he's consigning her to a dreary Jane Austenish spinsterhood. In the dream she'd objected – 'I might *like* a companion,' she told him, 'but I don't *need* one!' Even so, it was a concession she'd never have made when awake.

Sometimes she thinks the trouble with Tim was that there was nothing, really, to find fault with.

Tim was a considerate lover, trimming his fingernails regularly, always taking his watch off before he came to bed. Approaching her tender parts with scrupulous, spidery hands.

You're a lucky girl, her mother had said, *finding a man like Tim to look after you.*

The implication being that gratitude was definitely in order. But Ingrid didn't like having to be grateful, nor, it seemed, was she cut out for the symbiotic glue of marriage. She didn't like being soft, penetrable, like the jellyfish she used to scoop out of the Firth and hurl against the rocks. They'd lie there

87

helpless and upended, their bluish phosphorescence fading, their long stings shrivelling to sticky ribbons in the sun.

She thinks of the marital bed, with its aura of duty, its shudderingly cold sheets. Sometimes she thinks Tim has a lot to thank her for. Long before he retrained as a therapist, he'd learned his craft the hard, hands-on way, just from being married to someone like her.

When she props herself up against the pillows her head throbs. On the way back from the Medusa they'd stopped off at the Totem Bar, where she'd downed a bright blue cocktail which translated as a Poseidon's Kiss. Evidently it hadn't mixed too well with the *dopio krasi*.

They could have asked Madame Aglaia to call them a taxi, but instead they'd walked home through the darkness, Glenys staggering along on her wedges, giggling at glowworms: the cheery chappies, she'd called them.

She remembers the scent on the air: jasmine, mimosa, the smile spreading secretly across her face as the little worm of bliss unwound itself in her belly.

She remembers stumbling up the spiral staircase and collapsing into bed.

She eases herself up and pads across the white marble floor, smelling the sour odour of sweat. In the shower she turns the dial to cold and lathers herself quickly, standing on her cotton nightdress, virtuously trampling in the suds. The summer tourist invasion brings water-shortages, and although as far as she can see Greek plumbing hasn't advanced a great deal since the Bronze Age, she likes to think she's doing her bit for conservation.

Dressed and minimally combed, she goes out in search of milk and some good strong teabags.

Sophia the maid, in a faded pink vest and shorts, is sweeping dry leaves from the stairs. When she sees Ingrid she leans her broom against the rail and makes a strange undulatory movement with her arms and torso, as if miming a

88

drunken sailor. Her sweet lustreless face is unusually animated.

'*Sismos!*' she exclaims. 'You feel?'

'Earthquake?' Ingrid stares at her.

She remembers, now, waking suddenly in the night, some kind of dread clenching its fist in her stomach. The excitable echoes of the dance unfurling, peaking, tipping over into nausea. The bed had developed a tidal sway. When she sat up to steady herself the red light on the mosquito plug had shimmied sideways. She'd blamed the symptoms on the lethal cocktail; that there might be another explanation simply didn't enter her head.

'*Nai,*' says Sophia, with a vehement jerk of the head. '*Atichia!*' she promises, in a tone of avid fatalism.

Atichia, thinks Ingrid, fending off the afershocks of memory. *Bad luck.* A woman galumphing about in her combats, exhibiting herself on the dancefloor. So lost in her daft dream of beauty and pleasure that she forgot everything, even the possibility of scorn, the plain fact that she was past the age when those sort of antics might be indulged.

Tim is right, of course: he didn't do all these years of psychotherapy for nothing. She is, has always been, a wild card, which is why she can't afford to trust herself. Easy enough when you're young to rebel against family, church and state, to project all your ills on to society. But later you have to come to an accommodation with life, build your nest, find your niche, or whatever. Consolidate, perhaps, is the word she's looking for. At 43 her career profile is shapeless – a bit of teaching, a string of Research Fellowships, a few publications – and her relationships sporadic, ruled more by impulse than judgement.

If Tim's dream-message was chastening, maybe it's because she deserves to be chastened.

Seisismenon, she thinks. Shaken to the foundations. *Seisichthon,* Earthshaker: Pindar's epithet for Poseidon. If last night is anything to go by, when Evans pictured his Minoans as a confident, cultured people, lords of their island and masters of their fate, he factored out the vulnerability they must have felt, the constant apprehension of being at the mercy of chthonic forces.

In the Minimarket Demosthenes, who has lost some tiles off his roof, is sanguine.

'4.2,' he says dismissively. 'Not so big. The *epikentro* is not here, but in the *Peleponesus*. Athina is also having some damage.'

On the Flagstaff computer she finds an email from Texas, tagged *Alice Kober fan club*.

Attached is the memoir I mentioned – sorry about the delay. Eva Brann took AK's Classics 1 course at Brooklyn C. in the spring of '48. As she admits, it says as much about her as about Alice Kober – nevertheless, you may find it useful. Cheers, Hank.

She opens the attachment and prints it off, hoping Lynda won't object. Upstairs she makes her tea, takes it out to the table on the balcony, and flies through the text, flagging sentences.

Ms Brann turns out to be an astute observer, with a nice turn of phrase. Brooklyn College she sums up as '*no alma mater, but a dura mater*'; and while Alice '*projected a dry, refraining rigour, it seemed possible that there was a daredevil in her, and a romantic.*'

The memoir is long – some 30 pages – and valedictory. It's also imbued with what she recognises as the scholar's obsessive need to cover every angle, to leave not a single opening for criticism.

Like Professor Henry 'Hank' Yoakam, Eva Brann has no truck with the obvious analogy with Rosalind Franklin, the so-called 'Dark Lady' of DNA:

'*I want to enter my misgivings about skewing the direction of my teacher's life, by twisting it into a victim's life, co-opting*

90

it into current preoccupations with gender domination. This woman was masterful.'

Yes but, thinks Ingrid, nettled by what looks like a typical sideswipe at feminism. The intellectuals of Brann's generation have a tendency to deprecate theories they had no hand in formulating. It seems to be a point of pride with them – or else, maybe, of pure competitiveness. She weeds on through, trying to restrain her impatience. On page 15 she finds the crucial visual sighting.

'. . . she was, to coin a phrase, aggressively nondescript, or so it seems to me now. She wore drapy, dowdily feminine dresses; something mauve comes before my eyes. Her figure was dumpy with sloping shoulders, her chin heavily determined, her hair styled for minimum maintenance, her eyes behind bottle-bottom glasses snapped impatiently and twinkled not unkindly.'

Brains or beauty: the choice was far more cut and dried in Alice's time, of course – although even when she herself was young she'd felt it looming like a great divide.

If she thinks back to friends who didn't go on to the Grammar – Sandra Robson, Isobel Kennedy, Marie MacFarlane – what she remembers is the esoteric accessories that began to travel everywhere with them. Hairspray and blusher, eyelash curlers, eye-shadow palettes the size of tea-trays. Even before they left school it was as if they were already rehearsing for some witless kind of womanhood. Ingrid might have been top of the class, but in the meantime other areas of competence were being delineated. And although she can't remember exactly how the dividing lines were drawn, or how much her own scorn – defensive, no doubt – had contributed, she could remember to this day how inept their coded expertise had made her feel, and how excluded.

'*Dowdily feminine*', though, is both depressing and intriguing. It suggested that Alice hadn't taken the mannish dress option, which would certainly have been open to her – what could be more glamorous, after all, than Dietrich in a tuxedo, or Hepburn in sassy slacks? – but had chosen instead to be frumpish and schoolmarmy. In 1948, when Brann had met her, Alice would have been 41. An old maidish age, Ingrid supposes, for the times – but even if she'd decided by then to give up on the whole business, somewhere in herself she must have known that a woman would always be judged first and foremost on the image she presented.

There was no doubt that, 20 years earlier, she'd had options.

In the Hunter College photograph the young Alice had a soft bob, with a hint of a marcel wave flowing over one eyebrow. Without the bifocals, you could see eyes that were deep-set and intense, wide Slavic cheekbones, a fine straight nose. Hank had produced it with a flourish, slapped it down on the desk in front of her.

Alice Kober, Phi Beta Kappa. Treasurer of the Classical Club 1928. Costume Committee and Publicity Committee for Hippolytus. *In cast of German Christmas Play.*

'But how pretty she is!' Ingrid enthused, 'Without those awful glasses.'

She wore a dress or blouse of some muslinish fabric, with a faint geometric print and a frilled neckline low enough to reveal the curve of her collarbone, her pretty necklace.

'You can tell she hasn't given up yet. She's still making the effort.'

Admittedly Alice wasn't a glamour puss, like some of the other sophomores – the luminous Mildred Knag, for instance, or the pert doe-eyed Rose Kelder, with whom, Hank Yoakam joked, he was primarily in love, although Alice Kober came a close second – touching Ingrid's arm just in case she hadn't got the message that at 53 and thrice married he was still a man of impulsive affections, a man who got crushes on clever women. But if it was true that at 21 Alice looked a little sadder, perhaps, than she should have done, her half-smile a little too strained, no one would ever have called her unfeminine.

Ingrid had been wary, at first, of Professor Henry (Hank) Yoakam, for, engaging as he was – trim-hipped, fleet of foot, un-professorial in cowboy boots – he was, nevertheless, the Boss. His was the Archive, and his, crucially, the expertise, next to which her own grasp of the field was sketchy at best. (An M.A. Edin. in Classical Archaeology and Ancient Civilisations was hardly a match for a Chair in Classics, not to mention a D. Phil dissertation analysing different scribal hands on the Linear B tablets at Knossos.)

Fearing her own eagerness, and the vulnerability that made her interpret any coolness as criticism, it seemed safer to hide behind a barrier of reserve, to remain aloof, even standoffish. Over the week she'd spent at the University, however, he had grown on her, and finally she had to admit to herself that he was a kindly sort, generous and garrulous, with an artless show-offy vanity – a good egg, in fact, if a rather scatty one.

The trouble was that liking the man didn't make her feel any more at ease with him, but instead made her want to be liked in return, to be appreciated for her own qualities, not to mention the quality of the research documents she'd lugged down from New York – some of which he'd whisked off to xerox, but subsequently hadn't mentioned.

To her surprise, the grandly-named Aegean Script Archive turned out to be little more than a corridor linking his office with two smaller offices shared by other members of the Classics Faculty. Hank had cleared a desk in an alcove penned in by filing cabinets, and had piled it, not with the material she'd specifically asked for, but with material she had not. Instead of Kober's correspondence with John Franklin Daniel, which she'd repeatedly requested – to the point, she thought, of pestering – he had provided her with his own scarily erudite dissertation, sundry correspondence between Michael Ventris and Emmett Bennett from the early 1950s, after Kober was dead and gone, and also a lengthy unpublished monograph by Alice on the suffix -Inth or -Inthos in the Greek language.

Every afternoon around 4 o'clock she carried a briefcase full of photocopies back to her motel. The University campus – its walkways shaded by plutocratic trees under which students ambled, golden and privileged – was bordered on the east by a roaring Interstate.

'That'll be the Pan-American Highway,' the taxi-driver had said when he dropped her at reception. 'Yes Ma'am – all the way from Chicago to Mexico City!'

The Longhorn Motel – named, apparently, after the University football team – was a two storey building which squatted in the shadow of a flyover. From her first-floor window she counted ten lanes, with a conservative estimate of four more on the overpass, which was just too high for her to see. After the verticals of New York, she found herself with a view sectioned into horizontals: the lower lanes separated by steel barriers, then a strip of greensward planted with pink poppies; above that was a blurred line of distant trees, and a blue Texan sky neatly bisected by the parapet of the flyover.

Inside the room the noise was muffled by double-glazing, but outside it was unmitigated, deafening. In the mornings, pantechnicons sliced the low sun into strobic flashes so unnerving that she kept the heavy curtains shut tight, mindful of everything she'd ever heard about epileptic seizures.

The Longhorn's swimming pool was separated from the Freeway by a three foot wall surmounted by a signboard in the shape of a pair of steer's horns, some ten feet high and six feet wide. A lifebelt hung on the wall, its red and white paint flaking away; above it a faded notice prohibited eating, smoking, and the consumption of alcohol.

The interior of the pool had been painted standard turquoise, and although here and there swathes of dust gave the bottom the rugged look of a scree-slope, the water seemed clean enough.

When she lowered herself into the water and swam lustrally above the submarine scree, her peaceful passage disturbed not a teaspoonful of dust. Afterwards she climbed out and padded barefoot across the hot concrete surround. Spreading a hotel

94

towel on a decrepit lounger, she settled down behind the minimal sound-barrier afforded by the wall and opened the file that contained Alice Kober's -Inth monograph.

When she finished the last page late afternoon had become balmy evening; above the parapet of the flyover a pale crescent moon lounged lazily on its southerly bottom. Like a diver returning from the silence of the deep, she emerged into a different element. She was aware, once more, of car-horns, and the shriek and hiss of brakes. Tranced, she'd slipped beneath the surface of the world in which drivers forged single-mindedly towards their goal – sunglassed, look-ing neither to left nor right – and for an hour or more had managed to blot out the thunderstorms of sound.

Hank had told her he intended to publish the -Inth mono-graph, budget permitting. These days, he complained, funding passed on by without a second glance, alighting graciously on Petrochemical Sciences or Information Technology; next to those profit-generating giants, which were housed in glisten-ing ziggurats embossed with donors' names, Mycenology didn't stand a chance.

'Sometimes I think a return to the monastery system's the only answer,' he said bitterly. 'We used to employ a full-time archivist, but now Maryam does it *pro bono*. Jesus, we can't even pay for her flights down from Boston!'

Maryam was petite, gym-toned in blue jeans and a primrose polo shirt. Despite the early morning flight her skin was fresh, her eyes bright. She unfurled a roll of flex from her bag, crawled under the desk, and plugged it in.

'Excuse me, got to charge my cell.' Her movements were quick and economical, as if to emphasise that time was the enemy, the future a carrier of dust and dissolution. She pulled on a pair of white cotton gloves and opened the drawer of a filing-cabinet.'The cigarette-carton files' she explained, flicking a sable brush at something inside. 'Whenever I come down I just know I'm gong to find more silverfish skeletons!'

Paper-clips had left rust-shadows on the fragile yellowed slips of paper, cut from old Church announcements and Brooklyn college flyers, and packed tightly into the famous Fleetwood cartons. The Linear B signs had been drawn with a fountain pen, in brownish ink that had faded and furred over time.

Maryam pounced on a stray paper-clip and removed it. 'They react with the acid in the paper. One day, well.' Her smile was doleful. 'We did start to digitalise, but now, you know how it is, there simply isn't the money.'

Ingrid showed her the article of Hank's which mentioned the Kober-Daniel correspondence; she had even circled the foot-note in red, in the hope that sheer embarrassment would finally jog his memory.

'Letters from Daniel to Alice?' Maryam shook her head, frowning. 'I don't remember those at all. Let me check with the Finding Aid.'

She went into one of the adjoining offices and, reappearing with an open ring-binder, marched into Hank's office. Through the open door Ingrid could hear her scolding.

'Well if they aren't listed, Hank, where the hell are they?'

'Ah yeah.' he replied, helplessly.

Maryam emerged rolling her eyes. She took the Fleetwood cartons out of the drawer and carried them into the smaller office. 'Got to do my health-check.'

Some time later a rodeo whoop issued from Hank's room.

'Even a blind squirrel!' He appeared in the doorway barndishing a cardboard file. Lips pursed, he regarded it with mock astonishment. 'Haven't laid eyes on this since 1991!'

When Maryam emerged he spun on his boot-heel like a cowhand in a line dance, and gave her a bashful hangdog grin.

'You mean to say you found them?'

'Hey, who'd have known it?'

'Jesus, Hank!' Snatching the file from his hand, she rumpled her face at him. 'I'm going to xerox these damn things right away!'

Ingrid throws her uneaten toast into the waste-bin, retrieves her laptop from the wardrobe, and plugs it in. If work is what keeps her feet on the ground, perhaps it will also keep the ground under her feet. The power is on, the sun is shining normally; down on the beach the sunbeds stand, paired and ready, in their rows. Apart from the arid restless wind, nothing, fundamentally, seems to have changed.

16

On the drive back from the Medusa Yiannis hadn't been able to bring himself to come clean with Dora. Instead he'd played possum – yawned, feigned fatigue after the exertions of the dance, anything to avoid the plain truth that he didn't want to spend the night with her. Later, pretending to sleep, he'd lain in bed fuming, because despite all his good intentions, once again he'd let inertia be his guide.

This morning he'd stripped the bed as usual and dropped the sheets into the laundry basket. On his way back from the airing cupboard with clean ones he encountered Dora, half-dressed, in the kitchen. The laundry basket sat empty on the draining-board and Dora was crouching by the washing machine, setting the dials.

'You don't have to do that,' he said.

Dora smiled up at him complacently. 'Yianni, it's nothing.'

But Yiannis knew it wasn't nothing. If he'd mastered the un-macho skills of cleaning, cooking, and ironing, it was because of the draconian standards of equality Karen had enforced. She'd been a hard taskmistress – *How can you be a grown-up if you can't look after yourself?* she'd challenged – but she had taught him what no Greek mother ever taught a son: the basic humdrum skills required for independence.

He stood with the sheets in his arms, staring at Dora's neat body, the small breasts in their lace, the fuck-me G string cutting between her buttocks, and, perversely, he exploded. Dropping the sheets on the floor, he grabbed Dora by the arms and jerked her to her feet.

'Are you listening to me? Look around you! Do you see dust, do you see disorder? Do I look like a man who can't look after himself?'

He saw the shock on her face, and let go, trembling. As he stepped back his foot caught the edge of the cat's dish, which spun across the floor, spilling lumps of meat and jelly. Fleetingly it occurred to him that Kore had left her food untouched, and that this was something out of the ordinary. He watched the cat-bowl shatter against the fridge.

Dora began to cry. She ran into the bedroom sobbing and gathered up her clothes. Yiannis followed her, one part of him stricken by remorse, the other part frozen with resentment. Karen, who was physically courageous to the point of recklessness, would never have cowered away from him; she would have spat and kicked, she would have punched him in the face.

'Dora, I'm sorry.' His voice was leaden. He watched her haul her dress over her head. Her bedraggled face emerged from the red material, but as the folds slid down and settled over her hips she wouldn't look at him. Next door in the kitchen the washing machine started its cycle, toiling and moiling.

'You're such a shit, Yianni.'

'I know,' he said, half-hoping she would lash out or somehow lose control, yearning for the sheer relief of it. He tried to smile at her. 'But look, you were right. We have to talk.'

Dora's eyes darted at him. She went to the mirror and began to brush her hair with harsh, tugging strokes. He felt her fear fully now, and how it entrapped him. She'd decoded his words with perfect accuracy, but he couldn't take them back. He waited, his fists clenched, hating the power she had to turn him into her Lord Judge and High Executioner.

'So that's agreed, then?'

'If you say so.' Dora hurried her feet into her sandals and, chin up, swung her bag over her shoulder.

'We'll have dinner, right, and we'll talk.' He moved closer, meaning to touch her, to reassure, or at least to reinvoke some principle of friendship, but his hand froze in mid-air and wouldn't obey his command.

'Whatever you want!' she cried. Shrugging wildly, she fled

past him, ran down the hall, and slammed the front door behind her.

In the kitchen the smell of cat-food was overpowering. He'd thrown the shards of pottery into the bin and scooped up the scattered food mess with kitchen paper. Then he fetched mop and pail from the cupboard and, still in his underpants, began, painstakingly, to wash the kitchen floor.

17

Ingrid's towel glitters with sand, like the fleeces once used for panning gold by the shepherds of ancient Colchis. The scratchy grains have found their way into her crevices, and in between the pages of *Prehistoric Crete*.

She's decided that she's a little in love with Hutchinson. Dubbed 'The Squire' – 'tall, pacific, kindly' – Hutchinson had succeeded John Pendlebury as Curator of Knossos in the late 1930s, and remained in the post until the war forced the British School to evacuate the Villa Ariadne. The voice of the author of *Prehistoric Crete* has a kind of radiant modesty. Not for him the dashing heroics of the one-eyed Pendlebury, who famously demanded 10,000 rifles from the War Office to arm the Cretan Resistance. Instead, when Germany joined with Italy against Greece, Hutchinson closed up the Villa and shipped his ailing mother home to England, via Cairo, on a destroyer. It can't have been a very comfortable journey.

On April 30th, 1941, the night before he sailed away with his mother, 'The Squire' dined with John Pendlebury at the Officers' Club in Heraklion. Three weeks later the Germans invaded, and by 22nd May Pendlebury was dead, wounded in the Battle of Heraklion, captured, and summarily executed. Other Aegean archaeologists had also been co-opted by Allied Intelligence – Carl Blegen of Pylos fame, for instance, and of course John Franklin Daniel – but they had survived

The heroic paradigm, thinks Ingrid. Always it raised its head, subtly depreciating all other narratives. And of course there's no denying the allure of derring-do, even if it leaves poor Alice in the wings, sitting out the war at Brooklyn College, chivvying her girls through Juvenal and Catullus. As far as she knows, Alice waved no soldier off to war, drove no ambulance, sweated in no armaments factory; her adventures, like Hutchinson's were strictly of the intellect.

It's too hot to read, now, even under the shade of the umbrella, and also windy, everything flapping and flying.

She pays 5 euros to rent one of the red fibreglass canoes that live on the shelving pebbles by the jetty, and launches it into the shallows. Lining up the prow, she leaps in, digs hard with the paddle, and sets sail for the horizon.

The wind is stronger farther out, whipping up some sprightly waves. On the beach of bare-breasted ladies a gust uproots an umbrella and sends it spinning dangerously on the gyre of its pole, wreaking havoc among the sunbathers.

The canoe bucks suddenly as the waves slap against the prow. From the beach it must look quite dangerous – particularly if you don't know these broad-bottomed ones are almost impossible to capsize. The thought makes her feel adventurous: the dancing dip and rise of the canoe, the tossed sea telling a story of heroics and risks. She wedges her feet against the sides for purchase and throws all her weight behind the paddle, feeling the dark spine of the sea flex under her.

Farther out the waves abate, and she coasts on a rolling swell, the deep water indigo on the downslope and gun-metal grey on the rise. The shore is distant now, the land losing its grip on her. Spray has soaked her bathing suit and shorts, but the sun beats so fiercely on her head that she dunks her cap in the sea and clamps it back on. Her drenched hair pours runnels over her shoulders; light refracts through the water-drops on her sunglasses. Turning the canoe through 180 degrees, she points the prow at the shoreline and paddles with the weight of the waves behind her.

50 metres out from the beach she hits the breakers, catches one, and rides its momentum into the shallows. When the hull scrapes bottom she jumps out into the surf, and in what she

hopes is a seamless sequence of movements, throws the paddle inside, grabs the prow, and hauls the canoe clear of the waterline

Farther along the beach the Giffords are standing up by their sunbeds, watching the exhibition. Rinsed and triumphant, she waves to them, already thinking ahead to the pleasures of the Shoestring – her pens, her notebooks, how she'll sink into work like others sink into love.

*

Asaminthos: bathtub, or lustral basin
Erebinthos: translated shyly by Kober as membrum virile
Kerinthos: bee-bread or pollen
Labyrinthos: maze, large structure, even the Palace of
    Knossos itself

In her unpublished monograph, The Element -Inth in Greek, *Kober has methodically tracked down every Greek word containing the Cretan* -inth *or* -inthos *suffix, from* Akalanthis *– an archaic name for Artemis – to* Zerinthos, *a cave connected with the sacred rites of various goddesses, all of whom, Kober suggests, were manifestations of an ancient, chthonic goddess.*

For once, Alice Kober has allowed herself the luxury of speculation, of wondering, of romancing a little. Yes, her word catalogue is exhaustive, her foot-noting as meticulous as ever, but in the 'Inth' monograph her enthusiasm for the language of meadow and mountain shines through. Her tone is light and spacious, and, one might argue, inflected by a vigorous, almost a heroic longing. We can almost smell the minth *and the* hyakinth, *hear the bees in the heather, see the water glistening on cave-wall or naked skin. This is not the forensic investigator of the Linear B script, but a young woman of imagination, with a taste for the infinite – a woman who has not yet completed the serious work of reining herself in.*

Apparently Kober had got as far as circulating the -Inth paper for peer review, for in the margins she has collated the responses of her old Hunter College Professor Ernest Reiss, and also – profusely – the comments of John Franklin Daniel, the man she appears to have admired above all others.

Among Kober's private papers a University of Pennsylvania notebook belonging to Daniel reveals the similarity of their preoccupations in the early 1940s. The notebook contains a review of Evans' magisterial Palace of Minos, *Volume 1V of which, published in 1935, dealt with the three Cretan scripts.*

In the notebook we see Daniel puzzling over a Linear A inscription which appeared with remarkable regularity on votive objects and, in the earlier hieroglyphic form, on seal-stones.

This inscription, which Daniel believed to represent the name of the Mother Goddess, was later dubbed the Minoan Liba-tion Formula, and was to be a focus of interest to scholars for the next 30 years.

What Daniel rendered as e-sa-sa-la *would later be rendered as* ja-sa-sa-ra *– a persuasive reading, since the similiarity to the names of other goddesses of the East Mediterranean – the Luvian* Ashasara, *the Hittite* Ishasara, *and the Canaanite* Asherat *– was hard to ignore. That Kober had involved herself in this particular debate is evident from her observa-tion that the Hieroglyphic version Daniel discussed in his notebook would have to be read from right to left and from the bottom up to obtain the same reading as the Linear A version.*

A letter from Alice Kober to Henry Allen Moe of the Gug-genheim Foundation explaining that Daniel was intending to publish her -Inth monograph in the American Journal of Archaeology, *suggests that Kober and Daniel had been ac-quainted at least since the very beginning of the 1940s.*

John Franklin Daniel had been appointed Curator of the Mediterranean Section at the University of Pennsylvania

Museum in 1940, and was awarded his PhD there, on the Cypro-Minoan scripts, in 1941. In the summer of that year Alice Kober attended Professor Speiser's courses in Old Persian and Akkadian, but even if she and Daniel did not encounter each other in the Classics department of the U. of Pennsylvania, such like-minded scholars would certainly have met at one of the half-dozen learned societies of which both were active members – societies like the Classical League, the Linguistic Society, and the Archaeological Institute, which jointly convened annual Christmas meetings hosted in turn by Yale, Cincinnatti and other top-rank unversities across the States.

After being appointed to the University of Pennslvania as a lecturer in Greek, Daniel was released for war service. In 1942 he entered the OSS – the forerunner of the CIA – became a Commmanding Officer in Cyprus, and by 1943 was Lieutenant Colonel. It is tempting to imagine Daniel as an American version of the legendary John Pendlebury of the British School: a latter-day Homeric hero from the upper crust of Ann Arbor, bounding around the Mediterranean in baggy shorts. Tanned, athletic, with a devastating collegiate drawl.

In 1940 Daniel had married, in Fredericksburg, Virginia, one Ellen Alix du Poy. The name evokes gracious colonial mansions, stud farms, magnolia-shaded lawns – all the ease and privilege that was absent from Kober's background in the tenements of Yorkville and the South Bronx.

After the war, as Editor-in-Chief of the American Journal of Archaeology, Daniel was clearly a mentor to Kober, even a close friend. But one is tempted to wonder if there was a time when Alice the woman – the younger, dreaming Alice glimpsed in the -Inth monograph – had aspired to more.

18

The sunset had left its gold rim on the crouching profile of Mount Yuchtas. At the bottom of the garden, among the lemon trees his father had planted in the '50s, Yiannis smoked in the darkness, gazing up at the pinpoint lights of Neo Chori.

He had hosed the shrubs and the tree roots, but although the coolness of the water still hung on the air, there was a dryness in his mouth and a restlessness in his mind: a need for something unknown that was queasy, painful, and familiar. Only in the Karen years had it abated, alhough even then it could reappear on a certain kind of evening, one that was too pleasant, perhaps, too domestic: the sun sinking over the low hills beyond the western suburbs, the laughter of the neighbours in their yard, the sharp chlorine smell of swimming pools. The sheer smugness of the nice New World.

After work he and Karen would sit on their patio, flanked by banksia trees from which gaudy parrots noisily spat pips. They drank homemade lemonade opaque with crushed ice, made from lemons which were not Greek, which had ripened under a sun that moved contrarily across the northern sky.

At times like these the foreign light glinted mockingly, as if to say there were no secrets here, at least none it would unlock, and from his hollowness arose the thought that the paradise he was living in was one without shadows, and therefore bereft of dreams. When he'd tried to confide his unease in Karen, her face dulled with a kind of guilt he hadn't understood, at first. Her answer was flat, defensive. The dreamtime was the province of the Aborigines, she said – as a matter of fact it was all they could bloody call their own.

Karen had spent her childhood in Tasmania, and one summer before they were married she'd persuaded him to take a hiking holiday down on the South West coast.

He remembered the vineyards and orchards – sweet to his European eye – that bordered the Entrecasteaux channel, the oddly named villages: Sandfly, Snug, Tinderbox.

Farther south, though, the weather had turned bad. Bracing blasts of wind chased cold rain north from the Antarctic; rainbows arched above tall eucalyptus trees whose grey trunks wept desiccated tongues of bark. The coastal footpath was obstructed by dense groves of buttongrass and the bleached branches of fallen trees. Detouring around a silty inlet shadowed by rain forest, they'd stumbled on to an Aboriginal Reserve. Too late, they'd noticed the grassy burial mounds, the midden of oyster shells. A new weatherboard hut with a tarpaulin roof flew the Aboriginal flag. None of this, they agreed, had been marked on their map.

A thousand miles from the mainland, the wind had a southerly edge to it, and the first few spots of rain had begun to fall. In the lee of the hut a group of men and women were drinking tea around a brazier. They seemed ill-dressed for the climate, in sandals, T shirts, skimpy leggings.

Yiannis had wanted to beat a retreat, but one of the women beckoned them towards the fire.

'G'day,' Karen called cheerfully, taking off her rucksack and going over to warm her hands. They drank sweet black tea from tin mugs, crouching down beside the brazier, looking out across the sand.

To the south, nothing but sea-kelp between them and the pack-ice of Antarctica.

Tongue-tied, he'd handed round his cigarettes. His spoken English still in its infancy then. When something large leapt and splashed out on the water he said effortfully, 'Big fish. What kind is it?'

There was a rustle of laughter. 'She'll be a penguin, mate!'

'Not from these parts, is he?' he heard someone ask Karen, and Karen laughed too.

'Nah, Greece,' she said, as Yiannis nodded like the village idiot. 'He's a Greek, this one.'

A noticeboard was nailed to the door of the hut. On the board were laminated photographs, clippings from local papers, even a feature article from the *Sydney Morning Herald*. He read English better than he spoke it, and he could understand enough to get the gist.

The article was about the genocide of the entire Aboriginal population of Van Diemen's Land, some 5000 in all. In 1837, he read, the few survivors who hadn't died of disease or despair were transferred to their final settlement here at Oyster Cove, where, no longer a threat to the white establishment, they were dressed up and paraded at official functions. The last survivor, Queen Truganini, had died in 1876. As far as he could make out, her skeleton had been put on display in Hobart Museum, where it had remained until the Land Rights movement began in the 1970s.

In the old photograph Truganini's face, framed in a Victorian white lace bonnet, was so black as to be almost featureless. Conscious of curious eyes on him, Yiannis put his hands in his pockets and shivered. He couldn't have felt more displaced.

And then the pick-up truck had drawn up, stirring whirlwinds of dust. On the door was the logo of the Department of Aboriginal Affairs.

The man who jumped out wore Rangers' green. He had cropped pale hair and a furry dab of stubble on his chin; he was young and white and there was nothing accommodating about him. He advanced on them, jerking his thumb at the flag that flew on the hut.

'This is Aboriginal land! You can't just walk in here!'

Karen put down her mug and looked at him levelly. 'Yeah, sorry mate. We lost the path. Looks like you're not on the map yet.'

It had taken Yiannis a while to adjust to the pugnacity of Australian women. He saw the warning signs in her – the hands thrust into the back pockets of her jeans, the shoulders dropped, the mettlesome glint in her eye.

The Ranger's face was tight with anger. Yiannis sensed his inexperience. No way could a guy like this tolerate a public challenge to his authority.

'Sign says No Trespassing, it means No Tresspassing!'

Karen took a step forward.

'Beg yours? Like you're saying we can't have a yabber?'

She gestured towards the group at the brazier, but their hosts had fallen silent, drawing their hospitality back into themselves, eyeing her in the same way they eyed the Ranger, with a kind of neutral expectation. Clearly they were interested in the outcome, but Yiannis sensed there would be no support from that quarter.

'Let's go,' he said, scooping up Karen's rucksack and handing it to her.

They exited by a newly cindered track, through a checkpoint they hadn't noticed earlier. After a while the dirt road became a blacktop which led stubbornly inland. Karen grumbled along, stopping now and then to examine the apparently impenetrable forest for any sign of the coastal path.

'Some advert for the cause he was,' she muttered, struggling to hold the map flat in the wind. 'Bloody wowser!'

He remembered how he'd spotted two kookaburras, high up, staring each other out across a gap between branches. Australia's emblematic bird. Some advert for the New World, he said, pointing them out to Karen, hoping to raise a laugh. Although Karen the Aussie would hear nothing against them, to him they looked hunchbacked and irascible, like two old codgers suffering from gout. You could imagine each one saying to itself as it contemplated its mirror image, *Well, thank God I don't look like that ugly fuck!*

Despite himself, he smiled at the memory.

Was that why he'd picked the fight with Dora? So that he could smile to himself in the darkness, or equally give in to good honest melancholy?

Terpsikore wafted like a ghost out of the undergrowth and walked listlessly towards the kitchen door. He wondered if she was sickening for something; she hadn't touched the fish he'd tried to tempt her with at supper-time. He trod his cigarette butt into the dirt and followed her indoors.

*

Irini's salon was on Epimenidou, in the shadow of the old Venetian Arsenal. In the evenings the street was a favourite rat-run for kids on *papakis* but at 10 am, with the Heraklion rush hour over, it was reasonably tranquil.

Irini had taken on a new assistant, a bleached-blond Sicilian who called himself Nikki, although his real name, he confided – as if Yiannis was remotely interested – was Giovanni. He wore a brief mesh vest dyed in camouflage colours and a low hipster belt studded with brass cartridges. Peroxide Giovanni from Palermo, thought Yiannis as he waited, swathed in towels, to be washed and shorn.

'When are you due at HQ?' his sister asked.

'It's okay, the meeting isn't till 2.'

Her head was bent busily over a bride-to-be, a girl of no more than 18 who was wearing a crop-top and tight jeans. Although Irini's own hair was cut in an aggressively modern bob, like clipped crow's wings, she was teasing the bride's hair into the kind of bouffant her mother might have sported in the '70s, dancing nimbly round the chair while the girl sat before the mirror like someone sedated, staring at her reflection. On the counter below the mirror sat a coronet attached to a cloud of white veiling.

There was something disturbing about the girl's acquiescence, her abject surrender to antique tradition. A lamb to the slaughter, thought Yiannis. It had been hard enough to persuade Karen to go to the Registry Office, let alone to consider a white wedding. She'd been dressed in some kind of pale blue suit, high heeled shoes; wistfully he remembered that she hadn't bothered with stockings.

Tilting Yiannis' head back over the basin, Nikki adjusted the water temperature.

'Not too hot?'

'No, no. Perfect,' said Yiannis, closing his eyes and letting tiredness wash over him.

In the small hours of the morning a blast of gunfire had jolted him out of sleep. He'd put the pillow over his head, assuming the inevitable Cretan wedding party: they'd be letting off the customary fusillades, peppering the signposts with exuberant bullets. Then he heard music, and the crackle of American voices, and got up, cursing.

In the living room the television, inexplicably, was showing a black and white film; John Wayne's totemic face straddled the Greek subtitles. When he entered Terpsikore leapt off the sofa, clattering the remote to the floor. Had she stepped, somehow, on the button? When he scolded her she flattened her ears to her head and let out a wail of misery.

'What?' he demanded, clicking the off-button, staring at her. There was something about her posture that worried him: the way she had spread her haunches into a semi-squat, pained and ungainly. As he watched she began to drag her rear-end across the rug. He saw drops of fluid, pee perhaps. Then she squealed again and he saw that there was blood.

'What's wrong, Kore?'

Panic-stricken, he knelt down beside her, but the cat hissed at him and shrank from his touch.

Yiannis couldn't bear the broken-hearted sounds that were coming from her. For a wild moment he thought of calling Dora, who would know what to do. Then he remembered the flyer she'd given him, for an Animal Rescue Clinic run by one of her ex-students from the commune up at Neo Chori; Dora had worked as a volunteer for a while, campaigning about the stray problem.

He ran to the telephone and rifled through the small drawer under the table. The Clinic in Heraklion was closed, but a recorded message gave an out-of-hours number for emergencies.

A woman's voice answered sleepily in German, apologised, and launched into harshly-accented Greek. Near to tears, Yiannis gabbled back in English.

The woman listened for a moment.

'You know Neo Chori? Can you get her up here now? Take the first track on the right past the village signpost.'

Somehow he had swaddled Kore in a towel and bundled her into the cat-box. He'd driven up the hill like a madman, swerving round the hairpin bends, trying to ignore the eerie keening from the back of the car. Just before Neo Chori village a painted signboard on the right said 'Halcyon'.

The dirt road meandered upwards for a kilometre before he sighted habitation: beehives looming whitely in the headlights, a geodesic dome, polytunnels. The house was long and low, of whitewashed stone with new breezeblock extensions. A light-coloured jeep was parked outside, next to a battered pick-up truck. When he got out of the car an invisible dog barked at him from an outbuilding.

A woman dressed in a lab-coat over pajamas appeared on the porch, her dark hair scrubbed back and plaited in two long braids.

'I am Wiltraud,' she whispered, putting a finger to her lips. 'The children, you understand.' She took the cat box from him and hurried it inside.

In the kitchen she donned latex gloves, lifted Kore gently out, and set her on the table. The cat flattened herself, squirming away, her eyes aghast.

'Poor girl,' said Wiltraud. 'She's in much pain. Will you hold her for me? I must give some sedation.' She took a

112

syringe from a box in the fridge and soaked a cotton wool swab in something that smelled sharply, familiarly, of hospitals.

Yiannis held Kore down but could not look. Wiltraud's ears had parallel piercings from the lobe to a point halfway up the rim; he stared fixedly at the empty holes, willing the shot to take effect. She was stroking Kore's head, murmuring to her in German. The cat's movements grew weaker. Yiannis felt the flaccidity steal into her muscles like death.

Wiltraud glanced up at him. 'I think it's better to go out while I examine her. I will take some minutes.' Under the stark strip-light her eyes were blue and sorrowful in a wide sunburned face.

Yiannis nodded mutely, blinking back tears. He retired to the hallway, where red stickers forbade him to smoke. Spotting a noticeboard on the wall, he parked himself in front of it. What he assumed to be work rosters were neatly typed in English, with ruled columns in which people – some of them children, judging by the unformed writing – had signed up for domestic tasks: 'chickens', 'cooking', 'compost', 'laundry', and 'recycling'. He counted seven names, including Wiltraud's. He'd known of the place, of course, if only because it was on his patch, but since he'd never had cause to visit he assumed that whatever went on here was conducted in a fairly unobtrusive, law-abiding way. It certainly didn't correspond with the popular idea of a commune. No empty beer-bottles lolled on the porch, no ashtrays spilled over with the tell-tale cardboard litter of joints. He had a feeling it wasn't marijuana they were growing in their polytunnels. The impression he gained was one of orderliness and industry; he could imagine the six other communards, tucked up under their unbleached cotton sheets, sleeping the quiet sleep of the righteous.

Beside the work-roster there was an Internet printout in English, headed *Acropolis Meouw*.

'*Simply put, the feeling on the islands is that death from malnutrition, disease, or starvation (or poisoning, in winter,*

113

*when no tourists can see) is acceptable because it is 'natural'.
It involves no active intervention by humans, so it must
therefore be 'nature's way' and 'God's will' or what have
you. All intervention, especially surgical intervention, and
especially involving castration of males, is seen as unnatural
and barbaric.'*

He remembered now what Dora had said about the lea-
fletting campaign she'd been involved in: she'd been chastised,
even spat at, for taking the outsiders' line. If the leaflets were
as aggressive as the printout, no wonder they didn't go down
too well with the locals. He skimmed the statistics on health
benefits, and learned that neutering reduced the incidence of
prostate cancer, and spaying before the first cycle reduced the
risk of breast, uterine, and ovarian cancers.

Cold superstition nudged at the base of his spine. He stood,
rigid as a gun barrel, firing his pointless prayers at the gods.
He'd had no idea that cats could suffer from ovarian cancer.
By the time the pain arrived it was almost always too late: this
he'd learned, only afterwards, from Karen's consultant.

He went to the screen door and peered miserably out. On
the porch wind-chimes, stirred by the breeze, tinkled out their
spirit-message. Beyond the wooden deck were tubs of geraniums; a child's swing made from a car tyre dangled from a
shadowy olive tree.

He went outside and lit a cigarette. Moths fluttered at the
porch light. No sounds came from the kitchen. He shivered
and wrapped his arms across his chest, trying not to imagine
the tumour burgeoning unsuspected in Kore's slender belly.

At last Wiltraud emerged and beckoned him in. 'She has
cystitis, as I thought.' She handed him a small cardboard
packet; inside were several foil-wrapped sachets. 'You must
give her one powder twice a day with food.'

Yiannis almost sobbed with relief. 'That's all?' He looked at
Wiltraud apprehensively. 'You mean, apart from the cystitis,
she's okay?'

'Cysitis is unpleasant enough, I think! However, I would
like to keep her here tonight, so that I can check her again in

114

the morning. If you don't mind to pick her up tomorrow? Late afternoon would be convenient.'

Wiltraud had refused to charge for the treatment, telling him that the Clinic survived on donations. He'd given her 50 euros, but now he wondered if that had been enough. The commune, she said, were involved in organic farming. Already they sold their honey and vegetables through several health-food shops in Chania and Heraklion, and – surprisingly, he thought – they were also raising an organic herd. He'd assumed such an establishment would be strictly vegetarian, not to mention the fact that Crete wasn't exactly big on agribusiness: all the herds he knew of simply scratched around in the hills, so didn't that mean they were organic enough already?

'And how is Dora?' she'd asked as he got into the car. Startled by the question – he was aware Wiltraud had been a student of Dora's but he couldn't remember mentioning their relationship – he hadn't known how to answer.

He thought of the pathetic body on the sheeted table, the legs so boneless, the long tail limp as a hair-ribbon. Something in Wiltraud's expression had made him anxious; he couldn't quite believe she was giving him the whole picture. But then medics always seemed evasive to him, particularly when they were trying to reassure; that knowledgeable neutrality of theirs was an open invitation to fear the worst.

Sighing, he surrendered himself to Nikki's attentions. The Italian was massaging in a herb-scented conditioner. His thumbs circled up from Yiannis' temples to palpate his scalp, while the fingers worked gently at the knotted muscles at the back of his neck.

When Nikki rinsed he cupped a palm tenderly over Yiannis' ear to divert the flow of water from his face. Yiannis shut his eyes and let the water flush away the contagion of the night, its racking sounds and hospital odours. A tear slithered easily out of the corner of his eye and ran down his cheek, to be gathered up in Nikki's tactful hand and sluiced away in the current. Nikki patted his hair to soak up the moisture, and turbanned the towel around his head.

He got up groggily and allowed himself to be ushered to the row of chairs that faced the mirror. 'You're a magician,' he said sincerely, slipping the Italian a 5 euro note.

'With you in a minute,' said Irini, glancing across at him. She had clipped a hairpiece shaped like a snail to the crown of the bride's head, and was teasing out side-ringlets with a tail-comb.

Yiannis took an English magazine from the pile of *Vogue* and *Hello* and flicked through it. *Take a Break*, the cover invited, but the cheerful title belied the contents. The readers who, for a small fee, had submitted their personal stories, seemed to be either recently bereaved, suicidal, or afflicted with obesity or cancer.

An infant of five years old had eaten herself to death; an ex-athlete, having succumbed to the lure of junk food and gained 27 kilos, tried to drive his car off a cliff.

Spanking Men Cured my Depression, read one headline. He turned the page quickly. His eye fell on a column of household hints, also sent in by readers. *To stop a freshly-painted room smelling, leave a bowl of salt in it overnight.*

Ingenious, he thought, making a mental note to try it out at some distant time in the future, when he felt a definite urge to decorate.

Nikki was dealing with another customer, a cowed-looking woman in middle age who sat with her handbag in her lap and her eyes fixed glumly on his reflection. He had seized two hanks of her dull brown hair, which he held out on either side of her head; he was discoursing on highlights, a field in which he was evidently an expert.

'To colour the hair, it lifts the face.' He flattened his palms on her cheeks and stroked the skin upwards.'It's to be young and free, yes? Me, you see, I start as a . . . how is it . . . black-head, like the little goldfishes, but now, like them, I am a Goldilocks!' Nikki giggled. 'It's fun, no?'

116

Yiannis didn't think the client looked convinced.

He lit a cigarette and watched Irini position the wedding coronet on the crest of the girl's coiffure. She fluffed the long veil out, holding a hand-mirror behind the chair so that the bride could admire the full 360 degrees of her glory. A curl was tweaked here, a fold adjusted there, while the girl sat stock still in front of her new reflection, as if hypnotised by a rattlesnake. She murmured her approval, and the coronet was lifted off and replaced in its ribboned hat-box. A chiffon scarf shrouded the wondrous head. When she got up from her chair Yiannis glimpsed, above the low waist of her jeans, the intimate flicker of a thong.

'When's the wedding?' he asked Irini, while the girl texted busily on her mobile.

'This afternoon, at Ayios Titos.'

Outside the plate-glass windows of the salon a car squealed to a halt at the kerb, hooting. The girl moved gingerly across the tiled floor, touching a hand to the unwieldy chiffon edifice on her head.

Irini fussed around her, adjusting the chiffon scarf at the nape of her neck, flicking a clothes-brush across her shoulders. She handed over the hat-box and ran ahead to open the door. The girl followed cautiously, holding the box out in front of her, like a wedding cake.

'Ciao ciao!' Nikki cried, clapping his hands. 'I wish you a beautiful life!'

'My congratulations,' Yiannis called out, inwardly crossing his fingers, wishing her a husband with kind hands, and not, please God, some macho commissar or country oaf.

When she had waved the bride off Irini came to stand behind his chair, comb and scissors in hand. Her eyebrows questioned him in the mirror.

'So did you ring Mother?'

'Shit!' said Yiannis, who'd completely forgotten that the annual visit was fast approaching.

Every August since his return to Greece his mother had stayed for two or three weeks at his house in Katomeli –

which was fair enough, he reasoned, since Irini had more than discharged her filial duty over the years, and in any case the flat above the salon which she shared with Tassos was cramped and hot, and trembled with inner-city traffic.

Their father had died in the early 90s, while Yiannis was living with Karen in Melbourne. After the funeral Irini had asked him to move back to Crete and help look after their mother, and so he would have done, if Karen's first operation hadn't intervened. The full burden had therefore fallen on Irini, until Aunt Ioulia, who had also lost her husband, asked her younger sister to move to Athens and share her house in Pangrati.

'Is Ioulia coming, do you know?'

'No, she's off to Aegina with Anna's lot. And some of Petros' kids, I think.'

'Anna's lot' were their cousins, the Leandrous. Or perhaps they were second cousins? Yiannis could never remember: Irini, not he, was the proven expert on relations.

The smell of bleach wafting across from Nikki's trolley made his eyes water. Evidently the client must have succumbed to persuasion, for Nikki was now tiling her head with squares of aluminium foil, in which her small set face was framed like some hoplite in an armoured helmet.

'So who've they put in charge of the investigation?' Irini asked.

'Vasilakis.'

'Andreas? That's nice for you.' Irini's scissors paused above his head. 'Isn't it?'

Yiannis nodded doubtfully. He and Vasilakis had been rookies together years ago, but Vasilakis was now plain clothes, with the Criminal Division in Chania. It was at his request, Yiannis was sure, that he had been co-opted on to the team.

Irini was eyeing him in the mirror, lips pursed.

'You know, I still don't understand what keeps you with the Tourist Police. I always said you'd make C.I.D. if you'd only put your mind to it.'

Once again he was unnerved by his sister's capacity to read

118

him like a book. As Irini never tired of pointing out, she'd had neither the advantages nor the encouragement that he, as the favoured son, had enjoyed, yet despite this she'd gone on to make a success of herself. It was understandable if she had little sympathy with those who – as she saw it – were given opportunities but failed to grasp them.

'Maybe so,' he said, shrugging.

'Keep still!' Irini clamped an immobilising hand over his skull. The pressure was considerable, as if she wanted to thrust him down through the padded chair and the floor and into the very bowels of the earth. 'Maybe nothing,' she hissed, as the points of her scissors clipped a perilous crescent just above his ear.

19

By the 1920s Sir Arthur Evans had differentiated the Minoan scripts into Hieroglyphic, found on early sealstones and tokens, and Linear A, the syllabic script which he proposed as the predecessor – the Mother script, as it were – of Linear B.

Although Linear B was finally deciphered by Michael Ventris in 1953, Linear A is still keeping its secrets. For 60 years epigraphers struggling with the earlier script have made no substantive progress. Even though Linear A and Linear B share many signs, and the syllabograms are thought to share some sound-values, the Linear A script appears to represent no known language of the region – rather in the way that English and French both use the Roman alphabet, but are completely different languages.

Even the scholars of Alice Kober's day recognised that the objects on which Linear A featured were likely to have been devotional. Unlike the clay Linear B tablets, with their quotidian inventories of livestock, wool, and grain, it may be said that the Linear A inscriptions have always held out the promise of insights into religious and ecstatic practices.

The carved images on the early Minoan sealstones are tantalising, inscrutable. The Nature Goddess is yanked from the soil like a snake or a sheaf of barley; the Mistress of the Animals suckles goats and gazelles. There are male Adorants, certainly – up on tiptoe, their outstretched arms hoisted in a kind of heil, their bodies arched suggestively, pelvis forward, before the Goddess – but there are no masculine deities, not a *single one in sight. No woman worth her salt, one might think, could fail to be intrigued.*

It is tempting to wonder, therefore, why Kober had been so quick to dismiss Linear A as a suitable case for decipherment back in the 1940s. Although one cannot fault her rationale – there were too few Linear A finds, compared to the substantial Linear B hoard, a situation which still applies today – what is perhaps harder to understand is how she was able to resist its promise: the lure, one could say, of the labyrinth.

What one must remember is that the female scholars of Kober's era faced enormous difficulty and prejudice; their fear of the 'irrational' – that accusatory shorthand for 'feminine' – must have been so much more acute than ours. Perhaps clever Alice, minding her ps and qs, simply opted to leave the wilder epiphanies to the men, who could better afford to make fools of themselves. It goes without saying that, in those days, 'incisive' was generally guaranteed to earn more plaudits than 'insightful' – although the goalposts, of course, could always be shifted. Michael Ventris, for instance, described Kober's logic as 'prim but necessary', and even told an American woman colleague that her approach to decipherment was 'a shade too frigid and destructive' for his taste.

Any mention of Alice Kober, any recognition of her contribution, invariably came with a judgement: she had lacked the creative courage, the willingness to take intellectual risks, of the truly first-rate scholar. The balls, one might say. For Kober it was a no-win situation: since they could not fault her logic, they would damn it with faint praise. So if her decision to turn her back on Linear A was based on nothing other than common sense and cool ambition – and history, one may say, has proved that decision right – well then, all credit to her.

On her way to the bus stop Ingrid sees Zoe Shapcott approaching, in sports bra and skin shorts, jogging magnificently in the cool morning light.

'You're up early!'

Pushing back her earphones, Zoe stops, panting. Strands of

hair which have escaped from her ponytail stick sweatily to her forehead.

'Sometimes I can't sleep after dawn. That studio's so titchy.' Zoe gives a pretty grimace. 'And Dad snores, bless him!'

Ingrid hides her surprise. She'd assumed that the Shapcotts had a two-room apartment. They certainly look as if they could afford it. Picturing the two single beds, she wonders if such easy intimacy is to be envied. At Zoe's age, the thought of sharing with her father would have been, quite literally, unthinkable. Perhaps it bodes well for Zoe's sexual future. Then again, perhaps it doesn't.

'Off to town?' Zoe is looking curiously at her briefcase.

'The Museum calls, I'm afraid.'

'Are you, like, writing a book or something?'

'You could say.' Ingrid shrugs. 'It's about dead philologists,' she adds on a note of self-mockery, hoping to forestall the inevitable enquiries.

Zoe's face lights up. At close quarters, her skin is faultless, smooth and creamy as a new egg. 'Hey, that's really cool!'

Ingrid has to laugh. It isn't exactly the word she'd have chosen. In the face of Zoe's bounteous youth, her prehistoric logograms – not to mention Miss Alice E. Kober, deceased – seem deader and dustier than ever.

The Archaeological Museum is sheathed in scaffolding; flaking stucco and rust-veined extractors give it the look of some NHS hospital thrown up in the '30s and going to pot. In the gravel courtyard a bed or two of sorry shrubs lie smothered under fallen plane tree leaves, and an armless *kore* of the classical period stands next to a white block of Portaloos. From the door marked with the universal Ladies logogram, a woman emerges, flapping water off her fingers and frowning in exasperation.

She presents her ticket and walks into the dim glare of the atrium. A school party has arrived before her, armed with worksheets and clipboards. She zigzags through them, heading for Room V, where, according to the catalogue, the Linear B tablets are housed.

In the Old Palace Room there are finds from the hauntingly-named Anemospilia, the Caves of the Wind: a ceramic bull with tiny acrobats clinging to its horns, a pair of disembodied clay feet. She hasn't been there yet, but it's on her itinerary: a must-see, not a maybe.

The site on the shoulder of Mount Iuchtas had been excavated in the 1980s, and ever since then controversy had raged. The earthquake that destroyed the small temple had struck during a ceremony that apparently involved human sacrifice. Three skeletons were recovered from the west room, of which two seemed to be a priest and priestess. On top of the third skeleton- a boy of 17 or so, trussed on an altar – lay a large bronze knife. This poor soul, according to the forensic archaelogists, was already dead when the building collapsed on the others.

Everything she'd read dated the events at 1700 BCE, around the time of the catastrophic earthquakes that destroyed the first Palace. The hypothesis – credible enough, in her opinion, although still fiercely opposed by a few scholars hell-bent on portraying the Minoans as sublimely peaceable folk – was that the victim was offered up in a last-ditch attempt to propitiate the seisichthonic gods.

The clay feet, whose colour reminds her of American Tan stockings, stop just above the ankles, and have short wooden poles in place of legs. She imagines the wooden statue of the goddess on its ox-cart, jolting up the hill to the sanctuary, where the clay feet stood on the altar, waiting patiently to be slotted in.

Room V echoes with the click of cameras. She skulks past the crowd of baggy-shorted Adorants that surrounds the ceramic statue of the Snake Goddess. The statue is bold-eyed, bare-breasted, bell-skirted; next to it, she feels furtive, modern, and deprived.

In a glass display case in the corner are two glazed libation cups with Linear A signs written in cuttlefish ink on the inner rims. The brushstrokes are bold yet delicate, like Chinese calligraphy, but the captioning on the case is sparse, to say the

123

least. A readable transcription would help, but none has been provided. She peers through her own reflection, trying to identify the signs inside. As far as she can make out, none of them add up to the *ja-sa-sa-ra* sequence of the so-called Minoan Libation Formula.

Some of the schoolkids have escaped their tutor, and are milling about anarchically, emitting ringtones and sundry electronic beeps. From outside comes the periodic thunder of pneumatic drills. There's no air-conditioning in the Museum, and the windowless room is so stuffy it's a wonder the Nordic-looking tourists don't faint away in the clammy heat.

The case which contains the Linear B tablets is in the centre of the room. It's about the size of a coffee-table, waist-high and free-standing. Inside it there are so few tablets that she wonders if she's made a mistake. She checks the catalogue again, which confirms that the Linear B finds are housed exclusively here in Room V.

She shakes her head in disbelief. The Museum has a vast hoard of tablets; in no way is she looking at a representative sample.

There are only six 'livestock' tablets in the case. Tiny things, no bigger than a postcard, really. Postcards from prehistory. The tablets gleam dark gold in their preserving varnish. Although the script is needle-thin the signs are well-formed, as if written by a practised hand. They're made of clay, of course, but the material that comes to mind is beeswax. The visual analogue is oddly alluring. Beeswax, after all, would have been a supple, malleable medium, easy to recycle. A single pass with a hot knife and the surface would be smooth and blank again. But unlike clay, which had been baked hard by the fires that destroyed the final palaces, and thus preserved for posterity, beeswax would simply have melted away. Could this be the reason why Linear A finds were so scanty, compared with Linear B? Transience is the sworn enemy of archaeology; ceramic, stone, metal – those are the durable, desirable materials, the ones that bear the forensic traces.

A civilisation born out of silence, returning to silence: all the molten honey of its words pouring away down the open stone conduits of Knossos.

The only chair in the room is already occupied by a uniformed attendant. Clutching the transcriptions of the Knossos tablets in one hand – she doesn't dare to spread them out on the glass top of the case – Ingrid extracts her reading-glasses with the other.

Anticipation makes her clumsy, like a girl on her first date. She leafs rapidly through her photocopies, searching for a visual match with the tablets. Logograms and syllabograms dance before her eyes. For a moment she's back in the class-room, confounded by the incomprehensible symbols on the blackboard.

People passing by have stopped to stare, not at the tablets, which aren't particularly visually arresting, but at Ingrid, whose rapt attentiveness seems to have created a focal point. She spreads her elbows to clear a space for scholarship, hoping that its intimidating aura will drive the idly curious off towards the half-million other more charismatic objects they could, after all, be gawping at.

It dawns on her then that the logical approach – which she prepared for, systematically, only a few days ago, but in her jittery state has managed to forget – is to compare the numbers on her list with the numbers on the exhibits. And after a moment, there it is. H 304, with its improbable, galumphing herd of 100 male animals. Displayed so badly that the script is almost unreadable through the top-reflections on the glass.

She stares at it, feeling absolutely blank.

Alice would be calm, she thinks, methodical. She wouldn't stand here blinded by reflections. She'd get her hands on the thing, pore over it with a magnifying glass, subject it to thorough autopsy. Self-doubt wouldn't enter the equation.

The awareness makes her even more flustered. She forces herself to check off all the numbers on her list. To her dismay, H 304 is the only one of Alice's Livestock tablets in the case.

So where on earth are the others?

She should have waited, perhaps, for the Museum to respond to her emails. But how long would that have taken? Weeks? Months?

Her anger is restorative, propelling her back through the galleries to the atrium. To the left of the counter which sells postcards and catalogues, a stone stairway leads down to the basement. A notice on the wall warns *Staff Only*.

At the top of the steps an attendant stands guard: a stocky woman whose uniform shirt juts over a wedge of breasts. As she moves to bar the way Ingrid flaps the photocopies under her nose.

'These tablets are not on display! I must see the Ephor.'

'You have appointment?'

Ingrid frowns over her reading glasses: it's hardly her fault if she hasn't. 'I have come from England!' she says grandly, as if this should be enough to remind the woman who put the Minoans on the map in the first place. Sir Arthur Evans, she's sure, never took no for an answer.

A man comes light-footed up the staircase and pauses on the step below her. She glimpses a pale blue shirt, black and silver epaulettes.

'It's Ms Laurie, isn't it? There is a problem?'

With a shock of embarrassment she recognises the Sergeant 'Cherete,' she greets him, hoping against hope that he didn't hear her overdrawing on national credit. Whipping the glasses off her nose, she explains the dilemma of the tablets.

The Sergeant nods judiciously. 'So, an archaeologist.' It's not a question but a statement. Resting a hand on the banister rail, he speaks soberly to the female guard. Ingrid can't help noticing that he's assumed, consciously or not, the relaxed pose of the classical *kouros* – one bent knee producing the understated torque at the hip, the chest quiet, the head inclined slightly on the neck.

Apollo, not Dionysus, she thinks, with a little jolt of the heart.

A pall of respect has settled on the attendant's face. She glances at Ingrid and nods grudgingly.

'*Endaxi.*'

The Sergeant – Stephanoudakis, she remembers, is his name – turns back to her, trim as a pin in his uniform shirtsleeves. On his face is the scrupulous smile of officialdom.

'It's okay,' he says, standing aside to let her pass, 'You can go ahead now.'

Warmth rises to her cheeks. In broad daylight his self-possession gives the lie to the night and the music, confirming them in her mind as elements of some overheated dream, the kind you wake from embarrassed and alone. Despite herself, she feels the sting of rejection.

'Thank you so much!' she cries, smiling glassily. Stuffing the papers into her briefcase, she starts down the stairs.

'It's a building site down there, I'm afraid.' His frown is rueful and suddenly intimate. His eyes are on her, soft eyes, like a deer's. 'I hope you can find what you're looking for.'

Sergeant Stephanoudakis was right. She threads her way past tool-boxes and stepladders and circuit-boxes which hang from the walls, sprouting naked wires. A glass partition which used to divide the administrative offices from the corridor has been removed. Inside, ceiling plaster has been stripped back to the lathes, desks and computers swathed in polythene.

In a small office further along the corridor a semblance of order reigns amidst the wreckage. There's a potted begonia on the desk, a tray with a flask of coffee and a china cup. When Ingrid puts her head round the door a handsome, harassed woman with greying blonde hair looks up from her laptop.

'*Signome?* You are the Ephor? I emailed you about my visit, but received no reply.'

The woman places the object she's been holding carefully on the blotter; it's snail-shaped, made of terracotta, with regular piercings, around it a coiled snake in bas-relief.

'The Ephor will not be here until 4 today. Perhaps I can help you?' Although she's smiling politely, her tone betrays her unwillingness.

127

Ingrid produces her photocopies, stamped with the magic words *Ashmolean Museum.*

'I have come to see these livestock tablets, but I believe they must be in store?'

The woman's face lightens visibly. She shakes her head. 'Our storerooms are closed. I'm afraid it will be impossible to view the tablets at this moment.'

Ingrid stares at the snail-like object, realising that it is, in fact, a model of a beehive. 'Until when?'

The woman shrugs. Her hands describe a future that is limitless. For a moment Ingrid is speechless. A brick wall is the one eventuality she never stopped to consider. 'So what do you suggest?' she asks, if only to save face. She knows, really, that it's hopeless. 'I should email?'

'I'm very sorry. As you can see, we have chaos in the building.'

Outside in the courtyard light and sound merge into a single entity. The sun, high now, rages down on Ingrid; traffic hurries, hooting, around the roundabout of Platia Eleftherias. The feeling of failure flattens everything, spoils her for the ordinary world. Of course she can tell herself that 60 years ago Alice was in the same boat, but there isn't much comfort in the irony.

It occurs to her for the first time to ask why she felt compelled to see these particular tablets, what exactly she expected to gain. It isn't as if 3000 year old accounts raise her to a pitch of intoxication, as they would a genuine epigrapher. Idle curiosity aside, there's nothing on them that could tell her what she really wants to know about Alice. Like some pilgrim aching for a sight of Compostela or the Dome of the Rock, she simply let blind fervour drive her on.

The Museum Cafe, predictably, is closed for renovation. Putting her sunglasses on, she lights a cigarette and looks around for signs of coffee.

In the far corner of the forecourt a temporary kiosk is selling soft drinks to the tourists. Too late, she sees the Sergeant standing by the stall, one elbow resting on the counter; even the shadow of the awning can't disguise his air of patient watchfulness. Through the railings she sees the patrol car, parked casually on the kerb.

He hails her as she approaches. 'You had some success?'

Ingrid shakes her head. 'Total failure, to be honest.'

'I see. I'm sorry.' Sergeant Stephanoudakis has an inch of black coffee in a tiny plastic cup. His cigarettes are at his elbow, the lighter stacked neatly on top of the pack.

'*Ti thelete?*'

The man behind the counter is watching her impassively. She changes her mind about coffee and orders water.

Producing a bottle from the fridge, the vendor thumps it down on the counter. The sergeant frowns and flickers a finger, and a plastic glass materialises beside the bottle.

'Allow me,' he says as Ingrid tries to pay, waving aside her protests.

The small courtesy brings her momentarily close to tears. She pours water into the glass and takes out her cigarettes; the bottle is mercifully cold, misted with condensation. Already there's a slime of sweat under the bridge of her sunglasses.

'It's hot,' he agrees. 'You'd like to sit?'

After a moment's hesitation, she accepts. He's a Greek, after all, and Greeks believe in the little gallantries. Have her habits become so solitary that she can't accept a simple kindness?

Whisking two folding chairs from the stack beside the kiosk, he arranges them in the shade of a large plane tree. She sits down, cradling the cold bottle in her lap. The Sergeant sits opposite, cool and quiet, sizing her up.

'So you're studying our Minoans?' His black shoes are shiny and shipshape, as if no dust dared stick to them. A gun nests snugly in the holster at the back of his belt. 'I hope you're also taking time to enjoy the island?'

The protocol is pretty clear: it's his island, and he requires her to be happy on it.

'Oh of course,' she says airily, 'The sun, the sea, you know.' She waves an appreciative hand at the brilliant dome of the sky, understanding that, on this occasion, the inconvenient business of the corpse won't be mentioned.

'Of course,' he echoes, with just enough irony to make her wish she hadn't been quite so quick to relegate herself to the status of tourist.

Beyond a low jumble of rooftops the peak of Mount Yuchtas shows pale blue in the haze. She thinks of the sacrificial victim up on the hillside of Anemospilia, meek with awe and opium, succumbing to his fate. The torpid heat makes her feel heavy and hollow. With a sense of inevitability she waits to submit to the standard interrogation – the barrage of questions Greeks think not rude, but simply direct.

Ise pantremeni o eleftheri? Married or single, children, and so on.

By and large, she isn't in favour of talking about her family. After all, what on earth would she say? An only child, father dead, mother in a Care Home. No husband, children, or pets. It sounds lonely and maudlin, as if she were some kind of Orphan Annie. Not that she minds exchanging snippets of information, in a general kind of way, but she's not from a background where people talk freely about their feelings.

The Sergeant wears no wedding ring. His fingernails, she notices, are clipped and clean.

'Eleftheri,' she says, only because she can't remember the Greek for divorced. But the word sounds too assertive, literally, it means 'free.'

'Lipon, milate Ellenika?'

Ingrid shrugs apologetically. 'It's rusty. Ancient Greek isn't really the same, I'm afraid.'

He's in his mid- to late-forties, she guesses, but his body is lithe and exact. A disciplined man, then – one not given to excess – except, as she knows, on the dancefloor. His English seems fluent, idiomatic. Aussie English, he explains: the product of ten years in Melbourne.

'Ime apo tin Skotia,' she tells him, steeling herself for the usual whisky comments.

'Bonny Scotland,' he remarks, with a ceremonious smile.

With kinship sorted, politics can be addressed. The Macedonian question, where the Brits stand on divided Cyprus. Ingrid feels the slow drag of boredom.

'Well, obviously Turkey's over a barrel – if they're so keen to join the E.U., I mean.'

She knows she is floundering. It's always a good idea to read the newspapers before you come to Greece, work out a position. A dry leaf skims down form the plane tree and settles on her hair. Feeling his eyes on her, she says stiffly, 'It was good of you, to get me past the guard.'

'No problem,' he says, shrugging. Behind the portaloos a JCB strikes up a terrible noise and he waits, frowning, until it stops. 'I told her you were on official business from the British Museum.'

The duplicity startles her. 'But I'm not!'

'But you might easily be, no? I can't really see you as a thief, Ms Laurie. Or a forger.'

He's grinning straight at her now, a broad grin, unabashed. On his sleeve-badge something silver, perhaps a laurel wreath, winks in the dappling sun. To have power and to exercise it – is that what puts the gleam of pleasure in his eye?

'Not even a terrorist?' she counters.

The Sergeant ponders this, quirking an Olympian eyebrow. 'Mad, bad, and dangerous to know? Somehow I can't see it, Ms Laurie!'

Just then a small child darts between them, trips on a tree root, and falls face down on the ground. In one fluid movement the Sergeant rises from his chair, reaches the wailing boy and crouches down beside him. When the child sees the uniform his cries stop abruptly and his eyes grow wide. The mother is approaching, strolling placidly from the kiosk, dove-like sounds issuing from her mouth. She scoops the child up and sets him on his feet, shrugging ruefully at the sergeant, who returns to his chair brushing gravel-dust off his trousers.

'Not too young to be scared of the cops, then.'

His smile – understated, and undeniably appealing – invites Ingrid to agree that he could never, in a million years, be intimidating. It says that, under the uniform, he's an ordinary,

131

affable sort of guy – which he probably is, she decides, if a conceited one – and she nods indulgently, for if he wants to impress her a little, then where's the harm in it?

'So what brings you to the Museum, Sergeant Stephanoudakis?'

'Yiannis, please.'

'Ingrid,' she says, and they lean forward on their rickety chairs and shake hands awkwardly across the gap.

'Some objects came into my possession. Archaeological objects. They may be fakes but I don't think so.'

'That happens often?'

'More often than you'd think.' His shrug is casual, but something dark and doleful lingers on his face. 'This is Crete, after all.'

When his cellphone beeps he flicks it open and reads whatever is on the screen. Then he snaps it shut and looks around absently, as if he has lost the thread. As the silence stretches, it strikes her that the conversation may simply tail away to nothing; in a moment they'll get up and shake hands and go about their business, and that will be that. The prospect of this fills her with an angry ache, like failure.

She says in a rush, 'That dance you did the other night, at the Medusa. I meant to say, well, how impressive it was.' As soon as the words are out they sound not only gushy, but possibly intrusive. He's a Cretan, after all; who's to say what private relationship he has to the ecstasies of the dance?

'You were there?'

The surprise on his face is so clearly counterfeit that she's now quite convinced he saw her. Taking refuge in theatre, she spreads exaggerated hands, throws in the Greek word for Wonderful. 'No really. It was *exaretiko!*'

With an infinitesimal shake of the head the Sergeant nips his cigarette out between finger and thumb, and drops it into the plastic cup. '*Exaretiko?*'

'*Exaretiko,*' she insists.

'*Efkaristo poli,*' he replies, bowing his head in a parody of politeness.

'*Parakalo,*' says Ingrid.

132

20

Yiannis took lunch at a small *ouzeri* behind the Police Station. Spreading the latest edition of *Messoghios* on the table, he ate without conviction, his thoughts lingering on Ingrid the archaeologist.

A nun's face, he decided: intense and abstracted, but a body that spoke volumes. At the thought of this a kind of torpor overtook him. He scowled at a plate of pureed aubergine, and for a shameful moment Dora, imploring him with her eyes, took on the characteristics of the mushy food he hated.

Already he could see her facing him across the table: her clothes too considered, her face made up like a magazine cover. The way her fingers punished her napkin, while he, cringing, carried the burden of her hurt.

He pushed his plate away impatiently. He would ring her today, definitely: make peace, or at least make the break a clean one. Settle the thing before his mother arrived from Athens with her winks and nudges and coy little questions.

'Why can't you settle down with a nice Greek girl?' she'd demanded tearfully after he'd brought Karen home for the first time. 'Someone who'll look after you.' This, after all, was what she'd spoiled him for – so that a daughter-in-law could carry on where she left off. Yet even as a youth he'd shied away from the destiny she'd planned for him. Did this make him more of a man, he wondered, or less of a Greek?

Entering a humble plea of guilty, he stared unseeing at the Sports section. As far as he could see, his mother didn't have an ounce of subservience in her, and his father had been the mildest man on Crete. So why on earth had she brought her son up to be a tyrant?

133

He pulled out his cellphone and summoned Dora's number. Within seconds, however, he succumbed to a fit of childish rebellion. Guilt or no guilt, how could you adore a woman who'd been reared with the sole purpose of being at your beck and call? A man needed something to get his teeth into, and he couldn't simply transform himself to order.

As he leafed backwards through the newspaper his eye fell on a caption.

DO YOU KNOW THIS MAN?

Underneath the caption the fat boy's face stared starkly out at him. Kallenikos had opened the eyes, of course, for the photograph. The accompanying article took up the rest of the page. It was flagged *MYSTERY OF THE BEE MAN*, and it carried Martha Hourdaki's byline.

He let out a muttered curse. Hourdaki had been a media figure on the island for 20 years, and Yiannis had always measured his opinion of her by Karen's. An opportunist, Karen had called her, a bandwagon feminist out to further her career. And further it she had, from the first brief polemics of the 80s, to a shit-stirring column in *Messoghios*, and now a weekly radio slot, not to mention regular appearances on TV chat-shows, whose hosts adored a controversialist – especially one with a gravelly voice, a serious cleavage, and the snaking locks of a Medusa.

He scanned the first paragraph, nerves jumping. The police press statement had been particularly non-commital, steering well clear of disclosures that were now before him in black and white. The glaze of honey on the victim's skin, the cocktail of opiates in the stomach: exactly the sort of prurient detail that would make newspapers fly from the the stands, regardless of how much it might muddy the waters of any inquiry. Yiannis knew plenty of reporters who, in their vanity, aspired to be one jump ahead of the police, but Hourdaki, typically, seemed determined not only to conduct her own personal investigation, but also to try the case in court.

There was worse to come. '*Forensic evidence has led the*

134

police to suspect the presence of a third party of the female sex,' he read with alarm. *'Are we to assume that the hunt is now on for the Mystery Bee Woman?'*

Led the police to suspect indeed! Where on earth was the woman getting her information?

He rolled up the paper, threw a note on the table, and strode out to the car. There was a discomforting suspicion he couldn't quite banish from his mind. Martha Hourdaki was a smooth operator, and he could see that her particular blend of bullying and flattery might be formidably seductive. If she'd been snooping around the lab, was it possible that a vain man like Theo might have been susceptible?

The Incident Room was in a half-basement with square barred windows through which a tranche of pavement was visible, as well as the lower legs of assorted passers-by. The place had originally been a storehouse where Venetian merchants kept their bolts of silk and casks of spices, and although the stone walls must have been whitewashed countless times over the centuries, Yiannis fancied that the smell of the past remained: a smell of musk, salt-petre, and nutmegs.

Vasilakis tossed the newspaper into the centre of the table. 'What a bloody soap-opera!' His reddish-blond eyebrows flew as high on his forehead as wild geese in the skies of autumn.

Vasilakis had what Yiannis could only characterise as a stunned face, one that always appeared to be trying to come to terms with what life dealt out to him, the good hands and the bad. A face permanently awash with frowns of puzzlement, or blushes of surprise. But today he had heard Hourdaki on Radio Kriti on the way over from Chania, and Yiannis had rarely seen him so angry.

'For your information, guys, the first Oracle at Delphi was attended by bee-priestesses called the Melissae. And old Zeus, get it, was called Melissaios, the Bee man, because sacred bees fed him on honey when he was a baby in the Diktaean Cave!' Vasilakis snorted. 'Welcome to Neverland. I mean, who's she trying to impress?'

Outside the window a *papaki* rested against a lamp-post. As the rhetorical question hung in the air Yiannis saw a yellow dog hoist its missing back leg and water the wheel. Understandably, Vasilakis hated it when the press seized the initiative that rightly should be his. Not to mention the fact that a case which had most probably been headed straight for the files had now taken on a momentum of its own. The four of them stared glumly back at him.

It was Kyriaki who spoke first, brightly, as if to rally the troops. 'At least we've got a name for Miss X, sir.'

Detective Sergeant Kyriaki – Ioanna by name – looked as smart as a whip. She had a lean face with black eyebrows that crowded together in the middle, and a brazen white wave cresting at the front of her short dark hair. It was clear that she had every confidence in her boss's indulgence; clear also, from the glances exchanged by Kounidis and Mouzakitis, that the two junior officers would be glad to see her taken down a peg. Vasilakis had crimped his face into a frown. 'How so?'

'Melissa, sir?'

'Ai, Ioanna!' Eyebrows aloft, Vasilakis shook an admonishing finger. She might have been his naughty daughter, whose name Yiannis had temporarily forgotten. Given their respective ages, she could have been. Her ploy, though, seemed to have worked: egos had been obscurely soothed, and the atmosphere lightened perceptibly. Mouzakitis and Kounides shifted in their seats, brought out cigarettes, and allowed themselves a chuckle.

On the whiteboard Vasilakis had written. *M.O.? MOTIVE?* Beside *M.O.* he had drawn a bad hieroglyph of a bee. With a shrug that consigned the investigation to the status of a travelling circus, he picked up the marker pen and added *MELISSA?*

Spectral, the name stared back at Yiannis. He imagined long dark hair, moon-dapples like silver coins on the curving shadow of a back. For a moment the comely Zoe swam into his mind, but despite that Greek temptation to see all mischief, from nude bathing to sodomy, as vices imported from elsewhere, when he thought of the ghostly girl he couldn't pin a foreign face on her.

'No belongings, that's the real bastard!' Vasilakis glowered at the whiteboard like a man affronted. 'Otherwise, well, you'd think a sex-game gone wrong, something like that.' He sat down, took a gulp of his coffee, and pulled the autopsy report towards him. 'So. Nothing from Lyon yet?'

'No sir,' said Kyriaki. 'They're circulating it to the other national forces.'

Vasilakis sighed. 'No identifying marks, either. No scars or piercings, not a filling or a crown in his mouth.'

Yiannis hastily consulted his copy. 'No dental work, sir?'

'Absolutely zilch. Clean as a whistle.'

'Lucky sod,' Mouzakitis muttered.

Vasilakis withered him with a glance. 'Not lucky for us if it means no dental records.' He spread the photographs out on the table. 'So come on, guys. What *do* the photographs tell us?'

'He was strong and fit, sir?' Kyriaki offered. 'Almost like a professional athlete?'

'I agree,' said Vasilakis. He nibbled a fingernail, musing.

The fan which had been brought in laboured feebly against the preposterous heat.

Mediterranean origin, the report said. *Nationality unknown.* Yiannis loosened his tie and studied the body shot. On the chest, legs and arms the tan was still faintly visible, and more clearly demarcated against the paleness of the belly and genital area. Not a nudist, he thought, but did not say; it struck him that what was missing was the usual mark of a watchstrap.

The drone of the fan summoned up the timeless throb of the plane that had brought him back, all these years ago, from Melbourne. After the stretched day and the refuelling stop at Singapore, they'd entered a zone of continuous night, moving in a domain of darkness. He remembered that feeling of being held in the heart of it, as if in the dark waters of a mother's womb. Bad weather had diverted the plane to Vienna, and above him the blackness had been pricked by stars, and below him it was depthless, strung with the geometrical constellations of cities.

'So how did they get there? Hiked round the coast? *Papaki?* Car? They'd have had to park on the road. Someone must have seen *something?*'

Vasilakis cleared his throat noisily. 'Are you with us, Yianni?' His lips were pursed into a mode of tolerance but his eyebrows were exasperated. 'We're going to need house-to-house interviews in the Panomeli sector.'

'Yes, sir,' said Yiannis, abashed. Yiannis the dreamer. Yiannis the worshipper of dawns and dusks and shifting weather.

'And while you're at it, get the passport details of every damn tourist over there. I want a proper check done, is that clear?'

Shirt-sleeved, Vasilakis paced and smoked. Sweat shone on his bald patch; there was a brass-coloured fleece on his forearms, as if the years had contrived to transfer the deficit from his head to his extremities. He stopped mid-stride and fixed his gaze on Kyriaki. 'Get on to Forensics, Ioanna. I'm ordering another search of the scene. I want every last centimetre dusted, I want it sieved. I *know* there's trace, there's got to be.'

'Right you are, sir!' said Kyriaki.

Outside the window a woman pushing a double buggy stopped to answer her cellphone. From the buggy two identical faces gazed in, pop-eyed, at Vasilakis. Reaching the window, he saw them and stopped in his tracks, a soupy smile spreading over his face. When he fluttered his fingers at them, the infants opened their mouths and wailed in unison. As the decibels reached fever pitch the mother, cellphone still glued to her ear, bent down to investigate.

Kyriaki was grinning openly. Catching her eye, Yiannis wanted to laugh, but thought better of it.

Vasilakis turned and appealed to the room – What did I do? – his hands spread wide, his face a picture of perplexity.

*

As the car bumped down the track Kore mewed faintly but, Yiannis thought, uncomplainingly. She was no longer in pain, Wiltraud had assured him, although he must be careful to keep her on antibiotics for a week.

'If she is to be spayed,' she'd said, 'it should be soon. You will consider this?'

Her earnest blue eyes were so concerned for Kore's welfare that guilt made him say he would, but in the moment of saying so, intellect had cringed before instinct, and he knew that he couldn't, that his gut was Greek beyond reason.

In a rocky field on the left of the track two perched goats regarded him with hauteur. Part of the boundary wall had collapsed, and through the gap a man appeared, hefting a boulder. He was booted, sinewy in shorts; his hands were protected by industrial gloves but his head was bare under the blasting heat of the sun. His straight light hair was streaked with grey and tied at the nape with a red kerchief.

Yiannis slowed down and raised a hand as he drew level. 'Earthquake damage?'

The man set the rock down on a pile of similar grade and straightened up. There was white dust on his forearms and an English slogan on his T shirt. Yiannis read it with interest.

Cool eyes regarded him from behind rimless glasses. 'We have got off lightly, I think.' The shrug, he thought, was something more than stoical: *this time* was the lugubrious implication. The accent was precise, unmistakeably German. Yiannis summoned a commiserating smile. Far below lay the white houses of Katomeli, and the coiffured blond curve of the beach; beyond that was the sea, vast and calm and, at least for the moment, perfectly irreproachable.

'Lovely spot,' he observed – a prelude, he hoped, to a little pleasant conversation, about cats, maybe, or communes.

139

The German glanced briefly at the vista and, with a nod that was barely courteous, bent to retrieve his mallet and chisel.

Yiannis' eyes roved inquisitively, taking in a flask, a spirit-level, a small canvas rucksack. *Arbeit macht frei*, he thought sourly: you could always trust a German to get the job done properly. No doubt this new wall would be meeter and fitter in every way than the home-grown original. Like all cops, he was accustomed to the cold shoulder, and made a point of wishing the guy an affable Good Day. As he could have predicted, his *yassous* went unanswered.

He eased in the clutch and drove off thoughtfully. *BEE WARNED*, the slogan on the T shirt had said, *THE FUTURE DOES NOT NEED US.*

21

After the heat and bustle of Heraklion, the beach at Panomeli is a sleepy familiar haven. A late afternoon haze hangs over the sea; some way out, a group of sunhatted local *yia yias* float, gossiping, their rubber sandals double-parked along the shoreline.

Ingrid and Zoe lounge at the water's edge, cooling their feet in the shallows. A few metres higher up the beach, near a scatter of short-stemmed lilies which seem to have sprung up overnight, the Wilson-Wilsons are playing Snap in the deep shade of their umbrella. To their right Trish Ottakar, her ample breasts baking in the sun, is absorbed in Nabokov; to their left Mr. Shapcott sits neat and upright in a white cotton sunhat. He's reading *The Silence of the Lambs*, but without conviction, Ingrid suspects. As if someone has told him this is the kind of book you read on holiday, when really he'd prefer something more substantial, like Chomsky or Said, or Fiske's essays on the Middle East. She has the impression that, behind his sunglasses, he's keeping a beady eye on them.

'Alice didn't have a clue what the signs meant,' she continues, 'No one did back then. So she indexed all of them on tiny slips she cut out of old scrap paper, plus all the sign-groups, and filed them all in cigarette cartons.'

'Talk about low-tech!' Zoe shakes her head wonderingly at the dark ages.

'Exactly. Just imagine what she could have done with a Mac.'

Zoe is a surprisingly attentive student, and Ingrid is enjoying the tutorial. She thinks of the Script archive, the three of them working, monkish, among the tousled shelves: archaic listeners to dead voices. Yet here is Zoe, hanging on her every word, telling her that she's seriously considering archaeology at Uni – after her gap year, of course.

'What it did mean, though, was that she was the one who cleared away a lot of the bullshit and made room for an analysis of the linguistic structures.' She draws the sign-groups in the smooth damp sand. 'For instance.'

'If you look at the three alternative endings you can see the inflection clearly. Like – America, American, Americans.'

'Or Latin cases,' Zoe says intelligently. 'Dative, vocative, and stuff.'

Ingrid nods, pleased. 'That's what Alice thought, originally. "Kober's Triplets", the guys called them.'

Zoe pulls a face. 'Yuk. Sexist or what!'

'Isn't it just? Cruel too. She was a spinster, she didn't have children.'

Zoe gives her a fleeting, long-lashed glance. 'Have you?'

'Kids?' Ingrid is transfixed, momentarily, by Zoe's graceful body, perfectly unselfconscious in its sky-blue bikini. She shrugs, feeling defensive. The women of Zoe's generation are so organised, their courses plotted years in advance: college, career, partner, mortgage, children. They expect – no, demand – to reap all the benefits of equality. And good on them, too, she thinks, feeling vaguely that she has let Zoe down. She could, of course, point out, Cassandra-like, that everything isn't always possible, but the prospect threatens to put her on a par with the *yia yias*, so complacently asexual in their outsize bathing-suits, gossiping away the early evening.

'I got married too young, I guess. And divorced . . . and now, well.'

'You're not saying you're too old?'

'I'm 43.' Old enough, certainly, to be Zoe's mother.

Zoe gapes. 'But you can't be! You're too . . . cool.'

'Bless you!' says Ingrid, charmed.

'No, but I really envy it, you know,' Zoe goes on winningly, 'I see you up at the Shoestring, like, totally absorbed, totally fascinated by your subject. Must be so great, having a vocation.'

Not that fascinated, Ingrid thinks, but does not say. Right now she doesn't feel like dwelling on the downside of Alice's life – the loneliness, the constant chilly excitations of the mind. In the glow of Zoe's admiration her own life has taken on a winsome sparkle, and for the moment she wants to bask in it: to preserve, at least for a little longer, not only Zoe's illusions, but her own.

A large brown and white dog comes splashing towards them along the strand.

'Sweetie pie!' cries Zoe as it hurdles her outstretched legs. 'Look, he's just a puppy!'

He's a St. Bernard, in fact, huge and friendly and far from home. His paws are fat and floppy, his brown eyes melt with interest and concern. The owner follows, barefoot, saronged, carrying a large string bag and a coiled leash, a raggedy straw hat crammed over her brown braids.

From the other direction a black spaniel puppy appears, chasing a ball thrown by a thin tanned boy in his early teens. The two disproportionate dogs meet, sniffing; the woman cautions her dog in German, but the St Bernard has made a unilateral decision to play. The spaniel looks terrified, and shrinks back, shivering, behind the boy's legs.

The two owners shrug and smile. When the boy says

143

something in Italian the woman shakes her head in apology.

'I don't speak.'

In the string bag Ingrid sees the blue-black spines of sea-urchins, coiling and uncoiling.

Once the St. Bernard has ousted the smaller dog he chases it in and out of the sunbeds and then both dogs career back down to the water's edge, showering Ingrid and Zoe with sand.

Everyone is looking now; even the Wilson-Wilsons have abandoned their card game to watch the show.

Mr. Shapcott is suddenly on his feet, gesticulating. 'Darling, don't touch it!'

'It's a friendly dog,' Trish Ottakar protests, raising her sunglasses to stare at him.

Mr. Shapcott turns on her. 'You like dogs, then?'

'I like animals, yes – and people,' she replies coldly. 'Don't you?'

'I don't like foreign dogs,' he snaps, taking a few steps towards the water. 'Zoe, please. You never know, with rabies.'

'Oh Dad, it's not a stray,' Zoe scolds, as the panicked spaniel hurtles into Ingrid's lap and cowers there, trembling.

Instinctively Ingrid cradles it, surrounding it with her body: bare skin aginst sleek black fur. She wags an admonitory finger at the St. Bernard, which skids to a standstill and waves a hopeful paw at the fugitive. The spaniel's head is hot and smooth against her breast. She thinks of the *Potnia Theron*, the Mistress of the Animals. If the spaniel were a baby, it would be suckling.

'Got to get a picture!' Zoe scrambles to her feet, runs to her sunbed, and returns with her cellphone.

The puppy's heart pounds against Ingrid's ribs. It turns its head to gaze at her, its brown eyes seeking reassurance. 'He's only playing,' she urges, and the spaniel, plucking up courage, bats a paw out from its sanctuary. Zoe is down on her knees in the sand, aiming her cellphone, as the delighted St. Bernard skips back four-footed and flattens its muzzle along its paws.

But enough is enough. The woman snaps the leash on to the

144

St. Bernard's collar and coaxes him away, and Ingrid, opening her arms, surrenders her charge to the teenager. After a moment's hesitation the spaniel goes to him, waving its tail furiously, a bit of bravado in its waddle. Eyeing its departing adversary with what looks like regret, it even feints and growls at Zoe's cellphone.

Zoe sits back on her heels, giggling. 'What is he *like*?'

She can still feel the imprint of the puppy in her lap, its vanished heat a shadow on her skin. In the snapshot, though, nothing will be missing: the dog will be there, and the smiles, and the sea – a happy holiday moment captured for posterity. A small surf breaks across her calves, an echo of some far-out passing craft. Kober's Triplets have all but disappeared, rubbed out by a criss-cross of paw tracks and scuffed up sand.

She thinks of Yiannis, wonders if, long after the memories have faded, the photograph will fix on her face the aura of the morning, its secret sense of possibility.

22

In March 1947, preparing to set out on her first transatlantic voyage, Alice Kober brimmed over with excitement. To Myres she wrote 'I've timed myself, and I think I can copy between 100-125 inscriptions in a 12 hour day.' *Mindful that England had been suffering an arctic winter, she added a postscript:*

'I forgot to check my rate of work when my fingers were stiff with cold. I know it isn't a joking matter. But I feel, whatever the situation will be, I can cheerfully endure for 5 weeks what I learned to endure during the war.'

Alice liked England, and to Henry Allen Moe wrote sympathetically of its post-war privations.

'One of the tutors at St. Hugh's spent a week of her Easter vacation reweaving the elbows of her only decent tweed jacket. Sir John uses the gummed paper on the outside of a page of stamps to cover errors and changes in the *ms.* he's getting ready to publish. He can't get erasers or ink-eradicator. I left him everything I had in the way of writing equipment. He protested very feebly, and ended by saying the things would be "most welcome". All this in one of the countries on the winning side. Travel is most enlightening.'

There is further evidence of Kober's capacity for empathy with the privations suffered by her European colleagues in her letters to a new correspondent, Professor Johannes Sundwall of Abo University in Finland, whose work on the Minoan scripts she had admired for many years. Among the densely typed pages of technical discussion on Linear B, there are mentions of parcels she is sending, of oranges, sugar, Nescafe, even "rum-chocolates", in the hope that Sundwall is not a

146

"teetotaller". '(Kennen sie das wort? Es meint einer der ken Alkohol drinkt.)'

On March 28th an airmail letter, addressed c/o Sir John Myres, 3 Canterbury Road, arrived in Oxford. In it was what, with hindsight, one might characterise as perhaps the biggest failure of judgment ever made by the Guggenheim Foundation. Kober had requested a continuation of her Fellowship, in order to give her the time she thought she needed to complete her initial cataloguing of the Lnear B script. Henry Allen Moe wrote regretfully that the Committee had decided not to grant the renewal.

If Alice Kober was downcast by the refusal, there are no signs of it in her response to Moe, although there may be an implied rebuke in her acid reporting of the lack of progress in the decipherment field.

'Last year two more "decipherments" of Minoan were published, one by Hrozny, who has been "deciphering" languages right and left since he stated, long ago, and correctly, that Hittite was Indo-European, and so gave scholars the clue they needed for deciphering it. Since then, he has used the same system. That is, he states every unknown language is Indo-European. But I'd better not go on. Further nasty comments about it might be due to professional jealousy.'

Sir John Myres, aged 78 and housebound with arthritis, had asked Kober to go to Crete in his place and check the originals of the Knossos inscriptions, a task which had been impossible during the war years. The news from Heraklion, however, was discouraging. Shortly after Kober's retun to Brooklyn, Myres received a letter from the Heraklion Museum to say that the inscriptions, buried for safekeeping during the war, could not possibly be available in 1947. To Moe Kober observed, somewhat caustically,

'I suspect, although Sir John didn't mention it, that the Greeks do not have the money to dig them up again. At least, I know other Greek museums have told people interested in various exhibits that they would not be on display until money was forthcoming.'

In an era before fax, email, and cheap transatlantic flights, international collaboration was a slow and difficult business. It was also hindered by scholarly rivalry and protectionism, which Kober had experienced at first hand when Carl Blegen had refused her permission to see the Pylos material.

She complained later to Sundwall, 'although he [Blegen] criticised Evans bitterly for his slowness in publication and his selfishness in not permitting scholars to have access to the inscriptions, he himself seems to be following in his footsteps now.'

Although it is clear that she believed passionately in the free interchange of knowledge – at least between the very best minds in the field, of whom Sundwall was undoubtedly one – Kober was nevertheless forced to abide by the protocols of a league of squabbling gentlemen. At the cost of doubling her workload, she obtained Myres' permission to make copies of all the Linear B inscriptions, but only with the strict proviso that they would not be shown to anyone before the publication of Scripta Minoa II.

On her return to Brooklyn Kober did her best to advance the dream of collaborative scholarship by sending an article by John Franklin Daniel on the Cypro-Minoan scripts to Sir John Myres, and encouraging Sundwall to submit an article – which she would translate – to Daniel, who was now Editor-in-Chief of the American Journal of Archaeology. *Since Daniel was also Curator of the Mediterranean Section at the U. of Pennsylvania Museum, she passed on to him Sundwall's suggestion that an Institute be founded for the study of Minoan scripts.*

Living as he did in Finland, in the shadow of the USSR, Sundwall was very conscious of the effects of the last war, and also feared that a far more destructive nuclear war could be imminent. Minoan scholarship, he warned, could be safeguarded only if all the material currently available was

148

brought together under one roof; that it should be an American roof seemed self-evident.

Where such an institute might be housed was a moot question. Brooklyn College, Kober argued, did not have the money or space to accommodate such project, and she did not want it 'to come under Blegen, since he refuses to release the Pylos material.'

Although Franklin Daniel thought that Brooklyn was the obvious choice, since the material could be easily accessed by the woman who would make best use of it, he had no objections to Alice's suggestion that the University of Pennsylvania be the host.

He also responded with enthusiasm to her offer to translate Sundwall's article.

'I hope you don't intend to tackle the original Finnish, or maybe that presents no problem for you. His reprints and other publications will be most welcome as the first contribution to our "Minoan Institute of Epigraphy" (what are we going to call the thing anyway?)'

The Minoan Institute was not the only plot being hatched at the U. of Pennsylvania that autumn. When Kober commended Daniel to Sundwall as 'a very energetic young man', she wasn't exaggerating. The retirement of Roland Kent had left a position vacant in Indo-European Linguistics, and Daniel was determined to impress upon his colleagues that Alice Kober was the prime candidate.

'I am slowly boring from within toward this whole project, not the least part of which, of course, is trying to get you down here,' he wrote, adding that although he saw no difficulty about setting up the Minoan Centre as such, 'it would be rather lost without someone like you to look after it and use it.'

Daniel's 'nefarious schemes' were intended to kill two birds with one stone. As a Professor at the U. of Pennsylvania, Alice Kober would also be on hand to assume charge of the Minoan epigraphical centre to be established at the Museum.

'I have had some success in softening up the classicists and orientalists on the matter,' he writes gaily, 'and am about ready to make a frontal attack on the Dean . . . I would say that you are definitely considered a possibility for the job; the next step is to make you seem the *only* possibility. I certainly think it would be wonderful, for us at least, if this thing could be pulled off. It is just what we need to make this into a first class centre for the study of the Bronze Age in Greece and the Near East.'

In contrast to Kober's self-confessed pessimism, Daniel bursts with optimism about the future, and signs off with what is obviously a private joke: 'I must stop now and get back to my knitting.'

It took a brave man to assume the prerogative of teasing Alice Kober, and it is perhaps a measure of their intimacy that she responds in kind, reminding him with tart good humour that she only ever knits 'while reading detective stories.'

After submitting her magisterial paper, 'The Minoan Scripts: Fact and Theory' – *which Daniel thought an excellent and much-needed stocktaking – to the* American Journal of Archaeology, *Kober returned to her Linear B files.*

'Keep your fingers crossed,' *she wrote with unconcealed excitement,* 'I'm starting a tabulation of all the "cases" in the hope that I can tie them down. It gets very complicated, because some forms seem to be the same for two or more "cases", but I'm hoping for some results. If I can get them this way, just using my vocabulary and inscription lists, and the suffix and sign-juxtaposition file, I'll save a couple of years' work. If I can't get at it that way, I'll have to compile statistics on sign-use. You can figure out for yourself how long it will take to compare each of 78 signs with 78 other signs, at 15 minutes (with luck) for each comparison. That's about 1500 hours. I did it on the little slide rule I just bought to hasten the arithmetic I'll have to do.'

The letter ends on a gleefully bitchy note:

'I'm a malicious creature. Boy, wouldn't I like to decipher Minoan before Blegen publishes the Pylos material. But then he'd probably have to rewrite the whole thing, and hold everything up another decade or so.'

Clearly Kober knew she did not have to mince her words with John Franklin Daniel.

23

On the crude Flagstaff map Panomeli was roughly oblong in shape, bordered by the beach to the north and the main street to the south. The Totem Bar stood on the north-west corner, and the Shoestring on the south east. Little of the land between the beach-front and main street had been developed, leaving a sizeable central area to pomegranate trees, over-grown vines, and chicken runs.

At Yiannis' request, Lynda had scribbled the clients' names on the apartments. On main street, above the Minimarket, the Wilson-Wilsons were in the second floor *Kiki* studio, above Ingrid Laurie in *Stella*. Next door, in *Jasmin*, were the Shapcotts. All four Giffords had the larger detached house called the *Captain's*, a new-build villa on the eastern edge of the central wilderness

On the other side of the village, the Harknesses – who, despite their apparent distress, hadn't curtailed their holiday-were in *Kalliopi*, a first floor apartment in the new studio block opposite the Totem Bar while, on the ground floor, in *Daphne*, were the Misses Ottakar and Dodge.

In the office the desk and photocopier occupied most of the floor area, a space already narrowed by stacks of dry goods and brochure-laden shelves. There were Flagstaff posters on the walls, and a noticeboard given over to local ads which appeared to work on the principle, if it moves, hire it out. Yiannis wondered just what it took to secure a position on the board – the competition, he imagined, must be fierce. Favours would be called in, work done at discount, casks of wine deposited discreetly on doorsteps. In a tiny place like Pano-meli, it paid to keep in with Flagstaff.

Lynda had cleared the clutter off the desk, and Demosthenes had provided water, an ashtray, and two small *medio*s, one for Yiannis, and the other for Christos, who'd reappeared after a training stint at the Agios Nikolas station, and to whom Yiannis had entrusted the photocopying.

Yiannis had always found that as a nation the Brits were singularly attached to their passports. Even when the old navy blue one with its vainglorious royal crest had given way to the drab red EU model, their prideful attitude remained, as if they were clinging to some racial memory of the *laissez-passer*, the Grand Tour, and all the privileges of Empire. Although Lynda had suggested the clients drop off their passports and collect them from her later, he wasn't surprised when most of them refused, opting instead for an orderly British queue outside the door of the office.

The Wilson-Wilsons were first to step through the open door and approach the desk, the girl's wooden-soled sandals clip-clopping like shod hooves across the marble floor. They were ugly, presumably orthopaedic things, snub nosed, like jet-ski cowlings, and moulded from something hairy: goatskin, perhaps, or carpet underlay.

He opened the two passports and compared the details. Both, he noted, had been born in Wolverhampton, which he supposed to be somewhere in the north, where wolves once lived; presumably such sandals were manufactured there.

'If I could have a cellphone number, please.' He thanked them and handed the passports to Christos, who waited importantly by the photocopier.

From outside he heard a mellifluous laugh, easily identified as Zoe's.

'It's kind of glamorous, though, isn't it? Like being a suspect or something.'

'Well I think they've got a cheek!'

The indignant voice belonged to Miss Ottakar, and was clearly meant to be overheard. She swept into the room, passport flattened to her breast like a badge of honour.

152

Batting away the smoke from the cigarette which burned in the ashtray, she slapped the passport down on the desk.

'I mean to say, Officer, is this really necessary?'

'I'm afraid it is, Miss Ottakar.' Nettled, he crushed out the cigarette. Perhaps she thought that lesbians should be exempt from suspicion. For criminal, read heterosexual, was that it?

'Aye, love, and you're a suitable case for Interpol and that's the truth.'

The brawny Gifford man stood in the doorway, peeking through the plastic fly-strips. There was a loud Shush!, and laughter, quickly smothered.

Miss Ottakar bristled. Not the sort to take a joke, thought Yiannis. Probably in management; he could see her as a senior admin executive in some vast and cold-hearted bureaucracy – Health, or Tax, or Social Services.

Ignoring her protests, he gestured curtly at the photocopier – 'If you don't mind. My colleague will only take a moment' – and beckoned the Giffords in.

Since the office wasn't big enough to accommodate the whole family he dealt with the younger couple first, copying down their cellphone numbers and deflecting Ken Gifford's questions. Surprisingly, no one else had asked about the progress of the case. Either they were aware he wasn't allowed to discuss it, or else they were remarkably incurious.

The Gifford *yia-yia*, lipsticked and puckish in a straw stetson, steered her husband in. Yiannis offered her a chair, which she refused

'We're here for the third degree, Sergeant!' she chirped, waving two passports at him.

'What?' said the old boy, who appeared to be deaf.

Yiannis smiled and shook his head. 'I'm sorry to disappoint you, Mrs Gifford.'

Zoe came in apologising. 'Dad's having a lie-down, but I've got his passport here, if that's okay.' She wore a thin cotton shift with enough sky blue in it to be luminous; underneath Yiannis detected the shadowy lines of a bikini.

The visitation had frozen Christos in his tracks. His eyes were wide with reverence, the flood of colour plain on his face. Yiannis glanced at Zoe's birthdate and calculated that she would be seventeen in October. The address was in London – Hampstead, which even Yiannis had heard of. He took the details and passed her on to Christos, who received the passport like a votive offering, struggling manfully with his half-dozen words of English.

When Ingrid Laurie strode into the room he was so pleased to see her that for a second he forgot the occasion, and the need to find a face that fitted it. Her passport had a red spot on the front cover.

'It's a replacement,' she said anxiously. 'The last one was stolen when my flat was broken into.'

'Ah yes.' He flicked through the pages, pretending to examine the visas. 'This was in London?'

'Yes. Two years ago, I think.'

'I see. And your cellphone number?'

She looked back at him, wide-eyed. Embarrassed, he tapped the list of phone numbers with his pen. Surely she didn't think he was singling her out for special treatment?

Just then his own cellphone rang. It was D.S. Kyriaki, on her way to collect him, and could he please tell her exactly where the Minimarket was? He gave her instructions, feeling Ingrid's's eyes on him. When he snapped the phone shut he registered the white mark of sunglasses etched against the freckled bridge of her nose.

'Actually I don't have one,' she said.

A sixth of a second is all it takes. The synapses redirect the electrical signals to the limbic brain, the ancient, animal part. With a flush of shame he remembered that it was Karen who'd told him this, Karen up to her eyes in Psych. revision.

He stared at Ingrid, shocked. A taste had flooded his mouth, a sharp insistent sweetness, like leatherwood honey. He tried to remember what they'd been talking about.

'A cellphone,' she said, frowning.

'I see. Thank you.' He consulted his watch, as if to termi-

154

nate the interview, and pushed the passport across the desk. The breath of the fan was turning the sweat on the back of his neck to ice. His immediate thought was to get rid of her as fast as possible.

'Don't you want me to.?' she began, casting a doubtful glance towards the photocopier.

'Please, yes.' Yiannis cut her off abruptly, shooing her away with a tight smile and a flick of the fingers. He was already beckoning the next clients in. When they stood before him he took their passports and frowned intently at the photographs. Several moments passed before he recognised the Harknesses, and remembered that he ought to be sympathetic.

24

At first Pericles wishes that he hadn't come. He feels lost in the foreign crowd that throngs around the Palace, confused by the camera-flashes and the wide sun-dazed views. The place isn't at all as he remembers it, that day he brought his mother on the bus. The walls that were faced with sparkling white marble look limy and ruined now; whole buildings have vanished with their colours, to be replaced by roofless shells of dull sandstone, and the white horns he remembers – high up, red-striped like candy-canes – have vanished too.

He remembers a maze of alleyways, and in them, coolness, the smell of manure. Dark doors through which he'd glimpsed grindstones and olive-presses, the glow of a bronze-caster's forge. There were market stalls in the sunken square by the city gate, where ox-carts were unloading, and stone benches along the wall where grown men scratched their letters and their numbers on slates, just as he'd done himself in infant school.

Where before had been a laundry, timber-roofed and full of steam and shouts, Pericles sees only light and dust, as if there had been a war in the interim. Pericles wonders if this is possible. Jail was a world in itself, a seamless procession of keys and days; in jail everything passes you by, he knows that much. Everything but rumour.

That day his mother was wearing the black scarf she'd crocheted for church. She carried a heavy leather handbag and, inside, a plastic box full of fresh pineapple sliced into crescents.

He remembers his relief that she didn't seem to notice the women – not just those on the high balconies, but specially those bare-chested brazen ones on the great terrace, making their *volta* under the cedars. Childless and unguarded, like prostitutes, whispering like butterflies.

And old wrinkled ones too, with long dry dugs. He could no more grasp the meaning of them than he could understand a flower.

Their black eyes crawled over him till the heat burst in his head.

See how she looks at you, Pericles.

But still his mother had said nothing, seen nothing. Sinking down on a bench, she wiped her forehead, fanned herself, unlocked the box of pineapple.

Pericles sees a guide approaching, in white socks like a schoolgirl, waving a little flag. He counts twenty people in the party that follows in her wake. Ignoring him, she climbs right up on his bench and speaks to the group in French and in German, pointing at pillars. Surrounded, Pericles is invisible, his view restricted for the moment to broad bellies, rucksacks and brightly coloured shoelaces. The thought of the pineapple has made him thirsty: his throat is dry as dust and tugs at his tongue.

The guide jumps down and strides off, her party trailing after her across the wide courtyard. Once again the view spreads out before him, and now Pericles can see that gold and yellow daisies have sprung up between the paving stones, and that here and there are clumps of scarlet poppies. There are cedars on the far side of the courtyard, cypresses.

Suddenly his friends appear, darting out of the shadows and bursting into a glaze of sun. The short one and the tall one, both oiled and dark.They skip down the low tier of steps that surrounds the arena, waving their hands about excitedly, as if on their way to a football game.

Today the tall one has flowers, lilies maybe, tangled among his long curls. He stops at the bottom of the steps and shields his eyes with his hand, squinting across the bright space, pointing straight at Pericles.

The guide has left her bottle of water behind. Pericles wipes the top carefully, as his mother taught him, and tilts the bottle to his lips until he has drained it.

Only then does he risk another look at his friends. They are smiling, the tall one beckoning to him in a way that tells him what a really unmissable game it's going to be.

Embarrassed by the lilies, by their girlishness, Pericles covers his eyes with his hands. The other problem is that he has no money: every last cent had been counted out on the bus driver's tray, and even then the driver had been sharp with him.

The guilt comes into him again and curls in his stomach. He remembers how the gifts they'd given him went straight to the Sergeant, and now he has nothing to give them in return.

Pericles shrinks back into himself. Shrugging apologetically at his friends, he indicates his mother, who is moaning softly as she nurses her swollen feet. He can't just run off with them, can he, and leave the poor woman stranded with her big handbag on the bench. On the other hand, you don't want to disappoint people, do you, you don't want to insult their generosity.

He hears a peacock somewhere, crying like a baby, and remembers that they are blue and beautiful. Then the guide-girl stands before him, beak-faced, frowning at the empty bottle.

25

Androula had watched the couple walk up the track from the car – not a police car, although the man was in uniform – the girl making hard work of it in her tight skirt and high heels, the policeman pausing now and then to wait for her. Black blind eyes in sunglasses.

'I am Detective Sergeant Kyriaki,' the girl said, 'and this is Sergeant Stephanoudakis. May we come in for a moment, Kyria Zois?'

Kyriaki, she thought. Not a name that rings a bell. Ignoring her, Androula peered at the policeman. 'Not the son of Nikos Stephanoudakis the watchmaker?'

The policeman smiled. 'The same.'

Androula was delighted. A handsome boy, she thought, with the same twinkling eyes as his father. 'Do you know how many years ago he mended my old clock, and it's never lost a minute since!'

'I'm very glad to hear it, Kyria Androula.'

'And your poor mother? How is she?' Androula searched for a name. Was it Dimitria? She remembered a picnic just before the war, when they were all teenagers. Nikos and his Dimitria, her own dear Vagelis, Asterios and cousin Angelika. It was Nikos who had spread wild flowers all around the rug they'd brought to sit on. When a shower of spring hail crashed down on their heads they'd hidden underneath it, she and Vagelis holding hands in the scandalous darkness.

'Very well, thank you, Kyria. Of course she's in Athens now.'

'We're conducting an investigation, Kyria,' the girl cut in. 'We need to ask you some questions.'

Androula frowned at her. 'Questions?'

'About last Saturday night. Maybe you noticed something strange in the village, or heard something?'

'Me?' Androula threw back her head and clicked her tongue against her teeth. 'What would I notice from up here? As for strangers, the English are everywhere, you can't move for them.'

And with the English, she thought, comes nothing but trouble. Land-grabs, brawling and thieving, and now, as Asterios had said, dead bodies. Remembering her manners, even if the Kyriaki girl had forgotten hers, she invited them in.

'You'll want to talk to my brother. I'll wake him.' She led them through to the parlour and left them there. In the hall she banged loudly on Asterios' bedroom door, glad of an excuse to disturb him. It would remind him yet again that she hadn't forgiven him, and he needn't waste his time trying to talk her round. Not much a man could do – a man who needed a signature – if a woman dug her heels in.

In the kitchen she heated up the coffee and spooned cherry jam on to saucers. She rinsed two cups, filled two glasses with water, and carried the tray in. The Stephanoudakis boy – a gentleman if ever she saw one – moved quickly to take the tray from her, and placed it on the coffee table. The woman glanced around and seemed reluctant to sit, as if the parlour wasn't good enough for her, as if it wasn't as clean as a whistle and scented with polish and incense. At last, with a glance at her watch, she perched on the edge of an armchair.

Asterios came in buttoning up his trousers, bringing with him the stale smell of one wakened suddenly from a siesta. He wore a sweat-stained vest, and his grey hair was damp and awry. Seeing the surprise visitors, he mumbled a yassou and, without so much as a handshake, sat himself down heavily on the sofa. Androula was mortified. The man was behaving like a lout – an act put on, she was convinced, for the sole purpose of shaming her.

'What's all this, then?' Taking a half-smoked cigarette from behind his ear, Asterios lit up. He looked dourly at the photograph the Kyriaki woman produced from a cardboard folder, and shrugged. 'Never set eyes on him.' He eyed Kyriaki boldly. 'I saw the paper. It was a woman, wasn't it. Some tart getting her revenge.'

The Kyriaki girl gave him a frosty look. 'We can't discuss the case at this point. I need to know if you were in the vicinity of the Totem Bar last Saturday night.'

'I don't believe I was,' said Asterios, with such an air of innocence that Androula was astonished, since she knew for a fact that he spent most Saturday nights at the Totem, guzzling raki with Manoli Dimeros. She glanced at the Panagia for guidance. The candle on the altar flickered at the brazenness of the lie, but the Panagia didn't advise her one way or the other.

'Kyria?' The Stephanoudakis boy was watching her closely. She pursed her lips and folded her hands in her lap.

'Aach!' she said at last, shaking her head, for she could hold it in no longer. 'You should ask Manoli Dimeros, that's what! He's there every night after work, isn't he, sniffing around that Papaioannou girl.'

Asterios glared at her. 'Mind your business, woman!'

Androula tossed her head defiantly at him. Let him see that his scowls no longer had the power to silence her.

'Ask Sofia!' She turned to the Stephanoudakis boy. 'Sofia Benaki. My niece. She's a good girl, an honest girl. She lives opposite the place. If you want to know what goes on at the Totem, ask her.'

'I don't have to listen to this!' Asterios jumped up, hitched up his trousers and stormed out of the room, slamming the door behind him. A moment later the *papaki* engine sputtered, and snarled into life.

'No, no,' said the Stephanoudakis boy, when Androula tried to apologise. 'We were just leaving.' At the front door he turned to shake her by the hand. 'Thank you for your help, Kyria Androula.'

The intimacy of it brought tears to Androula's eyes. She held on to his hand just a moment longer, realising suddenly what it meant to be old. How hardly anyone ever asked you for help any more, let alone thanked you for it.

26

The Benaki house was a faded two-storey building in the shadow of a new apartment block, whose stark white balconies were tiered asymmetrically, to maximise the sun potential. When Yiannis rapped on the Benaki's door a woman leaned over one of the balconies, holding a large pair of secateurs.

'Sofia? She'll be at work. I saw her go off earlier with the boy.'

'Any idea when she'll be back?'

The woman shrugged. 'Me, I don't live here, I just keep an eye on the block.'

Although she was wearing sunglasses, Kyriaki shielded her eyes with her hand as she looked up. All afternoon it had been impossible to ignore the new engagement ring on her finger; but the determined way she kept flashing it made him just as determined to withhold the comment she clearly expected.

He glanced at the shuttered windows of the apartments. 'No one around, then?'

'You could try number 5. The Dutch gentleman. Weatherman,' she added helpfully, 'Works up at the observatory on Psiloritis. He's on the second floor.'

'Thank you, Kyria,' said Yiannis.

There was a smart new mountain bike on the second floor landing, as well as a snowboard, which Yiannis thought betrayed a certain optimism. There was snow in Crete, true, but not *that* much.

The Dutchman answered the door in silk boxer shorts, rubbing the sleep from his eyes. A giant of a guy, gym-toned and graceful. He had a broad open face marred only by a

162

small moustache, and blond bristle showing on a shaved scalp. The nipple ring announced that he was gay, just in case you hadn't already got the message.

When Yiannis explained himself in English, he said quickly, 'I understand,' and stood back to usher them in.

Yiannis saw woven rugs on the tiled floor, a low divan, and a slanted draughtsman's table spread with charts.On the wall of the studio were exhibition posters in clip-frames: Mapplethorpe, Ansel Adams; at the far end of the room French windows opened on to a triangular white balcony.

'I take it you've been here for some time, Mr . . .?'

'Jansen,' said the Dutchman, thrusting out his hand for Yiannis to shake. 'Jaap. Yes. I'm here for three months now, at the T.E.I. lab. From the University of Amersfoort. I do post-doctoral research. Image-modelling,' he added modestly. 'I design codes for incorporating seismic and meterological data.'

'Ah yes?' said Yiannis, frowning knowledgeably. Some moments later, his brain sagging under the weight of tapered wavelet analysis, cloud anomalies, and atmospheric precursors, he regretted having encouraged the Dutchman.

'*Milate Ellenika?*' Kyriaki demanded, giving Yiannis a reproachful look. He'd forgotten her English was limited, although he was fairly sure Jansen's spiel would have been no more comprehensible in Greek. It was another blot, he suspected, on his copybook.

'*Signome*,' cried Jansen, turning the full warmth of his attention on her. 'It's technical, I know. But excuse me, I must put a shirt.' With a brilliant smile at Kyriaki, he vanished into the bedroom.

There was an impressive arsenal of gadgets on the kitchen counter: a coffee grinder, some kind of steamer, a pasta maker, and two different kinds of blender. A man who likes to cook, thought Yiannis – a nesting Dutchman, rather than a flying one. Then he saw the photograph on top of the fridge-freezer. Jaap Jansen on his snowboard, performing a frighten-ing aerial manoeuvre against a fairytale Alpine backdrop.

There was another photograph, taken at a dinner table, in which Jansen was smooching a handsome mixed-race man with blue glitter on his eyelids.

The Dutchman reappeared in a long-sleeved linen shirt. He was still barefoot, and hadn't bothered with trousers. He took a string bag of oranges fom the fridge and began to cut them up.

'It is time for my juice, I think. You'll join me?'

Yiannis glanced at Kyriaki, who shrugged ungraciously but didn't actually refuse.

'You're very kind.'

The balcony faced west, with a view not of the sea but of the olive groves on the slope of the headland. Although a finger of sun touched the protruding beak of the balustrade, the table and chairs were still in shade.

Jansen settled a cushion on one of the chairs for Kyriaki and insisted that Yiannis take the other. Kyriaki sat down and examined her surroundings with an intently disdainful air: it was, Yiannis supposed, her way of pulling rank. Either that or she was one of those females who're allergic to gay men, who can't forgive them for turning their backs, so to speak, on women.

The juice, when it came, was delicious, and Yiannis said so.

Jaap Jansen beamed with pleasure. 'A carrot. My secret weapon. And I have picked blueberries on the mountain.' He leaned back easily against the balustrade, one bare foot propped up behind him. 'Raspberries I prefer, but of course one can't get them here. But in Holland, raspberries always.'

'So you're a meteorologist, Mr. Jansen?'

'Ah no. A geophysicist. I enjoy this – taking the pulse of the earth, you understand.' Since this elicited no more than a nod from Kyriaki, he turned his eager smile on Yiannis. Yiannis found himself smiling back. A likeable man, this Jaap, he decided, with his raspberries and his recipes.

'An obsession, then, rather than a profession?'

The Dutchman threw back his head and laughed. 'That's correct! Let me show you my earthquake escape route!' He

164

leaned over the parapet, pointing out the flat roof of the Benaki's back-kitchen extension; his hand described a wide straddle from there to a first floor balcony, and thence to the curved parapet of the ground floor patio.

'So you saw the quake coming?' said Yiannis.

Jansen shrugged, grinning. 'Not so much. Seismology is an infant science, Sergeant – we think we can predict, but Mother Earth, she plays with us, you know.?'

Kyriaki sipped fastidiously at her juice. Her engagement ring made an agreeable tinging sound against the glass.

'And were you here last Saturday night, Mr Jansen?'

'Ah yes!' He glanced at the olive grove, shaking his head mournfully. 'Poor guy. How terrible.' Sun silhouetted the tops of the trees on the upper slope; soon it would move round and turn the balcony into an oven. 'I was not on night shift on Saturday, so on Sunday morning I left early, about 6.30, I think.'

'Did anyone see you leave, that you know of?'

Jaap shook his head. 'I don't think so, no.'

'And you saw no one in the vicinity?'

'The German lady with the jeep, that's all.'

Kyriaki made a note. 'Where was this?'

'On the Katomeli road. By the Golden Sun studios, I think.'

'So this person could corroborate your statement?'

'Wiltraud?' Jaap frowned. 'Yes. I expect.'

Yiannis leaned forward, interested. 'Did she say what she was doing, exactly?'

'Delivering, I believe. To the wholefood shop in town. *Eleftheria*, where I get my bread and pulses and things – you know it?'

Yiannis scalp prickled. 'It's on Dedalou, right?' He made a mental note to check if *Eleftheria* was open on a Sunday.

'You have an address for her?' asked Kyriaki.

'It's the commune up at Neo Chori,' said Yiannis.

Kyriaki looked at him sharply. 'And on Saturday night – you heard nothing?'

The Dutchman spread his hands. 'On Saturday I was *dead*

to the world.' Realising that he had spoken in English, he begged Kyriaki's pardon.

'You were alone?' she asked abruptly.

'Yes,' said Jansen. Yiannis could have sworn that he blushed.

*

The fruit juice had acted like a depth charge on his innards. In the Totem bar he left Kyriaki to interview the Papaioannou girls while he hurried to the toilet in the back yard, opening the tiny net-curtained window to let out the choking smell of air-freshener.

Up in the olive grove they'd found the Crime Scene team standing around in their white bunny suits, scratching their heads.

'Looks like we're fucked,' said one whose name Yiannis recalled as Milo. He indicated the landslip which had strewn rocks, roots, and yellow earth across the site. Blue ribbons of police tape sagged among the debris.

'You've let D.I. Vasilakis know?'

The man pushed back his white hood and nodded glumly.

'*Not* best pleased. What do you think?'

Instead of toilet paper, squares of newspaper hung on a string. He tore off a couple and used them gingerly. The tap's jet was too powerful for the tiny foetus-shaped sink. He mopped his spattered trousers with a towel the size of a facecloth, and exited with relief.

Aphrodite was deep in conversation with Kyriaki. She wore a low square-cut top from which her breasts rose slippery and smooth, like boulders at the waterline. Above these riches, her lugubrious face expected the worst. When she saw Yiannis she jumped up.

'You'll take something, sir? An ice-cream, maybe?'

He wagged a finger at her, smiling. 'Don't encourage my bad habits, Aphrodite!'

Between the cool cupboard and the freezer where ice-creams were stored, the elder Papaiouannous sat side by side, he clicking away at his *komboli*, she in black dress and thick black stockings, basilisk-faced in the shade. They were too old, clearly, to be the girls' parents; too old, also, to chaperone them. Yiannis glanced enquiringly at Kyriaki, who warned him off with a slight shake of the head.

In the car Kyriaki filled him in. Manoli Dimeros had indeed patronised the Totem that night, as had Asterios Zois, and, briefly, Demosthenes and his wife, but Aphrodite had nothing unusual to report. Little Fotini had gone to bed at 10, as always, and Aphrodite had closed up at 1am.

Kyriaki had drawn a blank on the grandparents. 'He's stone deaf, and she's Turkish. Not a word of Greek. The girls' parents were killed in a car crash in Izmir 10 years ago, poor sods. They were over there visiting granny's side of the family.'

'And Aphrodite? What do you reckon?'

Kyriaki shrugged. 'None too bright.' She was driving fast and one-handed, her left elbow casual on the window rim, her fingers flattened fondly along the exterior bodywork, as if for optimum ring-exposure. 'Might be worth running a check on this Dimeros guy, though – see what he's got to say for himself.'

'I'll do it,' said Yiannis, 'I know the family.'

In Katomeli Kyriaki dropped him on Vassilikou and drove off without a wave. He headed for the corner, walking fast despite the heat, hoping against hope that Dora was indoors with the blinds drawn, declining nouns or conjugating verbs or whatever else she did in her air-conditioned classroom.

When he turned into Limonas Street he saw her on the tiny side patio, watering a tub of geraniums. Flat-eyed, she considered him for a second, then, without a word, she turned her back and went inside.

Hot-faced, Yiannis fled up the hill, and when he reached his house he went into the kitchen and ran the tap until the water was cold. He filled a glass and drank it, watched impassively by Kore, who was sunning herself on the windowsill. Then he headed for the shower, discarding his clothes as he went, throwing his shoes angrily through the open bedroom door.

Afterwards he lay on the bed for half an hour, trying unsuccessfully to nap. In the end he got up and went to look for clean pants in the chest of drawers. When his hand brushed against the condom box he stopped dead and stared at it. Although Dora was on the pill, he'd always insisted on using them. His mistrust, unspoken, evident in the act. The message must have been loud and clear but, typically, Dora had never told him what she felt about it. And, typically, he had never asked. But didn't he have reason for caution? Women without children – women of Dora's age, at least – were a law unto themselves. It was too easy for them, if not to play tricks, then to forget, accidentally on purpose, to present you with a *fait accompli*. And then, well, then you were really screwed, weren't you.

Yiannis listened to himself, and didn't much like what he heard. Perhaps he was turning into the sort of person who could always find good reasons for not doing things – one of those anal types who, out of ingrained conservatism, lets life pass them by.

Depressed by these bruising thoughts, he could bear the emptiness of the house no longer. He dressed quickly in T shirt and chinos, grabbed his cellphone, and went out into the back garden. All afternoon he'd managed, with some success, to deny that Ingrid was on his mind, but now he would deny it no longer.

Just as he was about to dial her number, however, his finger froze above the keypad. From the windowsill Kore was eyeing him with a certain irony. She knows a fool when she sees one, he thought, remembering that Ingrid had no number, because Ingrid had no cellphone.

He interred the phone in his pocket, uncoiled the garden hose, and advanced purposefully on the lemon grove at the bottom of the garden.

Insects floated, humming happily, in the soft radiance of the evening sun. It was 7 o'clock. Over in Panomeli, people would be taking a leisurely aperitif, deciding where to eat a meal: the Shoestring, or the Totem, or a shortish stroll to the Medusa. In Panomeli the choice of establishments was severely limited.

When he twisted the nozzle of the hose nothing happened. He must have forgotten to turn the tap on at the wall. One look back at the long stupid snake of the hose decided him. He threw the thing on the ground and ran indoors to fetch his car keys, anxious to get going before he could change his mind.

He was almost at the car when his cellphone rang. It was Sotiris at the station.

'Sorry, Yianni, but a call just came through from Knossos. They've been holding old Pericles at the ticket office. Something to do with thieving.'

Yiannis stopped with his hand on the door, thinking of the artefacts he'd delivered to the Museum. Could Pericles have filched the things from Knossos?

'Thieving what?' he snapped.

'Seems some tourist complained about a bottle of water.'

'Oh for Christ's sake! Haven't they got anything better to do up there?'

'Thing is, since he mentioned you by name, they said can you go and pick him up.'

27

As the autumn of 1947 turned to winter, John Franklin Daniel threw all his weight behind Alice Kober's candidacy for the Indo-European Linguistics post at the University of Pennsylvania. To Dean Morrow he made much of her work with Myres on Scripta Minoa, *describing Kober as the outstanding authority on pre-Hellenic languages and the Minoan scripts. He outlined how her appointment would allow her not only to take charge of the Minoan Linguistic Research Centre, but also to assist with any Lydian inscriptions uncovered by the Museum's projected excavations at Sardis in Turkey.*

'Miss Kober is one of the few people in this country who would be qualified to prepare this material for publication,' *he wrote to the Dean.* 'As I mentioned above, Lydian may well provide the key to the language of the Minoan inscriptions.'

Daniel's lobbying, however, met with opposition in the form of Professor H. Lamar Crosby, head of the Classics Department, who requested more information about Kober. Daniel wrote hastily to Alice saying that Crosby would be 'bowled over' *by one or two recommendations from well-known scholars.*

'He will be impressed if you can get somebody with a big name to write and tell him that you are wonderful. His trouble, strictly confidentially, is inertia. He is a very nice man, but he is also a lazy one. I gave him your opus on -INTH to look at but he was "too busy" to read it and just glanced at it a bit. Is there anyone at Harvard who can speak up for you? Crosby is very much under the Harvard spell.'

Cvs and references were duly mustered and sent to Philadelphia, where they were retyped by Daniel, with numerous carbon copies for tactical distribution.

*Daniel had been asked to organise an independent Depart-
ment of Archaeology at the University, and envisaged Alice's
appointment as straddling the Department of Indo-European
Linguistics,* 'of which you will be commander-in-chief', *and
Classical Archaeology,* 'of which I would be presumably
c-in-c', *an arrangement which would allow them to be* 'completely independent of the fuddy-duddies'.

*Always hard-headed, Alice Kober was cautiously making
plans. If the job actually materialised, she would not resign
from her Brooklyn position, but instead would try to get a
year's unpaid leave. In the meantime she intended to keep the
house she shared with her mother in Brooklyn, and come
home at weekends, so that Katharina would not be* 'completely alone.'

'In that way I can find out how it really works out, and if
I'm not as good as I think I am, can retire gracefully at the end
of the year, to everybody's relief, and come back here.'

Daniel's irreverence, however, was infectious – 'My own
Chairman is a fuddy-dud,' *Kober confided,* 'and you can leave
out the fuddy' – *and there is no mistaking the warmth of her
postscript:* 'I've never told you I'm grateful for all you're
doing. I am. It's been fun, too.'

*By now Daniel's expectations were running high. The
committee on the Indo-European appointment were* 'very
strongly impressed' *by the Minoan research library project,
and although one member was not yet convinced that Kober
was the proper person for the Professorship,* 'if we can
convince him that you are qualified to teach IE (and I think
we can), then I feel that your chances are excellent; I might
almost go so far as to say that it would be in the bag.'

*Not only did the University of Pennsylvania have world-class
scholars like Speiser and Kramer, it had big plans for expan-
sion in Anthropology, Indic Studies, and Egyptology. Daniel
wrote fulsomely to Kober about his ambitions for the Archaeology department, and proposed a rough schedule that was
far lighter than she could have dreamed of – four two-hour
courses in Linguistics, of which only two, or three at the most,*

would be given in any one year, with a course in Minoan scripts for Daniel's department. It was all graduate work, in very small classes; for the first time Alice would have a timetable which would allow her to concentrate on her Minoan.

Her response was immediate:

'Your latest letter has me sitting here with my tongue hanging out, and that's bad. I'm trying to preserve my equilibrium, so that I'll be happy no matter how things turn out. You're heartless.'

The temptation, it seemed, was almost too much for her.

'I've resolutely refused to think how wonderful it would be to have people like Speiser and Kramer right there in case Minoan starts swerving toward Semitic, Hurrian, Sumerian etc., and an Egyptologist on top so I can finally get to read it. Now you add a course in Minoan scripts!!!'

Just before Christmas, Daniel wrote anxiously that there had been a 'slight setback' and urged Kober to 'do everything in your power short of throwing hand-grenades to get E. Adelaide Hahn to send her testimonial immediately.'

What was still needed was a strong endorsement, not of Kober's Minoan expertise, but of her ability to handle Indo-European, and in particular Greek and Latin linguistics.

Daniel also advised Alice to do some lobbying of her own. The joint meetings held by the Classical societies were a regular Christmas feature; this year they were to take place at New Haven.

'Our entire Classics Department will be at the meetings and I trust you to take full advantage of the opportunity to make a favourable impression on Heffner and Crosby.'

In effect Daniel was telling Alice Kober to shmooze. For a woman who appears to have been well aware that she had been blessed with a first-class intellect, being judged by second-raters must have been galling enough, let alone having to kow-tow to them. Her pride smarting, she retreated into defensive scorn, writing back:

'As for Crosby and Heffner – well, I'll do my best at the

172

meetings. It will be hard. Neither has ever written anything I remember.'

And perhaps it was frustration that fuelled the uncharacteristically feminist query:

'Don't you think a lot of the opposition is really based on the fact that I'm a woman? Even if it isn't openly mentioned.'

In the meantime Daniel had become embroiled in interdepartmental in-fighting, and on Christmas Eve he wrote furiously to Alice, complaining that, in their determination to block her nomination, Crosby and Heffner had been drumming up inferior candidates.

'I am not being unduly bitter when I say that their controlling criterion seems to be mediocrity. They are third-raters themselves and simply do not want to get people who will show them up.'

His account of Crosby's machinations makes disturbing reading.

'On the day that I last wrote you, he called a meeting of the department but timed the notices so that I did not get mine until after the meeting. He didn't try to get me on the phone. At this meeting the department decided unanimously that you wouldn't do, and that Messing was their candidate.'

Only by petitioning both Deans had Daniel managed to get the decision overturned. The fact that the fight had become so dirty appears to have made him even more determined to win. He was also at pains to assure Alice that her sex had no bearing on the situation.

'[Dean] Williams even went so far as to say that it was a point in your favour, since it was time to rectify our male exclusiveness of the past.'

Daniel had not been in the O.S.S. for nothing, and one can only admire the guile with which he assesses the weaknesses of the opposition and lays out a strategy. He reiterates his advice to Alice to tackle Heffner, who is 'weak, lazy and impressionable', *and even Crosby, who* 'in the long run will have to be overridden, but it is certainly worth trying to bowl him over.'

That the whole business had taught Daniel a lot about human nature – the 'genus professoricus' *as he wryly puts it – is clear in his casually damning account of another department member.*

'Don't waste too much time on McDermott, though a smile would help. He has been an assistant professor for seven years and he told me perfectly frankly that he felt he had to oppose any appointment at a higher rank than that, because it would shut him out forever. Isn't that nice?'

The Christmas Conventions – a professional and, no doubt, a social must – were held jointly by the American Philological Association, the Archaeological Institute, and the Linguistic Society of America. The 79th Annual Meeting took place in New Haven from December 29th-31st. John Franklin Daniel stayed at the Graduate Club on New Haven Green, a beautiful clapboard building in the Federal style. Built in the 1800s, it was red-tiled, white-painted, and tree-shaded. In 1947 it was also all male.

Although no stranger to austerity, Alice Kober was staying at the Taft on College Street, at the time one of New Haven's finest and most modern hotels. She was 41, single, and on $6000 a year – which, given that her counterpart in an English university might have taken home £600, was a more than decent salary – so who could deny that she deserved, just for once, to spoil herself?

Records exist of the proceedings of the convention – for instance, at the dinner held on Tuesday 30th, Daniel, with Oscar Broneer and H.T. Wade-Gery, gave a symposium on the Homeric period. (Daniel was about to publish the Homeric issue of the American Journal of Archaeology.*)*

There is no record, however, of who networked with whom, who danced, flirted, or drank martinis, or whether Alice Kober managed to 'bowl over' Crosby, or anyone else for that matter.

We do know, however, that she talked to Oscar Broneer, who warned her that the prospect of seeing the Heraklion tablets in the coming year was 'none too rosy.'

As Kober felt even more strongly than Myres that Evans'
transcriptions should be checked against the original tablets,
Crete had been high on her agenda for the following summer.
Fuelling her urgency, as she confided to Johannes Sundwall,
was the fear that a nuclear 'war to end war' would soon wreck
what was left of the world. Understandably, she was dis-
appointed by Broneer's discouraging news.

A letter she wrote some weeks afterwards reveals that she had
also been feeling ill during the convention, and had only seen
Daniel in passing. She had heard nothing from him since New
Haven and, assuming from his silence that the 'Kent job
business' was over, had waited six weeks before writing.
Despite its apparent forthrightness, the letter exudes depres-
sion, and there are glimpses of a vulnerability Kober rarely
reveals.

'First, I did try to see you the last morning of the meeting,
and *saw* you at least five times, but each time you were deep in
converstaion, and didn't see me. I didn't want to interrupt.
The last time you were just saying to someone "Let's go
upstairs where we can talk without interference". I saw you
go up, and decided I'd go home, because I still wasn't feeling
right. Something I et [sic] no doubt.'

A common-or-garden hangover, one might assume, but there
is no evidence to suggest that Kober was a drinker. It may be
that the stress of an occasion on which so many hopes
depended was simply too much for her.

With hindsight, however, despite the casual quip about
'something I et', one is tempted to suspect that something
rather more sinister was at work. What appeared at the time
to be an ordinary stomach upset may well have been the early
warning signs of the malady that was to lead to her death a
mere two years later.

She empties her ashtray into the wastebin and carries half a
cup of cold coffee out on to the dark balcony. The air is less

stuffy there, but hardly cooler; it's the thought of Alice the wallflower that makes her shiver.

Ingrid imagines her in something mauve, her hands clasped before her waist, a clunky handbag like the Queen's dangling from her wrist. Her hair bobbed and permed, perhaps, for the big occasion, it's enough to make you weep. Invisible Alice, waiting and watching, and never being *seen*.

No one likes to go unnoticed, and sallow, stocky Alice didn't have glamour on her side. Impossible not to empathise with her as she hangs about, excluded, and finally, gathering the rags of her pride, flees from the convention.

Did Alice actually feel any of the emotions she imputes to her? She'll never know, of course, and, empathy or no empathy, she has no right to fill in the gaps. It's supposed to be a biography, not a fairy tale, and although she hates settling for these scholarly, mincing constructs – 'one' this and 'one' that – she can't risk assigning to her subject feelings she'd probably have strangled at birth.

The holiday apartments are silent and shuttered; all the tourists, sated by sun and swimming, are fast asleep. Glasses clink, though, on the terrace of Demosthenes' house, where an oil lamp glimmers through the canopy of vines.

She hadn't been able to face another night out with Hutchinson. The inevitable corner table with its single place setting, the pretence of reading. Not to mention the fear that Ken and Glenys would turn up and take pity on her. Instead she stayed in and composed a meal from odds and ends – fried potatoes and aubergines, with slices of hard-boiled egg and rounds of raw red onion – and ate it on the balcony with the moon for company.

Solitude, after all, has a lot to be said for it, and it's a whole lot easier to compose a meal than it is to compose a life.

She fetches the Metaxa from the kitchen and pours two inches into a tumbler: brandy to warm her, brandy to blot out a scene fraught with possibilities for humiliation.

Pantremeni o eleftheri?
He blanked you, Ingrid. Get over it.

The moonlight on the sea is pearly, like nail-varnish. She raises her glass to toast it (hasn't she always secretly believed that the moon is restorative?), letting the alcohol release all the wishes she could wish for Alice, all the pretty things that ought to be restored to her.

Here's looking at you, Alice, she says, willing the moon to work its magic, invoking her in her gleaming, princessly aspect, in her element -*Inth*.

28

Sofia wiped over the oilcloth on the kitchen table and dusted the plastic begonias for good measure. Ever since Andonis phoned from the depot she'd been going like a maniac. She'd rushed Spiraki up to Androula's, and begged first Marta, then Kristina, to cover for her, so that Kyria Evnochides wouldn't need to know she'd taken the day off.

It was typical of him, she thought, not to warn her in advance. Surely he could have phoned from Patras, or even from the ferry, given her a chance to sort things out.

She'd hardly had time to throw the lunch together, let alone blow-dry her hair and apply some blusher – Andonis hated to see her looking peaky – before he came bounding in the front door, grabbing for her.

'First things first,' he said, 'the shower won't run away.'

Then it was straight into bed and everything over in minutes – hardly long enough to crease the sheets. Long enough, though, to imprint on them the smell of all the miles he'd driven, of autoroutes and exhausts, night lay-bys, and petrol stations that never closed.

She began to lay out the *mezedes*. The *stifado* was in the oven, the beers icing in the fridge. Later he would kiss her and call her my lovely; later she might feel desire, but for the moment there was only anxiety.

A whole week together, he'd said buoyantly. How could she tell him she'd never be allowed a week off work without prior notice?

Andonis strode, sighing, from the bathroom, his skin fragrant with shower gel. He sank into his armchair, put his feet up on the *pouffe*, and plucked a newspaper from the pile she kept on the coffee-table in the hope that one day she'd get round to reading them. The hairs on his bare legs stood out stiffly, as if relishing the coolness. His face and arms were burnt dark from the sun in the cabin.

She hurried to fetch him a beer, loving him suddenly for his impulsiveness, remembering how his impatience had always been the strong wind which blew her along. Sometimes, after Spiraki was asleep, she'd find herself on the balcony, holding conversations with the sea, her hands weaving his presence from the empty air. Without him she was just a boat without a sail, and that was the plain truth of it.

When he took the beer from her she saw how his nails were broken and blackened with engine oil. She kissed the top of his wet head and turned quickly away.

At the back of the kitchen drawer she found the linen napkins Androula had sewn for her trousseau, and stood there fingering them, all the absences welling up behind her eyes. Five years already, she thought – have we really been married for five years?

She heard Andonis swear under his breath. He was staring at something in the newspaper.

'Sofia? Have you seen this?'

'Me? I never have the time,' she said gaily, 'I just save them up for you.'

'It's Ivo, I swear to God!'

'Who?' She dropped the napkins on the table and leaned over the back of his chair. When she saw the headline her hand went to her mouth. 'The one they found up on Stavlakis?'

'He was Albanian, poor bugger.' Andonis shook his head heavily. 'Nice lad, though, not like some of them. No drugs or any of that stuff. Said he was headed for some commune up at Neo Chori.'

With a jolt Sofia remembered what Androula had told her.

'The police have been round, Andoni. They've been asking questions.'

'For fuck's sake, Sofia! You didn't talk to them?'

Sofia shrank from his accusing tone.

'How could I, Andoni? I'm at work all day.'

'Well thank God for that, at least!'

Andonis took a gulp of beer from the bottle and shut his eyes for a moment. She'd set a glass and a coaster on the coffee table but he hadn't bothered with either of them. She watched him fumble for his cigarettes and light one with an unsteady hand.

'But if you know him, Andoni.' she said timidly, 'I mean, shouldn't we call, or something?'

When he thumped the arm of the chair beer spurted from the neck of the bottle.

'And get myself locked up? Are you crazy or what?' Sofia stared uncomprehendingly at the foam, and the stain spreading brown across his white vest. 'Who the fuck do you think brought him here?'

29

At noon Ingrid is ready to go, but the Giffords are definitely late. She smokes on the balcony, watching out for their hired red Renault.

Inside the apartment everything is shipshape, sorted late last night in a sudden flurry that's embarrassing. now, looked at with morning eyes. How ridiculous that, even when you know someone isn't coming, you prink up your house for him, clear the draining board of dishes, arrange and rearrange the fruit in the bowl. Automatic preening. The dust shaved from the surfaces, until everything waits like a still life, hieratic.

On the waste-ground across the road the cockerel, pecking among pumpkin flowers, sets up its mocking, discordant cry. She's aware of the ordinary world, but distantly: a car horn on the Katomeli road, a guitar practising somewhere – a down-swerving chord-sequence she recognises as the intro to *All you need is love* – the inevitable churn of a concrete-mixer. She's seized, suddenly, by a sense of necessity, a twinge of truth that flies in the face of the evidence. Her mind has constructed a memory which may or may not be false – of a hospitable face, a hospitable nature. What it can't do, however, is reconstruct the scene at the Museum; the details of this have vanished, like those in a novel read too fast, too greedily, so that all that's left is the thrall.

It's amazing, really, what you can concoct out of a 20 minute chat in the sultry shade of a city afternoon.

On the balcony next door Shapcott *père* appears in pajama bottoms, his bare arms stringy in the sharp morning light.

'Morning,' he mutters, spotting her, and nips smartly back inside. The balconies are separated by a gap of half a metre – too close, it seems, for comfort. Clearly convivial breakfasts – like foreign dogs – aren't on Mr. Shapcott's agenda.

What is it with him, she wonders – would it kill him to make a joke or say a pleasant word? It isn't as if she's smoking a joint, sunbathing starkers, or doing any other single thing a normal person might find offensive.

To her relief she sees Glenys emerge from the back door of the *Captain's* and hurry up the street. When Ingrid hails her from the balcony she stops on the pavement and looks up, flustered and lipstickless, her hair unstyled.

'It's Charlie' she says, 'She's had a bit of a turn. It's this arhythmia she gets, see.'

Ingrid is startled. Charlie is quick and lean and leather-skinned – a mini-Viking, not unlike her own mother in appearance, although it has to be said that Greta Laurie *née* Henderson had never done justice to her genes. Charlie could be a retired fell-runner; to look at her, you'd think she was indestructible.

'Is she all right?'

'Says she is, but we're running her to the doctor, just in case.' Glenys' face is wan, worry deepening her wrinkles and showing up her age. 'If you ask me it's just the heat, but you know, better safe than sorry.'

'Do you need me to come?' asks Ingrid, ' to translate or anything?'

'No love, you're fine. Lynda said they speak English at the clinic. Shame about our trip, though.'

Glenys trots away down the cobbled street, backless sandals slapping at her heels. Seized by an urge to get going immediately, Ingrid crushes out her cigarette and picks up her keys. A bus to Heraklion, pick up the Arkhanes one at the port; it's all perfectly do-able, even if it won't be the day she designed, the drive she was so looking forward to. A touch of tour-guiding in low-key, reassuring company; the

182

way the Giffords foster her, draw her into the bosom of the family.

On the bus she sinks back in her seat and watches the landscape as if through a mist. Disjointed villages, farm-tracks leading God knows where. A melon-field floats in the heat-haze.

Aimless walking, aimless looking. Already the thought of the day makes her feel leaden and exhausted, as if she were toting around some helpless small animal.

The bus stops in the dusty main square of Arkhanes and settles, sighing, on its suspension. It's siesta time, and hardly anyone is about; the air is heavy, loud with the drilling of cicadas.

At the *periptero* she stocks up with water for the hike and stands in the slice of shade under the awning, orienting herself. The printout tells her to take the left fork at the church, then it's a two and a half kilometre walk round the shoulder of Mount Yuchtas.

On the outskirts she passes polytunnels of tomatoes, a field of sunflowers whose ranked faces gaze up adoringly at Ilios. The road snakes uphill, treeless, through a hinterland of vineyards. After 45 minutes she discovers that it's also carless. Two and a half kilometres is, of course, pure fiction. Greek signposts are as imaginative as ever.

Mount Yuchtas rears up steeply on her left, drifted with grey scree and furze. On the skyline ahead the road breasts a col, to the right of which is a high beetling outcrop guarded by pines. She sees towers of yellow rock, free-standing and wind-blasted. Behind the trees, scooped caves are violet in shadow. The Caves of the Wind.

A car is approaching from behind – some kind of jeep with body-work sprayed an improbable shade of lilac. A dog's head pokes though the passenger window, ears flattened back by the draught. She lifts her thumb, but the jeep is already slowing.

'Anemospilia?'

'You're going there?' says Ingrid, recognising first the dog, and then the driver, who is already leaning over to open the back door.

'It's hot, yes?' the woman says in English, as Ingrid squeezes herself in beside several grain-sacks and a perforated plastic crate which smells rank and sweetish, like boiled hay. Scuffling and mewing sounds come from within.

The St. Bernard plants its paws on the back of the passenger seat and salutes Ingrid with rapturous barks. The woman is studying her intently.

'Not so many people visit this site. You are an archaeologist?'

Ingrid nods. 'I'm doing some research.'

The words sound self-important, even a little fraudulent. Alice was dead long before Anemospilia was discovered, and there's really no credible link between the two. She pats the eager muzzle of the puppy, which has powered itself halfway over the seat-back and is trying to lick her face.

'What age is he?'

'Six months only. Soon the baby will be too big for the jeep!'

When the woman smiles over her shoulder long silver earrings flick against her neck, delicate chains on the ends of which double-axes dangle like anchors.

Oh, here we go, thinks Ingrid, who knows her female symbols, but wouldn't be seen dead wearing them.

Just over the col the road swings left and contours a flattish bluff, on the right of which the land falls away to orchards, vineyards, and, in the distance, 180 degrees of sea. On the left, parched rocky ground slopes uphill, dotted with prickly shrubs. She spots a rusted chain-link fence with a padlocked gate, and a weathered sign in Greek and English which announces that the site is closed.

The jeep pulls into the delta of a short sandy track which leads up to the gate. As Ingrid gets out, the German woman tells her that there's a gap in the fence higher up. She drapes her bare arm

184

along the open window, her smile conspiratorial. 'To come alone is better, no? This way, you feel the power.'

'Ah yes,' she agrees, shrinking inwardly from all self-deluding sisterhoods. That's the trouble with prehistory – it's a blank slate on which anyone can write their own rituals, project their own shadows.

The woman engages the clutch and eases the jeep out on to the road.

'Enjoy your day!'

The remark falls oddly on Ingrid's ears, the German accent robbing it of all irony.

It's cooler up here, thanks to a sturdy little breeze shuting down from the summit of the mountain. She follows the fence and finds the hole at the highest point. From here the site spreads out below her, north-facing, bleak and birdless under a vast sky. The place has an orphaned, unwanted look; it looks as if no one has dug here since the 1979 excavations.

There are the remains of three small rooms, connected on the north side by what must once have been a corridor or porch. The walls are barely knee-high, one course of square-cut blocks surmounting another course of irregular boulders, set in crumbling mortar.

The west room contains not only a stone slab she assumes was the altar, but also, unaccountably, a cold-frame in which nothing grows but rubbish – a broken jam jar, an empty cigarette packet.

Near the north-east corner of the porch-structure she sees a pair of horns of consecration, barely two feet high. She goes over to take a closer look. They've been carved from a granitic rock, diorite, perhaps; judging by the hairline cement seam, they've been carefully restored. She crouches among chamomile flowers to run a hand over them. The surface is warm and retains a pleasing roughness; the stone has been ground, she thinks, rather than polished.

On a flinty bank above the site she sits down to eat her spinach pie. Her boots are rimmed with yellow dust. Burrs have stuck fast to the laces, and blood from a scratch on her shin has trickled down into her sock. When she puts her finger to the runnel and sucks she remembers Marinatos' monograph on sacrificial ritual. Before the blood to be used for the libation was poured over the horns of consecration, it was mixed with vinegar or red wine to prevent coagulation. Nanno Marinatos, that is, daughter of the famous Spiridon: you could always trust a woman to get right down to the recipe.

The water in her bottle has reached blood heat. She rinses out her mouth and wipes oily pastry-flakes from her fingers.

Bees cruise by, banking over clumps of thyme and heather. She sits in her heavy body, hearing her heart beat in the silence. Her very own perishability, pulsing away the seconds.

Somewhere below the lip of the site, two farm dogs strike up a conversation across fields. A moment later another, fainter, bark joins in, and then the message zigzags on down the hill like semaphore, diminishing plaintively into the distance.

The stones say nothing and everything: stories she can feel but can't hear, silent, insistent voices pressing against her skin.

The image that comes into her mind dates from the mid-nineties. The Turner Prize: a whole room filled with Anthony Gormley's terracotta midgets, massed in thousands on the floor. No more than tiny balls of clay with pinprick mouths and eyes raised to the heavens in some wordless plea for protection. They seemed to be drawing a collective breath, sighing in unison. Needing everything, like children do, and because of this, everything was what they deserved.

Looking at them, she could almost imagine how queens or gods might feel, when pressured by that enormous deficit – how you'd swell up like a cistern with spiritual credit, how you'd savour the duty to disburse.

My little Minoans. A small people, but perfectly formed.
Even if Alice's Linear B sign-groups and grids seem me-

chanical, inimical, Ingrid can understand why she focussed so stringently on structures, and steered well clear of anything as unscientific as empathy. It was her way of trying – and try she did, harder than anyone, perhaps – to give her Minoans a voice.

But surely, thinks Ingrid, hugging her knees and feeling tears mount up in her suddenly like a wave, surely they deserve more than that.

The milk. The honey. The warm enfolding arms.

30

If Alice Kober could be sisterly – even, on occasion, mildly flirtatious – with John Franklin Daniel, and flattering, in a daughterly way, to Johannes Sundwall – after seeing a snapshot of him at 70, she wrote coyly 'Are you sure you haven't made a mistake of about 20 years in your age?' – she appears to have been frosty, at best, with Michael Ventris.

Born in 1922, and educated at boarding schools in England and Switzerland, Michael Ventris had looked on Linear B as 'a hobby' since an encounter with Sir Arthur Evans at a Stowe School outing to Burlington House in 1936. Although at 14 he already showed precocious brilliance as a linguist, he was to follow architecture as a career and, unlike Kober, never undertook any formal study of Classics or linguistics. It was, rather, the sheer puzzle of the undeciphered script that seized his interest, and continued to fascinate him until his death in 1956.

As the first bombs fell on London in the autumn of 1940, Ventris, with youthful cheek, had sent an article to the American Journal of Archaeology *in which he proposed that the Minoan language was closely related to Etruscan. 'Introducing the Minoan Language' duly appeared in the last issue of AJA for that year, the author having omitted to mention in his covering letter that he was only 18.*

Ever since Sir Arthur Evans' death in 1941, Ventris had been in touch with Sir John Myres, and after his demobilisation in the summer of 1946 – he had served as a navigator in the RAF, and then worked with the Control Commission in West Germany – Myres invited him to Oxford to see the Knossos tablets for himself. He also solicited Ventris' help with the work on Scripta Minoa II.

Anxious to resume his studies at the Architectural Association, which had been interrupted by the war, Ventris turned Sir John down. One wonders, however, how differently things might have turned out for Alice Kober if he had not. Only a few weeks later Myres received Kober's first enthusiastic letter from Brooklyn, and jumped at the chance of having her skills at his disposal. It is unclear whether Kober knew at the time that she had not been, as it were, the first candidate for the job, but it is tempting to speculate whether this might have been one of the factors which coloured her attitude to the young decipherer.

By the beginning of 1948 Myres and Ventris were once again corresponding regularly about Linear B, and in March Myres sent a sample page of Ventris' drawings of the inscriptions to Kober in Brooklyn. She responded with praise – 'Mr. Ventris would have no trouble getting a job as scribe to King Minos. This is beautiful writing.' *– but also with criticism. The criticism took the form of 5 closely-typed pages which laid out a protocol in 8 points, detailing which rules and principles were to be observed in transcribing the Linear B texts.*

Kober sent Ventris a copy of The Minoan Scripts: Fact and Theory, *which was about to appear in the* American Journal of Archaeology, *and mentions in passing to Daniel that* 'Ventris has been added to my list of correspondents.'

His first letters to her – addressed to 'Miss Kober' – are boyishly expansive and fairly burst with enthusiasm. Quite quickly, however, a suppliant note creeps in – 'I hope I made amends for my Inthos mistake by anticipating its proper genderlessness in my last letter' *– he writes, and one begins to get the impression of an irresistible force meeting an immovable object.*

There is no doubt that Kober criticised Ventris for his methodology. She knew that Myres still wanted him on board, and that in all probability the two of them would be obliged to collaborate that summer in Oxford; one cer-

tainly gets the impression that she wanted to whip Ventris into shape beforehand.

By the end of May Ventris' tone is that of someone attempting to propitiate while still sticking to his guns.

'I hope my experiments with phonetic values don't seem completely arbitrary to you – I feel some of us must try out some hypothesis of linguistic relationship in order to clarify the possibilities.'

One can't help noticing that by this time Ventris has stopped addressing Kober as 'Miss' – had she pulled rank, perhaps? – adopting instead the more formal (and correct) Dr.

Earlier that month Kober had received bad news from John Franklin Daniel. Despite all Daniel's efforts on her behalf, the Indo-European post had gone to Hoenigswald.

'I am terribly disappointed,' *he wrote,* 'I was dreaming wonderful dreams of the terrific set-up we would have here with you and the Minoan collection.'

Kober replied stoically, 'Well, it was fun while it lasted. I can't say your news was unexpected, because I am a pessimist from 'way back, and always expect the worst – hoping to be pleasantly surprised.'

Daniel hastily concocted a scaled-down proposal for the 'Centre for Minoan Linguistic Research' and fired it off to the Director of the Museum, Dr. Froelich Rainey. Internal memos show that the University authorities looked favourably on the modest budgeting, which was to involve little more than the cost of refurbishing the small space next to Daniel's office. The only other action required, they noted, was the appointment of Dr. Alice Kober as Research Assistant, without pay. Far from being comfortably installed in the lucrative Indo-European chair, Kober was now to work for nothing, in what amounted to a broom-cupboard.

The prospect, however, seems not to have daunted her in the least. In any case, the Minoan project would be on hold for the summer, as she had promised to go to Oxford in July, and Daniel, meanwhile, was to set off for Greece on

September 10th, the day Alice was scheduled to sail back from England.

In Oxford, Myres was once again mired in publication difficulties with the Clarendon Press, and fretted that he might even have to make ' a very unsatisfactory facsimile publication of the earlier scripts and Cypro-Minoan.'

Alerted by Kober, Daniel immediately suggested that the AJA should publish the material, either in instalments, or as a monograph 'if funds can be raised, which is uncertain: we haven't yet got any more for your paper.' [*Kober's Element - Inth monograph, which still awaited publication.*]

As always the conduit between England and the U.S., Kober agreed to 'put in a plug' *with Myres, adding altruistically,* 'And for goodness sake, forget my monograph, if that money will do any good for this project.'

And here, with a brief discussion of final proof-corrections for her 'Minoan Scripts' article, and a breezy exchange of good wishes for their respective summers, the correspondence between Alice Kober and John Franklin Daniel ends. By a cruel twist of fate, the two colleagues were never to see each other again. If it can be said that the covetous gods had singled out both scholars for special treatment, it was the buoyant, energetic Daniel whom they clearly loved the best.

31

On his way to HQ Yiannis had taken a detour via Dedalou and stopped off at *Eleftheria*. The doorway was mud-brown, flanked on one side by sacks of organic compost, and on the other by a blackboard which advertised the healing benefits of rock crystals.

Inside he'd found a youth behind the counter, weighing soya beans into brown paper bags. His skin was pale as mother-of-pearl, his body skinny and tapering. Perched on the back of his head was a brown Fedora hat that would have been looked a whole lot better on Yves Montand

'So you're saying you're never open on Sundays?'

'I didn't say never. I said not that I know of.' The accent was more obtuse than Australian – New Zealand, Yiannis reckoned – and the face was petulant. 'We do need a day off sometimes, you know?'

Incense burned primly beside the till, as if to exorcise any lurking demons of commerce. A notice on the wall exhorted customers who required plastic bags for their purchases to kindly bring their own. 'Of course,' said Yiannis, who as far as he knew had implied no criticism. On the shelf behind the counter he saw detox products, cholesterol kits. For reasons best known to herself, Dora had once presented him with a self-test kit. The packet had nagged at him from the bathroom shelf until, suspecting that it was just the first item on a long agenda of reforms, he'd thrown it in the bin.'And last Sunday in particular?'

The youth shrugged listlessly. 'You'll have to ask Maria? She's the owner? She could have been doing the books and stuff?'

'She's here now?'

The brim of the Fedora jerked towards a hessian-covered door deep in the interior. To reach it Yiannis would have had to negotiate sacks of lentils, as well as stacked crates of leeks and avocados and lamentably shrunken apples.

He looked at the boy, who, making no move to help, looked back at him. His patience sorely tried, he said levelly, 'Can you fetch her for me, please?' *An epitrepetai,* he thought, *if I may ask*, fuckwit.

As soon as the kid had disappeared into the nether regions of the shop Yiannis was attacked by a fit of sneezing. He had a sense of healthful husks of grain hanging in the air; then again, perhaps he was simply allergic to all this righteousness.

He gazed bad-temperedly at the shelves, hoping to find cause for criticism. A brief survey revealed produce that had never grown in Cretan soil: lemon-grass, vanilla pods, Kenyan coffee. He saw pollen grains from Denmark, Thai fish sauce, buckwheat pasta all the way from South Australia. On the floor stood enough foreign bottled mineral water to fill a small reservoir. Gratified, he blew his nose loudly. Hypocrisy was the word that came to mind: if he wasn't mistaken, the place had a carbon footprint the size of King Kong.

Maria held the door open for Fedora boy, who was carrying a full tray of pastries. She came toward Yiannis wiping red workmanlike hands on a sackcloth apron.

'Can I help you?' Under a parched thicket of tawny hair her face was young and angelic.

Yiannis didn't elaborate more than he had to. 'In connection with an enquiry' was as far as he would go.

The girl cocked her head, listening. She was Dutch, he reckoned – a compatriot of Jaap the raspberry man. Up close, her skin looked desiccated, like an unhosed garden; there were flakes of psoriasis around her eyebrows. This seemed odd to Yiannis. Hydration, he thought – wasn't that the buzzword? Most kids her age could guzzle any old junk and still glow like gods, so how come wholefoodistas always managed to look so sickly?

'I shut the shop myself on Saturday night, and no one was here until Monday, I assure you.'

'And the German commune, at Neo Chori – they're regular suppliers?'

'Halcyon? For sure. They do cheeses, honey. Some vegetables like fennel and tomatoes.'

'But they definitely didn't deliver on Sunday morning?'

'As I said, no.' The girl knitted her dry brows at him. 'Please. They are in some trouble?'

He smiled non-committal. 'That remains to be seen, I'm afraid. Thank you for your help. We may need you to make a statement, however, at some point.'

The boy was decanting the pastries on to labelled plates, setting them out on the display counter. As Yiannis turned to go a label on one of the plates caught his eye. *Non-gender-specific gingerbread persons.* Were they serious? Pointing to the plate, he smiled sourly at the etiolated youth. 'That'll really change the world, won't it, mate?'

Outside he lit a cigarette and, good temper restored, strolled across the street to the *zacharoplasteion*. He could still produce a fair Melbourne accent when required. Karen, he reckoned, would have been proud of him. He left a message on Kyriaki's mobile, bought a baklava, and carried it to the counter by the window, where he pondered on Wiltraud, and her early-morning 'delivery'. A harmless lie, possibly, but his instincts told him otherwise. He had a sense of things coming together, massing.

The baklava looked like a bird's nest that had been woven from twigs and shreds, the pistachio nuts snuggling at its centre like eggs. It also looked like the perfect antidote to all things healthful. He waited while the girl eased it into a cardboard container, and carried it out to the car.

Even with the windows open the dustbin smell of Pericles still clung to the passenger seat. He'd seemed pleased to see Yiannis at first, and had scurried eagerly into the car, but had sat, all the way back to Katomeli, in a silent leakage of tears.

Yiannis could get no sense out of him; he seemed to have gone beyond the reach of scolding and chivvying. When they stopped outside the empty house he made no move to get out, and Yiannis had to go round to the passenger door and persuade him.

Clearly things couldn't go on as they were. Pericles had no sisters or cousins, not even a kindly niece to look in on him. Someone was going to have to step in, the Church, Social Services, fuck knows who.

Leaning against the bonnet of the car, Yiannis bit into the honeyed heart of the cake and stared blankly at the traffic, monitoring his sensations. The taste didn't exactly flood his mouth, as it had done yesterday in the Flagstaff office, but when your starting point was zero, everything was a matter of degree. The fact remained, though, that something in his damaged circuitry had been reactivated, and was transmitting a faint but detectable signal to his salivary glands.

*

Yiannis was chatting to one of the women constables in Missing Persons when Kyriaki rang back.

'Sorry, Yianni, we're up to our eyes. Only just got your message.' Her voice was resonant with recent drama, as if she'd just come off stage at Epidavros.

'What's up?' he asked, instantly alert.

'All hell's broken loose, that's what! You remember that ATM fraud over at Rethymnon? Well, we had a tip-off, right, a good one? So there was a raid last night up at Anogeia.'

'The Devil's Triangle?'

Yiannis was incredulous. Anogeia and its two neighbouring villages up in the Lefka Ori had become a no-go area for the police. Albanian bandits had moved in, planting their drug farms, turning a sleepy patch of rural Crete into a Wild West defended day and night by hand grenades and Kalashnikovs.

'Anyway, the gang took off – all but the grass, who got shot in the leg by mistake. So half the squad's in pursuit, and we've stretchered the casualty into the ambulance, when a couple of the bastards pop up again, out of fucking nowhere, Yianni! So then they force open the back doors of the thing, and just blast the guy. Right under our noses!'

'Christ,' breathed Yiannis, truly awed. For a moment he stood speechless, registering the hum of the ceiling fan, the anodyne click of keyboards. When the constable he'd been speaking to – a shy-looking girl in headphones, who could barely have been out of high school – flushed and lowered her eyes, he realised that he'd been staring at her. What a fucking cock-up, he thought but did not say.

'You got them, though?'

'The *papareli*? Sure we did, the little shits!'

Yiannis caught the note of hysteria in her voice, shock tightening the strings of her triumph. He decided not to ask about the big fish, the ones that got away. No doubt they were snug in their burrows by now: honour satisfied, they'd be twirling their moustaches and plotting more mayhem.

In the light of such a bloodbath his *Eleftheria* news faded into insignificance. As he filled Kyriaki in, Wiltraud's lie began to look grey or even white. Alternative explanations – ones that, embarrassingly, hadn't occurred to him till now – crowded his mind. What if she'd simply been sneaking back to the commune after a secret tryst? Or on some other early-morning scam she preferred to keep under her hat?

'So.' said Kyriaki, heaving an exhausted sigh.

'Look, don't worry about it,' he said, feeling decidedly sidelined. He glanced at his watch and made a decision. 'I'll go up there myself and have a word. I know the woman already. She's a vet, she treated my cat.' It sounded so pathetic that he immediately wished he'd kept his mouth shut.

'Do you need Mouzakitis?'

Did anyone ever need Mouzakitis? Yiannis wondered. Mouzakitis was a six foot hulk with armour-plated biceps. He had a low forehead from which his black hair was gelled straight back, a squared-off nose, and small, rather wistful, blue eyes. As Theo said, if he had a brain he'd be dangerous.

'It's okay, I can handle it.' Footslogging. It's what he'd signed up for, after all.

'Better take him anyway. You never know, Yianni.'

Kyriaki's voice was so awash with sympathy that for a moment he thought she would dissolve in tears. Catastrophe suited her, he decided: maybe it reminded her that she was human.

He was about to go in search of Mouzakitis when the fresh-faced constable came hurrying up to him.

'There you are, sir!' she said breathlessly, handing him a memo. 'One of the callers gave us a name.'

Ivo Kruja, he read.

'Did you get the caller's name?'

'Sorry sir, she rang off.' The girl looked crestfallen. 'She was Greek, though. She sounded, well, really scared.'

Yiannis looked at her badge. *Constable N. Constantinou.* 'N is for?'

'Nina, sir.'

'Thank you, Nina,' said Yiannis, wondering about the biochemistry of the blush, the seemingly autonomous dilation of blood vessels. Why boys grew out of it, but women didn't. It must, he supposed, have something to do with mating.

'She mentioned a commune, sir. I can't be sure, but it sounded like Neo Chori.'

*

'Last Sunday, in the early morning,' Yiannis said, 'I believe you told Mr Jansen you were delivering?'

Wiltraud gave an embarrassed shrug. When she bent to stroke the brown dog which panted in the shade of the awning, her breasts swung free under the thin white kaftan, and Yiannis saw the dark shadow of nipples.

'Between ourselves, Sergeant, I am a naturist. It's not the sort of thing one broadcasts, nowadays. So I must take my swim early, if you understand me.'

Yiannis inclined his head. It was well done, smoothly done. So why didn't he believe a word of it? Mouzakitis, he saw, was positively salivating: he might not have much English, but there wasn't a man in Crete who didn't understand the word 'naturist'.

197

When they'd got out of the car Mouzakitis had let out a whistle of admiration at the view: the grove of lemon and pomegranate trees sloping down to terraced fields and, far below, the beach of Katomeli, where the coastline blurred into a haze through which glinted the distant control towers of the airport.

'Some piece of real estate!' he'd said, shaking his head regretfully.

Wiltraud had been husking corn on the porch when they arrived, the dog comatose at her feet. A lilac-coloured jeep was parked in the yard, next to a battered pick-up, below which someone's splayed legs were visible. 50 metres away, in the parched grass of the perimeter, two children of about five years old were building a house out of straw bales.

'Castor and Pollux,' she'd told Yiannis, with a hostessy smile. 'Cassie and Polly to us.'

'The Heavenly Twins,' he'd observed, because even at a distance they were beautiful: gold-skinned, limber, with hair the exact colour of the bales they played among.

Margrit's children, she'd said. Margrit, apparently, was indoors making lemonade. The other communards, Prys and Jean-Yves, were still down in the fields but were expected back shortly.

When the the man emerged from beneath the pick-up Yiannis recognised the Teutonic wall-builder. Wolfgang, that was the name. He'd greeted Yiannis with a nod of recognition, but since then hadn't uttered a word. When they'd met on the track Yiannis had put him in his 40s, but he saw now that the guy was younger. His pitted complexion – had he had chicken pox as a child? – had given the impression of age.

Wolfgang wiped his oily hands with a rag and, straddling the low wall that edged the porch, began to roll a cigarette. Encouraged, Mouzakitis produced his own pack and made a general address to the air. 'I may?'

Wiltraud nodded. 'On the veranda, yes of course.'

Wolfang smoked in silence. Two spiralling white butterflies landed on his bare thigh where, reassured, perhaps, by some stillness in him, they settled down to copulate. Motionless, he observed them.

'*Lipon*,' said Yiannis, perplexed. 'You haven't heard anything about it in the media? On television?'

Wiltraud shook her head. 'We don't have one.'

Yiannis raised his eyebrows. 'No television?'

'People come here to find their centre, Sergeant, to learn about nature. Not to watch television.' Wolfgang had moved nothing but his eyes, which glinted severely at Yiannis over the Trotskyesque glasses.

Failing to come up with a suitably stinging rejoinder, Yiannis turned his attention to the love-struck antics of the butterflies. Kore would have stalked them, in increments of motion so tiny that only geological time could measure them; then, in an instant no camera shutter could capture, she would reappear a metre away in her other, killer, guise, the pretty wings clamped between her jaws.

'And you've had no one staying here by the name of Ivo Kruja?'

'No we have not!'

Wolfgang leaned his head against the whitewashed wall of the house and shut his eyes, as if the business of entertaining two policemen was simply beneath his dignity.

'This happened last Saturday, you say?' Wiltraud put in quickly. She gave the ghost of a shiver. 'How awful.'

A woman appeared in the doorway, carrying a tray laden with a pitcher and glasses.

'Margrit!' Wiltraud cried, jumping up with evident relief and taking the tray from her. Wolfgang and the butterflies, Yiannis noticed, stayed put. A hollow-cheeked blonde in her thirties, with greyhound-thin shoulders, she wore a pale yellow vest and a skirt tiered in long flounces. She limped to the edge of the veranda and semaphored her arms at the children. When she sat down in the basketwork chair Wiltraud had pulled out for her, Yiannis saw the prosthesis which replaced her lower left leg, and the trainer, incongruously big and boatlike on the end of the slender steel pole.

The twins came running towards their mother, chattering in a language Yiannis didn't recognise.

'English now,' Margrit commanded, pouring two glasses of lemonade. 'Say hello to the officer.'

The one Yiannis took to be a girl, if only because of the longer hair, looked him straight in the eye.

'Hello officer. My name is Cassie.' Polly, who was apparently a boy, hung back until nudged forward by his sister.

'I am Polly,' he mumbled, blushing fiercely.

'I'm impressed,' said Yiannis.

'English is the *lingua franca* here,' Wiltraud said pleasantly, handing him a glass the rim of which was crusted with sugar, like an old-fashioned American cocktail. 'Danes, Germans, a Frenchman and a Welsh – as you see, we are like the United Nations!'

Mouzakitis accepted the glass Wiltraud offered, and even thanked her in English. He sipped at the drink dubiously, as if it might be spiked with ecstasy. The children had settled down on the deck, leaning their backs against the unprotesting dog. Making a trollish face at them, Wolfgang licked a finger, dabbed at the sugar, and popped it into his mouth. The twins copied him immediately, giggling themselves silly, as though white sugar were a rare and guilty treat.

An Edenic scene, thought Yiannis to himself.

Mouzakitis was standing with one foot on the bottom step of the porch, blowing prissy smoke-plumes at the yard, and making what appeared to be an expert assessment of the wind-chimes. The impression he gave was that of a man trying to blend into the background, with about as much chance of success, Yiannis thought, as a dinosaur in a duckpond. Feeling a distinct desire to distance himself from the photos, he decided to let Mouzakitis be the carrier of contagion. At least it would give him something to do.

'My colleague is going to show you some photographs of the victim.' He looked at Margrit, hesitating. 'But not, perhaps, the children?'

It was Wolfgang, however, who answered. 'Cassie and Polly are commune members. I don't think we should exclude them.'

Margrit gave him a sharp glance, but nodded in agreement.

'As you wish,' said Yiannis.

When Mouzakitis lumbered up the steps with the file, Yiannis told him to hand round the prints. There were two sets; Kallenikos had taken full-face, profile, and several oblique shots. From every angle, the boy looked equally dead.

Wiltraud glanced at them and let out a gasp, covering her mouth with her hand. Margrit leafed through them slowly, her face impassive. As she passed the prints across to Wolfgang the dog sniffed at them and let out a mournful growl; the butterflies, panicked, uncoupled and fluttered away.

Cassie was up on her knees, craning eagerly to see. After a second she said in a small voice, 'What's wrong with Pema, Mummy?'

For a moment Yiannis thought she meant the dog. Then Margrit said emphatically, 'No, darling, it isn't Pema.'

'Pema?' said Yiannis.

Cassie had edged closer to her mother. Suddenly babyish, she drooped her head against Margrit's knee, or whatever stood in for it under the flowing skirt.

'Just someone who stayed here for a while,' Margrit said, holding Yiannis' gaze. 'The photograph resembles him, perhaps, a little.' Her eyes were dark and depthful, the pupils dilated. She could have been a doper, but he doubted it: contact lenses over a certain magnification could produce a similar effect.

'And this Pema – when did he leave?'

'About two, three months ago?' Margrit said, glancing at Wolfgang for confirmation.

Handing the file back to Mouzakitis, Wolfgang nodded. He had hardly glanced at the photographs. Polly's eyes were round and scared, watching him. His thumb had slipped into his mouth.

Mouzakitis glanced at the boy and raised his eyebrows at Yiannis, who replied with a slight shake of the head. Enough was enough, whatever the commune protocols. There was no sense in upsetting both the children.

'He was here for how long, exactly?'

'Exactly, Sergeant, I couldn't say. People come and go. Commune life does not suit everyone.'

There was a sneer, Yiannis thought, in Wolfgang's voice. He was beginning to lose patience with all this studied vagueness. If the rota on the wall was anything to go by, those were no dreamy hippies, but folk who dotted their i's, crossed their t's, and organised their every waking moment.

'The name Pema – it's German, or.?'

Margrit's hand was on Cassie's head, stroking her hair. The fingers were extremely long, the joints enlarged and arthitic-looking. 'This was not his real name, I think. It was the name he took.'

'And his real name?'

'We are not the Gestapo, Sergeant. We don't interrogate our members.' This with the hint of a softening smile.

'Pema was a student of Cultural Anthropology,' Wiltraud interjected, in a voice that sounded muffled and somehow lifeless, 'from the University of Tirana.'

Yiannis remembered that Theo had recently attended a conference in Tirana. The new Mayor, he said, was painting the city all the colours of the rainbow, but you could still drown a sizeable rat in the road potholes. He thanked Wiltraud and made a note. He was glad someone was trying to be helpful.

'You have an address for him?'

Wiltraud shook her head. 'I don't think so, no.'

Surprise surprise, thought Yiannis. Putting his notepad back in his pocket, he stood up decisively.

'I'd like to see the room he stayed in, if I may.'

'Margrit uses it for her yoga now.' There was something hushed and deferential in Wiltraud's tone that made Yiannis wonder, not for the first time, who ruled the roost in this chicken-run.

Margrit hesitated. He could feel her taking the measure of him. Swallows were whistling in the eaves of the outbuilding; on a high rocky bluff behind the house goats grazed nimbly on sparse tussocks. At last she set down her glass, shrugging.

'Okay. No problem.'

Yiannis followed her delicate shoulderblades along the corridor, past the work rota and the kitchen door. This part of the building was new, built of whitewashed breezeblocks and carpeted in coir matting.

Margrit turned right and limped up a short flight of stairs, her silk flounces eddying and rustling. On the landing a bathroom door was ajar; to the right of it was another door, which she pushed open.

Inside, a dark pink crocheted curtain dimmed the light from the window. There was a single bed with a rolled-up foam mat on it, a trestle table, and a camp chair. In one corner fat candle-stubs sat in a huddle on the bare floor. They were unlit, but their scent persisted in the room: lavender, he thought, cypress, and something sweet and heavy, like jasmine.

'You do yoga here?'

'And meditation, yes.'

Yiannis was suddenly conscious of his uniform, his polluting pistol. He imagined how she would light the candles after he'd gone, fumigate the space, chase out the bad karma. He saw several cardboard boxes stacked under the trestle table.

'These boxes belong to Pema?'

'His books, perhaps. He was working for his Doctorate.'

Yiannis looked at her sharply. 'You expect him back, then?'

Margrit shrugged. 'I really have no idea.'

He took a pair of latex gloves from his pocket and pulled out one of the boxes. Margrit sighed audibly but did not protest; she sat down on the divan, straight-backed, watching him.

The box was unsealed. He turned his back on her and opened the lid. Inside he saw a pair of jeans, some socks, a heavy woollen waistcoat woven in garish Aztec zigzags. Underneath the clothes were several books whose covers were familiar: paperbacks of Castaneda and Hesse, and Gimbutas' tome on the Great Goddess, which Karen had bought years ago but had never managed to finish. At the bottom of the box were two A4 ring-binders.

'Looks like he left rather a lot behind.'

Margrit laughed sharply. 'You are wasting your time, Sergeant. The man in the photograph is not Pema.'

Yiannis felt a great stubbornness overtake him; the more she denied it, the more he felt inclined to prove her wrong.

'Nevertheless, he has to be eliminated from the enquiry. Which is why I have to trace him.' He leafed through the binders, looking for an address or a telephone number. The pages were closely typed, in English, with handwritten notes in the margins. He turned to Margrit. 'Why would he write in English?'

'Maybe he wants to publish, who am I to say? To my knowledge there are no publishers in Albania, Sergeant.'

Yiannis replaced the books and folded the clothes on top. DNA, he thought, would have a field day.

'I'll need to take these in for examination.'

Margrit laughed in his face.

'You know, of course, that I can't allow that! You will have to get a warrant.'

She had drawn her legs up under her in a lotus position; her long hands lay, palm up, in the lap of her silk skirt. Under the silk, the steel, he thought, convinced she was enjoying the confrontation.

'Fair enough,' he said, controlling his anger. 'You'll have it first thing in the morning.'

*

On the way back to Heraklion they got stuck behind a vast refrigerated truck. On a mural painted on the back and sides baby Eskimos ate ice-creams in a frozen landscape of *seracs* and ice-floes.

Yiannis and Mouzakitis crawled behind, sweating like pigs, as the truck swayed round the hairpin bends, mincing hedge-rows and ripping off overhanging olive branches.

Yiannis got on the radio and requested the Tirana check, hoping the task would fall to the obliging Nina. For such a big bruiser, Mouzakitis was as timid as a mouse behind the wheel: at this rate it would take an hour to get down to the coast road.

Seeing a fork ahead, he lost patience and leaned across to blast the horn.

'Take him!' he cried, and Mouzakitis rammed his foot down on the accelerator, and veered across the entrance of a track which joined on the left. As the wheels mounted the verge, he corrected wildly, missing the truck by inches. Yiannis was left with an impression of the driver's blank face, framed by earphones. He hadn't even heard them coming.

'*Gamoto-mou!*' He glared at Mouzakitis. 'You can open your eyes now, I'm taking over.'

He made short work of the coast road, and twenty minutes later the odorous roar of Heraklion engulfed them. He parked behind the police station and left Mouzakitis to return the photographs. After gulping a coffee at the counter of the Sportcafe on Yianari, he hurried back towards Dikeosinas Street.

On the way he passed an old, headscarfed Roma woman who was crouching on the pavement, holding out a packet of Softex and an imploring hand. Under her black skirt her legs were invisible, and her posture made her look boneless and collapsed, like someone who's fallen from a 10 storey building.

Although the shrunken figure occupied no more space than a largish dog, something in the way the good citizens of Heraklion, while managing to give the impression of not having noticed her at all, stepped carefully around her, made Yiannis stop dead, go back, and press a 2 euro coin into her hand, for which he received two small packets of tissues and a veritable outburst of blessings.

He walked on through the crowds, dialling Dora's number as he went. Her automated voice told him in Greek and English that she was unavailable, and promised to ring back as soon as possible. He left a message asking her to meet him that evening, and, spotting a convenient wastebin, dropped the tissues in.

32

Ingrid orders three fairly reliable items from the otherwise unpromising menu: courgette fritters, the garlic and potato paste called *skordalia*, and grilled sardines *horis tipota* – without the fries, the rice, the sodden pitta. The sardines are a main course, while the other dishes are starters, but she wants them all together.

Ola mazi, she insists, bracing herself for the skirmish.

'*Ola mazi?*' The waiter's eyebrows arch in protest. The Shoestring does its best to cater for foreign tastes – witness the egg-and-chips on the menu, whimsically called the 'Shirley Valentine' – but apparently her request is a bridge too far.

'*Parakalo,*' she says firmly, staring him down.

Once again she's dining with Hutchinson – not, unfortunately, in person, although there would be plenty of room for him at the four-seater table she's been granted, for once, at the outer edge of the terrace – presumably because most Greeks prefer dining in the mezzanine, which is roofed, marble-floored, and protected by storm-sheets of sand-blasted polythene. A stubby date-palm shaped like an outsize pineapple hides her, at least partially, from curious eyes. Through its razor leaves she can see the Wilson-Wilsons, already eating, and a large family party celebrating what appears to be a birthday or name-day, since at the circular bar in the middle of the terrace a waitress is loading a tray with tall ice-creams spiked with sparklers.

On the way to the Shoestring she'd called in at the *Captain's* to check on Charlie.

'Right as rain,' Glenys had told her. 'But you know how it

is, she just needed to hear a medic say so.' She was lying down, Glenys said; evidently she'd had an anxiety attack, cured by a couple of valium. 'Ken wants to keep an eye on her, though. He picked up some pizzas in town, but we might pop up for a drink later.'

In the Minimarket she'd searched for a postcard that would suit her mother – something gay and glamorous, on which to write an appropriately up-beat message. A bright white cove, bright turquoise sea, a bright red *caique*.

She extracts the card from the pages of *Prehistoric Crete*, where it's been serving as a bookmark, and squares it up on the paper tablecloth. Greta will show it off to her fellow inmates and boast, glassy-eyed, about her daughter.

Dr. Ingrid Laurie, not the medical sort, you understand, the clever sort.

Sometimes she thinks that's all Greta ever wanted – to be the top dog, the belle of the ball. Certainly she seems to be thriving now – happier in her fantasies, it appears, than she ever was in real life. And still with spite to spare for her dead husband, even though it was his foresight which funded the bay-windowed suite in Buncranna House, with its chintz curtains and ensuite bathroom, and even a corkboard on the wall for the display of exactly such trophies as postcards from globetrotting daughters.

Down on the beach the sunbeds have been put to sleep and dusk is falling on an empty sea. A lone man stands thigh-deep in the shallows, operating a toy speedboat by remote control, putting it through its paces. His small son looks on, yipping with excitement, while the mother – dressed in a matronly navy-blue beach-dress and bucket-shaped hat, although the sun set half an hour ago – fusses a beach towel over the boy's shoulders. It's young Sofia the maid, she realises: Sofia the foreteller of catastrophes.

The waiter unloads oil and vinegar from his tray, a *miso* of white, a wicker basket of bread. The paper tablecloth, strapped down by an elastic band, has a map of Crete printed in the centre. Around the borders are nautical designs of hawsers, knots, tillers, as if to remind her that she's mistress of her own ship, and anything's better than confinement in a chintz armchair, currant-scones in the hushed tea lounge, and the contemplation of a life wasted.

She turns the postcard over, picks up her pen, and stares, defeated, at the blank space. She knows her mother won't even try to read between the lines; she's never shown any sign of wanting to decipher her daughter. So why this nagging hope that one day a happy point will come when they can dispense with fiction, when some new and fragile language will be conjured up in which they can communicate?

Oh come on, she thinks. Tell her what she wants to hear. Minimum effort, maximum reward. Would it kill you to give her a little pleasure?

Around the terrace and in the eaves of the mezzanine, lights come on, fake carriage lamps which make even the children's faces look florid and strained. Smells gust from the kitchen; on tree-boles, in doorways, the cats are gathering.

Her view of the mezzanine is partial, through a gap between two plastic storm-sheets. She sees a trouser-leg under a table, a bare foot in a brown leather loafer. It's the ill-tempered tapping of the foot which has caught her eye. She glimpses two female feet in high-heeled sandals, below wide-legged white trousers.

A red-haired woman leans into the frame, supporting her chin on one hand, gesticulating at her companion with the other. She's wearing a bronze kaftan made of some kind of sheer material, over a low-necked white vest. There's a metallic flicker of rings, a man's hand caught in the act of pouring wine.

Ingrid shrinks back behind the leaves of the date-palm. She doesn't have to see the man's face to know whose hand it is.

Her food is arriving, *ola mazi* as requested. The waiter arranges the plates on the table, his expression hovering between doubt and mockery. He nods graciously at her ardent *efkharistos*.

Then several things happen, in rapid sequence. First the cicadas turn up their volume to a deafening pitch, less like a song, suddenly, than the sound of knives sharpening on carborundum stone. Something must have alarmed or angered them; they sound, in fact, deranged.

Next Yiannis pulls the storm-sheet aside and peers out, frowning. There's no doubt that he's seen her, and no dodging the sudden quake she feels, so that when all the lights go out abruptly, she's lightheaded, drowning in darkness, some cellular memory harking back to the original darkness of the cave. For a second the silence is total, but then laughter sighs out from the mezzanine, stoical and Greek, because it's only a power-cut, and power-cuts are par for the course in the Cretan summer.

Every light in Panomeli has gone out, and beyond the point of the headland the westernmost straggle of Katomeli has also vanished into darkness; all that remains is the faint dazzle of a trip-boat in the bay, a sunset cruise, perhaps, nosing its way towards the blacked-out harbour.

She removes the glass canopy from the little oil lamp on her table, winds up the wick, flicks her lighter, and adjusts the flame to a steady sootless glow. People are filtering out of the mezzanine, following the children out on to the terrace to hover by the rail, their faces lit by the transient gleam of cigarettes. When the children twitter with excitement their delight is so palpable she can't distinguish it from her own. It's as if they've all suddenly remembered that what they've been missing is the wondrous, the event tinged with half-remembered terror that will snatch them up in its inclusive arms.

Even her modest meal looks ceremonial, as if it has finally found its proper place in the scheme of things. The sardines, she discovers, are delicious: crisp, lemony, and uncluttered, apart from a dusting of coriander and diced red onion.

In the black void of sky above the headland, the stars have become admirable. She nibbles at her food, admiring them.

The hum of the emergency generator sets up a ripple of applause and disappointment. The bar stereo picks up where it left off, and on the mezzanine the carriage-lamps pulse feebly and settle to a dim glare. The waiters are buzzing about again, skittish in the shadows, smiling broadly.

When she risks a glance at the mezzanine she sees an arm with a wristwatch, a hand draped over the mouth of a wine glass. The man's legs are stretched out under the table, ankles crossed. The red-haired woman has disappeared.

The first lights to wink on are in the villages high up on the shoulder of Mount Yuchtas. Then Katomeli's coastline sparks into life. Ingrid watches the power flow eastwards to feed the street lamps of Panomeli, the Totem Bar, and the bluish-white balcony lights of the new studio apartments by the shore.

The night recedes, defeated, and the stars go out. Even the cicadas have subsided. She can no longer see the Milky Way; she can see both too much and too little.

When Yiannis appears before her she's conscious that her senses are on overdrive, absorbing in a fraction of a second Van Morrison's wailing prayer to Madam Joy, the cellphone in Yiannis' hand, the thumb that strokes sideways across his chest in that Greek way, the mixture of arrogance and shiftiness in the way he glances around and doesn't quite look her in the eye.

The absence of a smile confuses her. She manages a nod.

'Please,' she says, indicating a chair. She looks around for the red-headed woman. 'And your friend?'

'Dora?' Yiannis shrugs, but doesn't sit down. 'She's gone,' he says, at least that's what she thinks he says. His mouth is set defensively. 'Something that was overdue, I think.'

Heat flames in her face for the casual way this Dora has been dismissed. Her immediate desire is to take the hard fact and scoot off with it, get the measure of its weight, its density. Set it on her private shelf and contemplate its glitter.

'I see,' she murmurs, although she doesn't, at least not yet. Not one to waste time, then, a voice warns her. He's wearing a black T shirt and chinos that are neatly pressed: if he's going to be so businesslike, shouldn't he be in uniform?

When the cellphone rings he doesn't say excuse me, but steps aside and listens, expressionless, nodding out at the blankness of the sea.

Ingrid centres the postcard on the tablecloth map.

Dear Mother . . . It's stamped and addressed, but the message space still waits for the flattering fiction. The single wine glass looks spinterish; if there were a spare one on the table she could at least offer him a drink before some important villainy drags him away.

He snaps the cellphone shut and poises on the balls of his feet, as if about to launch into a brisk *zembetiko*.

'*Signome*. I have to go, I'm afraid.'

'Ah yes,' she says, with a commiserating nod.

Yiannis scans 180 degrees of terrace for signs of disorder and, apparently finding none, says curtly, 'There's dancing tomorrow at the Medusa. You'd like to come, maybe?'

Sweat flares and cools almost immediately on her skin. She curves her shoulders forward, resisting the urge to clamp her arms across her breasts. 'You'll be dancing, I take it?'

Now he looks simply perplexed. He glances at his watch and then at her. 'That wasn't exactly the idea.' The skin of her face feels hot and papery, as if his eyes could set it alight. 'You're in *Stella*, aren't you?' She nods, startled, but of course it's his job to know these things, isn't it. 'I'll pick you up around eight, then.' He raises a hand in salutation and, turning away, speeds past the raffia-roofed bar and melts into the darkness.

A night bird calls from a bush. From somewhere behind her comes the click of backgammon counters. She lights a cigarette and gazes at the remains of her dinner: half a dish of *skordalia*, a mound of courgettes, three large sardines staring her out. The Greeks haven't quite got the knack of solitary dining; they invariably serve enough for two.

211

Inside the mezzanine there's the flash of a digital camera: the birthday party, if such it is, is in full swing. The men are grouped together at one end of a long table, the women and children at the other. The men, whether young or middle-aged, are all well-fleshed; they sit squarely in their chairs with their elbows spread wide, bellies stuck out, and flip-flops kicked off under the table. They stroke their chest-hairs, their arms dangle expansively, hands busy with cigarettes or worry beads.

She sits back and listens to her own breathing, trying to spread out to fill the space.

Below the terrace there's the flicker of a torch, and Ken and Glenys come puffing up the steps, Ken resplendent in an England shirt with a red crusader cross and a pair of crop pants printed with pink flamingos.

'There you are!' cries Glenys, pulling out a chair and collapsing into it.

Ken indicates Ingrid's empty glass. 'What'll it be, then?'

'I'm okay, thanks.' She shows him the tin of wine, which is almost half full.

'Was that our friendly local plod, then?' His eyes are on her, keen and blue in the solid tan of his face. He leans over the back of Glenys' chair, palpating her shoulders with his big builders' hands. 'The best laid plans, eh?'

'Oh give over,' Glenys chides, pouting up at him.

'What?' says Ingrid, baffled.

Glenys grins apologetically. 'To be honest, I had you paired off with that Shapcott chap.'

'You did not! The man's a pain.'

Ken grins triumphantly and gives Glenys a conclusive little pat.

'What did I tell you?' Fishing his wallet from an invisible pocket in the flamingo trousers, he says, 'The usual, love?' and winks over her head at Ingrid. 'She likes her banana daiquiri, does Glenys!'

33

As the car bumped up the track to the commune he scanned the article in that morning's *Messoghios*.

On the Queen's mating flight, he read, *which lasts an average 13 minutes, only the fastest and strongest drones can keep up with her. Because of the intricacies of his anatomy, the drone can mate only when the rush of air forces open the lower part of his abdomen, freeing his genitals to enter the Queen's open vulva. There is a pop – his genitals are torn from him after he enters; his abdomen ruptured, he falls to earth paralysed, his male organ left behind dangling from the Queen like a trophy.*

'Charming!' he snorted. This time Hourdaki was really scraping the barrel.

Above the text was a line drawing from the Museum, subtitled *Goddess and priestesses dressed as bees dance together on a golden seal buried with the dead.*

'Makes you think, though, sir.' Mouzakitis took one hand off the wheel and cupped his genitals protectively. 'The queen does it with 17 drones, did you see that bit? Till she's got enough, you know, for a lifetime?'

Yiannis threw the newspaper into the back seat. For a second he was surprised that Mouzakitis could actually read. 'Hourdaki's source must have dried. She's just filling the space with any old shit she can dredge up.'

As they approached the commune he saw that a new notice had appeared on the gatepost, exhorting visitors to turn off their mobile phones.

'Did you see the notice?' Mouzakitis asked.

'What notice?' said Yiannis.

The porch of the house was deserted, apart from the St. Bernard dozing on the deck. This time it was not Margrit who came to the door, but Wiltraud, dressed in a white blouse, narrow black skirt, and black heeled pumps, like an office girl setting out for the city. She had makeup on, and her long braids were coiled neatly on top of her head.

Yiannis presented his warrant, and the two of them followed her inside. When she pushed open the door of the room it was immediately apparent that the burnt-down candles had been replaced with new ones. He turned on her angrily. 'My instructions were that no one was to come in here.' He pointed to the tall new candles. 'I explained quite clearly that nothing should be touched!'

'I'm sorry. Perhaps the twins have come in? They like to melt the . . . stubs?. you know, to make new ones.'

Oh very cute, thought Yiannis: an everyday tale of recycling folk. He looked suspiciously at the cardboard boxes under the desk. Were they exactly as he had left them? 'And Margrit – where is she today?' He could not keep the sarcasm from his voice.

'She took the children to the dentist,' Wiltraud said. 'They should be back soon, I think.'

Yiannis drew on his gloves and waited while Mouzakitis did the same.

'What are we taking, sir?'

'Just the boxes.' The room would be contaminated to hell: Margrit had been using it for months, not to mention the kiddies practising their little handicrafts. On second thoughts he said, 'And bag the bedcover.'

Wiltraud had taken a bunch of keys from her handbag and now stood in the doorway, clinking them impatiently.

'I have a clinic in town, Sergeant. If I don't leave now I will be late.' There was just enough *hauteur* in her voice to chase from his mind any remaining gratitude for the rescue of Terpsikore. He remembered how coolly Margrit had asserted her rights, and decided he'd had enough of the master race, with their rotas and schedules and *verboten* notices. They'd had him dancing to a German tune, so now he would introduce them to a Greek one, make them hop and skip about a bit.

'The procedure,' he said icily, 'is this. You will wait until we have finished here, and the room is secured. Then I will fill in a receipt form for the articles, which you will read and sign, and of which you will retain a copy. Then, of course, you will be free to go.'

Even Mouzakitis, who was hoisting two of the boxes in his ample arms, raised an eyebrow at this piece of pomposity. Yiannis was pleased to see that Wiltraud looked as shocked as a schoolgirl, and was almost standing to attention. How gratifying for her, he thought, to be face to face with a fascist at last.

34

From Brooklyn College, she'd calculated, the walk home down Flatbush Avenue would have taken Alice fifteen minutes door to door.

To the European eye, 1050 E.43rd Street wasn't exactly a pretty house. It was too narrow for its two and a half storeys and steep pitched roof, rather like a house that had been sliced in two, and separated from its other half by a lane which revealed it was also too deep for its width. The facade was of glazed bricks, their pinks and blues and yellows faded to the watery, ersatz shades of an old tinted photograph.

Aspirational was the adjective that had come to mind. Alice the single professional woman had bought a house that was too big for her – bigger by far, certainly, than the cramped tenements of her childhood.

She'd been aiming the camera when a black man emerged from the front door and ran down the steps, cell phone clamped to his ear. She'd opened her mouth to explain why she was standing in the road, snapping away like some shady realtor, but the man rushed past her, dismissing her with a glance, and jumped into an SUV parked at the curb.

She'd written from London to ask if she might be allowed to see the house, but no one had replied. Most likely the current owners had seen her letter as some kind of scam – a philologist (a whaaaat?) who deciphered ancient scripts (are you kidding me?). Watching the SUV drive off, she wished she'd been quicker to accost him. It seemed like a chance missed – to get inside, to see how many rooms there were, and how disposed; to step into Alice's ivory tower (surely in the room at the top with the small dormer window) and imagine her typing at her desk, or on summer evenings knitting on the stoop, reading her detective stories.

A scholarly solitude, an elderly mother to care for: this was certainly the impression given by Alice's letters, but now Hank Yoakam, bless his little cowboy boots, has forwarded the email, and Pamela D. has opened the door, has filled the gloomy little house with characters. After months of effort – apparently fruitless – to find a single living relative, the emergence of a great-niece has come as quite a shock. Pamela D. is the granddaughter of John Gruber, Katharina's brother, which in Ingrid's reckoning actually makes her Alice's second cousin, but no matter.

On the balcony she tries to reconstruct the Gruber family tree. According to Pamela, the Gruber forebears *came down the Danube in the time of Maria Theresa*', and settled in the Banat region of Southern Hungary. Although they were ethnic Germans, since political boundaries kept changing and school was taught in one language one year and another the next, they also spoke Hungarian and Romanian.

Alice's grandparents, Michael and Catherine Gruber, had married in Budapest, and of their five children four had emigrated to the USA. Bertha, the eldest, had left first, followed soon afterwards by Katharina and Anna, and finally by Pamela's grandfather John. Joseph, the youngest, was the only sibling to stay behind, although Anna – Anna the eighteen-year-old cook of the Statendam manifest – eventually returned to Hungary.

'*Family was their life*', Pamela has written, '*and they all liked to visit one another.*' She herself was seven years old when Alice died, and what she remembers of her own youth is '*grandparents, aunts and uncles – their accents, their laughing faces, card games, food and friendly ways – what a group they were!*' 'Tante Katie' – Katarina – she recalls as '*kind and very loving,*' as were her grandmother Susanna, and Aunt Bertha.

217

All the women were '*great cooks*', reportedly having cooked for some of the wealthiest familes of Europe.

In Ingrid's mind Katarina Kober had etched herself as a timid widow, elderly and rather frail, but now, as Tante Katie, she emerges as a jolly, fulsome 60-something, a competent house-keeper and gourmet cook. It's suddenly begun to sound like a very comfortable *ménage* at 1050 E. 43rd Street. Alice the breadwinner was well fed and watered; she probably never had to lift a finger. Many a working woman, Ingrid imagines, would have envied her. So much for her own attempts – as assiduous as any matchmaker's – to provide Alice with a sexual life, or at least with the comfort of a partner. Instead, here she is, ensconced in a kind of matriarchal hive, one that was evidently doting, industrious, and fiercely protective.

Alice enfolded, Alice looked after hand and foot. Alice with nephews and nieces to fuss over.

As an only child, from a family of late (and, it seemed, reluctant) breeders, Ingrid finds this new nexus hard to swallow. It's a bit like learning Greek: at first you see the sounds phonetically, in the familiar Roman letters, then, much later, you feel the alien Cyrillic alphabet gradually muscling in to take their place. Nor is she sure she really wants to absorb it. Rather than being relieved to discover that Alice was far from deprived on a daily basis, she can't help feeling, per-versely, that she's been deceived.

When Alice was anticipating the Indo-European job at the University of Pennsylvania, hadn't she told John Franklin Daniel that she planned to go home at weekends for the first year, so that her mother wouldn't be 'completely alone'? She'd hardly made a single mention of her brother William – 'Cousin Willie', as Pamela calls him – who now turns out to have been living, for at least some of the time, right there in the Brooklyn house. It's as if he didn't exist. Yet here he is, large as life, his notepaper headed with the E.43rd Street address. 'A mathematical type', according to Pamela: an inventor, a consultant engineer who designed cockpit breathing apparatus for the U.S. Air Force. Here he is on the golf course, playing volleyball on the beach, setting up a telescope in the back yard to show the Brooklyn stars to little Pamela and her brother.

Nor had Alice made any reference to the greater Gruber clan, to their cooking and joking, to the card-games conducted in umpteen noisy languages, to the fragrances that must have drifted up from the kitchen – caraway and chives, roast goose-liver and sour cherry soup. The image she projected in her letters was of someone who dwelt exclusively in an exalted realm where nothing quotidian, nothing domestic, was allowed to trespass on the meeting of true minds.

Hungarian cooking was famously heavy: goulash soup with noodles, curd dumplings with bacon, pancakes in paprika-cream sauce. If Alice was a plump wee body, perhaps that was because they were stuffing her like a goose.

In 1948, setting off on that second trip to Oxford, she'd crammed her trunk with foodstuffs – not for herself, she pointed out, but for Myres and her other English friends. *'I plan to be austere for 6 weeks,'* she wrote, *'it will do me good.'*

It strikes her that Pamela may be able to help with the Death Certificate. As a relative, surely Pamela will be granted the access flatly denied to Ingrid, and also – despite his U.S. citizenship and top-flight credentials – to Professor Henry 'Hank' Yoakam? Since Pamela lives in Manhattan, it should be easy enough to call personally at the Public Health Department in Worth Street.

Cause of death is what she needs. Place of interment. Death, though, is a delicate matter – far more delicate, even, than sex. She'll have to be circumspect.

Across the waste ground she can see two generations of Giffords taking a late lunch in the oleander shade of their terrace. Down on the beach a large family of newly-arrived blonds – Dutch? Swedish? – seem to have claimed the sunbeds vacated by the Giffords, dragging them out of the pairs so painstakingly arranged by Androula and rearranging them in a solid phalanx along the shore-line.

Her concentration is shot now, her mind overstuffed with new input. Anxiety kicks in at the pit of her stomach. Jumping up, she clatters the dishes into the sink and sets feverishly about the washing up. The shape-shifting Grubers, she decides, have unsettled her.

She imagines Yiannis surrounded, Yiannis on the dance-floor, egged on by his extended family, his *parea*. For all she knows he might come mob-handed, complete with accoutrements. With the best of intentions, he might try to fit her in like some deserving stray, oblige her to be grateful for his Cretan hospitality.

In the bedroom she hurries the sheet smooth across the bed, gets the iron out of the wardrobe, and plugs it in. The symbols on the foreign temperature dial are indecipherable. She spits on the iron to test the heat and slides her green silk skirt on to the ironing board.

Another scenario comes to mind, one that's more intimate, and even more alarming. On second thoughts, a skirt might make too strong a statement: there's always the risk he'll think she's making too much of an effort. She hasn't forgotten how he cut her dead the other morning, but now, it seems, he expects her to jump to his command.

As she stands with the iron in her hand a drift of wind from the open French windows excites the material of the skirt, lifting and slithering it along the ironing board. In a sudden flash of temper she considers calling the whole thing off. Silk is such a supple, elemental thing, but silk is so easily crushed.

35

Aglaia had kept a table at the edge of the dancefloor, and when Yiannis asked instead for something on the periphery she gave him an old-lady smirk and winked slyly. He let Ingrid go ahead of him, observing her shoulders with their fine spray of freckles, and the shape of her hips under a skirt that was silvery-green in colour, like the underside of an olive leaf. He scanned the bare upper part of her back for tattoos, and was relieved to find none: tattoos, on the whole, repelled him, being too reminiscent of brands on livestock.

The restaurant was already crowded, but not, as far as he could judge, with Greeks, which would at least cut down on the gossip-mongering. Through the throng he saw the shaved skull of Jaap Jansen, who was deep in conversation with a Turkish-looking type with bleached teeth and hair lustrously layered in the style of the tallest, prettiest BeeGee. Where had he dug him up? Yiannis wondered. He caught a glimpse of two angelic blond heads before Wiltraud turned full face to stare at him. As he acknowledged her he saw Ingrid nod and smile in greeting.

'You know her?' he said, surprised.

'She gave me a lift to Anemospilia, up on Mount Yuchtas.'

He pulled out a chair and waited while she sat. 'You were hitch-hiking?' It sounded more disapproving than he'd intended. 'So what took you up there?'

'I'm not sure, really. Chasing ghosts, you could say.' Her earrings were Greek, he noticed: little silver dolphins with chips of turquoise for the eyes. The sort you could pick up for a few euros anywhere in the islands. He was surprised by the brilliance of her smile.

'You know the story, then?'

'The human sacrifice?'

'And do you believe it? Speaking as an archaeologist, I mean?' Signalling for ouzo, he lit a cigarette.

Ingrid swivelled her chair seawards so that she could put her feet up on the low perimeter wall. 'I guess so, yes. The evidence is pretty strong.'

He watched her smooth her skirt down over her knees. He knew he was talking too fast, too nervously. She rummaged in a large raffia bag and brought out a glasses case, a hardback book stamped 'Institute of Archaeology' and a handful of pens accompanied by a small shower of sand. Finally she retrieved a packet of cigarettes and slid one out. When he leaned over to light it for her he smelled a jasminey perfume mixed with the lemon-butter scent of some unguent on her skin. He picked up the menu, although he didn't feel in the least bit hungry. 'So what do you fancy? The food here is, you know, so-so.'

'*Etsi-ketsi,*' she agreed. 'Maybe I'll just have souvlaki.'

A flyer on the table caught his eye. *We regret that the Hatzidakis are unable to perform tonight due to a family bereavement. They will be replaced by the wonderful local group, 'Exadelphi'.* This wasn't part of the plan at all. *Cousins*, indeed, he thought. More likely the kitchen staff decked out in cummerbunds. He threw down the flyer with a sigh of disappointment.

'They're not so good?' Ingrid was watching him anxiouly.

'There's no comparison! The Hatzidakis are very authentic, very Cretan.'

The ouzos came, with *mezedes*. He poured water into Ingrid's glass and watched the viscous liquid turn as white as milk. He couldn't help noticing that her short hair was no longer straight and spiky, but curled softly above her brow in a style that reminded him of the young Mercouri as Stella, the wild bouzouki singer, for whom love and freedom went hand in hand. An iconic film of the fifties: obligatory viewing, he'd told Karen, if you really wanted to understand the Greeks.

Determined to force Stella into marriage, the domineering Miltos had wooed her not with roses, but with a lit stick of dynamite. Karen had loved the film; she'd even allowed that it was feminist before its time. But she'd been reared on Hollywood happy endings, and couldn't condone Stella's final defiant walk towards Miltos and his knife.

Love is a switchknife, as the song went, *with a double blade of joy and pain.*

There was an 80s compilation on the PA system, in deference, presumably, to the demographic of the audience. The Heavenly Twins had taken to the floor, and were innocently jigging about to the camp and flippant strains of the YMCA. He wondered what age Ingrid was – in her mid-thirties, maybe? Older by a decade, certainly, than Mercouri in *Stella*. He must have noted down her birthdate with the other passport details, but in his funk had simply forgotten it.

'I tried that once.' Ingrid pointed the tip of her cigarette at a small boat that was puttering across the bay, a storm-lantern mounted in its prow; smiling wryly, she bent her arm back and swung it in an arc, as if operating a tiller. 'It's not as easy as it looks. I've never said sorry in so many languages!'

Yiannis laughed. 'It takes practice, I agree. Of course in Greece we more or less grow up on the sea. I still have my father's boat, as a matter of fact, down at the quay. Perhaps you'd like to try it again?'

'Are you kidding?'

Her face was so wide open and unwary that for a second he stared at her, transfixed by her excitement. Almost immediately a thought struck him, one that could only embarrass them both. He pressed on, hoping she hadn't noticed.

'So you're here for how long?' For once he'd come dangerously close to blushing.

'Another week. I wish it could be more.'

'A week!' he exclaimed. 'But you need a month, two months. No one can know Crete in less.'

Ingrid spread her hands and shrugged regretfully. 'Of course, but.'

He saw he had been too stern. Buffeted by obscure currents of distress, he frowned at the Dimeros boy, who had arrived with bread and wine. Dynamite, roses, whatever; he'd definitely forgotten the art of flirting. Already she was slipping through his fingers, getting ready to morph herself into a laurel tree and make her escape like some Daphne or Thetis.

There was an elemental quality in the impatience that flared in him. His hands frisked about the table, looking for something to pick up.

'Davidoffs,' he observed casually, his hand alighting on her cigarette packet. Some default mode his mind had slipped into had already set the trap. He picked up a pen, wrote on the packet, and slid it across the tablecloth.

'What's this?' She held it away from her, squinting at the inscription. He watched her retrieve her glasses from their leather case and put them on. She hadn't turned a hair, which made him feel not only relieved, but also uncomfortably conscious of the way his mind was serving up all the wrong questions, while the right ones remained unasked.

'Now that *is* wierd. The thing is, it's all one word.' Taking the pen from him, she wrote quickly. 'Like this. *Akakallis*. Actually Hutchinson has her as a Cretan candidate for the Great Goddess.' She tapped her book, which indeed bore the name Hutchinson. 'She was Minos's daughter, supposedly-so, Ariadne's sister, half-sister of Asterios the Minotaur.' She had slipped so effortlessly into scholarly mode that Yiannis felt rather as if he was back at school, and no star pupil at that. 'Seemingly she had several sons by Apollo, who were suckled by wolves, or goats. Phylakis and Philander – they were twins – and there was Kydon – as in Kydonia?'

Yiannis nodded. Kydonia, now Chania, had been the ancient capital: that much he did know.

'Kydon was suckled by a bitch, I think.' Pausing mid-lecture, she gave him a look which was nothing short of imperious. 'This is to do with your case, is it?'

'Possibly.'

'Which you can't talk about?'

'Which I can't talk about.' The reading glasses magnified her remarkably pale eyes. For a moment Yiannis, dazed, felt as if he was falling into the moon.

'If it's any use to you, Akakallis is also a name for the narcissus.'

His memory flagged up Theo's tox report. *Narkiso*, he thought, startled. *To grow numb.* He saw Manoli Dimeros advancing with a tray, and a sea bass swam into view and settled on the table in front of him, garnished with singed branches of thyme and chunks of lemon. 'Is it, indeed?'

Ingrid was watching him with a pursed, challenging expression. She had moved her chair back into place, so that they were now sitting side by side, with hardly a hand's breadth between them.

'So did I pass the test?'

'With flying colours,' said Yiannis.

And is there someone in London? he thought, but the question refused to ask itself. He imagined her in lamp-black London clothes, on the arm of a large and professorial Englishman. A woman with her looks – not to mention her brains – surely wouldn't lack admirers.

He stripped the spine cleanly from his fish and laid it on a side-plate. 'So how is your work?' he asked, vaguely recalling their conversation at the Museum. Had she said that she was writing a book?

Ingrid laughed. 'Off the record?'

'Sorry about that! Goes with the territory, I'm afraid.'

He touched her left wrist an inch above the silver links of her watchstrap, shaking a penitent head at himself. His fingers tingled with some kind of static charge that brought a film of sweat to his forehead. When he took a forkful of bass the forgotten flavour of the sea flooded into his mouth.

He ate steadily and tried to listen. He learned that her scholar, Alice Kober – he'd heard 'Cobber' until she spelled it out for him – had died two years before the Linear B script was finally deciphered, and had therefore failed to reap the reward for her superhuman efforts.

An English architect called Michael Ventris appeared to be the villain of the piece: announcing his decipherment on the BBC, he hadn't even bothered to mention her name. A very bad show indeed, Yiannis agreed, nodding dutifully. Of course he knew about Sir Arthur Evans, all Cretans did, since the tourist trade more or less depended on him, but he wasn't entirely sure that he'd heard of Michael Ventris.

In the kitchen a quarrel erupted and died.

'The utter determination of the woman.' Ingrid continued, spreading her hands helplessly, as if words were about to fail her. The reading glasses, forgotten, were perched on top of her head. A ripple of smoke from her cigarette curled back into her face, and she coughed abruptly, her eyes watering. '. . . it just beggars belief.'

The expression that passed across her face was so furtive and haggard that Yiannis sensed he was being asked to endorse not only the unsung struggles of her American, but also something more personal, some proud and effortful aloneness that was all her own.

On the PA system the 80s hits had given way to a Greek selection, although there was still no sign of the so-called Cousins. He recognised the irresistible tune of *Dimitroula-mou*, and in his mind's eye his mother threw her sewing aside, her arms slithering up above her head. Fingers clicking, she rose as if spellbound from the sofa, her apron falling from her, to dance in front of the radio.

'If you ask me, she simply worked herself to death,' Ingrid said.

He sipped his wine and nodded sympathetically. It was very sad, he agreed, that Alice Kober had never made it to Crete. Already his fingertips were drumming on the table, his hips beginning to pitch and toss to the beat.

'An old favourite of my mother's,' he explained. 'Dimitroula is her name – short for Dimitria.' He caught sight of

Aglaia in the doorway, rose-petals at the ready; she was turning to exhort the Cousins within, urging them to sally forth and, he suspected, massacre the Wedding Dance.

'I suppose I came here, in a way, because she couldn't,' said Ingrid, as if to herself.

Yiannis' patience was wearing thin. He turned and looked her squarely in the face.

'Well I'm very glad you did. Whatever the reason.'

There was a silence in which Ingrid tidied grizzled green pepper slices to the side of her plate. A pelican flew low across the shallows, encumbered by its heavy, burdened beak, and a memory of Karen shivered and settled for a moment in the pit of his stomach.

Yiannis felt angry with himself. Why couldn't he just accept the evidence that they weren't on the same wave-length, and could not, despite his best efforts, arrive there?

'You know what I think?' he declared. 'I think she's haunting you, this Alice!'

He saw with relief that the dancers were filing out: three boys and three girls, not one of them a day over eighteen. One of the girls had a wall eye; the other he recognised as one of the sales assistants from Evnochides' dress shop. He and Ingrid clapped energetically.

'*Tavrokatharpsia*,' she said suddenly, darting a glance at him.

'Excuse me?' The word meant the bull-jumping games of Minoan times, but beyond that he didn't know what she was getting at.

'Is my accent that bad?'

Katharpazo, he remembered, literally meant *to take the bull by the horns*. The understanding dawned in his knees, rose up warmly through his chest, and broke out in a beam on his face. He leaned across and clinked his glass against hers.

'*Yamas!*'

'*Yamas!*' she echoed, grinning at him.

In the centre of the floor the dancers were doing their best, skipping stiffly about and side-stepping for all they were worth. Ingrid watched raptly, swaying along with the music, craning to check out the footwork. She turned to him with that wide-eyed, winning look.

'You can always tell, can't you? Which ones really *have* to dance.' She pointed to a stocky girl with black bouncing curls. 'That wee one there – you'd think she'd just got on a direct line to God!'

Yiannis studied the eloquent limbs, the joy barely contained on the round young face. He nodded, his heart thumping against his ribs: that was it exactly; he couldn't have put it better himself. He put his hand over Ingrid's and left it there.

Afterwards Yiannis had no idea how long they had sat there. What he could remember was a series of discrete ritual actions: things said or seen, or danced, or merely imagined. The spine of the sea bass on his plate, as neat and clean as though Terpsikore herself had eaten it; the dancers guzzling Cokes at the table by the door, tapping onanistically at their mobiles.

Children were taken home, the oil lamps on the tables burned low. Jaap and his paramour, not quite touching, strolled casually away along the skinny shore that led round the headland to Panomeli.

'You said your wife was Australian?'

'Yes. She died ten years ago.'

'I'm sorry,' Ingrid murmured. 'She must have been so young.'

'Thirty-three.' And then he'd added, truthfully, 'I'm still adjusting.'

The relief of the admission had washed through him like a tide. They'd been dancing by then, in the formal way of schoolkids at a ballroom class, keeping a decent distance between them; underfoot, the stone floor was sticky with crushed rose-petals.

None of these elements linked together into a narrative, for in his euphoria narratives belonged not to the past but to a future which contained the story-to-be: of the bed, his father's boat, the picnic, and thereafter the many introductions that would need to be made, as well as the doubts and protestations that would have to be overcome, or simply swept aside.

His hand on the nape of her neck. In the greenish light from the dashboard, a vertiginous kiss. Afterwards she drew away and laid her hand against his cheek.

'Not yet,' she said, and he could feel her trembling, and hear the leafy rustle of her skirt. He took her hand and kissed it. He hadn't bargained on such restraint, (but what did he expect? That she'd fall into bed at the first opportunity?) 'You don't mind?' she'd asked, and he'd laughed, exhilarated, for how could he mind a constraint that delivered him, in ways he couldn't have explained, from his own impediments?

And after she got out of the car he watched her run up the alley and turn up the spiral stairs, letting her go with the sudden certainty that he and Fate were in accord, for once. He would do the loving, would be the adorant, not the adored, and this was not only how it *would* be, this was how he *wanted* it to be.

With this thought in his mind he'd driven off with both hands on the wheel, singing at the top of his voice, '*My heart and I agree, She's everything on earth to me.*' – 'Stella by Starlight', the 1947 Frank Sinatra version – knowing he was probably going to make himself ridiculous, but not giving a shit. Caution had been his bedfellow for too long, and he was more than glad to see the back of it. He took the bends on the back road at a lick, feeling the car whipped by bamboo fronds and trailing briars, and when he passed the Katomeli signpost he felt like shooting the thing up, just for the hell of it.

36

The day is windless, the sea in the bay flat calm. From this distance the beach is a featureless strip dotted with identical blue sun umbrellas, although Ingrid's own umbrella is distinguishable by the red sarong dangling limply from the spokes. A marker flag, on days of powerful currents, to show her how far downshore she has drifted.

One hundred metres out she turns on her back and floats, shutting her eyes and letting the sun beat down on her eyelids. The sea limns her sweetly, seals her in a bubble of skin. High overhead a plane shines like a needle, stitching its way towards Africa. Blue above, and blue below.

When she'd arrived at the beach it was almost lunchtime, and the Giffords were already ensconced. Ken pushed up his sunglasses, sardonic.

'Been hard at it, eh?'

Glenys was washing two peaches, dousing them with a bottle of mineral water. She handed one to Ken and dried her hands on a Kleenex. 'We called by last night to see if you wanted a bite or something?'

This was the moment she'd been hoping to avoid, when she'd have to admit where she'd been. Sweat oozed from her pores, the oily sweat of indoors. She made light of it, stirring the sand with her toe, glad of the sunglasses that concealed her eyes.

Ken greeted the news with a grin and a 'Good on you, girl.'

Glenys blew on her fingers and flapped them, as if the thought was too hot to handle. 'Well, I don't mind saying, love, I wouldn't mind being in your dancing-shoes!' Wide-eyed, avid for gossip, she swung her feet off the sunbed to make room for Ingrid, swishing the sand away hospitably with the flat of her hand.

There was no sign of the Gifford parents, and the sunbeds on either side had been claimed by the new Dutch families, the men smoking silently behind thrillers, the women – cropped-blonde, bare-breasted – digging three naked infants into a foot-deep hole in the sand. She'd found a spare sunbed nearby and claimed it quickly. Putting a safe distance between herself and the Giffords, noticing with a shock of dismay that one of the Dutchwomen had had a mastectomy.

It was the left breast, she remembers now, that had been removed. The surgery had left very little scarring: what was disturbing was that from one side she looked female, and from the other, entirely boyish. Also that she didn't seem to care whose eyes were irresistibly drawn by the missing symmetry. She thinks of the tanned flatness of the torso, the visible configuration of ribs. Half-boy, half-woman. Wavelets of unease lap at her stomach, taking her back to the adolescent country of the in-between.

She remembers running the gauntlet, the boys calling out from their huddle outside the chip shop, spitting the words angrily out of the corners of their mouths.

Hey blondie! Hey brainbox! The same boys she'd played with only the year before, hut-building innocently in the reed-beds, picking mussels on the cold seaweedy shore. She'd known how to trade insults then, how to face them down. But these new games had a new sting of humiliation. For the first time she was conscious of a handicap – something that wasn't quite right in her, even a part that was missing.

Yes she had a clever tongue in her head to brush them off like burrs, but how was she supposed to know – as the other girls, in some deep ingrained way, seemed to know – what the jeers really meant, how they were supposed to be taken as tribute?

Most of the night she'd been hard at work, cutting her high hopes down to size. Only when she'd edited the story down to

231

one she could believe in did she feel normal, and fell into the blanked-out sleep of the thoroughly deflated.

If she were in London, eating with Maxine and Hilary in the cosy, noisy Euro-restaurant on the corner, how would she tell it? Maxine and Hilary are on her side; they can always be counted upon to lend an empathetic ear.

There would be a post-mortem with giggles, advice, strategies. Her excitement – absorbed, applauded – would settle into place. She might even be able to accept it herself.

Perhaps she should call them, let them soak up her overspill of nerves. She can't just close her eyes and take a leap at the thing, for she knows exactly where that will get her. When you're careless with your life, other people – alerted, like sharks, by asymmetry – will zero in on your unwariness. She's no longer capable of following the kind of instincts that tumble you into unsuitable beds, and also, which is worse, turn you against the suitable men, the ones who want, perhaps, to love and keep you there.

She had made herself eat breakfast, had even worked a little, although not enough to feel virtuous. After drafting several versions by hand, she'd finally replied to Pamela D.'s email, conscious that Pamela might well be granted access to the Death Certificate, but, as a relative, might not wish to divulge the actual cause of death. However the request was phrased it sounded prurient: somehow she couldn't quite convince herself that she – or the public at large – really had a right to know.

As she swims slowly back towards the shore, the beach separates itself into contrasting horizontal stripes: bright blond sand, and, under the sunlit domes of the umbrellas, deep violet shade. She locates her umbrella by the beacon of the red sarong, but then, with territorial annoyance, notices someone sitting under it – a dumpy, old-ladyish figure, which appears to be wearing something mauve. Unless that's merely a trick of the shadow.

232

It must be Androula, she decides: who else would dress like that on a midday beach? Except that Androula normally makes her rounds at 10.30, then again at 3, and the rest of the time sits sharp-eyed under a raffia-roofed shelter where the steps lead down from the road. It simply isn't her habit to plonk herself down on someone's sunbed and wait impatiently for her money.

Anxious now, she strikes up a fast crawl and steams towards the shallows. At the edge the sea laps noiselessly at the Dutch excavations, whose ramparts are melting away now and filling the pit with greyish silt. When she wades out she sees her towel folded on the sunbed, her sunglasses and sun-cream on top, just as she left them; there's no sign whatsoever that anyone has been there.

Ken is sitting astride his sunbed, bent over a copy of the *Daily Express*. Water-drops glisten on his oiled shoulders.

'The old girl?' he says, squinting up at her. 'Nah, gone off for her siesta, most like.'

Glenys unloads a two litre bottle of Fanta from a plastic Minimarket bag and drops a packet of postcards on her sunbed.

'I ran into Lynda up top, she said there was a call for you.'

Ingrid's heart leaps with alarm. Flashing on the corkboard on the wall of her mother's room, the still unsent postcard, her mind clocks up every catastrophe that could possibly happen in a Care Home. If anything 's gone wrong, it'll be Aunt Elsa who calls, not Buncranna House: Elsa isn't only the archivist of the family, but also the rock-solid repository of travel details.

'Did she say who from?'

Glenys puffs out her cheeks. 'I *think* she said the police.'

'Looks like you're in trouble, love.'

When Ken lets out a snort the penny drops. The glance he and Glenys exchange makes Ingrid cringe, but there's still a residue of alarm, enough to dull the embarrassment. She stands dripping, screwing up her eyes against the glare.

'I'd better go up, then.'

'Aye,' grins Ken, 'Better had.'

Lynda is at the photocopier when Ingrid arrives. She's wearing shorts, for once, which make her look fatter, but also younger, and her blonde hair is tied in two Spice-Girl bunches above her ears. She spins round, one hair-bunch flipping forward over her shoulder.

'Oh great. You've saved me a trip You had a call.'

'Was it urgent, do you know?'

Lynda shrugs. 'He didn't say.' She dumps a pile of photocopying on the desk and tears a square of paper from a memo pad, which she passes it over to Ingrid, along with a flyer which advertises a day-trip to the windmills of Lasithi.

Ingrid indicates the phone on the desk. 'Do you mind if I use your land line?'

'Sure, yeah, help yourself.'

Lynda looks surprised, as well she might. If Ingrid has held out against cellphones it isn't only because of her superstitious distrust of all microwaves, but also because she hates the idea of being wide open to invasion at all hours of the day and night. Her mother's grasp on time, like her ability to recognise boundaries, has always been fragile, and recently she seems to have relinquished it altogether.

Under the red sarong her bathing suit is still soaking wet, so she bends over the desk and punches the numbers standing up. The sweat is slippery on her fingers. What will happen if she hits the wrong key, makes a hash of it?

The voice barks out, unrecognisable, from a cavern of noise. '*Nai, embros.*' She hears phones trilling in the background, and the light pitter and patter of keyboards.

'*O Yiannis Stephanoudakis ine ekei?*'

There's a pause, and a sighing outflow of breath. A door closes, and the noises recede. 'It's Ingrid?'

The room seems too bright suddenly, dust-hazed. Turning her back on Lynda, she shields the mouthpiece with her hand.

'I'm in the Flagstaff office. Is anything wrong?'

'Wrong? No, nothing's *wrong*.. I want to see you. When can

234

I see you?' His voice is so peremptory that she feels ambushed. 'Tonight?' he says. 'I can be with you by 8.'

Backed up against the desk, she passes a hand across her eyes. Faced with the definite possibility that his version of events may not be the same as hers, her first reaction is that she won't allow him to dictate. Obviously he hasn't thought it through like she has, isn't the type to question his own judgement.

That's the trouble with Greeks, she decides. It isn't just the machismo. They're just so much better at drama, at deceiving themselves. She studies her feet, which are sandalled, salt-crusted, and sensibly on the ground.

'Okay,' she hears herself say, 'Tonight, then.' But even though her voice sounds cool, almost offhand, some liquid, intangible element is beginning to short-circuit her brain. Her nostrils prickle, remembering her cheek against his, the faintly juniper smell of him. She sneezes several times, apologises, and gropes in her beach bag for a Kleenex. Yiannis says something that sounds like Bless you.

The signal is begnning to break up; sonic beeps and crackles are reducing the language to stray phonemes, syllables adrift on some powerful current of feeling.

She hears him swear in Greek. 'Losing you,' he complains.

Behind her the photocopier whirrs into life and starts up its rhythmic thud, spitting out another bunch of flyers.

'Okay!' she shouts into the phone, 'I said Yes!' She replaces the receiver and stares at it with disbelief, wondering how she managed to convince herself that nothing was going to happen.

37

From Essenes to Adorants: Redefining Masculinity in the Prehistoric Aegean and Near East.

Stretching his legs across a chair, Yiannis sipped his *medio* and stared, confounded, at the title. The fan had been filched, and it felt hot and claustrophobic in the barrel-vaulted basement.

Kyriaki had relayed his instructions down the phone.

'You're the one with the English, Yianni – enjoy!'

That English, however, was proving no match for the discourse of academia – even the title had him running upstairs to borrow a dictionary. Nor had anyone explained to him the exact purpose of the exercise, so he wasn't at all sure what he was looking for.

Kyriaki had rung him first thing, her voice thrumming with good tidngs. 'These prints forensics got from the commune stuff ? They're a perfect match for our victim!'

Yiannis hid his excitement. 'Right,' he said, as if bulls-eyes were what he hit every day, and therefore only to be expected. 'And is there DNA?'

'Not through yet – but it's him, all right. Hang on, the boss wants a word.'

Vasilakis' voice boomed down the line. 'Nice one, Yianni! I always said you had a nose!'

The Co-Ops team had also had a result – remarkably, Yiannis thought, given what he knew of Albanian bureaucracy. An Ivo Kruja was indeed registered as a PhD student at the Univeristy of Tirana, and the local police had confirmed a family address on the outskirts of the city. However, apart from the mother – an ethnic Roma, currently resident in the acute wing of a State asylum – no living relatives were on record.

So far, so good, then. All the same, he couldn't help feeling, as usual, that the action was elsewhere, while he was stuck with the reading.

The typewritten pages were double-spaced and dense with handwritten inserts: the 'thesis' was clearly more of a work in progress. On the inside front page a Table of Contents listed 9 chapters, each with a digest. In the hope that by reading these he might avoid having to plough through the whole thing, he forced himself to concentrate.

Chapter 1 appeared to deal with the dawn of the Neolithic, the domestication of animals, and the shift from hunter-gatherers to settled farming communities. He glanced through the synopsis and looked at Chapter 2. This focussed on Catal Hoyuk, wherever that was, and promised to supply '*skeletal and iconic evidence for gynocentrism*'.

He ran his eye quickly down the page, but the terms used throughout were so specialised that he couldn't be certain he'd grasped the meaning. A word he did understand, though – and one which cropped up rather too often for his liking – was *castration*.

According to the digest, the final chapter focussed specifically on the Kouretic cults of ancient Crete. This, presumably, was what Kruja had come here to study.

The initiated *kouros*, Yiannis learned, was a ministrant of the Goddess. Once initiated as *eniautos*, he became eligible for the position of Consort. Consort to whom? he wondered, realising that to find this out he'd have to tackle the whole damned chapter.

He got up and went along the corridor to the Gents Toilet. At the sink he splashed cold water on his face and dabbed himself dry with a paper towel. His eyes in the mirror looked bloodshot, the pupils strangely dilated.

Beyond a faintly toxic aura of New Agery, the text conveyed little to him, the images it conjured up a muddle of happy pagans in goatskins, pan-pipes, and eco-druids genuflecting to the sickle moon. The sort of thing he could imagine the pietists of *Eleftheria* getting up to in their spare time. And the communards of Halcyon? he wondered, as he returned to his studious seat, but somehow he couldn't see it.

Lighting another cigarette, he stared glumly at the headings. *Pre-nuptial selection rituals of the eniautos* were listed by number:
  1) by foot-race
  2) by bull in the *tavrokatharpsia*
  3) by bees in the *melipnois* or *kerinthophagia*.
Yiannis froze. In his mind's eye he saw the bees, torpid or dying in the dappling shadow. He remembered the boy's hand, half-open, the fingers curled softly like a calyx. Inside, two or three bees, gold-striped, investigating.

The words were clearly Greek, but it wasn't a Greek he knew. Hoping to find clarification in the actual text, he grabbed the second binder and fanned through the pages till he found Chapter 9. The chapter, however, was barely a page and a half long, and ended abruptly in mid-paragraph. Still shaken, he stared at the last sentence:

'*How else are we to interpret the dedicatory posture of the eniautos as he thrusts forward his pelvis, offering his genitals to the Goddess?*'

Just then the door opened and Theo pushed in, carrying two bulging supermarket bags and using his behind to manoeuvre. A bunch of leeks protruded from one bag, and from the other, a sheaf of tiger-lilies. He wore a red polo shirt and white jeans that were one size too small, and cased the room with what could have been described as a slouching pout, his eyes flicking here and there as if he expected a nymphette to be hiding in every alcove. A strong smell of prawns assailed Yiannis' nostrils.

'Off your usual patch, aren't you?' he said warily.

Dumping his bags on the floor, Theo tapped the side of his nose.

'Things to do, people to see.' He produced a video cassette

from one of the bags and slid it across the table; it was *Alphaville*, Yiannis' favourite Godard, just ahead of *Breathless*. 'Thanks a lot,' he said, with a regretful glance at the cover, 'That Anna Karina's really something.! They've got these flat faces, haven't they, Frenchwomen. And these big smeary sort of mouths.'

'Karina was Polish,' Yiannis pointed out, eyeing a globe-shaped vegetable which had spilled from one of the bags and was now rolling across the floor; it was rutted and greyish and looked like a small planet, recently deceased. 'So what's with the shrunken head?'

Theo the footballer caught up with it and blocked it neatly with his foot. 'It's celeriac.'

'Looks more like a souvenir from the mortuary. Been shopping?'

'It's Livia's birthday. I'm on barbecue duty.' He gave Yiannis a sidelong look. 'Don't say it. Livia already asked Dora, so . . .'

'No problem,' Yiannis said quickly, feeling the slight but definite sting that comes from exclusion.

'Unless you're having second thoughts, of course?'

'I'm not. Wish Livia my best, will you?' He scanned Theo's face for signs of malice, waiting to discover why he had really come.

'So how's it going?'

'So-so,' Yiannis grunted, resisting a schoolboyish urge to cover the open page with his hand.

On Theo's face suspicion wrestled with amusement, and lost. 'Are you holding out on me?'

And screw you too, thought Yiannis. He decided it was high time he confronted him. 'So how do I know it won't go straight into *Messoghios*?'

Theo gave an aggrieved laugh. 'Is that what you think? Jesus, Yianni!'

Immediately Yiannis felt defensive. He scowled at Theo. 'Well, some little bird's been whispering to the big bad she-wolf!'

'Don't look at *me*! How many sticky fingers d'you think

tox reports go through, for Christ's sake?' Extracting a squashed packet of cigarettes from the back pocket of his Levis, he lit one and blew smoke out sullenly. 'Not my style, Yianni, you should know that. Not my league, either.'

Shrugging, Yiannis pushed the ashtray towards him. The relief he felt was tainted by remorse. His suspicions had so paralysed him that he hadn't even been able to call Theo. He wasn't proud of his capacity for avoiding confrontation; all the same, he wasn't quite ready to apologise.

Theo shook his head sadly. 'You know your trouble, my friend? You've got a nasty suspicious nature.' He was fingering a necklace made from plaited strands of leather, which was rakish, rather hippy and, in Yiannis' opinion, far too young for him.

'So *did* you talk to her?'

Theo shook his head sadly. 'But hey, you know, so what if I had? All's well that ends well. You got your case, didn't you?'

There was no answer to this one; it was both cynical and undeniable.

'We've got an identity,' he admitted. 'Albanian student. Looks like he sneaked in without papers.'

'Well, there you go,' said Theo, nodding sagely.'Any more on our mysterious female?'

Yiannis tried to dismiss a residual tremor of unease: after all, what else was instinct but a judgement with no supporting evidence? 'Not yet.We're still waiting for the DNA.' Relenting, he said, 'Look, how about a coffee?'

'No way. I'm under heavy manners from Livia.' Theo began to assemble his shopping bags, fussing elaborately with the blush-pink heads of the tiger-lilies, which had become entangled with the handle. 'Rumour has it, by the way, that you were spotted at the Medusa last night.'

'I was?' said Yiannis innocently, undersanding that this was the real reason for the visit: nothing Theo liked better than to keep abreast of the gossip. He flicked open his mobile and studied the screen, as if perusing a text message of some import. If he couldn't deflect Theo's enquiry, at least he could delay it.

'And do I know the lucky lady?'

As he shook his head Yiannis felt the smile spilling out across his face. 'You don't. She's English. Actually, Scottish.'

Theo studied him through a cumulus cloud of cigarette smoke. '*Panagia-mou!* If I didn't know it was impossible, I'd swear the man was actually blushing. Does she have a name?'

Yiannis hesitated. 'Ingrid.' Despite himself, his mouth tingled at the utterance. He heard the church clock of Agios Titos chime three times as he held his breath, trying to suppress the flood of pleasurable sensations.

'Ingrid,' echoed Theo, sounding out the syllables in a lecherous, lip-smacking way. 'A noble name indeed.' He cocked an eyebrow at Yiannis. 'I hear she's a natural blonde, too.'

At the thought that he would at some point be obliged to expose Ingrid to Theo's priapic aura, Yiannis felt a primitive surge of jealousy; he wished, now, that he had left her name unspoken, that boastful pride hadn't simply got the better of him.

Once, after an evening out during which Dora had flirted cheerfully with Theo, Yiannis had demanded to know if she found him attractive.

Dora had laughed and looked at him with incredulity.'You mean you haven't noticed the dodgy thumb?'

He had indeed noticed, he realised, but long ago in the mists of boyhood and – in thrall, perhaps, to Theo's sexual prowess – had somehow managed to erase it from his consciousness. Even now he had to force himself to look directly at the item – a truncated, hoof-shaped digit from the knuckle of which sprouted long curly hairs – to convince himself the flaw existed.

'Back off!' he retorted, pointing a warning finger.

'I did think you were looking unusually, shall we say, twinkly? Uncle Theo doesn't miss much, you see.' Theo made a comedy of ducking down behind the tiger-lilies, and Yiannis laughed, his good humour restored.

Glad to put dissent behind him, he gave in to a simple urge

to confide. He heard hiself say with mock solemnity, 'Actually, I'm in love.'

After a dumb-struck pause Theo let out a whistle.

'Ai Yianni!' He gave Yiannis a pensive look. '*Are* in love, or *want* to be in love?' Yiannis was startled by the distinction: on the whole he wouldn't have credited Theo with such subtlety.

Theo was regarding him with what could fairly have been called a melting smile. 'Well, that's great news. Congratulations, *pedi-mou*, what can I say?'

Although velvet was an element Theo usually reserved for the female sex, his pleasure was apparently so sincere that Yiannis, caressed by warmth, was quite touched.

Crushing out his cigarette, Theo put his hand over his heart. He wiped an imaginary tear from his eye, reciting:

'*Qu'est-ce qui s'allume la nuit en lumières?*
– La poésie.'
'*What is it that lights up the night?*
– Poetry.'

If the words were soulful, the voice was robotic. Theo jerked his prehistoric thumb towards the video of Alphaville. 'Lemmy Caution interrogated by computer. Didn't know I spoke French, did you?'

'Fuck off,' said Yiannis, who was also quite capable of reading English subtitles.

'No honestly. I envy you, I do.' Wreathed in smiles, Theo loaded his arms with plastic bags. At the door he turned and said, 'Don't be a stranger, Yianni!'

38

Under the awning of the grocer's shop the cool concrete step is flanked on one side by a postcard-stand and a stack of tomato boxes, and on the other by displays of melons, artichokes, and twelve-packs of mineral water bottles tautly shrouded in plastic. People trot in and out on last minute errands; some of them even stop to acknowledge Pericles with a nod or a smile. When ringed fingers press three euro coins into his hand he sees that it is Kyria Dora who lives on the corner, her pretty feet in silver sandals, her wide red skirt swishing past him like a wave of wind.

As the sun moves on its grand journey overhead, Pericles remembers the gold light on cypresses, the sounds and colours of welcome falling like honey from the air. In his ears the buzz of celebration still echoes, but the truth is that he did not go with his friends when they invited him, and because of this their disappointment is like a rheumatic in his bones.

Beyond the shadow-line of the awning ants run in and out of cracks in the pavement. When he lets his head rest sideways on his knees the world tilts and the ants scale precipices. The tomato-boxes and the postcard-stand yawn out over space. Passing cars ascend an impossible gradient, or else zip down from heaven and dissolve into the oleander bush on the corner, below which a vertical sea plunges, like his memories, into the abyss. But even on a slant the world reveals no entry-points, no way he can get back in. If he goes back there he will be arrested, this is what the Sergeant says, but if he cannot go back, nor can he go forward, with his dishonourable pockets and his head swollen with unsaid Sorrys.

Earlier Markos had brought him a Coke, coming out of the store in his apron and snapping the ring-pull open, so that

243

noise fizzed out into the air. Pericles raises his head to suck on it and feels the cold liquid run down inside him. Two children are coming up the street: a small girl with a large handbag, unsteady on her mother's high-heeled shoes, leading a bandy-legged toddler by the hand.

'Mind the man who's drinking, see?' she warns importantly, 'I'll show you the way.'

As they climb the steps, skirting him carefully, Pericles catches the little boy's eye.

'Say Yassou,' the girls instructs.

'Yassou' the boy chirps obediently. His gaze is clear and grave, his skin luminous in the shade of the awning.

When they have gone inside Pericles looks at his feet, suddenly ashamed of the gnarled old arches and the antler-like spread of raised blue veins.

He thinks of a little wooden train, blue and white for the Greek flag, with two open carriages filled with pebbles and snails. He thinks of his toy spade, and the day he met a snake coiled sleeping on the garden path. He thinks of killing the snake like a brave soldier and trundling it in to show his mother. He thinks of the clip-clop sound of the train wheels on the tiles of the kitchen floor, and then the slaps echo in his head like the night-noise of the bombs that fell on the harbour.

He clutches the coins, their copper and silver imprint on his palm, and thinks of what is owed. He thinks of dropping the coins into their hands, so that the friends will understand he wants to go with them.

When the children emerge from the shop the toddler stops to show Pericles his red and white striped ice-lolly, his eyes wide with amazement. The girl tugs him on down the steps, but he resists, turning to look over his shoulder, the lolly held high like an Olympic torch, until Pericles sees that he must in some way acknowledge the wonder of it. Only when he raises his hand in a salute does the boy smile and allow himself to be led away.

Markos has already begun to cover the displays of fruit; soon the shutters will roll down with a clatter and the street will

244

thicken with lunchtime heat. Pericles wipes his mouth with the back of his hand, hugging to him the infant's borderless pride. He feels the great festival swell inside him, with its bull-games, its bare-boobied ladies, its circus stripes.

39

Waking before Ingrid, Yiannis found himself in a character-less bedroom, white-walled and white-tiled, in which two single beds had been pushed together to make one. To the left of the bed was a low pine locker on which sat a packet of English biscuits, a half-empty bottle of mineral water, and a pair of small wax earplugs; on the right an identical locker held his own cellphone and wristwatch. Against the opposite wall a desk was piled with books and files; next to it, squeezed into the corner of the room, stood a generic pine wardrobe. It was a scene so stamped with transience that he felt his heart tighten with home-sickness, as if it were he, rather than Ingrid, who'd landed in a foreign country.

On the white expanse of the bed she lay curled on her side, clutching the sheet to her throat. It stretched tautly over her hips like a toga, leaving the curve of her back tender and bare. The loose tendrils of hair at the nape of her neck were dark and sticky with sweat.

She'd looked the words up for him in a big hard-backed lexicon, licking a fingertip and leafing rapidly through the pages. *Melipnois*, literally translated, turned out to mean *honey-breathing*. *Kerinthophagia,* however, was nowhere to be found. Reconstructing it from its elements, she'd come up with *pollen-eating*.

'Fabulous word!' she'd exclaimed, 'Wherever did you dig that up?'

Over dinner at the Shoestring – he remembered how they'd rearranged their cutlery countless times, smoked a lot, and managed to eat almost nothing – he mentioned his problem with the thesis. She seemed genuinely intrigued, and listened with her chin propped on her hand, nodding gravely.

'It's the bee connection, then?'

He looked sharply at her. He'd been careful not to say anything about the identity of the writer. 'What makes you say that?'

'Well, I did read the newspapers.' She shrugged and sat back, wrapping her arms around herself. He sensed her withdrawal, but although the distance pained him, he'd already said more than he ought to. After that, she'd seemed muted and self-conscious, and had offered no more interpretations. At last, light-headed with ouzo, he admitted he was completely out of his depth with the thing and – without wanting to take advantage, of course – would really value her input. At the time it had seemed such a brainwave that he'd pushed to the back of his mind the obvious problem of authorisation.

On the bedside rug his trousers lay in a concertina'd heap, as if he had just stepped out of them. Ingrid's underthings had joined the papers on the desk; her skirt was draped silkily over the back of the chair. Easing himself out of bed, he tiptoed to the desk, removed the skirt, and carried the chair over to the French windows, where he sat down, straddling it. The windows were wide open, and through the diaphanous curtains he could see it was just after dawn. The sky over the sea was filling up with watercolour blue, and the roofs of the houses down by the beach were beginning to emit a warm earthy glow.

Seen in the light of a new day, his happiness took on a more solid outline. In the night he'd been all too aware of the layers of history he brought to the encounter: what techniques he'd practised, and with whom; what pleased one lover, but left another cold. He was also conscious of how ignorant he was about Ingrid's experience. As yet she'd said nothing about the men she'd been with, and it was hard not to feel that his performance was being scrutinised by these ghostly, unknown

247

lovers, who stood in the wings comparing notes, and critically assessing his every move.

He'd worried, too, about his lack of finesse, even as he sensed that finesse was not one of her priorities; for, to be honest, there were things she had done – direct to the point of indelicacy – that had shocked him a little. Once she'd committed herself, her focus was absolute: she made love, he thought, as if hypnotised. There were no athletics, no cinematic archings of the back or vehicular collisions of the hips. It was as if her body commanded, and his own was more than thrilled to respond to its imperatives; at no point, mercifully, did he get the sense she was trying to flatter him. Her orgasm, when it came, was fruitful and full-throated, and left no room for doubt. The simplicity of it had brought tears of gratitude to his eyes. Afterwards, holding her, he'd felt ubiquitous, like a prince. When he tried to extricate his arm from under her body she let out a grunt of protest; she was breathing heavily, already half asleep. He gave up then, grinned to himself in the darkness, lay still and felt the moonlight cooling his sweat.

Overhead there were sounds of movement: the soft shuffle of bare feet on floorboards, a tap running. Outside Demosthenes' house a workman was ferrying breeze-blocks from a pick-up truck and stacking them on the terrace.

He crept over to the bed and retrieved his watch. It was later than he'd thought. He bent over Ingrid, who snoozed on, apparently oblivious of the fly he now brushed tenderly from a nose which in most of the English-speaking world would be called Grecian, and in Greece, Roman, and as for the other, far-flung territories, well, who knows what name such noses went by in Samoa, for instance, or Tajikistan.

He kissed her ear and whispered, 'Good morning, my love.'

She stirred, opening an unwilling eye. 'What time?'

'Early. I have to go home and change.'

'Not yet,' she grumbled complacently. Her arm came up

and groped its way around his neck; he received a sleepy, dry-mouthed kiss. He was tempted to gather her into his arms and sink back into the rumpled white depths of the bed, but at that moment he heard rapid footseps on the external staircase, followed immediately by a thundering at the door.

Ingrid sat up abruptly, reaching for her nightshirt. 'God, what now?' she exclaimed, but he was already out of bed and pulling on his trousers. 'No, I'll go,' she protested. Ignoring her, he put on his T shirt and padded into the kitchen.

When he opened the door the boy almost fell into his arms. He was barefoot, dressed only in pajama bottoms. Yiannis tried to recall the double-barrelled name: Watson-Johnston? Weston-Wilson? He thrust a mobile phone at Yiannis. 'It's my wife, she needs a doctor! I can't get through.'

Ingrid's head came round the bedroom door, her face wary and concerned. 'Is something wrong?'

The boy was breathing hard, dancing from foot to foot. 'She's bleeding. Please . . . can someone come?'

Yiannis nodded at Ingrid and followed the boy up the spiral stairs. For one so young, he was badly out of condition – thick-waisted and ungainly, gripping the rail for support and wheezing his way up like an old asthmatic.

The top floor studio was a large oak-beamed room with a varnished wood floor and sloping eaves. The girl lay in the centre of the double bed, her head flung back on the pillows. She was waxy-pale and appeared semi-comatose.

'She's pregnant,' the boy muttered, his eyes reddening with tears.

Yiannis sat down on the edge of the bed and put his hand to her forehead, which was cold and sweat-slicked. 'How far on?'

'Three months.'

'Okay,' said Yiannis, 'What's her name?'

'Kylie.'

'And yours?'

'Darren.'

He reached for the girl's wrist and felt the rapid flicker of her pulse. 'Kylie? Can you hear me?' Her eyelids stirred and a tremor of pain puckered her face. 'Do you know where you are?'

Darren had crossed his arms over his bare chest and jammed his thumbs into his armpits; he was grey-faced, shivering. 'Is she all right?'

'Probably in shock.'

Yiannis heard Ingrid's footsteps on the outside stairs. She knocked tentatively and came in.

'Listen, Darren, I'm going to call an ambulance. In the meantime, tea. Hot, weak, and sweet. Is there a blanket anywhere?'

'On top of the wardrobe,' Ingrid said immediately. Grabbing a kitchen chair, she climbed on to it and retrieved two blankets made from a brown furry fabric.

Yiannis dialled Control and spoke quickly into the phone. He took the blankets from Ingrid and spread them over the girl, swaddling her to the neck. 'Try to relax,' he said. She nodded weakly, her eyes fixed on him. He shooed Darren into the bathroom to get dressed.

Ingrid was filling a kettle at the sink. She took cups from the draining-board and set them on the table, pushing aside a deck of cards laid out on the oilcloth: evidently someone had been halfway through a game of Patience.

He gestured to her to follow him outside. A tall date-palm grew up from the garden below, its fronded leaves drooping over the landing; the wiry stems which projected from the trunk bore yellow explosions of fruit.

'Poor kid. She's miscarrying, I reckon.'

Ingrid gripped the railing with both hands and leaned out over the garden; she looked bleary and ragged, as if weighed down by the transactions of the night.

'Look, you don't have to stay,' he said quickly. 'I'll wait with her till the ambulance gets here.'

'It's not that, it's only . . . I feel such a pig.'

He stared at her, baffled. 'She's young, you know. She'll be all right.'

She gave him a woebegone smile. 'You should go back in. No really.'

Darren looked up hopefully when Yiannis re-entered the room; he had dressed and was sitting on the bed with his arm draped in an awkward arc across the top of the pillows, like a teenager in the back row of the cinema.

'Don't worry,' said Yiannis, 'They'll be here soon.'

Ingrid had made tea in a pot, in the English way. He found milk in the fridge, spooned in sugar, and carried the cup over to the bed.

'Try to get her to drink some of this.' When the boy took the cup Yiannis saw that his hands were trembling. 'Careful,' he warned, 'it's hot.'

The girl jerked her head away and shut her eyes, but not before Yiannis had seen the flash of fury in them. Her lips were seamed tight, refusing. Concerned that she might be seriously dehydrated, he retrieved the cup from Darren and, taking his place on the bed, tried to induce her to drink a little.

When he heard the siren he went out on to the balcony to signal to the crew. Two male paramedics bounded up the steps with the collapsible stretcher. He spoke to them briefly outside the door and followed them in. As they unfolded the stretcher Kylie looked wildly at him, her face tense with the anticipation of pain. He smiled at her, since nobody else had.

'They're going to take you to hospital, Kylie. You'll be more comfortable there.'

The alarm beeped on his wristwatch and he turned it off. 7 o'clock. Somewhere outside a cockerel crowed in agreement. When they shifted her on to the stretcher he turned his head away from the bed and its spreading scarlet stain.

At the door of the ambulance he waited while a female paramedic fixed up a drip. Darren stood beside him, splay-footed, his hands in the pockets of his tracksuit bottoms. His eyes were downcast, his lower lip jutting. After a moment he said aggressively. 'Don't I get to go, then?'

'Of course.' Yiannis gazed at him in surprise. 'You have your documents?'

'Documents?'

'Passports, insurance? You'll need them for the hospital.'

Darren shook his head. Yiannis looked impatiently at the sloping, defeated shoulders.

'Well go up and get them, then!'

In the white hygienic gloom of the ambulance the patient was strapped up and ready to go. The woman paramedic crouched next to the stretcher, her hand laid protectively across the blanket; she was talking to Kylie in a low, murmuring voice.

Yiannis remembered now what he'd dreamt in the night. There was a white room in the dream, in which two operating tables stood side by side. He lay on one of them, pale and still, under a sign that said *nil by mouth*. Theo was leaning over the other table, where Dora was stretched out, stark naked; he had a crab's claw for a hand, with which he was incising her torso, painstakingly, from pubis to base throat.

Yiannis stepped away from the door of the ambulance and, lighting a cigarette, inhaled with relief. After the first brunt of the recall he was struck by the anomaly: why had Dora featured, rather than Karen? It was almost as if the dream, in its mercy, had superimposed a protective layer, like a scab across a wound. He thought of Nicole, his so-called 'grief counsellor', whose terminal optimism had so enraged him. 'Closure' had been her watchword, even when Karen was hardly cold in the ground. Nicole would have pounced on the dream, shaken it like a happy terrier. 'Do you think.' she'd have said – disingenuously, when 'I think' was what she actually meant – 'Do you think it's trying to tell you that you're on the way to healing?'

The driver had already got into the cab and started up the engine, and the other paramedic, a square-bodied man in his fifties whose stomach strained against his tabard, came over to stand beside Yiannis. Hands on hips, he squinted up at the top floor balcony.

'Is the kid coming, or what?'

Yiannis crushed the cigarette out under his foot. 'Sure, just give him a second.' For the first time he felt a stab of sympathy for the angry boy who couldn't be a man. 'Will she lose it?' he asked, with no particular expectation of an answer. The medic looked at him dourly. A razor rash stretched from his Adam's apple to the outer angle of his jaw.

'Maybe, maybe not.'

When Darren reappeared he was carrying a bulging plastic Minimarket bag. His eyes appealed to Yiannis. 'I didn't know if she'd need her toilet things and stuff?'

'Good man,' Yiannis said approvingly.

He stood back while the medic shut the boy in and locked the doors. The lights of the ambulance flashed feebly in the strengthening sun. He watched it creep slowly down the cobbled street until it reached the corner, where the siren started up again.

40

'Hallo? Are you there?'

Ingrid gets up from the computer and goes out on to the balcony. Zoe is leaning over the half-metre gap; she's wearing an outsize Greenpeace T shirt and sequined ballerina pumps, and she looks relieved to see her.

'Dad saw the ambulance, earlier, and we were worried that . . .?'

'It was for upstairs,' she says quickly, 'looks like she had a miscarriage.'

'Oh grim! That's awful. Is she going to be okay?'

'I expect so,' Ingrid says, wondering with a twinge of guilt if Zoe feels the same as she does about the Wilson-Wilsons. 'Some holiday for them, though.'

'Yeah. They must be gutted.' Zoe frowns absently, the sunlight gracing her gleaming hair. 'Was that our nice sergeant?' she adds, in a neutral tone, and Ingrid realises her French windows had been wide open all night, as indeed had the Shapcotts.

Zoe's underclothes hang, flagrant, on the drying-rack: bikini briefs, flimsy balconette bras, thongs. Ingrid thinks suddenly of the washing-line in the back yard, stretched between two iron poles: her father's vests and long-johns pegged out indiscriminately among her school knickers and her mother's brassieres and slips. She'd slink past with eyes averted, trying to ignore the careless, promiscuous mingling. She watches Zoe collect a couple of items from the rack and finger others which are still damp, evidently, for she leaves them there. 'We went for something to eat,' she says, deciding that it would be stupid to deny it. She

254

adds mendaciously, 'He wanted some help with a manu-script.'

Zoe nods, accepting the retreat into the formal, the im-personal, but she seems pent-up and distracted, as if there's something on her mind.

'Cool,' she says, removing a beach towel from the railing and rolling it up. 'He's quite attractive, though, isn't he?' She sighs, and frowns sadly at the sea. 'Sometimes I really wish Dad would get himself a girlfriend. You know, like Internet dating or something?'

Dating isn't a word that sits easily with Shapcott *père*, any more than it does with Ingrid.

'I guess that's how it's done these days,' she agrees, with a pang of sympathy on his behalf, but also on behalf of his putative partners, who'll find themselves competing with his stunning daughter.

'Whatever,' Zoe says, her face clearing. 'I've actually man-aged to persuade him to go to the Museum this afternoon, if you need a lift or anything.'

'Actually that could work. I've got things to do in town.' She decides not to mention the Police Station.

'In about an hour? He's a bit of an old slowcoach in the morning.' Zoe arches her back, thrusting her breasts forward, and now her ams flow out and up, her hands coiling and uncoiling in the air, like smoke or serpents. She grins reso-lutely at Ingrid. 'Can't wait to see these snake ladies!'

Ingrid fills the sink with cold water, washes the silk skirt, and takes a shower. Conscious of dressing the part, she puts on a cap-sleeved white blouse and black linen trousers: urban armour, cool but businesslike. She transfers pen, notebook and reading glasses from her tote bag to her briefcase, adds a bottle of water, and goes out on to the balcony to wait for the Shapcotts.

She remembers how Yiannis drank his coffee standing up at the sink; how she'd wanted to touch him somewhere, but couldn't shift the authoritative barrier of air between them.

Although he was in civilian clothes she'd almost said the stupid words aloud.

Every girl loves a man in uniform.

It would be just like her to strike a wrong note. She's never learnt the knack of graceful, grown-up partings.

*

The Police HQ in Heraklion is tall, Venetian, built of honey-coloured limestone, with a sentry-box outside the main entrance. Inside the foyer the floor is laid with patterned ceramic tiles, and plastic flowers adorn high arched niches which might once have housed ikons. There are basketwork chairs, and shelves filled with technicolour tourist brochures; were it not for the uniforms, she could be in the foyer of a 3 star hotel.

In the foyer she waits, briefcase in hand, while the receptionist rings through for Yiannis. Already she feels as though she'd stepped into one of those police procedurals that the networks trot out on weekday evenings. Stock characters, formulaic plots. The female profiler wheeled in by the scriptwriters to inject glamour into the grubby, sandwich-scoffing milieu of the copshop. If you're ill or depressed there's something to be said for the anaesthetic effects of pure plot stripped of messy emotions, but its hardly her favourite genre.

When Yiannis appears he acknowledges her with a slight inclination of the head, and signs for her as if she were a parcel. Behind the reception desk a flight of stone steps leads down to the basement. The treads are worn and concave, their edges blurred by centuries of feet. At the bottom he stops with his hand on the handle of a heavy oak door.

'They're keeping Kylie in overnight. I'm afraid they couldn't save the baby.'

'You went to the hospital?'

'I rang an hour ago. She's okay. Resting, as they say.' He shows her into a low, barrel-vaulted room which smells

256

reassuringly of cigarette smoke. In the centre four tables have been pushed together to make a conference table; around the walls are stacks of newspapers, computer paper, and a jumble of keyboards and monitors waiting to be assembled. 'It's not great,' he says, 'But at least we won't be disturbed down here.'

'It's fine,' she says, although in fact it isn't. The makeshift look of the place makes her uneasy, in case it reflects the state of the investigation. She'd like to think of the police as a competent bunch, dissecting the forensic evidence, communing with Interpol, relentlessly chasing down the bad guys. Scotland Yard, the Criminal Justice System – all the things her father, with his chauvinist certainities, insisted the Brits did, not only first, but best. *No one to touch us, Ingrid.*

There are two ring-binders on the table, next to several cardboard boxes. On top of one of the boxes lies a pair of white gloves.What she hadn't realised is that the material hasn't been xeroxed. It will have to be read *in situ,* here in the room with sealed windows and trapped oppressive air.

It isn't as if she hasn't got enough on her plate already. So why is she sweating in a basement when she could be lying on the beach, taking a little time to adjust? Out of professional curiosity? – *melipnois* and *kerinthophagia* had certainly appealed to the sleuth in her – or simply because she was so flattered to be asked for help?

Yiannis collects used styrofoam cups from the table and crushes them into a brimming wasetbasket.

'Are you sure you're all right with this? I'm trying to get you a fee, but . . .'

'Don't worry about it,' she says quickly. She's already decided to keep the thing on an informal footing, at least till she's sure she can handle it.

He's been home to shower and change; in her mind's eye she sees him take his uniform down from its hanger, lace up his shiny black shoes. Men can just walk away, of course. Egos topped up by the night's elixirs, a brief kiss goodbye and then back to business. Maybe she should have warned Zoe about mornings like these, when there you were, toughing it out, while underneath you felt, well, *gutted* would do, *gutted* was the perfect word for it.

Stiff-armed, they stare at one another. Yiannis produces an awkward smile. 'Not exactly what I had in mind – "A professional relationship."'

'What *did* you have in mind, exactly?'

'I should have thought that was obvious by now.'

When he encloses her in his arms she tenses, smelling aftershave and smoke.

'Don't worry, there's no CCTV in here!' His voice is conspiratorial in her ear, a pillow-voice, breathing the night back into her. As his hand slithers up the nape of her neck she pulls away from him. Rage mounts up in her skull, like a pressure that can't be released. Until it clicks back into the compartment she usually keeps it in, she doesn't trust her skin with anyone.

'So,' she says brightly, 'Is there coffee, by any chance?'

He steps back and looks at her, perplexed. 'Sorry. I can get some, of course.'

Left alone, she sits down at the table and folds her hands in her lap, anxious not to do anything that could be construed as tampering with the evidence. The faint smell of incense that comes from the cardboard boxes is redolent of the funeral parlour. The white gloves are made of latex, not cotton, as they would be in the Ashmolean. They look alien, surgical. She eyes them squeamishly, thinking of the dusty box-files in the Myres archive. Alice's letters, written or typed on paper frail as insects' wings.

60 years is a long time, almost three generations. Death at a safe distance, rather than death in close-up.

Yiannis has told her that the body has been identified. Ivo Kruja, born Albania 1986: a boy young enough to be her son. How much time has to elapse, she wonders, before a corpse can decently be disjoined from the personal, the familial, and become public property? Surely she ought to know by now, where exactly Archaeology draws the line.

When Yiannis comes back with the coffee she asks if she has to wear the gloves but he says no, everything's been dusted for prints already.

'So what am I actually looking for?'

He sets one of the styrofoam cups in front of her and cautiously opens his own.

'At this stage, I guess, anything that strikes you. What kind of guy Kruja was? Any signs that he was a suicidal type, for instance?'

She points out that she's no pyschologist, to which Yiannis replies that he's no archaeologist, either. As he bends over her to open the first ring-binder she feels his breath warm against her cheek.

'Even if you just ran your eye over the chapters on Crete, it would help a lot.'

His cellphone rings abruptly, and he turns away to answer it. Although the conversation is in Greek she makes out her own name, pronounced importantly as *Kyria Lo-ri*. Wrinkling his brow, he covers the mouthpiece with his hand.

'Okay if I leave you alone for a while? I have to run over to Chania.'

Clearly it's a rhetorical question: already he's delving in his pocket for car keys. Ingrid nods; if anything, she feels relieved. Without Yiannis hanging over her, she might even be able to concentrate.

'If you need anything, just ask at Reception. I should be back by six.'

Halfway to the door he turns and eyes her with such intent that for a second she imagines he's going to lock her in with the evidence.

'I was hoping we could have dinner later, at my place.' He hesitates, squinting in a shaft of sunshine; although he's smiling tentatively the strain shows through, hollowing his cheeks and deepening the shadows under his eyes.

'In town?' she says, as her stomach performs a furtive somersault. She realises she has no idea where he lives.

'In Katomeli. If you'd like that?'

Before she can tell him whether she likes it or not, he surprises her by bursting out laughing. It's a youthful, artless laugh, one that simply doesn't countenance the possibility of being disappointed.

'I hope you realise,' he says, 'Before we go any further, I have to introduce you to my cat!'

She opens the first binder gingerly, but it smells of nothing. The first thing she notices is the small label stuck inside the front cover: a logo block-printed from a wood- or lino-cut, like something a child might produce in primary school. The two signs that make up the logo look remarkably like Linear B.

She takes her notebook out and checks her Mycenaean glossary, just to be sure. The first sign turns out to be *pe*. There are only half a dozen words on the list that begin with *pe*, so the second is easy to establish as *ma*.

Pleased with herself, she makes a note:

Linear B: *Pema*.

Greek restoration: *sperma*.

English translation: *seed*.

She puts on her glasses, lights a cigarette, and studies the Table of Contents.

Chapter 1: The Anatolian Hinterland

Hunter-gatherers to Neolithic settlers – maternal practices contrasted. Contraceptive effects of breast-feeding on demand (to 5 years) versus early weaning (1-2 years) in settled agricultural communities. Development of cereal crops and herds ensures ample food supply, resulting in population explosion. Domestication of animals requiring 1) male kill-off strategies 2) castration of majority of males.

Chapter 2: Evidence for Gynocentrism

Organisation of early Neolithic settlements mirrors organisation of the herd. Spread of human castration practices 6200-

4500 BCE mirroring historical development of animal castra-
tion. Mortuary evidence at Francthi Cave, Catal Hoyuk Level
V. Scarcity of adult male skeletons; Infant male skeletons
greatly outnumber infant female; Absence of male figurines;
Grave goods – important burials overwhelmingly female.

Chapter 3: The Iconic Evidence
No males represented after Level V1 at Catal Hoyuk. Bulls' or
cows' horns in the sacral chambers? The case for the horned
benches as loci for cult sacrifice. The chamber walls: clay
breasts with nipples of vulture-beaks and weasel skulls. Dis-
cussion of Melanie Klein's concept of the 'bad breast.' In-
culcation of fear and awe of the Great Mother. Arguments for
a symbolic transfer of potency from the wild bull to the
domesticating theoi. The matriarchal oikos linked to bull-
cults and bucrania.

Chapter 4: Death and the Harvest in the Near East
"The Last Sheaf" sacrifice for the ripe corn – killing of reaper
with spades and hoes. Bones of Adonis/Tammuz ground in mill.
Body-parts kept in seed-storage bins. Young dying vegetation
gods – Tammuz, Osiris, Dionysus, Attis, Orpheus at Eleusis.
Anat/Astarte "plaques" with depictions of seeds. Yearly cere-
mony of "Osiris beds" attested since Pre-Dynastic Egypt.

Chapter 5: The Sickle Moon and the Horned Mother Goddess
Canaanite Anat, the Heifer. Ugaritic Anath. Ashera of Pales-
tine. Ishtar of Uruk. Hathor the Cow-Goddess. Akakallis of
Crete. Sickles and castration tropes from Gaia to Anat. The
"sickle of adamant" used by Kronos to castrate Ouranos.
Canaanite Harvest Hymn of Anat: "with a sickle she winnows
him". Miniature clay cult-sickles in the Cretan zerinthos.

Chapter 6: The Dedication of Potency: Drones, Priests and Scribes
"Asinnu" as followers of Inanna – "maker of eunuchs". Isis
and Osiris. Essenes eunuch priests of Ephesian Artemis, head
priest Megabyzos or King Bee. Statue of Artemis hung with

offerings of bulls' testicles. Eunuchs and "officers" in the Old Testament. Arab essendelees. *Scythian* enarees *in high political and military office. Phrygian Kybele and the Mysteries of Attis. Ouranian Aphrodite in her castrating bee-form. Thracian cult of Dionysus. Freud's search for the phylogenetic or species memory of the "castration complex".*

Chapter 7: Kouretes and Korybants
Idean Dactyls – Mount Ida in Crete or Mount Ida in Phrygia? Kouretes/Korybants of Rhea/Kybele. Kybele = kybilis, the double axe. Willets: Kouretes founded Knossos and initiated cult of Kybele, Kouretic cults of Crete and Thracian cult of Dionysus substantially the same. Kouretes as protectors of infant Zeus in the Idean cave, aided by sacred bees or meliai. *Ida and Adrasteia* nymphoi *and "honey-nurses" to Zeus. Kouretes in myth first to domesticate cattle and discover the art of bee-keeping.*

Chapter 8: The Kouros as *Eniautos* or Year-Spirit
Periodicity – yearly death and resurrection of the young god. Minos as ennearos *– "9 year" or "full-grown" king? Inititation of the Kouros as* eniautos. *Rituals and rites of the Kouretic cult: the* dromenon *– mimic death and resurrection in the womb-cave of the* zerinthos; *Mimetic dance of the* hyporchema *at the July* Kronia *festival; Sacramental feast of the* omophagia; *Hymn of the Kouretes, "for fields of fruit, and for hives to bring increase".*

Chapter 9: Kouretes and Adorants
Artemis as Kourotrophos. *Apollo and Artemis as Kouros and Great Mother. The bull-sacrifice on the Hagia Triada sarcophagus. Kouretes as ministrants of the* Potnia Theron, *Mistress of the Animals. The fruits and flowers of the* eiresione *carried by the Kouros. Discussion of the dedicatory posture of the* eniautos/ adorant. *The* hieros gamos *or ritual marriage. Selection rituals of the* eniautos: 1) by foot-race 2) by bull in the tavrokatharpsia 3) by bees in the melipnois or kerinthophagia. *Inauguration of the new Year-King at the festival of the* Kronia.

41

Yiannis would have preferred to wait to hear Ingrid's take on the thesis, but when Vasilakis asked for an update, you provided it, and when he summoned you to Chania, you went.

The building which housed the Serious Crime Unit had recently been renovated, with the addition of silent, efficient lifts, and double-glazing on the windows to mute the bustle of the street below. The air-con, tuned to U.S. levels, flowed icily through his nostrils, putting a spring in his step.

Vasilakis had greeted him warmly, and ordered drinks from a young woman constable: coffee for Yiannis, mint tea for himself.

'For the digestion,' he said, patting his paunch. 'At our age, you know . . .'

They gossiped for a few moments about the Devil's Triangle while they waited for the drinks to arrive. On the desk Yiannis saw a framed snapshot of a young woman with a chubby infant in her arms. With an effort he remembered her name.

'It's Viktoria?' he asked, recalling that Vasilakis' daughter had been caught up in the anti-global protests in London some years ago; there had been a photograph of her cavorting on the steps of the Stock Exchange, in green dreadlocks and a pink tutu. The photo had eventually found its way into the pages of *Haniotika Nea* – another little scoop, he remembered, for the many-tentacled Martha Hourdaki.

'It is.' Vasilakis gazed adoringly at the snapshot. 'So I'm a grandfather now, Yianni, how about that?'

'A boy?' said Yiannis with a pang. Vasilakis was only a year older than he was: a proper age, indeed, to be a grandfather.

Vasilakis nodded. 'They've called him Andreas.'

'Congratulations, sir!' said Yiannis.

The drinks came with a saucer of *loukoumi*, baby-pink and powdered with icing-sugar. Vasilakis bared his teeth at the sweets and pushed the saucer towards him. Yiannis shook his head and was about to light a cigarette when he saw the No Smoking sign on the wall.

'So – this hippy Halcyon of yours.' Vasilakis tapped the report Yiannis had faxed through from Heraklion. 'How involved do you think they are?'

'They know a lot more than they're saying, sir. For a start I'd lay a bet that the Kruja kid didn't move out two months ago. I think he was there a lot more recently than that.'

'And there's no question he had company that night?' Vasilakis curled his lip. 'Our mysterious Melissa.'

'That's what I'm thinking, sir.'

Yiannis thought of mentioning the strange bee reference in the thesis, but in view of the Hourdaki connection he decided against it. If he was going to send his boss's blood pressure sky high, better to wait until the evidence was so solid that he could no longer avoid it.

'Well!' said Vasilakis, rubbing his hands together enthusiastically. 'I think it's time we pulled them in for questioning, don't you? Ask them nicely, of course . . . but make sure you put it out to the press, see if we can rattle a few cages.' He took a sip of his mint tea and gave Yiannis an avuncular grin. 'First thing is to get the paperwork on your side. Check everything – residency, bank statements, business licences. Scare them a bit. They run some kind of clinic, don't they? So, medical qualifications, whatever you can drag up.'

Yiannis tried to conceal his pleasure. 'And DNA samples, sir? From the women?'

Vasilakis nodded. 'I'm trusting you on this one, Yianni.'

'Thank you, sir,' said Yiannis. On second thoughts he took a piece of *loukoumi* from the saucer and popped it into his mouth. It was firm, yet gelatinous, and definitely tasted of roses.

'You'll have Abbot and Costello, of course.'

'Fine, sir,' said Yiannis insincerely. Abbot was obvious, spatially speaking, so he supposed the runty Kounidis must be Costello.

'And I'm putting Kyriaki back on it full time. Poor girl's been a bit strung out lately, she needs a change of scene.'

'The ambulance shooting?'

Vasilakis shrugged.'Well, that too. Her fiance dumped her.'

'I'm sorry to hear that, sir,' said Yiannis.

*

On the way back from Chania he reviewed those items he thought were in the fridge, and those he still had to purchase. He would do lamb kebabs with peppers, he decided, roast sweetcorn, sardines with fennel. He'd have to hose down the fly-blown garden chairs, fire up the old barbecue and hope it didn't punish him on grounds of grave neglect.

His body, meanwhile, occupied that no-man's-land between memory and imagination. His lips smiled dreamily, his palms on the steering wheel felt tender and alert. Although he couldn't actually remember Ingrid touching him there, the inner margins of his arms seemed to possess a prickling life of their own, as if there was an invisible seam beneath the skin along which his body, originally conjoined with hers, now itched to be restored to its greater Platonic whole.

He was aware of oleanders twinkling at the roadside, a tanker gliding far out at sea, heading for Souda Bay. As he came over the headland the main beach of Georgiopoli came into view, jam-packed with sunbeds and umbrellas. The smaller beach to the west of it, the one favoured by Greeks and a few discriminating tourists, was tranquil and poplar-shaded. The sand there was almost pure white, the water cooled by two deep clear streams which flowed down from the heights of the Lefka Ori. He and Dora had canoed up the larger stream one blistering afternoon, and had spotted huge turtles, peaceful and purple-shelled on the sandy bottom. There was a good fish taverna at one end of the beach, and at the other a rickety bar roofed with palm-leaves, with a sign in English announcing it as *The Cretin Club*. He'd never had the heart to tip off the owner.

Just past the Georgiopoli turn-off a rescue truck passed him at speed: there was some kind of blockage on the westbound carriageway, about 500 metres ahead. As he got closer he saw an ambulance, police motorbikes. A tour bus was angled across the inside lane, its nose half way up the verge. Sprawled across the tarmac was the steel mesh of a snare, its trident-like teeth glinting in the sun. A second snare had become entangled with the back fender, and trailed behind like a wedding veil. Slowing, he flashed his lights and did a tight U turn.

There was a strong smell of burning rubber, although fortunately no sign of flames. He got out and went over to a traffic cop who was standing with arms akimbo, staring bemusedly at the front axle of the bus.

'They sure know how to make a tyre, these Germans! Bloody bus went straight through three snares before we stopped it.' When he kicked the tread the tyre subsided, expelling a breath of acrid air.

'What's up?' said Yiannis.

'He only stole it, didn't he!' The cop jerked his head at a youth who sat on the verge, holding a wad of cotton wool to his forehead; a paramedic crouched beside him, fiddling with a blood pressure cuff. 'We've been chasing the wanker all the way from Heraklion!'

The boy looked all of 14, hardly old enough to shave – just a skinny schoolkid in laundered shorts and a blood-spotted white T shirt. A school satchel spilled books on to the scrubby grass beside him.

'Drunk?' Yiannis asked.

The cop shook his head. 'Not a trace. Says his girlfriend dumped him. Spots the bus with the keys in the ignition and decides to take a joyride.' He shrugged lugubriously at the queue of cars. 'So here we are.'

Traffic cones had been laid in an arc, and two officers were directing the backed-up westbound traffic into the eastbound lane. In both directions the long flat ribbon of the road lay under a luminous haze of exhaust fumes.

'A rush of blood to the head, eh?' said Yiannis.

'Hormones, more like.'

Yiannis looked at his watch. It was already 5.30. 'You're okay here?'

The officer's sigh was long-suffering. 'Yeah, we're good.'

Yiannis said his yassous and got back into the car. Angry citizens glared at him as he slipped back into the eastbound lane and accelerated past the growing queue. In his rearview mirror the sun-struck scene receded: they were beginning to winch the bus up on to the flatbed. With its muzzle suspended a metre clear of the road, its great glossy bulk looked netted and helpless, like a felled bull.

42

She reads with growing fascination, snorting sceptically from time to time, shaking her head in exasperation at the audacity of the thing. If Kruja were her student, she'd have a thing or two to say about his wilder extrapolations, and the way he bases them on highly selective evidence. Certainly she'd be going through the footnoted references with a fine-tooth comb.

The trouble is that the sheer obsessiveness of the piece is infectious. Seeds and sickles, the castration complex – all heady stuff in this day and age. It's a far more absorbing read than the dissertations she usually supervises – by students with an eye on their career prospects, who're careful to parrot the pet ideas of their professors and quite content, it seems, to document minutiae until the cows come home.

Cigarette ends mount up in the ashtray. The fluorescent strip-lights bolted into the barrel-vaulted the ceiling are giving her a headache.

She follows the trail of the *sperma,* from the Harvest-hymn of the Canaanite goddess Anat to the royal funerary rites of Middle Kingdom Egypt. She learns that barley seeds were sown in silt-filled wooden moulds made in the form of the god Osiris. The 'Coffin Texts', from which Kruja quotes at length, specify the number of days the seeds must be watered until they sprouted, which apparently marked the moment when the dead monarch transmuted into 'the life that comes from Osiris.' Without pausing for breath, Kruja's whistle-stop tour of the Near East proceeded to Syria, where women sowed 'Adonis gardens' of herbs and barley in yearly rites to commemorate the death of Adonis/Tammuz, Aphrodite's lover.

Outside the high barred windows, bare summer legs pass by on the pavement. Sunbeams slant off the polished bodywork of parked cars. Without a doubt, Kruja's compass is far too ambitious, his arguments totalising, and his conclusions dubious. But couldn't you say the same of Graves, of Gimbutas? Their work doesn't exactly meet the rigorous criteria of scholarship, but they've never been off the best-seller lists. In fact she can think of several publishers who'd snap the thing up – the same ones, naturally, who wouldn't touch her own little book with a bargepole!

To be cynical about it, Kruja's material is quite sexy enough for a bidding war – which with the best will in the world couldn't be said of Alice Kober. Nothing sensational about Kober's devotion to solid proof and peer review: nothing that would sparkle or catch the light. Just careful clearing of the ground, and progression in minute, shadowy increments. A stark contrast, indeed, to Kruja's wild epiphanies.

Chalk and cheese, she thinks. Logic and analogic: the old antithesis of science versus art, ritual, the ecstatic imagination.

Linear B as Left Brain, Linear A as Right.

Chapter 3 has her referring to the appendices at the back of the binder. There's a photocopy of one of Mellaart's drawings of the excavations at Catal Hoyuk. The huge clay breasts that protrude from the walls of the underground chamber look every bit as lethal as they sound in Kruja's text. Plastered white, with those beaky, persecutory nipples. Breasts that symbolise the power to give life, but also the power to snuff it out.

According to Melanie Klein, the mother's breast was feared and hated by the infant just as intensely as it was loved. Ingrid has a nodding acquaintance with Klein's theories, but no desire at all to snuggle up to them: if you want to sleep at night, there are some strata of the psyche you'd do well not to excavate.

In Mellaart's drawing, the chamber looks like the ideal dreamscape of a sado-masochist. The stone benches in the chamber resemble nursery cots, fenced in by barricades of horns. Kruja is arguing – with noticeable relish – that the benches were the *loci* for sacrifice. Ingrid is inclined to agree. Between the horns there's a space about 2 metres long, and just wide enough to tie a young man down.

The more she reads, the more a sense of disturbance grows in her. If Kruja is so in thrall to his themes, isn't there something perverse – perverted, even – in his entrancement? She feels breathless and overcharged, and shifts uncomfortably in her seat. The poor kid is dead, and that's bad and sad enough. So why this reflexive urge to giggle? Taking off her glasses, she smooths her brow with her fingers. For a second she teeters on the edge of hilarity, as if Kruja has tapped some gleeful sadistic source in her.

Maxine, she decides, would have summed him up. Back in the old days, Maxine had been merciless. While Ingrid was doing her Teaching Certificate, Maxine was working shifts at a feminist magazine in Bloomsbury, manning – or rather womanning – the switchboard.

A surprising number of her callers, she said, were men.

'They start off all supportive,' she complained, 'wanting to do their bit for 'the Movement', saying how much they admire strong women, and so on, and if you don't stop them right there you can bet your bottom dollar they'll end up begging to lick your Doc Martens or hoover your living-room in the buff!'

Maxine's theory was that those sad and ludicrous masochists had been lurking under the surface all along. Hosts of them, like lugworms waiting for the tide to turn. 'Poor lambs. Must have been tough on them, having to be macho for so many millenia.'

Although it's already 5 o'clock it's still hot as hell in the basement. Her linen trousers stick damply to the canvas seat of her chair. She checks her face in her compact mirror: her skin looks bleached under the strip-lights, the few freckles standing out blackly. In her eyes there's a glazed, hectic expression.

It's time to take stock, to deliver her considered opinion.

She kicks off her sandals, rolls her trouser legs above her knees, and tries to be objective.

Kruja is attempting to lay out a bold cultural-anthropological hypothesis about the origins of modern civilisation and gender relations. Arguing from the first instances of animal domestication around 7000 BCE, he proposes a parallel development in human populations. This is along the lines that, just as management of the herd meant controlling the disruptive sexual energies of the male animal, so the burgeoning human settlements of the Neolithic, first, killed off a proportion of males in infancy and, later, castrated a substantial proportion at the onset of puberty.

With regard to Neolithic religious cult, Kruja argues for
(a) a symbolic transfer of potency from the now-conquered wild bull to an all powerful 'domestic' goddess (unfortunately oikos, *with its larger connotations of homeland, clan, settlement, has no direct equivalent in English).*
(b) fertility cults of death and rebirth, arising from a new dependence on the agricultural year, with its revolutionary technologies of sowing, reaping, threshing etc.

To back up his arguments Kruja employs an impressive battery of references from recent work in animal paleopathology, forensic archaeology, and skeletal analysis.
He then attempts to trace a continuum from the castrated/dismembered gods of the Near East to the Kouretic cults of Crete, although in the Cretan story the emphasis seems to be less on actual physical dismemberment than on offertory rituals of tribute and submission.

The young male as intermediary vis-a-vis the Goddess is not new territory, but, having taken as his starting-point such a radical premise, Kruja pushes his conclusions much farther than most scholars would care to venture, and certainly farther than anything produced by the 'Engendering Archaeology' feminists, whose work he draws upon.

271

*However, his argument falls apart somewhat in the final – unfinished – chapter. It's possible, of course, that he simply ran out of time, or out of steam, but frankly, if I were his supervisor I would have serious concerns about some kind of mental breakdown.**

*See Appendix 23, which I'm 90 per cent sure is a fiction. Kruja has given the source as Book V1 of Diodorus Siculus, but this is completely spurious, given that Books V1 to X1 of Diodorus were lost centuries ago. It's also written in the first person, which Books 1-V certainly were not, and which in any case is unlikely to have been in usage in such a form as early as 60 BCE. It looks very much as if Kruja, for whatever reason, has simply abandoned academic discourse here, and taken refuge in overheated fantasy.

43

Yiannis got to the Chania Gate just in time for the rush-hour snarl-up, and sat sweltering under the shell-scarred section of the CityWall where martyrs had been made, once, and where nowadays the gay fraternity liked to cruise riskily by moonlight.

Since it was now too late to detour via the Market he went straight up Kalokairinou to the station, where he found Ingrid, not in the basement, but sitting at a borrowed computer in the bustle of the Co-ops office.

'Just finished,' she said, glancing up at him; she looked flushed and pleased with herself, bright with the patina of collective industry. 'How many copies do you need?'

'Can you do four? Sorry, five – you'll want one for yourself.'

She pressed Print and stood up, flashing a smile at the young constable who stood waiting to reclaim his machine.

Downstairs Yiannis collated the copies and filed them in the dossier. The air seemed cooler than before, and the ashtrays had been emptied; he saw that Ingrid had procured a fan from somewhere, which was more than he had managed.

'Aren't you going to read it?' she asked, with such schoolgirlish eagerness that he wanted to pat her on the head and give her the gold star she so clearly wanted. His mind stopped a millimetre short of picturing her at fifteen, sixteen.

He shook his head, smiling. 'Later. You've got your copy?'

She shrugged and patted her briefcase.

'Then I think it's time we got out of here, don't you?'

'Hang on a minute.' Opening one of the binders, Ingrid

273

extracted two pages from a section at the back. 'I think you should xerox this bit.'

In the car he slipped a bouzouki cd into the player and beat time on the steering wheel as they crawled through the evening traffic. At the lights at the top of Ikarou he glanced over at her, smiling with disbelief. She looked so demure with her briefcase on her lap, bloused, trousered, and ladylike – deceptively so, he thought, but did not say.

'What?' she demanded.

'I'm just checking you're actually here in the flesh!'

Ingrid laughed. 'Well I'd say so. Although I couldn't be a hundred per cent sure.'

She asked permission to light a cigarette, and blew the smoke conscientiously out of the window. He watched her covertly, finding it hard to transpose her unfamiliar presence into the known confines of his house, let alone into the unknown spaces of his future.

Beyond the perimeter fence of the airport the coastal strip was a desert of dishevelled sand dunes and old concrete Air Force bunkers. A light haze of benzene fumes spread a glittering veil across the sea.

'Amnisos!' Ingrid exclaimed, pointing out a battered sign-post.

He looked at her, surprised. 'You want to go there?'

'Just for a drink, maybe? You know it was the ancient port of Knossos?'

Yiannis hesitated, thinking about the shopping and, more particularly, the cooking, which wasn't a task he liked to hurry. He was also conscious of the mounting pressure of the case. Judging by what Vasilakis had said, there would be very little resembling leave from now on, so he could kiss goodbye to his days off, and thus, he feared, to time he wanted very much to devote to Ingrid. Amnisos, as far as he knew, was a dump, but she was gazing so longingly at the wind-blasted landscape that he made a snap decision. He signalled left and turned off on to the winding road that hugged the coastline.

Ingrid nodded, smiling gratefully. 'I could really do with some air.' As she spoke an Airbus 340 blundered overhead, straining to slow down in time to rendezvous with the runway.

Yiannis laughed. 'As long as you're not too fussy about the quality.'

A couple of kilometres to the east, almost directly under the flight path, the village of Amnisos comprised a straggle of houses, a handful of shops, and one or two beach tavernas.He stopped beside one which was little more than a concrete platform roofed with corrugated plastic sheeting. Seaward of the concrete a few tables and chairs had been placed on a strip of sand. The place was deserted, which was no surprise to Yiannis. Ingrid, however, was already out of the car, and heading with a singularly determined stride towards the shore.

He left the car windows open and followed her past tubs of wind-tattered geraniums to a table at the edge of the sea.

'It's okay here?'

'*Exaretiko*,' she enthused. She had moved a white plastic chair so that the waves lapped at its very ankles, and now she slipped off her sandals and, grinning happily, submerged her feet in the sea. Linking her fingers, she stretched both arms above her head.

'A-mi-ni-so' she recited, 'A-mi-ni-si-jo, A-mi-ni-si-ja.' She wriggled her shoulderblades, her breath sighing out in a small explosion of contentment

He raised his eyebrows, waiting for a translation which didn't come. 'Don't worry, your secret's safe with me.'

Ingrid's eyes sparked at him. 'Sorry – Amnisos, Amnesian men, Amnesian women. It was in one of Kober's triplets. You could say Amnisos was the word that cracked the code.'

He gazed at her, baffled. 'Amnesian' conjured up memory and the loss of it; for a second he imagined gangs of geriatric citizens tottering along the shore, beachcombing for scraps of a long-lost past.

'*Ti thelete?*' A youth in flip-flops had wandered across the road from the *zacharoplasteion* and now presented himself

275

in front of them, his eyes flickering over Ingrid's indecorous feet.

'*Tha ithela mia portakalada*,' she enunciated gravely.

Before the youth could smirk at this quaintly polite locution, Yiannis frowned at him and ordered a beer.

'How so?' he asked.

'Well, an identifiable proper name was worth its weight in gold. Like Ptolemy and Cleopatra in the decipherment of Egyptian Hieroglyphic.' She hesitated fractionally, darting a sideways glance at him. Her hair was haloed by sun, gilt-edged as an ikon against the sombre blue background of sea. 'Are you really sure you want to hear this? It's pretty technical.'

Stroked by the breeze, he smiled hospitably. 'No really. I'm curious now.' Noticing that the wavelets were encroaching on the table legs, he put his feet up on a chair; when in uniform, you didn't take your shoes off.

It was a question of word-endings, he gathered. The Kober woman had identified clusters of them on the Linear B tablets; meanwhile, the Ventris guy was trying out different sounds against the various signs, to see if he could come up with anything that resembled a known language.

The drinks came with a dish of small green olives wrenched too early from the tree. Ingrid drank deeply and wiped her mouth with her hand.

'Since the triplets were only found on the Knossos tablets, he reckoned they might refer to local place names. Good guesswork, as it turned out.'

Ventris, she went on, had already allocated the values 'a' and 'ni' to two of the signs (hypothetically – it all sounded very hypothetical to Yiannis). Going on the basis of A-mi-ni-so, he'd postulated 'mi' and 'so' for the remaining two signs in the sequence. Then – by a process of reasoning which even Ingrid faltered over, and Yiannis didn't even attempt to grasp (he'd always been useless at crosswords) Ventris had deduced other combinations. When applied to some of the sequences in the other triplets, these syllables had produced Ko-no-so (for Knossos) and Pa-i-to (for Phaistos).

'Eureka!' said Yiannis, who felt like giving the guy a round of applause.

Ingrid pursed her lips. 'Well, not quite. But at least it put him on the right track. It's what finally persuaded him that Linear B was actually an archaic form of Greek, not Etruscan or whatever.'

'So what did your lady scholar make of that?'

'Alice?' Ingrid frowned faintly. 'This was 1952. She'd been dead two years by then.'

A silver grey fighter streaked towards the coast, on an exact parallel with the horizon. It banked almost overhead and slunk down, shark-like, to belly-skim the sea. He had a split second to admire the plane before the roar caught up with them.

Ingrid ducked and covered her ears with her hands.

'Jesus!' she said, staring after it.

Her face was so affronted that Yiannis smiled wryly at her; he didn't like to say I told you so.

*

Yiannis fetched the old leather bellows from the shed and gusted air into the stubborn black heart of the charcoal. The barbecue wasn't responding to his persuasions; never a natural arsonist, he seemed to have lost skills learned at his father's knee and perfected, or so he'd thought, in the back yards of Melbourne.

'You're actually going to cook?' Ingrid had asked; she'd sounded so surprised that he immediately placed the patio out of bounds. If he was going to make an idiot of himself, he preferred to do it unsupervised.

Banished, she'd taken her ouzo down to the end of the garden, where she appeared to be communing with his father's lemon grove. Watching covertly, he saw her pinch the fruit to test its ripeness, rub the gloss on the leaves between thumb and forefinger, and examine the undersides of the leaves for parasites, all with the kind of rapt attention she

277

might have bestowed on an artefact dug up from some royal Mesopotamian tomb. Kore, meanwhile, sat at her feet, looking up inquisitively to see what on earth she found so interesting.

He was reminded of the way his father had pored over the intricate machinery of watches, their tiny cogs and springs. It struck him that he would have liked Ingrid, that they shared, in fact, some silent, avid quality of concentration.

He lit the citronella candles he'd bought and placed them on the table. The fennel and sweetcorn waited on a plate, sprayed with oil from the labour-saving aerosol Markos had recommended, and the souvlaki were ready on their sticks. At the check-out Markos had eyed Ingrid curiously, expecting, no doubt, to be introduced. Conscious that Dora was also one of his regular customers, Yiannis had denied him that particular pleasure.

The coals in the barbecue were giving out no more than a shy and hesitant glow. He picked up the bellows and redoubled his efforts; having hefted the charcoal from the shop, he wasn't going to give up so easily. After a moment or two sparks began to scatter out like fireflies in the dusk, and flames licked around the nozzle of the bellows, sucking at the jets of air. A pungent smoke belched from the barbecue. He stood back and wiped sweat from his forehead, realising he should have started it earlier, given the heat time to consolidate.

Ingrid had drifted up from the garden, and now appeared through the pall of smoke.

'Hephaestos at his forge,' she observed, setting two lemons on the table. 'I see we could be here for quite some time.'

'Go!' he said, waving the tongs threateningly.

Ingrid grinned at him and slipped through the open French windows into the sitting room. Cold-shouldering the sardines, the cat followed her. He could see the two of them inside, pale-haired and prowling in the lamplight.

He spread tinfoil on the grill and laid on the souvlaki sticks and the quartered fennel. Remembering that corncobs were best done on the bare rungs, he gave them an extra spray of oil for good measure.

Ingrid had reappeared in the doorway. 'Is it safe to set the table?'

'I guess so. Sardines don't take any time at all, do they.' He eyed the coals doubtfully; at least the meat was beginning to sizzle. He heard her clattering around in the kitchen. After a while she came back out carrying a tray of plates and glasses.

'Just sit!' she ordered, pouring him a glass of wine.

He drank gratefully and lit a cigarette. There was oil everywhere, on his fingers, on his shorts, a forensic splatter on his T shirt. Even oil-stains, now, on his cigarette. He watched her set out plates, napkins, cutlery.

Beyond the garden wall some girls passed by on the road, chattering about shampoos and earrings, and Ingrid cocked her head, listening.

'You look so young' she said suddenly. 'In the wedding photograph.'

Yiannis felt his chest tighten. 'I was twenty-five.'

'That *is* young.'

'Yes,' Yiannis said.

'Karen's lovely. So full of life.'

As she said it he felt a surge of hopelessness; for a second he could have howled like a dog for his lost love, and his oil-stained fingers, even for the jilted schoolkid and his hare-brained joyride. Apparently it wasn't enough to have his heart broken, he'd wanted to break his stupid neck as well.

Jumping up, he seized the tongs and began to turn over the souvlaki.

'I'm sorry. I didn't mean to intrude.'

He shrugged, his back turned to her. 'It's time I put them away, anyway.' Even to his own ears it didn't sound convincing.

'But why should you?'

Yiannis could think of no reply to this. He felt worn out suddenly, his nerves run ragged. He began to lay out the sardines carefully, in military rows. There was a smell of hot oil and charring fish. Kore stalked out on to the patio and sat at a safe distance, ogling him expectantly. He glowered back at her, weighed down by the pressure of wanting everything to be perfect. He began to transfer the souvlaki to a serving dish.

Ingrid had picked up a knife and was cutting lemons into quarters. After a concentrated silence she said, 'So what happens to his things?'

He looked at her across the barbecue. Through the blue heat-shimmer she wavered like an apparition.

'Kruja's?' he said reluctantly. A solitary priest, he thought, a decent burial paid for by the State. There were people whose job it was to arrange such things. He had no idea what would happen to the personal effects, and wondered dully why she had brought up the subject.

'I'm not sure.' He thought of the patched jeans, the socks and undershorts, the intricately woven waistcoat. A mother would have held them against her cheek, inhaling the smell of him; she would have traced each darn precisely, like a cartographer of pain.

Karen's mother had cleared the wardrobe of trouser-suits and dresses, rarely worn; she'd packed them into black bin bags and driven them to the local St.Vincent de Paul's. She'd distributed medical books, tennis raquets, and scuba gear to Karen's friends, and arranged for the sale of the furniture. He'd never known what she did with the underwear she cleared from the chest of drawers. He had kept only the necklace he'd given Karen, a lozenge of New Zealand jade on a silver chain. That and her wedding ring.

He stuck a skewer in the fennel and turned the corn-cobs over to check the rate of their cremation. It would be winter in Melbourne now, the South-Westerlies bringing their cold drizzle in across the sea. Hardly the barbecue season.

The sardines were almost ready. He squeezed lemon on them and watched the juices fizz and sputter on the tinfoil.

'You've got a serious amount of food there!' Ingrid observed, and they both started laughing, for it was true, there was more than enough to feed a family of five.

'I really hope you're hungry,' he said.

*

Yiannis read through the photocopied appendix, his hand clamped firmly on Ingrid's knee.

Not to fear the bee
nor to hate it
but to learn
to be meet and fit
to live in the honeycomb

The name of the eunuch is Melikertes, the honey-cutter, he who tends the hive on the west terrace.

This sour person must be flattered and sweetened constantly. Should he express a wish to have the blinds drawn over against the sharpness of the light, or a sudden thirst for a jug of barley beer, I must say yes please, and jump to it. Also must fetch for him his necessaries among which is the stinking urine of pregnant mares, said to wither the little growth left in the beard, and soften the ugliness of a face such as his.

Although I myself have seen no improvement, I must lie, and say yes to his queries, and hold the mirror before his face so that he may admire himself. He is like a great golden pear, with smooth nails, red lips, and long cunning toes like a monkey.

This person who is not my ally, unhappily must become so. His eyes feast on my oiled limbs as I flex in preparation for the somersault. His nostrils scent for my blood, just as mine smell his wish that my comrades will fail to execute the catch, and the bull trample and gore my fallen body, as is its holy nature.

This person deliberately leaves the palm-leaf screens ajar so that I may witness certain services he performs for the lady in the course of her bathing. Pride oozes from him like meko-

281

nium juice from a poppy – but how, tell me, is there cause for pride, when everyone knows he is only permitted to serve her because no issue can come from it?

Those of us who are eligibles are taught that the bees are the truest and final test, but all of us know the rumours. The bees may be pacified with cypress-wood smoke, or angered by echoes or cymbal-clashes. And he who has the trick of this can twist fate one way or the other.

Ever since the cutting of the forelock I have been made ready. Like a horse in a stable I have been bred for her, fed and watered for her. I have completed the tests of the taurokatharpsia for one year without a scar, and can stand before her unmarked.

The eyes of the lady tell me I please her, but the last word will come, as the first did, from the bees.

The one that the bees love will be Prince of the Lilies.

'Maybe he just downloaded it from some cheesy website,' Ingrid suggested. Kore had draped herself along the back of the sofa. Her blonde head was inches from Ingrid's, her green gaze fixed adoringly on her hair, as if she'd just discovered a long-lost sibling.

'Maybe,' he conceded, but he didn't think so. He finished his Metaxa and set the glass down on the coffee table. Already his mind was sketching out a love story, a tale of trial and tribulation. The lover braving hell and high water to win his girl and find his happy ending.

Ingrid was looking at him dubiously. 'The test by bees is pretty hard to imagine.'

'Even if you wanted to imagine it!' he retorted. The image of the body etched in his memory was one of abandonment, in every sense of the word. But if the corpse now turned out to have a voice, and that voice implied a degree of collusion? Something in him recoiled from the thought; he felt as though he'd stepped inside the sticky flesh, shared in its arousal. Squaring up the pages, he slapped them down on the coffee table to rid himself of the contagion.'You reckon he was a bit unhinged, then?'

282

'Well, don't you find the castration stuff just a touch perverse? In a man, I mean?'

Yiannis thought for a moment. He said a little defensively, 'And in a woman it wouldn't be?'

'Maybe more understandable, though?'

When he opened his mouth to object twin pairs of pale eyes stared back at him: a female cabbal, daring him to contradict. 'Why do I get the feeling that you're ganging up on me?'

'You know what I really think? It may be a new variation but it's the same old theme: all women are maenads at heart.' Yawning, Ingrid seized the cat and transferred her unceremoniously to her lap, where she rolled on her back in ecstasy and showed off every shameless thing she'd got. 'Isn't that right, Kore?'

Yiannis laughed. For a second he felt almost dizzy with relief, just to see Ingrid at his side, warm, soft, and smiling at him like an ordinary mortal. She tapped the cat's brow lightly, as if bestowing a curse or a blessng. 'As for this little honey-breather, she's going straight into my rucksack!'

'No way,' he said automatically. '*She'll* never leave me.' The emphasis had been unintentional. He leaned over to tickle the cat's snowy belly, avoiding Ingrid's eyes. 'Exhibitionist,' he scolded her. As if sensing a change in the atmosphere, Kore righted herself, slipped off Ingrid's lap, and strolled out into the darkness.

Yiannis was getting tired of sitting sedately, thigh to thigh on the sofa. It was getting late. Moths which had come in through the open windows banged blindly at the lampshades.

In the silence he touched his fingertips to the nape of Ingrid's neck. She closed her eyes, shivered, and went absolutely still. When he took her hands and pulled her to her feet she looked at him from some distant, dazed place.

'It's been a long day,' he said, and led her through to the bedroom, where nothing, by any stretch of the imagination, could be said to be sedate.

44

Ingrid wakes to the sound of a shower running. When she opens her eyes she sees a white cat sitting on the end of the bed, washing itself. Then Yiannis pads into the room, a sarong tied round his waist.

'So who were you fighting with?'

'Fighting?' she says, taken aback.

'In the night.' He towels his wet hair, grinning at her. 'I barely escaped with my life.'

The image that floats back to her is of someone or something creepily sewn up in a sack, like a pauper's corpse. In the dream she was flailing around, feeling for light switches in the blackout. A smothering darkness, an invisible assailant so swaddled and padded that she couldn't land a punch on it.

'Coffee's on,' he announces, drawing back the curtains. 'If you get up now I can give you a lift.' He has brought her a bath-towel, a thick fluffy navy-blue one which is pleasingly masculine. 'Hungover? he enquires, clean-shaven, clean-limbed, and smiling sweetly through a sunbeam.

Groaning, she shields her eyes with her hand. Although she wasn't drunk last night – she had no more than a couple of glasses of wine, and a Metaxa after dinner – she's dull and decentred, at the stage of knowing that depressives shouldn't drink at all. Hungover, though, isn't exactly what she feels. What she feels is belligerent. She only wishes he'd give her a reason to be.

She remembers lighting a cigarette afterwards, Yiannis with his hands clasped behind his head, watching her. 'It's a bit like sleeping with Jean-Paul Belmondo' he said pleasantly, and chuckled. Or perhaps she dreamt that too. She decides to resent him in any case, for putting her at a disadvantage. 'Too

284

much pleasure,' she complains, ramping herself up against the pillows. 'Mr. Knox always gets his revenge.'

Yiannis laughs. 'Sorry about that!'

'What else do you expect from a Scot?'

She watches him pull a pair of spanking white pants from the dressing table drawer. Smirking, he drops the sarong and steps into them. His penis dangles, relaxed. The colour isn't that aggressive sort of red, but a smooth cafe au lait tinged with rose. He opens the wardrobe and takes out his black trousers; inside she glimpses a uniform jacket on a hanger, its bright buttons glinting behind polythene. The trousers go on, then the short-sleeved uniform shirt.

At the bedroom door he pauses, tucking the shirt primly into the waistband of his trousers. She wonders where he keeps the bulky belt that holds the radio, the holster, and the gun.

'Do Scots take milk in their coffee?'

'They do. At least this one does.' She knows she should smile but she isn't going to.

She gets out of bed and picks up the navy-blue bath-towel. The cat blinks up at her, purring. The only mirror in the room is on the inside of the wardrobe door. She stands in front of it, warming herself in a shaft of sun. The sight of her body reassures her. Her stomach is flat between her hip bones; her breasts, on which no child has suckled, would certainly still pass the pencil test. Against the suntan her nipples are innocently pink: no sign of Kruja's vulture-beaks or weasel skulls, nothing that could possibly scare the pants off a man.

Next door Yiannis is clattering in the kitchen, talking to the cat in Greek. 'I'm making toast,' he shouts, 'if you want some.'

*

The sun glares through the windscreen straight into her eyes. She puts on her sunglasses and pulls the visor down. A flatbed truck is bowling along ahead of them; on the back of it a wheelbarrow lies upside down on a mound of gravel. Chained to the side of the truck, a snouty hound perches precariously on top of the mound; it looks like the dog on the old HMV label, the one that smiled ingratiatingly at the bullhorn. It looks happy, she thinks, in its chains.

'You don't have to go, you know,' Yiannis says suddenly. 'You could stay till the end of the month, at least.' His eyes flicker at her, questing. 'I can have a word with Gaylene. It shouldn't be a problem to change the ticket.'

For a moment she's speechless. But of course he can do that sort of thing – pull strings, call in favours. Swing it for her, so that she'll be well and truly beholden. She fumbles in her bag for her cigarettes, takes one out, and lights it with an unsteady hand. HMV, she remembers, stands for His Master's Voice. When the truck ahead signals and swerves sharply to the right the hound corrects expertly, like a pillion rider. Just watching it makes her feel queasy. She knows she's as capable as the next woman of following a man around abjectly, like a dog.

To the north the expanse of the sea breathes out, glimmering. From here, London feels like a planet you'd never want to land on, a toxic grid of noise, dirt, interference. She pictures the return: the descent through cloud-stricken skies, the cramped 30's semis of the suburbs, the testosterone Turks blasting their horns at pedestrians on the zebra crossings in the Square. All the hyped up kids on the buses, texting, bellowing, chucking Macdonalds' cartons on the floor. Gnawed spare ribs sticky with barbecue sauce, whole heaps of chips under the seats. Who but a masochist wouldn't choose to stay here in blueness, on a sea-girt island rising from the haze?

'Look, I'll be sorry to leave, of course I will, but . . .'

'But?' Yiannis echoes, impatience thrumming in his voice. The air is so dry that the smoke stings her throat; she gives up on the cigarette, crushing it out in the ashtray. After a moment he announces, 'You're not happy in your life.'

Her first instinct is to lie, to invoke fictitious Summer

Schools, Publishers' deadlines. The more she compares her life to his, the more it loses substance, won't stand up to close scrutiny, and the truth – that no immediate commitments, personal or professional, call her back – threatens to leave her without a leg to stand on.

'What gives you that impression?'

Yiannis shrugs at the road; his profile has a dark-browed, determined look to it. 'I *know* this.'

She looks at him incredulously. 'Which means I can change it, just like that?'

Yiannis clicks his tongue against his teeth. '*Change!*' he says haughtily, '*Change* is the one absolutely certain thing in life. Of course, whether it will be the change you *want* . . .'

This Socratic pronouncement stops her short. 'How fatalistic can you get?'

He eyes her, his face sardonic. 'What else do you expect from a Greek?'

She sees the Panomeli signpost approaching at speed. Sighing, Yiannis signals and turns left on to the old road.

'So where are we going with this, Ingrid?'

The Apollo Studios loom up ahead; on the balconies people are already breakfasting, tilting their faces to suck up the early rays of the sun.

'Going with it?' She looks at him, dismayed. 'Isn't it a bit soon for . . .?' For what, she wonders: regrets? Apologies? Ultimatums? A sluggishness seems to have overtaken her mind; in her lap her fingers are tentacled together, thoroughly entangled, as if she's literally wringing her hands. 'Can't we just leave things . . . as they are?'

As soon as she's said it the heat rises to her face. She's heard that lame old line too many times not to know it simply won't wash.

When Yiannis steps on the brake she braces herself against the dashboard. The car swerves, and stops with a jolt half-way up the verge. 'For Christ's sake!' she cries.

He snaps the ignition off, throws his hands in the air, and

thumps them down on the steering-wheel. 'Is this how it's done in London? Is it? You'll sleep with me, but you'll never say my name?'

In the wing mirror a crocodile of white-legged tourists straggles out of the gate of the Studios. Encumbered by buggies and airbeds, they're heading along the road towards the car. The engine, taken by surprise, ticks and cools.

'Say it now, Ingrid!' Seizing her hands, Yiannis yanks her round to face him. 'Say "Yianni"!'

Instinctively she resists, and there's a small ridiculous scuffle which she lets him win, if only because the first of the tourists are passing by: a sunhatted guy with a paunch, and a fat young woman pushing a toddler in a buggy. They glance shyly at Yiannis' uniform and murmur hopeful *kalimeras*. Receiving no response, they exchange affronted looks and plod on silently towards the beach.

When she realises he's still pinning her by the wrists fear rises up in her throat and mushrooms hotly in her head. It isn't exactly a fear that he will harm her, more a sense that some crucial control barrier is about to crumble and leave her drowning and defenceless. She wrenches her hands from his grasp and gropes for the clip of her seat-belt.

'Fuck off *Yianni*!' she shouts, and dives for the door.

*

Head down, keeping her eyes on the road, she marches back to Panomeli. Disappointment seething vengefully in her veins. In the village the Minimarket, unusually, is already open, the Flagstaff minibus parked outside. Through the tinted windows she glimpses the Harknesses, and a solitary Trish Ottakar. Clearly the Lasithi Windmill trip is somewhat undersubscribed.

When she goes in to buy stamps Lynda spots her from the office and hurries through, brandishing a card.'Can I nab you for a second? Just to sign this for Kylie?'

The card is elaborately quilted in some kind of shiny fabric, with an inappropriate pink silk bow; it looks like the kind of thing you'd send for a christening. All that's missing is the stork. The legend in Greek says Get Well, but Kylie Wilson-Wilson isn't going to know that, is she.

Opening it out, she scribbles her message next to the others – *Hope you're feeling better. I. Laurie* – and hands the card back to Lynda.

While Demosthenes sorts out her change she stares at the phone cards on the shelf above the till. 10 euros, 25 euros, in little stacks secured by elastic bands.

The post-box is a flimsy tin affair mounted on a telegraph pole across the road. She sticks a stamp on her mother's postcard and stuffs it into the slot with no great confidence that it will get there, rather than end its days in some Cretan hedge or horse-trough.

We'll soon have you on your feet, says her mother's voice, twanging with false cheer, and her mind flashes on the clay feet of the statue, stolid as shoe-trees on their wooden shafts, waiting to be slotted in. *You'll be as right as rain in no time.* Such an odd expression, she thinks, particularly in a place like Dunelg, which had so much rain it was hard to see anything right about it

At the time, her response to both rain and remarks about it seemed to be silence. It wasn't so much that she refused to talk, rather that what she felt and the words to say it parted company, quite politely, like lukewarm acquaintances who're secretly glad to see the back of one another.

Her mother was only trying to help, of course: the trouble was that up till then she hadn't exactly given grounds for confidence. It was Aunt Elsa who'd come to pick her up from the Halls of Residence: Elsa the 'tough cookie', as Greta called her, who could always be relied upon in emergencies. Ingrid used to fantasise that Elsa was her real birth-mother, that through one of those family pacts not uncommon back then, Greta had stepped in to save her unmarried sister's bacon.

Not that Elsa would have had a spare minute to be a mother. Without a husband to fall back on, she'd worked all her life, first as a Warden in a Young Offenders Unit, later as a Probation Officer in Perth. Now, in 'retirement', she'd transformed her back garden into a plant nursery, specialising in magnolias.

On the drive back to Dunelg Elsa fed her cigarettes and peppermints, and didn't try to break the silence, not until, unloading Ingrid's suitcase from the boot, she sighed and said, 'Doctors don't know everything, pet. Although in my experience they think they do.'

From Aunt Elsa's lips, the words had the ring of authority.

She remembers a head like a china egg, pale hooded eyes behind half-glasses. Outside, the drizzle clearing to unmask a high blue Edinburgh sky. Sun shafting in through the tall Georgian windows, casting a decisive sheen on the desk and lancing off the doctor's gold wedding ring.

You smoke so much because you want to bite and tear at the penis.

Dr. Stein and his antique Freudian claptrap. He'd seemed such a puny little man, and so very old – at least as old as her father. He wore a spotted bow tie and a silk waisctcoat patterned with fleur-de-lys, and regarded her over steepled fingers, unsmiling. Half an hour into the assessment he said flatly, *You should settle down, find a good man. Have six children.*

What he really meant, of course, was: *That'll settle your hash.* In the leather armchair she chain-smoked, sweating under his unblinking stare. Trying to put a curtain of smoke between them, trying to blot out the eyes which said he was the Word and the Law and she was a nympho and a nobody.

The day is blowsily bright and inviting, but Ingrid wants nothing to do with it. What she wants is to crawl into bed with a valium ('valium for flying' says the medical record on the Health Centre computer screen), blot out all light and sound. Opt for the anaesthetic silence of the stones.

When she thinks of Yiannis her head aches, and so does her heart. The good man, to whom the Dr. Steins of this world would have her submit – those old school Freudians, so fixated on their precious phallus. As she climbs the stairs to the apartment it strikes her that what Dr. Stein said might not actually have been *the* penis, but *my* penis. *You want to bite and tear at my penis.*

Dream on, she thinks, with a small shock of embarrassment. No doubt he'd have said the exact same thing to Alice.

45

That Alice Kober was undaunted by her failure to obtain the Indo-European post at the University of Pennsylvania is evident in a letter she wrote to Johannes Sundwall in June 1948, shortly after hearing the news of her rejection. In it she expresses her satisfaction that plans for the Minoan Institute, albeit revised, are going ahead, and seems sanguine about the absence of a salary, writing airily, 'Money means very little to me, as far as Minoan is concerned.' *She outlines her ideas to form a kind of co-ordinating centre for the collation of casts and photographs of the inscriptions, and includes a list of the scholars she thinks should be invited to join – Myres, Blegen, Emmett Bennett, Carratelli, Peruzzi, Grumach, Bossert, Hrozny, Ktistopoulos, and Ventris.*

'Quite truthfully, there are a few I would rather not ask, but do not see how it can be avoided'

One wonders if Blegen was one of the scholars she would have preferred to snub, since she had only recently received the Pylos transcripts, at second hand, as it were, through Sundwall.

'It was most kind of Professor Persson to make them available,' *she writes,* 'though I confess that it was most unkind of Professor Blegen to give copies to some people and not to others.'

On July 21st Kober set sail for England on the Mauretania – 'I was fortunate enough to get passage, although only in First Class, and it makes me shudder to think of what it will cost' *– and on July 28th she arrived in an England inured to post-war austerity, lugging suitcases which contained not only her Linear B files and reams of writing paper, but also*

292

luxuries like coffee, sugar and tinned meats for her British colleagues.

Thanks to her tireless work of creating in the 'cigarette-carton' files the equivalent of a modern computer data-base, Kober now knew more about the signs, texts, and patterns of Linear B than any other scholar of the time. Nevertheless, the work that awaited her in Oxford was fraught with problems. She had repeatedly tried to persuade Myres to eliminate signs that Evans had mistakenly read, and still thought that Myres' own signary often ordered signs in categories that relied on arbitrary judgements. Alice Kober was not someone who had any patience with the arbitrary, as we can see from her peremptory description of her method of compiling the Linear B sign-lists.

'I discard all readings not in agreement with photographs immediately. I am interested only in what the Minoans wrote. When I have no photograph, I accept what other people say is there. As soon as I have a photograph, I discard these. In the case of a dubious sign, I consider my own guess to be as good as anyone's, but I record the sign as dubious.'

Earlier in the year Kober had added to her list of correspondents Emmett Bennett Junior, Blegen's former Doctoral student, to whom he had entrusted the analysis of the Pylos tablets, and who was, in Kober's words 'A very nice young man when he can be.' In June she had borrowed his dissertation from the University of Cincinnatti library and, in a pre-xerox era, spent 2 weeks reading and absorbing the contents.

Bennett, meanwhile, was continuing to labour on the thousands of text characters found on the Pylos tablets, with the aim of establishing a list of syllabic signs, and a second class of pictographic signs he believed were used as logograms.

Bennett's method – painstaking visual comparison, combined with comparison of the contexts of all the characters on the tablets and a frequency analysis of signs and sign combinations – met with Kober's approval. Not until the following year, however, in exchange for showing Bennett the Myres/

Evans Knossos material, would Kober be able to see and draw the Pylos material for herself, and find confirmation therein for some of the deductions she had already made from the Knossos inscriptions.

It has been said that in the history of the decipherment, Bennett's work may be likened to 'clearing the terrain of jungle and straightening the path' while Kober's was more in the nature of proposing a methodology that would enable the decipherment to move forward along the path to progress. In the summer of 1948, however, the two scholars were still labouring independently, Bennett at Yale, and Kober in Oxford.

Meanwhile, the man who would ultimately reap the benefit of their work was touring Europe in an old Ford army van. On a camping holiday with his wife Lois and two Architectural Association colleagues, Michael Ventris was visiting the highlights of modernist architecture in France and Italy. While in Tuscany Ventris had also taken the opportunity to do some private research on Etruscan, which he still saw as a contender for the language of Linear B, but he apparently said nothing about this to his companions. They were therefore taken aback when he refused a proposed trip to Corbusier's workers' flats, currently under construction in Marseilles, saying that he had to return immediately to England.

What Ventris had omitted to tell them was that back in June he had given Myres an assurance that he would spend much of August and the early autumn in Oxford, working with him on Scripta Minoa. This secrecy was, perhaps, a measure of his ambivalence about the Linear B project – an ambivalence which may have stemmed from the conflict of loyalties he felt between architecture and decipherment, but which may also have been heightened by the awareness that in Oxford the formidable Alice Kober awaited him.

One suspects that Ventris contrived to be rather late for his appointment, for it was not until the end of August that he arrived in Oxford. The meeting took place around the Bank

Holiday weekend and, to put it mildly, was not a success. The upshot was that Ventris pulled out of the collaboration and immediately fled Oxford, writing a tortured apology to Myres which is headed, Oxford Station, Monday night:

'You will probably think me quite mad if I try and account for the reasons why I'll be absent on Tuesday morning, and why I should like to ask Miss Kober, or the other girl you mentioned [sic] to complete the transcription.' . . . 'But however much I tell myself that I am a swine to let you down after all my glib promises and conceited preparations – I am hit at last by the overwhelming realisation that I should not be able to stand 6 weeks' work alone in Oxford, and that I am an idiot not to stick to my own last.'

Although there is evidence to suggest that on his return to London Ventris told his wife Lois that he had had 'a terrible row', *what happened at the meeting remains shrouded in mystery. We do not know whether there actually was some kind of altercation, or whether Ventris' abrupt withdrawal was caused by a crisis of confidence. However, judging by a hurried, cryptic apology Kober sent Sir John a few days later, one suspects that she too had cause to regret her behaviour. The note is dated – wrongly – August 4th (she must have meant to write September 4th) and ends, uncharacteristically,* 'Quite chastened, Alice.'

One has to sympathise with the kindly, mild-mannered Myres, who cannot have anticipated that the meeting would turn into a clash of Titans!

46

On the main road Yiannis put his foot down. His breathing was fast and shallow, a turmoil in the upper sector of his chest. He slammed his hand on the horn to clear a minibus out of the fast lane: speed, even more than time, was of the essence. Speed for its own sake, to cancel out his racing thoughts and shut down his mind.

He was aware of strobic light flickering sideways through the cypress trees that lined the road, a confetti of insects sacrificing themselves on the windscreen. His inner eye offered up fragments of a film in black and white. A woman in the uniform of an air stewardess, a woman in a cab to the airport. A woman standing on the steps of a plane, smiling her stewardessy smile. Although his memory refused to yield up the title, he recalled with a sense of dread that the central theme was of a man who had missed his moment, a man who had acted too late, and whom fate had duly punished. It could have been by Truffaut but he wasn't sure. Françoise Dorleac, sister of the glorious Catherine Deneuve, had played the part of the air hostess, Jean Desailly the married academic with whom she was in love. The lovers had quarrelled, he recalled, and Dorleac had ended the affair.

What stood starkly in his memory was the phone kiosk that was occupied when Desailly tried to call – a plot-point made redundant, now, by the advent of the cellphone, but devastating back then. Although time is running out, the indecisive Desailly doesn't eject the wretched caller; instead, he stands there, polite and desperately impatient. When at last he gets through the phone trills in an empty apartment. The propellors roar into action, stirring dust-plumes on the tarmac. The plane takes off. The plane crashes. End of story.

That, at least, was how he thought it ended, although he had an inkling that there was more. What he did remember was an irony that chilled his heart. Dorleac herself had died soon afterwards, in a car wreck on the Autoroute du Sud. He'd always found her even more beautiful than her sister.

The thought of Ingrid hollowed him out. He'd watched her walk away, back rigorous, briefcase clutched in her hand. If he'd made the decision not to go after her, it wasn't, he hoped, an executive one.

When he reached the Station he was late, although not as late as he might have been. At a desk in the Co-ops suite the jilted Kyriaki, pale-faced in a brave red suit, was smoking concentratedly. She looked up dully when he greeted her, and if she didn't exactly smile, nor did she reprimand him.

Heartsick or not, Kyriaki was a fast worker. Her desk was awash with printouts, and she'd already assigned tasks to the ever-eager Nina, teamed up on this occasion with a sweating, jug-eared constable called Stelios.

'Halcyon,' she said, passing a typed list to Yiannis. He noticed that the diamond engagement ring had vanished. She hadn't even worn it long enough for the sun to print its demarcation on her finger. 'They produce food up there, don't they? So there'll be Min of Ag certification, business licences. Same goes for that clinic place on Odos Evans.'

'VetAid,' Nina supplied, looking up from her list and acknowledging Yiannis with a shy nod.

'VetAid, right. Stelio, you're in luck. You get the easy bit. Residence Permits: they're either on file here or at the nearest station – Katomeli, I guess.'

After half an hour at the computer Yiannis managed to consign to limbo that part of his mind which was still waiting for his cellphone to ring. He felt just shaky enough to be glad of the tedious work of cross referencing, and even more grateful than usual for the balm of Nina's blushing assistance. When he rang the VetAid number the voice that answered was female, English, and irascible.

'Another check?' the woman snapped. 'We *are* fully accredited, you know!'

Another incidence of police harrassment, he could hear her thinking. 'All the same, if you would fax through the documents right away. Including your HVA certificate,' he added, just to rub it in.

'One moment.' She spoke rapidly to someone in the background; he was fairly sure the voice that replied was Wiltraud's. 'As you wish. I'll do it directly.'

He spelled out the fax number and rang off, satisfied. Nina would double check with the tax people and the Chamber of Commerce, but neither he nor Kyriaki seriously expected to find infringements. Catching Kyriaki's eye, he raised a thumb. She glanced at her watch and stood up, swinging her bag purposefully over her shoulder. Her nostrils had the flare of a horse at the starting gate; she no longer looked beseiged, nor in the least bit humble.

'Shall we get going, then? I think they've had just enough time to get the wind up.'

As Kyriaki's car rounded Platia Eleftherias he felt himself brushed by the wings of excitement. Abbott and Costello were in a squad car behind, followed by the family liaison officer – a bespectacled woman in her fiftes called Mrs. Leandrou, who was accompanied by a female constable. Since the traffic was unusually light, and what vehicles there were scattered before the flashing police beacons, within half an hour they had turned off the coastal highway and were heading into the hills.

If he'd expected to find some degree of consternation at Halcyon, when they drove through the gate his eyes fell on a calm and bucolic scene. Chickens pecked around a compost heap, while a commune cat dozed in the shade of the great olive tree in the yard. A wheelbarrow full of bedding plants stood next to a brand new water butt. There were no vehicles in the yard, so the three cars parked with relative ease.

Stepping out into a pervasive smell of fresh manure, he made a point of waiting for Kyriaki to join him before advancing on the house. Apart from a brace of watermelons ripening on the deck, the porch was empty, but he'd caught a glimpse of movement in the shade at the side of the out-building. He saw it was Margrit, thin as a supermodel in a black vest and jogging pants, her hair falling in elegant wisps over her face. She might have been on the cover of Vogue, had it not been for the horned head wedged firmly between her thighs.

Seeing them, Margrit spoke over her shoulder to Polly, who had been squatting under the goat's belly, and now crawled out clutching a plastic pail. Although he gaped at the spectacle of the police cars and flashing lights, he stood up slowly, careful not to spill a single drop of milk.

With a cool look at the visitors, Margrit unstraddled the goat, led it over to a post, tethered it, and limped back towards them. She squinted as she emerged from the shade, the noon sun showing up the fine wrinkles around her eyes. Despite himself, Yiannis was impressed. A class act, was what you'd call it.

In the absence of the interpreter, who was to meet them back at HQ, Kyriaki had agreed that Yiannis should do the honours, but now she produced the paperwork from her bag and flapped it under Margrit's nose.

Margrit gave the papers a cursory glance. 'I have expected this,' she said with a sigh. She took the pail of milk from Polly and laid a protective hand on his shoulder. Dismissing Kyriaki with a quick once-over, she looked imperiously at Yiannis. 'So. Are you arresting us, Sergeant?'

'Not necessarily. But I advise you to cooperate.'

A pick-up truck laden with hay-bales nosed through the gateway and stopped dead. Wolfgang jumped out and hit the ground running. Cassie tumbled out of the passenger seat and raced after him A stream of German assailed Yiannis' ears: a harsh, abusive sound, guaranteed to get anyone's back up.

Mouzakitis and Kounidis were immediately on their mettle.

Hands hovering over their belts, they squared up to Wolfgang, each with the degree of menace commensurate with his stature.

It was Margrit who stayed Wolfgang with a warning hand and a few muttered word in German.

'We'll also require your computers and laptops,' Yiannis continued.

'On what grounds?' Wolfgang demanded.

'Let's see.' Yiannis shrugged, considering. 'We could start with obstruction.'

'Cellphones too,' Kyriaki reminded him sourly.

Yiannis sensed that she was losing patience. She issued a sharp order and Kounidis and Mouzakitis headed for the house. He saw two men emerge from the polytunnel. The white man was stocky, bow-legged; his dungarees were baggy and mud-streaked, the bib dangling loose over a packed, muscular chest. Over his shoulder he carried a wide-pronged rake. The black man with him was well over six feet tall, with the princely posture and fluent gait of a Premier League footballer. Yiannis heard Kyriaki swear under her breath.

Spotting the reception committee, the short one dropped his rake and ambled towards them. His Little House on the Prairie act didn't fool Yiannis for a second: that compact, contained aïr could only mean one of two things – either he was ex-military, or an ex-cop.

'All right, lovely?' he said quietly, stopping beside Margrit. He hitched up his straps and assessed Yiannis. 'Helping the police with their enquiries, is it?'

'They want our cellphones, Prys!' Wolfgang's expression suggested derision rather than anger. Yiannis wondered what the joke was.

Prys was grinning openly. 'Not possible, Sergeant. Decommissioned by popular vote. Sorry about that.'

Yiannis remembered the notice on the gate. He glanced at Kyriaki, wondering how much she'd understood.

'Disposed of – ecologically, like. Sent them all off meself.'

'The reason being?'

'C.C.D. Colony Collapse Disorder. You should read the

newspapers, Sergeant.' Prys was plainly enjoying himself. 'Nasty things, these microwaves. Fuck the hives up something dreadful.'

A haze descended on Yiannis' brain. His first instinct was to dismiss the whole thing as one of these Internet effusions so beloved of the apocalyptically-minded. But the coincidences were too frequent, and too bizarre.

Wolfgang was standing with his arms folded and his jaw squared, tapping his foot impatiently. Yiannis thought of the man on the track, sporting his alarmist T shirt. He translated quickly for Kyriaki, who raised her eyes to the heavens.

'Now I've heard everything! Who *is* this wanker?' Suggesting succinctly that it was time they got shot of this dungheap, she began to wave her arms about like a belligerent schoolgirl, matching personnel with cars.

There was a delay while Margrit asked to fetch some things for the children, and had to be escorted indoors by the young policewoman. The matronly Mrs. Leandrou, meanwhile, had hunkered down beside the twins, and seemed to be asking them about their pets.

After a moment or two Mouzakitis emerged from the house with a computer and carried it across to the squad car, trailing the flex behind him in the dust.

The sunlight was filmic and dazzling, the yard a set on which each actor played his part: Prys, casually dowsing his underarms at the water butt, Jean-Yves, the black boy from the *banlieues*, batting away burning strands of tobacco which floated from the end of his roll-up. Yiannis looked on, feeling faintly nauseous. The thought that it was he who had set the whole pantomime in motion was suddenly impossible to contemplate, and for a second he hovered in the realms of the godlike and unreal.

'No handcuffs, Sergeant?' Wolfgang sneered, as Kyriaki shut him into the car. Her face was sharp with concentration, her jaws working determinedly at her nicotine chewing gum. If she was prey to the same self-doubts as Yiannis she gave no sign of it. In the bright sunshine her suit was a scarlet beacon which hurt his eyes.

He went over to help Leandrou with the twins, who were not responding to her motherly blandishments. Cassie was half in and half out of the car; she had braced her feet against the door frame and was yelling blue murder. Polly was already in the back seat, observing her with interest. 'She wants her teddy,' he explained soberly.

Yiannis pasted on his face his most persuasive smile. 'Now then, what's all the fuss about?' For this he received a truculent scowl and a kick in the shins. Seizing Cassie by the waist, he scooped up her legs and swung her bodily into the back seat.

'Look Cassie!' Leandrou cried, 'Mummy's coming.'

Shrugging, he went back to join Kyriaki. It was the second time that day he'd felt like a brute.

Prys was in the back seat of the car with Wolfgang, sucking on a damp roll-up and dripping all over the upholstery. Kyriaki was chewing away madly, drumming her fingers on the wheel. Yiannis got into the passenger seat and buckled himself in.

Kyriaki sucked in her breath. 'Will you take a look at that!'

On the porch the young policewoman, carrying a basket of toys, was helping Margrit down the steps. Yiannis saw that she had changed her clothes for the occasion, and now wore a yellow sun-dress which clearly revealed the shiny steel pole of her prosthesis. At the bottom of the steps she unfolded a Japanese fan and flapped it in a way that made him think of a broken-winged butterfly.

As if hypnotised, he and Kyriaki watched the frail figure progress haltingly across the yard.

'Are you thinking what I'm thinking?'

Yiannis nodded. If the press got anywhere near her they'd have a field day. She'd definitely win the sympathy vote hands down.

47

Silence has fallen on the Zois house, a thick swarming silence that pulses through the empty rooms. Asterios goes hungry to work in the mornings and, returning to a bare larder, guns his *papaki* down to the Totem Bar to eat a disconsolate meal.

In the kitchen garden the aubergines and zucchini go unwatered, and the chickens in the coop unfed. On the beach the sunbeds lie higgledy-piggledy, and the tourists, finding no one to pay, have set up a yoghurt pot on the chair under the raffia shelter, into which Dutch, Germans and British dutifully drop their fees.

Androula packs her cleaning things into a plastic bucket and toils up the hill to the cemetery of Agia Stephanou. She fills the bucket at the tap in the wall; kneeling on the gravel in front of her parents' grave, she scrubs down the marble headstone and surround and washes the glass which protects the yellowed photographs. Then she picks stray leaves off the gravel and rights the plastic begonias in their vase. Having done her duty by them, she allows herself to hope that, just for once, they will take their daughter's side and make her godless brother come to his senses.

The interior of the salt-white chapel is cool, the light dim and dusty. Candles flicker on the altar, beside posies of dying flowers and votive tokens left to remind the saint of the particulars of a prayer. A deaf ear, stamped in dull tin, asks to hear again, a lone leg asks to walk. Someone begs for a beaten brass baby. Lighting a beeswax candle from one of the others Androula sets it in a holder, crosses herself, and kneels on the prie dieu to address the Panagia.

'Sofia says to me, oh Auntie, it's only the old field he's talking about, not the house, and that husband of hers says, Asterios is the man of the family, it's his duty to secure your future. But it's *my* field he wants to sell to the English, Panagia-mou, left to me because I didn't have a husband to look out for me, my mother told me herself a week before we buried her. "And what do you want with that stony patch of thistles?" he says. "It's as barren as you are, you old fool. You can't grow a grape or even graze a goat on it. Show me the deeds," he says, and he hands me the key of the bureau because he knows I don't know about these legal things. "Find me a document to prove it. Find me a signature." And when I told him he was going against the word and wishes of his own mother, what did he do but smile as if he was glad of it. "It's your word against mine," he said. Even though the woman's long since dead he'll cheat his own flesh and blood to get back at her.'

Androula's hands are cramped from gripping the prie-dieu. She kneads them together and feels the pins and needles pricking inside her fingers. The very thought of Asterios makes the blood boil up in her head. It strikes her that if he was the one who'd gone away to join the *andartes*, rather than her own Vagelis, things would never have come to such a pass. For a moment she sees her brother mown down and lying raggedly against the City Wall and the vengeful vision makes her cross herself and beg the Panagia to forgive her for a sinner.

'I'm at the end of my tether, Panagia-mou. I've waited on him hand and foot, I've done my duty. And this is the thanks I get?'

Androula tries to catch the Panagia's eye, but her lids are downcast and keep their counsel. She gazes enviously at the votive offerings which crowd the altar: with all those pleas and prayers clamouring for attention, how will the Panagia ever hear her voice? If only she had a bright tin token to offer – a house or a field, even a thistle. For if the Panagia wouldn't reach down from her heaven and help an old woman, who on God's earth would?

48

On the drive to the south coast Ken keeps the windows shut and the air-conditioning on: the day has turned into the hottest yet, windless and unsparing. The winding road over the mountains is mercifully quiet, the hill villages deserted, for those with any sense have shuttered their houses against the midday heat and are lunching in the leafy shade of their terraces. At the last moment the elder Giffords had thought better of the trip, opting instead for a lazy afternoon at the beach. Ken and Glenys, however – those indefatigable sight-seers – pooh-poohed the idea that a mere 40 degrees Celsius might be a deterrent; they'd missed out on Anemospilia, so they weren't about to forgo a trip to Phaistos.

Pa-i-to, thinks Ingrid, dry-mouthed from her brief valium doze, swigging water in the back seat.

Ken has brought CDs for the journey, old standards like Blondie and Fleetwood Mac. When 'Heart of Glass' comes on he sings along in a creditable falsetto, while Glenys jigs around in her seat.'Yeah, swing it, Debbie!' he whoops as the track ends. 'Now there's a lass who didn't need to sing in her underwear. Not like some of the slappers nowadays. With what they're earning you'd think they could afford a frock, eh?'

'They're just kids,' Glenys objects. 'They don't know any better. It's these money-men, isn't it, telling them what to do.' She stares straight ahead, her chin tilted belligerently.

Ken shoots a glance at her and says no more. When he catches her eye in the mirror Ingrid looks away quickly. The Giffords have a daughter at college, she remembers; Ashley, she thinks, is her name. She pictures her own First Year students at the Institute: curvy girls with tumultuous hair, who trot into lectures in hotpants. Perhaps Ashley is the slapper he's sniping at.

The road breasts a high bluff, and the sea glitters darkly on the horizon. Ken stops the car on the gravelly shoulder.

'Now there's a view and a half! You girls want to step out for a smoke?'

On all sides the land falls away, revealing the pale line of the Aegean to the north, the Libyan sea to the south. 'Two seas!' says Ingrid, stretching her arms wide at the edge of the bluff.

'It's grand,' Glenys agrees. They light up and smoke quietly. From the open door of the car music tumbles out and spills over the juniper-clad precipice.

A few metres away a granite stone, roughly carved, squats at the roadside. There are names on it, painted in black, and a date. 1943. A bunch of dog-daisies withers on the ground beside it. Ingrid counts ten names on the stone; four are from one family, six from another. 'Martyrs,' she explains, when Ken comes over to join her. 'They massacred whole villages up here.'

'No getting away from history, is there?' Ken stands with his hands in his pockets; his voice, for once, is dour and humourless. 'And now they're crawling all over the beaches, eh?'

The prejudice jars, but she decides it isn't worth the argument. After all, she's taken advantage of the subtler forms herself. In Greece the older generation often assume she's German. *Yermanika?* they ask suspiciously, eyeing her hair. *Ochi, Skotsesa*, she shoots back, knowing this puts her firmly on the side of the angels. Everyone loves the Scots, with their castles and kilts. The Highland Regiments with their piper, marching to the rescue. The war graves near Chania are full of them.

She stubs her cigarette out on the sole of her boot and stows the butt in the pocket of her shorts. 'Fire risk,' she says when

Ken looks quizzically at her, although it's simply a matter of respect.

The car park on Kastri hill is almost empty. They park under an olive tree and buy tickets at a kiosk beside the cedar-shaded Tourist Pavilion. Spread out across the levelled summit of the hill like a table laid for the sky-gods, the site has a lofty overview of the sea and the rich crop-fields of the Mesara plain. When they come out on to the Central Court, the sun hits them like a blow.

'My word!' says Glenys, groping in her bag for her digital camera. The court – 55 by 25 metres, the printout says – is south facing, edged on three sides by the low foundations of walls. From the north-west corner a broad flight of steps, partly carved out of the rock, leads down to the theatral area. At the south end the paving has fallen away because of earthquake or erosion; a clump of pines leans out over the abyss, next to a single mimosa tree.

The first thing that strikes her is the contrast: no tour-groups or guides here, none of the scaffolding or roped walkways which keep visitors at a safe distance from the frescos and artefacts of Knossos. The second is the silence. There's hardly anyone around – maybe a dozen other visitors scattered around the site, aiming cameras or sitting, hushed, on the tumbled walls, as if succumbing to an invisible spell.

Remembering her role as tour-guide, she consults the printout. What they're looking at, she tells the Giffords, is for the most part what remains of the Second Palace, built after the first was devastated by an earthquake. Even so, it predates Knossos, and constitutes the earliest palatial building in Crete.

Ken whistles. '2000 BC! You wouldn't credit it, would you?' He smooths a hand across a concave indentation on the top of a low stone pillar. 'Oil lamps, you think? For their *son et lumière?*'

When Glenys aims her camera Ken steps aside, but she beckons him back. 'No, stay there, love. You too, Ingrid.'

Slipping his arm around Ingrid's waist, Ken squares up to the camera. She can feel the damp heat of his skin through her T shirt.

By common consent they take shelter under the shade of the pine trees. 'Mercy me!' says Glenys, mopping her face with a kleenex. She sinks on to a bench and flaps the front of her blouse to cool herself.

In the rubble around the tree carved stones lie higgledy-piggledy. Ingrid crouches down to examine a triangular stone incised with a trident glyph. Nearby are other glyphs – a broken Z, chevrons, crosses. Ingrid checks the printout, but there's no reference to the carved signs. She takes out her notebook and begins to sketch, as if drawing the things will somehow lay bare their meaning.

'Crikey!' says Ken as he leans over her to peer. 'That your Linear B, is it?'

'It looks more like a cross between Hieroglyphic and Linear A.' She grins up at him. 'Then again, it could just be 4000 year old graffiti.'

'They don't give you much of a clue here, do they. Not like they do at Knossos.'

Somewhere she's read that the word 'clue' derives from 'clew', meaning a ball of thread or yarn. It came to mean 'that which points the way' because of the Greek myth in which Theseus used the ball of thread given him by Ariadne to find his way out of the labyrinth. 'They're a bit light on the labelling side,' she agrees, although actually she prefers it that way: at least no one's trying to tell you fairy tales. She hands the printout to Ken. 'Want to have a look?'

Ivo Kruja himself would be hard put to weave a narrative from these bare traces. On one account, though, his instincts were correct. Mother Nature takes pride of place here: the transit of the sun and moon across the sky, the cycle of the seasons, of sowing and reaping. The smell of the *minth* and the *hyakinth*. On the basis of something she can't yet define, she feels a strong affinity with the place. No amount of scepticism can diminish the sense of being brushed by microscopic vibrations from the past, as though atoms of ecstasy have been stamped on the very air.

Among the tangled tree-roots is a stone with a glyph that resembles a pair of spectacles on legs. When she bends to study it the eyepieces stare right back at her, mocking her with their emptiness. She straightens up abruptly, feels the wash of dizziness. She wonders for a moment if Yiannis finds her as incomprehensible as she does herself.

A few metres away Ken stands splay-legged by Glenys's bench, turning the site-map this way and that. They've been rubbing in sun-lotion, donning sun hats in brilliant colours. 'Sunken grain-pits,' Ken recites, pointing. From the mimosa shade she sees them move out into the dazzle of the Great Court, Ken's orange baseball cap a bright blot against the bleached paleness of the stones.

When she rejoins them, Ken is standing on a low wall gazing down into what remains of a small oblong room. Glenys is inside, sitting on one of the stone benches that line the walls. ' "Dressing chamber for athletes or performers",' Ken reads. 'So it's their locker room, yeah?. You can just see the lads getting their kit on.' Glenys calls him inside for a photo and he poses, grinning, on the bench, belly thrust out, arms spread along the low wall. He might be in an Essex pub with England on TV: all that's missing is the pint.

It's Ken who leads the way down the stone staircase to the theatral area. At the bottom he turns to squint at the steps. 'Now that's what I call skill. See that convex curve? Same as they did on the Parthenon.'

'But a lot older,' Ingrid points out, pedantic. 'By about 12 centuries actually.'

'Well it certainly gets my vote.' He flattens one hand to a vertical and the other to a horizontal and squints judiciously. 'That's about 20 centimetres, I reckon'

Pleased that the craftsmanship has gained his professional

seal of approval, she agrees that it certainly is a masterly piece of construction

There are more glyphs on the paving stones where the bottom steps abut the north wall. She crouches in a hot sliver of shade and sketches busily, pausing to smile up at Glenys, who has wandered over with her camera. Maybe later she can compare these proto-signs with actual Linear A signs: not that she'll be able to make any sense of them, but at least she might feel more like a scholar.

A ring-tone jangles out, startling her. Ken fishes his mobile out of his pocket and clamps it to his ear.

'It's not Ashley, is it?' Glenys's hand has flown to her throat; under the pink sun-hat her face is beaded with sweat.

Ken shakes his head irritably and turns away. He begins to pace, his voice booming out across the bare courtyard. Glenys is hugging her bag to her chest and gazing around distractedly, as if muggers might be lying in wait among the ruins.

'Are you all right?' Ingrid asks.

Glenys nods, putting a brave face on it. In her eyes there's a lost, anguished look. 'Just a bit wobbly, love. Think I'd better go up to the caff and cool off a bit.'

'I'll join you in a minute, okay?' Ingrid says, glimpsing for a moment what it must be like to be a parent, to be gripped by fear for your nearest and dearest.

The acoustic of the court amplifies Ken's voice to performance pitch. The dissonance grates on her nerves. But in any case her concentration is shot now, she's only going through the motions.

'I'll seriously consider that,' he's saying, 'Yeah, definitely, definitely.' He turns and paces back towards her, blind-eyed, his forehead creased tightly into a frown. 'Look, mate, I'm a hundred per cent person, okay?'

She finds Glenys on the terrace of the Pavilion with a frappé in front of her, her bag and sunhat booking the other chairs at the table. 'Better?' she asks, claiming a chair and sinking into it with relief. Glenys has washed and powdered her face, and looks somewhat revived.

'Much. That heat, it's like you can't breathe!' A breeze trembles the winged branches of the cedar and ruffles the flowers on the oleander bush above her head. Geraniums grow in pots on the low balustrade that surrounds the terrace, interspersed by the blue-green spikes of lavender.

'Heavenly spot,' Ingrid observes, and Glenys nods vigorously as she sucks her frappé up through a straw.

They watch Ken emerge at the top of the steps and make his way towards them, the cellphone still clamped to his ear.

'Who was it, love?'

'Just Manoli. Sounds like the old girl's digging her heels in.'

'You mean his wife?'

'Sister. Turns out she owns a half share. Wish I'd bloody known that at the start.' Ken kicks off his sandals and subsides into his chair. 'Manoli's trying to sort it with old Asterios. He's a savvy lad, that one.'

'Beer?' asks Ingrid, getting up quickly.

'You're a star!' He pulls off his baseball cap and drops it on the table. On the crown of his head his reddish hair is plastered flat with sweat.

The interior of the Pavilion is cooled by whirring fans. She takes two beers from the cold cupboard, pays at the counter, and carries them outside. As she sets Ken's beer down in front of him she sees that he's been doodling something on the back of the printout. A house with a pitched roof, schematic, childlike. Over his shoulder she reads the legend, and wishes she hadn't.

She sits down beside Glenys and decants her own beer into a plastic glass. 'Is that what he had up his sleeve, then?'

Glenys doesn't seem to register the disapproval. She glances at Ken, grinning indulgently.'That's him all over – starts off as a holiday home, now it's a bloody construction company!'

Minos Construction. Ingrid wonders whose bright idea it was to call it that. Is it naive of her, to be shocked? After all, most Brits see Crete as a paradise where profits are ripe for the picking. So who is she to sit in judgement?

'In for a penny, in for a pound, love!' Ken swigs beer straight from the can and wipes his mouth with the back of his hand. Putting his feet up on the lavender-laden balustrade, he assesses the view through narrowed eyes and chuckles contentedly. 'Always did see myself with a Karaoke Bar, like! "The Lancashire Hotspot" – Manoli reckons it would go down a bomb.'

49

The Interview Room was some 15 metres square and contained a formica-topped table with tobacco stains decorating the edges, a moulded plastic chair for the interviewee and, facing it, two others which Yiannis and Kyriaki currently occupied. The interpreter, a capable Italian woman he knew by sight, sat a little to the side, on Kyriaki's right. The walls of the room had been painted a dull institutional mustard, although the colour could equally have come from decades of nicotine. High in the wall a small wire-netted window gave out on to some kind of shaft and let in not light but a smell of canteen cooking and drains, and the periodic sound of a flushing toilet.

Yiannis shifted in his chair, unsticking the soles of his shoes from lino which clearly hadn't been washed for weeks. Even if you were as innocent as the driven snow, five minutes in this fetid hutch would convince you of your guilt, there being no other possible reason for suffering such a punishment.

Margrit sat straight as a sunflower in her yellow dress, her hands loose in her lap, her nostrils flaring minutely as her chest rose and fell in what he supposed to be some kind of yoga breathing aimed at repelling the miasmic exudations of the State. She had refused food but asked for water, which had been duly fetched; meanwhile, elsewhere in the building, her co-communards were being served an oleaginous and distinctly non-organic canteen meal. Yiannis wished them joy of it.

Kyriaki had spread out the photographs like a deck of cards. She spoke curtly in Greek, which Ridotti translated. 'We now

314

know for a fact the the victim was Ivo Kruja, an Albanian student. Do you continue to deny that you knew him?'

Shrugging, Margrit fixed her blue gaze on Kyriaki.

'To us he was simply Pema. We do not ask for passports, Sergeant. We are an intentional community, not the Border Police.'

Kyriaki scowled as Ridotti translated. 'Intentional community' was every bit as baffling when rendered in Greek. Yiannis wanted to tell her that she was wasting her time. Locking horns with Margrit was pointless: in any confrontation Kyriaki could only be the loser.

'Do you have links with any particular religious group,' he asked. '*Neokorai*, for instance?' When Ridotti translated his question Kyriaki looked askance at him, as if to say: You've been doing your homework. Which, indeed, he had, with a little help from his friends, the obliging Nina in particular.

A quick sweep of the Internet had netted a plethora of New Age groups: polytheists, monastic pluralists, Hellenic revivalists, invokers of Demeter or Apollo. He'd originally read the name as *Neokouroi* – under the influence, no doubt, of Ivo Kruja's outpourings. *Neokorai* apparently meant The Temple-Keepers. They had 25 members, and boasted a spiritual retreat for truth-seekers and an esoteric library of over 2000 volumes. The joining fee, he noted with interest, was given as 'all assets'.

Margit was regarding him with the weary tolerance of a teacher faced with the class dunce. 'We are not pagans, Sergeant. Although we do believe in building alternatives to a spiritually bankrupt society.'

She produced the Japanese fan from her bag and opened it with a loose-fisted gesture that would have done credit to a Court lady of the Heian era, flickering it at the stale air until tendrils of pale hair levitated above her forehead. He saw a bridge spanning a phantasmagorical gorge, over which a procession of kimono-clad ladies wended towards a spindly snow-capped mountain. Their black eyes were elongated, down-drooping, their mouths bee-stings in enigmatic oval faces. Despite himself, the deft lines and delicate colours – so incongruous in the sordid room – lulled him into a landscape of longing, and for a moment all thought of present procedures wavered and lost substance in his head. Perturbed by the lapse, he said on impulse, 'And would you describe yourselves as feminists?'

Detecting a flicker of interest in her eyes, he watched her closely. If he fanned the spark, gently at first, would it produce a flame, would the ice-maiden melt in the fires of her own fanaticism?

'Only in that we would say men have become egotised. They have lost their proper relationship to the feminine.'

'But they can regain this?' Although the fixed gaze of faith made him shiver, he forced himself not to look away.

'I believe so. It's a question of cultivating the correct state of mind.'

What state would that be, he wondered. Resting his chin on his hand, he adopted an expression of humble interest. 'You mean to say, through fasting, meditation, things like that?'

With an admonitory shake of the head Margrit snapped the fan shut and placed it on the table. 'Surely you don't expect me to discuss our practices under duress, Sergeant? Of course, you're very welcome to come to one of our open days – you might find it of great benefit.' Her lips were twisted into something of a smile. Yiannis was in no doubt that he'd been rumbled.

Beside him Kyriaki rustled through the paperwork, pretending to examine bank statements, licences, and residence permits, as if hoping the display might unseat Margrit from her high horse. Clearing her smoker's throat, she barked in Greek, 'Can you account for your movements on the night of Saturday 3rd July?' Without taking her eyes off Margrit, she folded her arms while Ridotti translated.

'Last Saturday?' said Margrit, musing. 'I took yoga class in the early evening. Then cooking, I suppose. And I gave the twins an English lesson.' She ticked off each item on her long fingers, bending them back at an angle which suggested double joints, rather than yoga.

Kyriaki eyed her beadily. 'You're certified to teach yoga in this country?'

'We do not charge for our services, Sergeant. If the students wish to make a donation it's up to them.' Margrit rearranged her legs under the table, grimacing a little, as if the prosthesis was causing her discomfort. The play for sympathy, if such it was, was lost on Kyriaki.

'You have their details? Cellphone numbers?'

Margrit shrugged. 'Of course.'

When Kyriaki's phone rang she switched off the tape recorder and flicked it open. Yiannis took advantage of the pause to check his own for messages, succumbing to the temptation he'd been resisting all day, with the zeal of a seminarist refraining from self-abuse. There was one message from the Co ops room and one from Katomeli station, but nothing, as he'd feared, from Ingrid.

'Right!' Kyriaki snapped her phone shut and glanced triumphantly at Yiannis. She said in English, 'Crime scene boys turned up something.'

Yiannis raised his eyebrows, wondering if it was a set-up. Whether it was fact or fiction, the news had no apparent effect on Margrit, whose expression was not one of alarm, but annoyance.

'Are you charging me with anything, Sergeant? If not, I would like to get back to my children.'

Ignoring her, Kyriaki turned the tape recorder back on, checked her watch, and informed the machine that the interview was terminated. She pressed the buzzer under the table and the female constable came in.

'The officer will take you upstairs for DNA testing. Then you can see your children.'

For once Margrit was shocked into silence. When the constable made a move to help her up she rebuffed her angrily. She stood up and brushed down the skirt of her dress, as if sullied by the encounter and, head held high, limped towards the door.

As soon as Margrit had gone Kyriaki's face creased into a smile. 'Organic compost bag. Looks like someone buried it in the olive grove but the landslip turned it up.'

Yiannis stared at her. Old Stavlakis was a man of the donkey-dung era; he'd have laughed himself silly at the very idea of organic compost.

'Where was this?'

'Higher up the path, near the Katomeli road. They're running tests now, but he said they've got some kind of dog-hairs.'

'Have they, indeed?' He had an image of Wiltraud on the porch, bending to stroke the St. Bernard. 'The jeep,' he said suddenly, 'They haven't checked it out, have they?'

Kyriaki gazed back at him. 'Shit. I'll get straight on to them.'

Yiannis felt like rubbing his hands. If Margrit knew when to feint, when to block, and when to concede, Wiltraud, he sensed, was more vulnerable, less of a tactician. He decided he was really looking forward to interviewing Wiltraud.

While Kyriaki went to snatch a bite in the canteen Yiannis headed outside for a cigarette. At the main entrance the first press men were staking out their positions on the pavement, smoking and eyeing each other with that hunch-shouldered, hunterly look. Just then Margrit emerged from the door, a child clutching each hand. Mrs. Leandrou followed in her wake like a faithful handmaiden, lugging the basket of toys.

Madonna and twins, he thought, as the posse closed in, bellowing for quotes, aiming their cameras at the shining prosthesis. As the little group, shepherded by Leandrou, reached the waiting squad car, a NET van screeched to a halt at the kerb and Martha Hourdaki bundled out, insofar as one can do so in a skin-tight skirt and five-inch heels. The frilled jabot on her blouse failed to conceal the magisterial bosom on her, and he had the impression that she didn't really shoulder her way through the throng, rather that the photographers parted before her bust in the way the Red Sea had before Moses. She had a tape recorder on a strap over her shoulder and a cameraman in tow. As she thrust the mike under Margrit's nose her cameraman backed away, lining up his shot.

When Yiannis heard the word 'harassment' he ground his cigarette out under his heel and turned away. He didn't need to wait around to hear the rest. He could watch the whole show on the evening news, like every other punter on the island.

50

On the way back from Phaistos they say little. Glenys texts busily on her mobile, then leans back against the headrest and lapses into a doze. Outside the window the panorama changes from mountain scrub to green valleys in which lemon groves lie tranced under the long evening shadows.

When Ken puts Ella Fitzgerald on the CD player the lazy purity of the voice gives the lie to the spoilers of the world, who go boldly where there's money to be made, who reduce things to the lowest common denominator. Ingrid's mouth quivers childishly and her eyes sting with the onrush of tears. She knows she's outnumbered; her political party would have a membership of one. Conscious that Ken can see her in the driving mirror, she shuts her eyes and lolls her head back in a pretence of sleep.

The main street of Panomeli is quiet in the dusk, moths inhabiting the first tentative aureoles of the street lamps. Only the Minimarket shows any signs of life. Ken stops the car outside and, keeping the engine running, gives Glenys's shoulder a squeeze. Glenys opens her eyes and looks at him blankly. 'Wakey wakey! I reckon you girls need an early night.'

Relieved, Ingrid agrees. An early night isn't actually on her agenda, but nor is dinner à trois with the Giffords.

On the terrace outside the Minimarket Demosthenes' two young children are down on their knees, prodding a small animal. It's a young hedgehog, tottering on skinny legs – too young to have learned the defensive reflex of coiling itself into a spiny ball.

'Hedgehog,' she says, because she doesn't know the Greek.

The little boy points at it, looking up at her. He says a word that sounds like *okantksochiros*.

'He lose his Mamma,' the girl announces sadly.

Inside, Demosthenes is cashing up. Apologising, Ingrid grabs a small bottle of ouzo from the shelf and, on second thoughts, asks for a 10 euro phone card. Demosthenes smiles wearily at her as he extracts it from the pile.

Upstairs she showers and puts on a cotton wrap. Sofia the maid has been in: the marble floor, washed clean of sandy residue, is smooth and cool underfoot. In the kitchen the crockery has been cleared from the drying rack, which stands upright on the gleaming draining-board; she has even refilled the ice tray in the fridge.

It's cooler now, although thunder rumbles distantly in the north, and a brilliant fork of lightning stabs suddenly at the dark meniscus of the sea. No sound comes from the Shapcott's studio next door, but she can hear murmurings from the balcony above. If Kylie is back from hospital, shouldn't she be visited? The thought crosses her mind but, like the guilt, is swiftly suppressed. Traumatised Kylie might be, and deserving of sympathy, but the odds are she'd still be capable of biting the hand that feeds.

Tipping ice-cubes into a glass, she drenches them with ouzo; finds olives and half a packet of pistachios in the cupboard, and takes them through to the bedroom. The beds she and Yiannis pushed together are single and separate again, spread with sheets that still bear the rectangular creases of the iron. She switches on the bedside light, retrieves her laptop from the wardrobe, and plugs it in.

51

Kober sailed for New York on September 10th, just as John Franklin Daniel, on the other side of the Atlantic, embarked for Turkey. She arrived in Brooklyn on September 18th, having encountered a hurricane en route. As she wrote to Myres,

'We were at its edge about 18 hours, apparently because we might have to go in to succour some ships in distress.'

It appears that, in the meantime, Myres had decided to revoke his previous sanction, for at the beginning of October Kober wrote to Sundwall that she now had permission to release her drawings of the Knossos inscriptions, arranged according to her classification, to all the scholars interested.

'This made me very happy, but required a great deal of work, since I had not made the drawings for such a use, but simply to be used in connection with *Scripta Minoa* when it appeared.'

She was mailing to him, under separate cover, a set of reproductions, with some corrections.

'I know only too well how inadequate you will consider them. No matter how carefully I draw the signs, the process of hectographing blurs them, and makes them hard to read. Also, hand-drawing results in errors and checking these will take a long time. All the same, I feel that in your case, the sooner you get these drawings, with all their faults, the better.'

In fact Sundwall is being given a preview. Kober lists the other scholars who will receive copies later, once she has compiled a comprehensive list of corrections:

'When I have sent the inscriptions to Ktistopoulos, Hrozny, Pugliese Carratelli, Perruzi, Grumach, Daniel, Bennett and Blegen, we can all exchange ideas.'

Ventris's name is conspicuously absent from the list, and in none of her letters that autumn is there any reference to their disastrous meeting in Oxford. On that subject, apparently, Kober's lips were sealed.

Scripta Minoa II *dealt only with Linear B scripts, but Myres also wanted to publish Evans' Linear A corpus, in the form of a proposed article for the* American Journal of Archaeology, *and despatched to Brooklyn the batches of Linear A material which Kober had not had time to copy. Charged with this extra responsibility, on top of a backlog of college work – 130 exam papers to correct from all five classes – as well as at least one visit to Philadelphia to organise the Minoan Research Centre, she wrote peevishly to Sundwall,*

'First I have to type [Myres'] handwritten manuscripts with the typewriter and then I have to read everything through very carefully because he makes so many mistakes. The truth is that he is not really capable of reading Minoan scripts. Perhaps his eyesight has deteriorated and he does not want to admit it.'

What Kober did not confide to Sundwall was that she had become ill in September, either on the boat or soon after her arrival in Brooklyn. Her family had become worried about her, and blamed her malaise on the fact that 'she didn't eat properly in England.'

In a letter written on November 9th she finally confessed to Myres,

'My health is, unfortunately, not what it should be. I was again *[sic: does this imply that she had had previous treatment for the same complaint?]* in the hospital for almost six weeks and just returned home a week ago. I managed to acquire something very unusual, and it took the doctors more than a month to find out what it was – and then they were stumped about a cure. I think I am on the road to recovery – I hope so. I am not bed-ridden, but am at present house-bound, because 10 weeks in hospitals in the last 12 have weakened my legs so that I cannot manage stairs. But enough about that.'

Kober's account of the timing is curious here: if she arrived in New York on September 18th, she had not been back in the U.S. for more than 7 or 8 weeks – unless we are to assume that she was also in hospital in England, which seems unlikely. It was not in Kober's nature to make special pleas for sympathy, and it is hard to believe that a woman like her would have resorted to exaggeration. It is notable that she made no complaint about the extra work Myres' Linear A article would involve; rather, she stalled.

'Daniel may give up the editorship [of the A.J.A] since he wants to go excavating and can't be editor at the same time. There's nothing I can do until he gets back.'

Daniel was not expected back till February. In the week before Christmas, however, news came that he had died suddenly, near Antalaya in southern Turkey.

On Boxing Day Kober wrote to Myres,

'I heard last Tuesday that Daniel had died in Turkey, at the age of 38, of a heart attack. The news came as a terrible shock, as you can imagine. Daniel was a friend of whom I was fond as well as the person on whom practically all of my Minoan plans for the immediate future depended. I don't know what's going to happen about the Minoan Research Center or about your ms.'

To Sundwall she reiterated her worries about the Centre, adding sadly,

'In ihm habe ich einen Freund, nicht nur einen Kollegen verloren.' *(In him I have lost not only a colleague, but also a friend.)*

On the same day Kober wrote to Dr. Froelich Rainey, Director of the University of Pennsylvania Museum, anxiously seeking assurances and proposing a meeting in January.

'It occurs to me that the Minoan Research Center depends very much on the Curator of the Mediterranean section, and it is possible that the new curator may not think of it as Daniel did.'

Even if it was Kober's habit to suppress her personal feelings and focus her energies on her scholarly work, such hard-headedness seems inappropriate, not to say callous. The following day she set off for St. Louis, 1800 miles away, where the annual Christmas meetings of the Archaeological Institute and the Philological Association were to take place. For Alice Kober, evidently, it was a case of the show must go on.

Depression, not surprisingly, took over. Although her letters in the following weeks are overwhelmingly technical – she and Bennett were preparing to exchange sign-lists, and Bennett had worked out a system of counting for the Pylos words that she intended to adopt – a mood of almost cosmic gloom pervades them.

'You are a busy man,' *she wrote to Sundwall in March,* 'with lectures, and articles, and Linear B – at least it will take your mind off the <u>Iron Curtain.</u>We all need to keep busy these days, so that we will not think too much!' *And again, a few days later:* 'I am afraid our civilisation is doomed. Whatever happens, the freedom of the individual will be lost, and for generations we will live in war or under the threat of war. The prospect is too gloomy to think of.'

Sundwall may have suspected that what ailed Kober was something rather more deep-rooted than the Cold War angst she gave voice to, for he appears to have prompted her about Daniel's death. On March 19th she wrote a brief reply.

'I did not write more about Daniel because I myself had no information. He died in Turkey, while he was exploring for a site to excavate for the University Museum. He was with Rodney Young, who is now his successor at the Museum. Young came back for a few weeks in January, and told me all I know. Daniel seems to have died of a heart attack – although I suspect the doctors there did not examine him too carefully. They had just finished inspecting a site, and were in an automobile, going to another place, when Daniel, who had apparently been in the best of health, complained of feeling ill. In half an hour, he was unconscious, and in two or three hours more, was dead. He was taken to Cyprus, and buried at Episcopi. It is very sad. I still can't believe it.'

What Kober omits to mention – possibly she was not consciously aware of it – is the tragic coincidence of the dates. Her dear friend John Franklin Daniel had died on December 17th, the same date on which her father had died 13 years previously.

52

If he'd expected Wiltraud to be a pushover, Yiannis had been sorely mistaken. The initial interview had been a washout. Severely businesslike in her blouse and skirt, Wiltraud had sat with her hands clasped in her lap and answered his questions without expression. Yes she had been at the commune that night, helping Wolfgang with the tax returns. Later she'd baked a strudel with the children and had gone to bed early. Prys and Jean-Yves, she said, had been away that night, delivering to outlets on the south coast.

'You say that 'Pema' went back to Albania?'

Wiltraud shrugged and studied her hands. 'I think so. I don't really know.'

'Did he return at any point?'

Wiltraud shook her head. 'No'

Yiannis was losing patience with the seamless insistence that Kruja/Pema had left 2 months ago;, not least because, despite himself, he was beginning to be convinced. Kruja and Pema were undoubtedly the same person, but what if that person had indeed left Halcyon, and had got himself into trouble all on his lonesome?

'And he didn't communicate with you in any way?'

'No,' Wiltraud said again, with a glance at her watch.

By now he was hardly listening to the answers, rather playing for time as his mind sped off up various winding hill roads which might at any point turn into impassable goat-paths. If what they were saying was true, Kruja could have left the commune but remained on the island. Maybe the poor kid had simply had enough of life in the Berchtesgarten, and had sloped off to shack up with some hippy girl for the duration.

Alternatively, he could have been purged. Karen had regaled him with hair-raising tales of psychological terrorism in the commune she'd belonged to in Melbourne; the main reason she'd run away to Greece was to put such hot-house experiments behind her. Kruja might have transgressed in some way – coupled up with one of the women, perhaps, become jealous and troublesome, upsetting the equilibrium of the group . . . and later, perhaps, sneaked back to meet her in a secret tryst?

He gazed at Wiltraud, undecided. This was clearly getting nowhere. In Greek he asked Kyriaki if they could break off the interview. 'Let's get the guys in. See if a good long wait won't take the gloss off her.'

Prys and Jean-Yves had indeed been delivering, it seemed, to shops in Matala, Makriyalos and Soudia.

'And the proprietors?' asked Kyriaki, who once again was running the show. 'You can provide details?'

'No problem.' Prys's eyes wrinkled into a smile that said he knew a fishing expedition when he saw one. 'Want me to write them down?'

Although possessed of a broken front tooth, the prominent pointy ears of a goblin, and a face which had weathered several dirty wars, his sexual aura was palpable; he had Alpha Male written all over him. Yiannis couldn't help noticing the disturbing effect this had on Kyriaki and Ridotti – if such things can be judged by the crossing and recrossing of legs, and the way their fingers fussed with shirt-neck or skirt-hem, as if to button down tight against the enlivening assault of pheromones.

Kyriaki looked up from her notes. 'I see you served in Iraq.'

'That's right, ma'am. Second Battalion, the Parachute Regiment.'

'And why did you leave the army?'

Yiannis knew she was just going through the motions: even from here he could see the words 'honourable discharge' on the sheet.

'You could say I felt like a quiet life.'

Prys responded to the rapped out questions with a radiant good humour. Yes of course he knew Pema – a quiet type, didn't give much away. Good with animals, although he didn't know shit about organic farming. But a willing worker, right enough.

'Was he particularly close to anyone?' Kyriaki asked. While Ridotti translated Prys cocked his head, eyeing Kyriaki with the friendly appetite of a man about to tackle a fillet steak.

'You mean a girlfriend? Not that I know of. More's the pity, eh?'

Yiannis raised a finger, and Kyriaki nodded her assent. 'Was pressure put on him to leave?'

'Pressure? No way. We could do with more like him, to be honest.' His gaze drifted back to Kyriaki, who by now had a definite rose in her cheeks.

'And his state of mind? Was he unhappy in any way? Did he behave strangely, for instance?'

With obvious reluctance Prys focussed his attention on the less appealing figure of Sergeant Yiannis. 'He could be a bit of a star-gazer, if that's what you're getting at. But the lad was no space-cadet. Hey, he had a university degree, for starters!'

Yiannis glanced uncertainly at Kyriaki, who signalled her agreement.

'That all, then?' said Prys, stretching lazily.

'For the moment.'

Prys planted his hands on his thighs and eased himself up. 'By the way, I wouldn't waste your time on Jean-Yves, unless the lovely lady's French is tip-top.'

The prediction, unfortunately, proved to be right. The boy from the *banlieus* spoke no more than a few basic words of English, and Ridotti was unable to follow the few French sentences they managed to squeeze from him. For most of the time he sat in a frozen slouch, his long legs stretched out under the table, on his face an expression of sullen fright which suggested more than one run-in with the Paris *flics*.

Finally Kyriaki slapped her file shut and stood up, and Yiannis followed suit. Clearly it was time to call a halt; until another interpreter could be brought in the whole exercise was pointless.

'Are we holding him?'

Kyriaki gave him a hard look. 'Is it really worth it?'

Yiannis shrugged. Probably it was not. All the same, the implicit accusation made him feel defensive. Understandably, she was frustrated, but it was hardly his fault if they seemed to be hitting a brick wall. Ridotti, too, looked despondent, as if infected by the atmosphere of failure that pervaded the room. Obviously it was time for an alternative approach, but right now he had no idea what that was.

'So it's your German friend next?' Kyriaki sounded resigned.

The prospect of crossing rapiers with the steel-rimmed Gauleiter did little to lighten his mood. Another factor was that he hadn't eaten for hours, and what little blood sugar remained in his system certainly didn't seem to be making it to his brain. On impulse, he said, 'Look, he'll keep. Why don't we go round to the *Foka* for half an hour?'

Kyriaki glanced at her watch, frowning. She shrugged. 'Well, I could certainly do with an *ouzo*.'

They took a table indoors, away from the noise of the traffic which jostled at the chaotic 5 way junction. While Kyriaki nibbled glumly at olives, Yiannis tore through a mixed mezedes of *gigantes* in tomato sauce, grilled sardines, artichoke hearts and stuffed vine-leaves. Sated, he felt ready, if not for anything, then for most things this long and difficult day might yet decide to throw at him.

When Kyriaki tipped her head back to drain the last of her ouzo, her exposed neck looked pale and vulnerable, the jugular vein pulsing blue under the skin. Staring at the tiny crucifix that lay against her clavicle, he realised what he wanted to do.

'Let's get Wiltraud back in,' he heard himself say. 'Forget Wolfgang for the moment.'

53

When she shuts down the laptop Ingrid feels immensely sad, in a familar, autumnal way: that sense of fruitfulness being at an end, that panicky grasping at the remnants of summer.

Switching off the light to deter mosquitoes, she opens the French windows to air the stuffy room. From the balcony she can see the fairy-lights of the Shoestring terrace glimmering through the trees. She hears music, too, in some melancholy register, but she can't make out what it is.

In a fit of rebellion she drags her silk skirt out of the wardrobe, and the silk top that goes with it, and puts them on. At the mirror – she tells herself she's dressing up for Alice, and if the patrons of the Shoestring see her as a lone female on the prowl, then good luck to them – she feels a stir of anticipation, as though a slippery part of her mind has managed to erase the tape – the morning, after all, seems a long time ago – so that she can look forward in all innocence to the pleasure of facing Yiannis across the table, twining her fingers through his, taking him home, afterwards, to the passionate civilities of her bed.

In the dim light of the balcony she paints her nails defiantly silver, and holds them up to the moon for comparison. There are exhalations of jasmine on the air, and a faint smell of roasting meat drifting across from Demosthenes' garden. Down on the beach empty sunbeds are scattered at odd angles, like an abandoned gypsy camp; the waves lap at sand which has the metallic grey gleam of mud.

If she were to ring him, bite the bullet, what would she say? That those you need too badly turn you to jelly, and you hate them for it? That when you're accustomed to thinking of yourself as unlovable, giving up the idea isn't just difficult, it's like abandoning your native country?

She slips Hutchinson into her bag, cigarettes. The phone card is in her wallet but that doesn't mean she has to use it.

54

Self-conscious under Kyriaki's surveillance, Yiannis was losing confidence. The critic who'd taken up residence in his head told him he should start again from the beginning, neglecting none of the details that had previously appeared trivial, and proceed in a logical manner. But as he gazed at Wiltraud a sense of unreality overtook him. There was something stagey in her dress and demeanor that brought to mind the various manifestations he'd encountered so far: the efficient, melancholic medic, the shy seductress in her see-through kaftan, and now this pin-tucked Madonna of the boardroom.

If Margrit was a monolith, he decided, Wiltraud was protean – the many-faceted goddess indeed.

'Someone was with Kruja that night,' he said flatly. If the slow erosion of questioning wouldn't rock her foundations, maybe outright confrontation would. He saw her pupils dilate for a split second before she lowered her eyes. 'It was you, wasn't it, Wiltraud. The saliva swabs we took will prove it.' Ignoring the faint intake of breath from Kyriaki, he stared at Wiltraud, willing her to break. If the allegation was false, all the better, for in a moment of almost extra-terrestrial lucidity he'd sensed that the more unjust the accusation, the more gravely it would disrupt her sense of moral rectitude. 'There was, shall we say, an exchange of bodily fluids.'

Wiltraud flinched visibly. She ran the tip of her tongue over her lips before folding them tight. The message her eyes sent was pure martyr: how could he deal so unfairly with one whose healing skills had succoured his beloved cat?

How indeed, thought Yiannis.

'He was alone.' She spoke with such quiet vehemence that for a moment he wondered if he'd heard correctly. In a silence dense enough to lean on, he felt Kyriaki tense, and prayed that she'd say nothing. 'It was I who found him.' Wiltraud's voice was thick with emotion but the words were distinct. She put her head in her hands, her shoulders shaking suddenly with sobs.

Yiannis and Kyriaki looked at each other, astonished. There was nothing sham about the tears that seeped between Wiltraud's fingers like a mountain spring from a rock, nor, indeed, about the drops of blood that simultaneously appeared on her sparkling white shirt-front. Buffeted by the pressure-waves from her epicentre, he felt as though he were witnessing the collapse of an entire civilisation, a disintegration all the more radical for being long overdue.

'Nose bleed!' Kyriaki snapped. Digging a packet of Softex out of her bag, she pushed it across the table. 'Tell her to put her head back.'

'Put your head back,' he and Ridotti said in tandem. Automatically, Wiltraud complied, groping for a tissue and holding it to her nose.

Kyriaki buzzed the constable in – a new one, a compact, wary-faced woman with the look of a wardress. 'Get some ice from the kitchen, and a roll of paper towel.'

Wiltraud's body quivered with the spasmodic effort of her breath. 'I tried to stop him going, but he wouldn't listen.' The admission brought on a fresh outflow of tears, and a concomitant increase in gore.

'Take deep breaths,' Yiannis advised. 'Don't try to talk now.' When Kyriaki frowned at him he rotated his forefinger in a gesture that said, All in good time. He certainly didn't intend to wring a confession from someone in such a state – not to mention the state of her shirt, the implications of which should surely have struck Kyriaki by now. He could already hear the jeers of the press pack outside: *Gave her a good going over, did you, Sergeant?*

The constable reappeared with a plastic bowl of ice-cubes and a roll of kitchen towel. Stripping a length from the roll, she wrapped it round some ice cubes and, supporting Wiltraud's head with one hand, held the pack to the bridge of her nose. Presently her breathing slowed, although it was still perturbed now and again by staccato sighs. The flow of blood had stopped, as had the tears. She sipped from the glass of water the constable held to her lips and gazed around with the dull, distant look of one who has temporarily forgotten where she is.

'You'd like to wash your face?' Yiannis suggested.

Wiltraud nodded, and was ushered out. When she returned he saw with relief that the front of her blouse was soaking wet: either she or the constable must have mopped it down, and had managed to get rid of most of the stains. He waited until she had composed herself.

'You're okay to continue?'

Wiltraud inclined her head. She looked, he thought, relieved; her face was softer than before, more open, as though washed clean not only of blood and tears but also, perhaps, of deceit.

'So you tried to stop Pema,' he prompted.

'Doing what?' Kyriaki said, taking the words out of his mouth.

Wiltraud's lip quivered. 'He was young. He was impatient. You should not tamper with such things, not without preparation.' She brushed damp strands of hair back from her forehead, her eyes appealing to Yiannis. 'I asked Margrit to stop him but she said it was his own journey, we should not interfere.'

Yiannis watched her pull another tissue from the packet and harry it between her fingers. 'This journey of his – what was it, exactly?'

'I don't know.' Wiltraud hesitated, glancing primly down at the shredded tissue. 'It is the men's affair. Between them and . . .' She looked not at Yiannis but through him, her eyes focussing on the wall behind, like someone trying to decipher the tiny letters on the bottom of an optician's chart. '. . . the Goddess.' Although her voice had sunk to a whisper, as if merely pronouncing the word was a transgression, her shrug betrayed a vestige of embarrassment.

335

Kyriaki's response was instant and denigratory.'*Po po po po!*' she exclaimed, the plosives tripping off her tongue like the sound of distant artillery.

With an effort, Yiannis controlled his expression. 'This was an initiation of some kind?' he asked, with a sangfroid he was far from feeling.

Kyriaki interrupted before Wiltraud could answer. 'Ask her about Wolfgang. He was there that night, wasn't he?'

Yiannis asked.

Wiltraud sniffed and brushed away new tears with the back of her hand. 'Wolfgang tried also to stop him. There was an argument, I heard them shouting outside. Then Pema went off.'

'To?' said Yiannis, restraining his impatience.

'Anemospilia. This is where the men go for . . . their gatherings.'

For a moment he was thrown off balance. 'The hill sanctuary? How did he get all the way up there?'

'I don't know. Hitchhiked maybe.'

Yiannis looked at her reproachfully. 'Come on, Wiltraud. You drove him, didn't you.'

'No!' she cried, shaking her head furiously.

He raised his eyebrows in disbelief. 'So you followed him?'

Wiltraud gave a minute nod. 'All night I was worried, I couldn't sleep. When he didn't return I got up and drove there.'

'Alone?'

'Yes.'

'And you found him there?'

'His body, yes.'

Kyriaki was on the edge of her seat by now, ready to pounce. 'Ask her if it was clothed!'

Wiltraud shook her head, squeezing her eyes shut as if to defend herself against the memory.

'You're quite sure he was dead?' Yiannis asked.

'I have a medical training, Sergeant. There was no mistake.'

There was no mistaking the condescension either. Old habits die hard, thought Yiannis. Back on her high horse, even when she knew it was a worn out nag fit only for the knacker's yard. He said sarcastically, 'Yet you didn't feel the need to call the emergency services? You realise, surely, how serious that is?'

Although Wiltraud said nothing, her face betrayed her agitation. She knows she's in deep shit, he thought. Outside the tiny window a door slammed open, filling the shaft with noise: the clatter of crockery, fierce roars from a broadcast of a Panathinaikos game. The commentator was describing the match as a friendly but it didn't sound very friendly to Yiannis.

'And then the body just rose up like Lazarus and strolled all the way down to Panomeli?

Wiltraud sat back in her chair, a sullen twist to her mouth; guilt, he thought, was written all over her.

'Did you move Pema, Wiltraud?'

The dead, Yiannis knew, were heavy beyond belief, as though only the soul itself had fended off the forces of gravity, and once it had gone, the body succumbed with relief to the age-old pull of Mother Earth. 70 kilos could feel like 100, and Wiltraud was neither tall nor particularly strongly built. No way could she have transported the corpse to Stavlakis' olive grove.

Ignoring him, Wiltraud addressed herself to Kyriaki. 'I wish to have a lawyer,' she said, with a defiant tilt of the head. He didn't have to look at Kyriaki to know how suprised she was that Wiltraud hadn't asked before.

With a shrug of resignation Kyriaki began to reel off the formula. He dived in before Ridotti could translate. 'Someone helped you, didn't they? Who are you protecting, Wiltraud?'

Ridotti gave him a reproachful look, and he signalled his apology. 'You may retain your own counsel,' she intoned, 'otherwise we will appoint a duty solicitor.'

Wiltraud rifled through her wallet and produced a business card, which she passed across the table to Kyriaki.

They already had enough to charge her, if not with murder, then on a string of counts ranging from concealment of evidence to conspiracy to pervert the course of justice. What frustrated him beyond measure was the thought of all the questions that would never be answered, now she had the protective cover of a solicitor.

His mind seethed with possible scenarios, and a few impossible ones to boot. All young people believed they were immortal, and he had personal experience of the methods they used to cull themselves – base-jumping, sky-diving, hard drugs, alcohol. Over the years he'd come to see solid sense in the ways so-called savage peoples formalised their rituals of manhood; without such regulation, young men seemed compelled to invent their own, ever more lethal, rites of passage. What he was beginning to suspect was that Kruja's steamy fantasies could no longer be written off as ravings. If he'd tried to turn them into action – with or without the aid of a third party – well, he wouldn't be the first, would he? Even so, in Yiannis's personal catalogue of entirely avoidable accidents, this had to be one of the saddest, and the most bizarre.

55

Ingrid takes the beach route back from the Shoestring, sandals in hand, paddling a little unsteadily through the shallows. She'd drunk quite a lot with her meal, wanting to brazen it out, float on the hot sweet breath of the evening. Hutchinson was open, as always, on the table, but only for camouflage: without her glasses she couldn't read a word. It had been less of an ordeal than she'd expected. By the time she arrived the foreign tourists were paying their bills and heading home to bed, while the Greeks – self-contained units whose infants dozed in buggies with frilled sunshades – gave her casual glances which never quite turned into stares. The waiter, obviously recognising her, treated her with such respect that she assumed he'd seen her with Yiannis, and was minding his ps and qs.

She weaves her way through the scattered sunbeds, climbs the steps from the beach, and pads up the street, stopping to rinse the sand off her feet at the outdoor shower in the alleyway. As she puts her key in the lock she sees the note peeping out under the door

The rush of gratitude weakens her knees, the surprise like a secret she's been keeping from herself. Yiannis can't call her, this she knows. But of his own free will he has come looking for her. Pushing the door open, she picks up the note and searches impatiently for her reading glasses.

Dear Miss Laurie, she reads, and for a split second the formality taps a chilly reservoir of disappointment.

Elsa Henderson phoned, your to ring her, its urgent. Regards, Lynda.

She sits down at the kitchen table to get her breath: Elsa is the least alarmist person in the world – she'd only call if things were critical. Heart hammering, she grabs her bag and dashes out of the apartment.

The call-box is on the corner where Main Street joins the tarmac road which leads to the Totem Bar and the new holiday apartments. There's a rusty bus-halt beside it where nothing ever stops. She punches the numbers in by the light of the street lamp and gets straight through

'Elsa?'

'Speaking.' The voice is wary, but determined. 'Ah, it's you, pet. I was in two minds about calling.' The line is so clear that Elsa might be in the bus shelter two feet from the kiosk. What sounds like BBC Question Time is playing in the background.

'It's Mother?'

'I'm afraid so. Not the worst news, mind you, but not the best either. She's had a stroke, or maybe several. TIAs, they call them. Transient Ischaemic Attacks.'

'She's in Hospital?'

'No, pet, they've moved her to the High Care Unit for the moment.'

'Jesus, Elsa!' She shuts her eyes, remembering. She'd gone out for a cigarette, lost her way in the labyrinth of corridors, and stumbled on the enclosed courtyard. Outside the glass doors High Care patients lay in padded chairs shaped like a cross between chaise longues and hip-baths, their heads lolling back, their faces tilted up helplessly at the sky. No one talked. In the eerie silence their eyes followed her. 'Nurse! Nurse!' one of them cried, and she saw then that these old folks were of no interest to one another. All their hopes were focussed on the ambulant, of which she, at that moment, was the sole repre-sentative.

'Is she conscious?'

'Aye, she's conscious all right. It's affected her speech mainly.'

'She can't talk?'

There's a pause in which Ingrid hears the tell-tale click of a cigarette lighter. 'Well, after a fashion.'

'After a *fashion*? What sort of things is she saying?'

Elsa coughs dryly. 'I'm not a speaker of Mandarin, pet, I couldn't rightly tell you.'

Outside the kiosk insects blunder around the street lamp, foreign and phototropic. Her mind seems to be on overload, most of its functions given over to the questionmark that has suddenly appeared over her mother's place in the universe. 'But she could get her speech back?'

'Anything's possible, even at her age. They're not ruling it out, at any rate.'

The moon is high and distant now, as though preparing to renounce its bond with the Earth and soar off on some independent track. 'Do you think I should come?' she says hopelessly, knowing she has no option.

'When do you fly back?'

'Not till Saturday.'

Elsa clears her throat. 'It's just, well, they've stabilised her for the moment, but they seem to think she could have another of these TIAs at any time.'

Ingrid watches her fingers winding in the telephone cord, separating out the spirals. There's a vacuum where her stomach should be, as if some ghostly surgeon had sucked the contents out through the navel. Elsa hasn't once said she needs you but she doesn't have to. She takes deep breaths, her energies marshalling themselves around a series of practical tasks – tests to run, doctors to chivvy, consultants to contact – tasks which mean that Greta will be shored up, reinstated, and set to rights. The alternative – she has a bathetic vision of her mother, wandering about like mad Mrs. Rochester, lost in the ruins of language – simply can't be entertained.

'I'll get the first flight I can,' she says, before the black hole can catch up with her.

Elsa hesitates. 'I think that's best, dear.'

'I've got to go, Elsa, I'll let you know.'

'Mind and take care of yourself, now!'

'I will, Elsa.' Without a pause for thought she locates the cellphone number in her wallet, and punches in the numbers.

341

Yiannis answers immediately. '*Nai, embros*'

'I have to get home. My mother's had a stroke.' Her voice trembles on the last word but doesn't break.

Yiannis listens without interrupting. 'I'm very sorry to hear that,' he says at last.

'You said you could get on to Gaylene if . . .'

'Of course. I'll ring her straight away. You know, however, that the airline offices won't be open till the morning?'

His tone is cool and formal: it might be a conversation between two computers. She hears the background rumble of traffic, passing laughter. A car door slams shut and the acoustic changes. 'I'm just leaving the Station. Give me half an hour.'

'You're coming here?' she asks stupidly.

'Well, what else do you suggest?' says Yiannis.

Shock has turned her stone cold sober. Back at the apartment she throws herself into the practicalities of packing, lining the bottom of her holdall wiith the cardboard folders which contain her Kober notes, wrapping her Liddell and Scott in a beach-towel that's board-like, stiff with sand and salt. Once she's stowed her laptop in its case she pulls clothes from their hangers and flings them on the bed. Thanks to Sofia's ministrations the place, at least, is shipshape. From the drawer where she keeps her passport and currency she sorts out a note for her tip. At the back of the drawer she finds her house-keys and a handful of English notes and coins which look unfamiliar now, faintly fraudulent, like Monopoly money.

When the knock comes at the kitchen door she hurries through to answer it. Yiannis has already pushed it open, and stands on the threshold. His face is drawn, his eyes bloodshot. He looks like a man who has had a hard day and doesn't expect it to get any better.

He nods when she gestures him to come in, but doesn't greet her. 'Gaylene doesn't think there's anything free on the charters. You may have to go Olympic via Athens.'

'Fine,' she says. This means a seven hour journey, as well as the Glasgow shuttle from Heathrow, but right now it doesn't seem to matter.

'She's going to check and call me first thing in the morning.' His face is careful, wiped clean of expression. It occurs to her that he intends to stay, although it isn't clear what this implies. Are they to sleep chastely in the beds Sofia has separated?

As if in confirmation, Yiannis pulls out a chair and sits down at the kitchen table. Producing cigarettes from his shirt pocket, he lights one and lines the lighter up meticulously with the packet. Perhaps he means to see her safely to the airport, use his authority to oil the wheels. She imagines saying goodbye at Passport Control, submitting herself to the serial abuse of electronic security. Passing beyond his jurisdiction into a tunnel between worlds. She considers all this briefly and from a distance, feeling her status subtly altered to that of a person for whom allowances must be made.

'I should finish packing,' she says, looking around distractedly. Yiannis drums his fingers on the oilcloth, which Sofia has wiped clean of crumbs; she has also replaced the vase of plastic begonias, centering it neatly on its white lace doily. 'You'll have a Metaxa?'

Yiannis shrugs. 'If you are.'

She fetches the bottle and sets two glasses on the table. Her hand trembles as she pours, spilling brandy on the oilcloth. He stands up and takes the bottle from her. 'Let me.'

Snatching the pristine doily out of range, she finds a cloth and wipes up the spreading puddle. Yiannis waits until she sits down again and hands her a glass.

'*Yamas!*' he says, raising his own, but his voice is flat, the gesture constricted. Suddenly she misses that lively eagerness of his; she wishes she could give it all back to him, conjure up his boyish gleam.

'I'm not fun company, I'm afraid.'

'Fun isn't what I came for, Ingrid.' The Greek glower

343

reminds her that an offence has been committed, for which she hasn't been forgiven.

A light wind blows in through the open door, fluttering the curtains and stirring the ash in the ashtray. She can see the dark fringes of the palm tree in the garden and, beyond it, a sky pierced by the bright insistent points of stars. Already Crete feels like a lost Eden, a country she can't re-enter, while Scotland is still as insubstantial as a dream. The air that strokes her skin is soft as silk but tomorrow it won't be, when she steps out into the cold Gasgow rain.

Through the open bedroom door she can see skirts and trousers draped across the single bed. She wonders briefly what she would say if he wanted to make love to her. That sex would feel sacrilegious, like fucking on a grave? Call it fate, call it what you like, the trajectory has a grim inevitability. Going home, returning to the chthonic realms of the mother.

She retrieves the dishcloth and uses it to corral the ash that has drifted across the table. 'You look shattered,' she says. 'You've been interviewing?'

Yiannis shrugs impatiently, as if to say there are matters of more consequence than tiredness. 'That thing Kruja wrote? Looks like it might not be so far from the truth after all.'

She stares at him, cradling her glass in both hands. 'The piece about the tests?'

'As if life didn't set enough tests of its own!' Leaning forward, he seizes the bottle and pours another inch into his glass. He glances interrogatively at Ingrid, who shakes her head, covering her glass with her hand. 'Maybe he was desperate for a result. Purification, Instant Karma, who knows? At this point I have absolutely no idea.'

Ingrid hesitates. 'Should you be telling me this?'

'No,' he admits, with the twist of a smile.

Nocturnal noises come from the studio above: a toilet flushes, bedsprings creak complainingly.

'The *hieros gamos*,' she says suddenly, changing her mind and reaching for the bottle, '- the marriage between mortal

344

and incarnated god. Couldn't these terms of Kruja's – honey-breathing, pollen-eating – be epithets for sex?'

A spasm of anger crosses Yiannis's face. She watches his hand make a fist and release it.

'Let me ask you something. If you wanted to have it off with the immortal, would you choose a god-forsaken dump like Anesmospilia to do it?'

The crudeness hits her like a slap. 'It's not the kind of place I fancy spending the night in, if that's what you mean.'

'Well, Kruja did, whatever the fuck else he was up to.'

Her mind flashes on the wind-burned hillside, the short moon-shadows of the stones. She stares at him, confused. 'But surely he was found at Panomeli?'

'Someone moved the body.' Yiannis has turned his head away, as if contemplating his separate future; half of his face is in shadow, and on the other half the light cast by the table-lamp strikes gold glints from the evening stubble on his jaw.

'But you don't know who?'

'That's what we're trying to find out.'

Ingrid stands up and pushes her chair back. 'I'd better get moving.'

'You're not on the plane yet!' Extending his forefinger, Yiannis rotates it backwards. 'We still have time.' He gives a perfunctory laugh. 'Well, at least you'll be spared the pleasure of meeting my mother!' His eyes meet hers for a second and flicker away. He shakes his head. 'I'm sorry, Ingrid. Forget I said that.'

As the misery crowds in on her she shakes her head, not trusting herself to speak. She thinks of Elsa at the airport in her anorak and golfing cap, the red Fiat heading north through the dense dripping fir forests that flank the A9. Beyond that is a blank, a closed door behind which everything or nothing waits to be done.

Yiannis jumps up and, taking a swift step towards her, squats down beside her chair. 'Look, London's only three hours away!' He takes a bracing grip on her knees, like a coach trying to inject confidence into a flagging athlete. Frustrated energy radiates from him. 'You'll be back. I *feel* it.' Over his shoulder the moon has moved into view above the silhouette of the palm tree, on the wane now, its right sector deflated.

She smiles weakly, wishing she could believe him. 'Do you?'

Straightening up, he stands above her, hands on hips; his eyes dart around but his torso is rigid, his jaw set mutinously against fate. 'I want to hold you!'

She nods, speechless, and bursts into tears.

56

There were few people about at such an hour: an early water-skier cutting delicate arcs across the calm sea, an old man plodding along the verge with a basket of newly picked figs, his singlet visible through his cheap nylon shirt. Yiannis drove slowly, with one hand on Ingrid's knee; she had placed her own hand over his, and kept it there.

Earlier, watching her apply mascara with ritual concentration, he'd wondered just how beautiful a woman had to be before she believed it

'Can't fly without it,' she explained. 'Keeps the plane in the air.' Her smile was brittle, the grey of her eyes paler than ever in the dark fringe of lashes. He'd understood then that she had to paint some kind of safe place for herself, even if each stroke of the brush set her farther apart from him.

In the night the barriers had fallen, and he thought he'd seen her for what she was. He remembered the limp curls of her hair on the soaked pillow, the storm of weeping that had followed their love-making. When a woman cried like that after orgasm, you couldn't help but think that the tears had flushed away all the doubts she'd been casting on love.

At the airport the first tour buses were already decanting a horde of travellers who, although bound for chilly northern cities, were still optimistically togged out in scanty beachwear. A long white awning had been erected on the forecourt to shield the growing queues from the heat of the sun. He saw surfboards, souvenir sombreros, youths downing cans of lager at 7 in the morning.

The PA system in the Terminal squawked out instructions

in three languages, all of them incomprehensible. He carried Ingrid's bag to the Olympic desk, flashed his warrant card, and was directed to the priority check-in. According to the TV monitor the Olympic flight was already boarding.

Hurrying her through Security, he smiled at her guilty face framed in the scanner gate. People were glancing at them curiously

'I feel like your prisoner,' she muttered as she retrieved her laptop from the conveyor belt.

'Perhaps you are,' he replied, on a reckless surge of optimism.

They reached the Boarding Gate just as it was closing. There was a brief skirmish with the Olympic girl before she let them through. Outside the glassed-in building the dazzle made him squint. He put on his sunglasses and lugged Ingrid's bag down the white-hot steps and across the apron, where operatives in fluorescent tabards waited to wheel away the boarding gantry.

At the bottom of the steps he held her to him tightly, like a teenager, and kissed her hard, without giving a shit about who was looking. As she bent to shoulder her holdall he noticed a label sticking out at the back of her T shirt. He tucked it in, laid a hand against her cheek, and let her go.

From the car park he watched a Lufthansa plane land and taxi back to the apron. Then the Olympic airbus lumbered to the end of the runway, turned slowly, and with a bullish roar of engines, thundered past the Terminal building. The plane lifted just in time to clear the sea, and soared up, banking, into its proper element

As the wheels tore themselves from the ground a ragged gasp came from his mouth. The confidence that had buoyed him up emptied out in a rush, and a hospital blankness descended on his mind, as if the future had turned tail before his eyes and angled back towards the past. Dry-mouthed, he felt the *dipsa* rise in him like a waiting demon, shrinking his innards and crawling like ants across his skin.

The cigarette was making him feel nauseous. He stamped it out and leaned against the roof of the car, winded, his knees as fragile as straw. He had an urge to head for the nearest bar and throw down first one brandy, and then another. He knew it was crucial not to think about Karen, nor about the fate that had delivered him up to a woman who could vanish like a migrating bird, a woman who didn't know who or what she belonged to.

He forced himself to dwell on his responsibilities – to Vasilakis and the case, not to mention his dear Mama, who'd be flying in next week from Athens. He imagined her stepping gingerly down the metal ramp in her best high heels, her grey hair rolled up in the strictest of coils at the back of her neck – she refused to let Irini cut or style it, and dismissed any suggestion of colour rinses as the work of the devil. She'd expect him to play host, to chauffeur her around the island to visit with old acquaintances, second cousins, and sundry ancient relations-by-marriage; she'd expect him to take leave, although right now leave was the last thing he wanted. In that respect, the Kruja case might yet turn out to be a blessing in disguise.

It was too late to go home, but still too early to arrive at HQ. He got into the car, shaved quickly with the electric razor he kept in the glove compartment, and drove out of the car park. At the airport roundabout his procrastinating instincts took over. Instead of heading for Heraklion he found himself turning on to the old coast road: perhaps the sight of the sea would settle his nerves and put him in some kind of shape to face the day ahead.

A maroon camper van was parked in a small roadside lot, its roof loaded with luggage. There was just enough room for another car. He parked behind it, got out, and pushed his way through undergrowth to the scrubby shore, where a concrete jetty jutted a few metres into the water. At the end of the jetty a red-headed boy with alarmingly white skin stood beside an older man, presumably his father, who was ostentatiously muscled and wore a pair of skimpy black bathing trunks. The two of them seemed to be gazing at a huddle of small boats, moored to orange buoys, that floated just offshore.

Yiannis sat down on a rock and listened to the little slap of waves against hulls. In a daze, he watched a huge white yacht slide into view past the point and proceed with imperial grace across the bay, towing an inflatable behind it. A flicker of colour on the jetty caught his eye: the red-headed boy had unfurled a German flag, which in the absence of the slightest breath of wind neither flew nor flapped but drooped impotently.

Barking some kind of command, the father backed up a few steps and fiddled with the lens of an expensive-looking camera. The boy hoisted the flag above his head, stretching it taut between both hands, and posed like some victorious invader.

Yiannis couldn't believe his eyes. Where the fuck did they think they were? At the very least such tricks were tactless, whether or not you'd lived through the war. He jumped up, put his hands on his hips, and glared menacingly at them. Although the father glanced in his direction, he made no response whatsoever and, evidently aware that arrogance wasn't in itself an arrestible offence, continued to snap away happily. Frustrated, Yiannis turned on his heel and strode back to the car.

As he turned the key in the ignition he saw a traffic cop cruising round the bend ahead. He flashed his lights and the motor-bike slowed. When it drew up alongside he recognised Haris Kazantzakis, popularly known as Nikos, although as far as Yiannis knew he was absolutely no relation to Crete's most famous writer. He indicated the camper van.

'Do me a favour, will you, Hari? Just slap a ticket on this one.'

Haris grinned beneath his goggles. 'My pleasure!' Nowhere was there any indication that parking was prohibited, but Yiannis knew he wasn't the type to ask questions. Any excuse to harrass our foreign friends was good enough for Haris.

'Thanks,' Yiannis said. 'I owe you one.' Momentarily

cheered by the encounter, he put the car in gear and drove off towards Heraklion.

Like a javelin hurled from afar, the jealousy ripped into him. Now that Ingrid was out of his sight, all his ghostly competitors stepped from the shadows, rubbing their hands. He saw a good-looking American cross his chino-clad legs and lean towards her, flirting determinedly in the cramped intimacy of the plane seats. He saw tweedy university colleagues, tennis-partners, the hungry ex-husbands of Ingrid's girlfriends, circling the bright halo of her hair like moths.

The sudden injection of adrenalin made his mind stall. The image that floated up through the fog was primitive and pre-Olympic. With a shiver of recognition, he let out a groan. What if the Kruja kid had been writing not about a test but a contest, some crazy ritualised competition over one of the women? Although only the DNA tests would tell which one, he himself would be betting on Margrit. With that autocratic sexuality, she was by far the likelier candidate for the Queen Bee role.

A furious toot from behind alerted him to the fact that the car had drifted across towards the inside lane. Correcting quickly, he raised a hand in apology. Shaken, he took a firmer grip on the wheel. The winner takes it all, he thought. And the losers? Well, no silver or bronze for them; the losers, in this case, lost everything.

*

Yiannis was getting tired of beating about the bush.

'Did you or did you not help Wiltraud to move the body?' he demanded.

'I did not,' Wolfgang replied, without a flicker of expression.

A night in the cells had done him no favours; unshowered and unshaven, he looked somewhat the worse for wear. Although previously Yiannis had discerned nothing remotely attractive in Wolfgang, he now found himself wondering how

351

the frigid, monkish-looking German would appear if assessed by the jealous eye of a rival. Now that the idea had planted itself in his mind, through its altered filter he could detect a certain grace of movement, a slender musculature, the decisive line of nose and cheekbones.

'But you're familiar with Anemospilia, aren't you, Wolfgang.'

'It's common knowledge that our members go there sometimes, there is no law against it.'

'Leaving aside the law of trespass!' Yiannis retorted.

Wolfgang bristled visibly. 'People gossip about us. They are envious.'

'Envious?' said Yiannis, interested.

'Everyone *wants* the dream, yes, but they won't *live* it. They don't have the courage to follow their hearts!'

A Greek would have spread his hands in an appeal for consensus, but Wolfgang's remained stubbornly clenched. Q.E.D., thought Yiannis, as Ridotti muttered the translation to Kyriaki.

'This dream everyone wants . . .' he began, but Kyriaki interrupted.

'We are charging your colleague with perverting the course of justice,' she said impatiently. 'She will be interviewed in the presence of her lawyer this afternoon.'

Wolfgang's gaze did not waver; instead it grew icicles. 'The guy was already dead.' The slight shrug of his shoulders suggested that little love had been lost between them. 'If Wiltraud tries to protect our commune – everything she has worked for – I see no crime.' He looked challengingly from Yiannis to Kyriaki. 'If you charge her with this you must charge us all!'

Don't tempt me, thought Yiannis, picturing a happy band of heretics chucking themselves collectively on the pyre. He left it to Kyriaki to point out that in this case 'protection' meant removing evidence and supplying false information to the police. 'I'm warning you,' she added, 'it won't help your case if you keep refusing to tell us exactly what happened that night.'

As they listened to the translation Wolfgang brought out tobacco and papers, and began to roll a cigarette. Thin cigarette, thin lips, thought Yiannis. Last night's ashtray had not been emptied. With a frown of distaste, Wolfgang pulled it towards him. In the flare of the match his face looked lizardly, the pockmarks standing out on his skin. He muttered something that included the word 'mistake'.

Yiannis pounced. 'Who made a mistake? Pema?'

Studying the hand that held his cigarette, Wolfgang muttered something that in German sounded insulting. *Stupid arsehole*, or some such.

Kyriaki glared, but Yiannis shook his head at her. He could see that Wolfgang was working himself into a lather. If he read his palm for long enough, maybe it would tell a story. The savage muttering continued, a kind of abusive internal debate. It was hard to tell whether he was swearing, praying, or berating himself.

Finally Kyriaki lost patience. 'English!' she demanded.

Wolfgang heaved a godly sigh. The hand with the cigarette scythed, teacher-like, through the air.

'Fucked up men, doormat women. They have their precious little cars, their washing-machines. Then – Poom – man abuses kids, slits throat of wife. Son mugs old folk to buy drugs. Big surprise, yeah? Big media. – Where is community in this? Where is value?'

The aggressiveness of German became cold sarcasm in English. Yiannis waited while Ridotti translated the bombast for Kyriaki. Mainly the tirade made him feel very old. There was a time when he would have agreed wholeheartedly with the German's critique of consumer society, but life seemed to have blunted most of the axes he'd had to grind. If Wolfgang's socio-political theories held little interest, however, what did intrigue him was the venom of the delivery.

The details forwarded from Germany had been scant. Wolfgang Muller was born in 1972, in a well-off suburb of Munich, the only son of Erhardt, a financial lawyer, and Elfriede, a housewife. After gaining good qualifications at school, Wolfgang had studied dance-theatre in Wuppertal, and thereafter did youth work and part-time teaching in Bonn and Stuttgart. Apart from one shoplifting conviction while a student – the fine promptly paid, presumably by Daddy – he had not attracted the attention of the police. After a normal, comfortable childhood, if, perhaps, a cossetted one – it appeared that Herr and Frau Muller had been in middle age when they produced their only son – by all accounts he had grown up to be a law-abiding citizen. There was certainly nothing in the file to explain such bitter animosity towards the society that had shaped him. Although the same could be said, of course, about the backgrounds of the infamous Red Army Faction.

Kyriaki pushed her chair back and beckoned Yiannis to follow her out. In the corridor she thrust her hands into her hair and tugged furiously, as if to wrench it out by the roots.

'Do we really have to listen to all that shit? Is it me, or is he getting loonier by the minute?'

'He's an angry lad,' Yiannis agreed. 'Chip on his shoulder the size of the Bundesbank.'

Kyriaki looked at him, wide-eyed. 'Give me a cigarette, Yianni.' He handed her one and flicked his lighter. She sucked at it greedily but blew the smoke out in clouds, without inhaling. 'But was he *involved*, when it comes down to it?'

Yiannis shrugged. 'Maybe not directly. I'd say he was all bluster, but that's just gut instinct. Maybe he did try to stop Kruja, as Wiltraud says . . .'

'Fuck it! We've got enough to charge him already.' Just then Kyriaki's phone rang and she fumbled to answer. 'Vasilakis,' she said, covering the mouthpiece with her hand. 'Right, sir. We'll expect you, then' She slipped the phone back into her bag. 'There've been developments on the DNA.'

Yiannis pricked up his ears. 'Did he say what?'

Kyriaki shook her head. 'He's on his way over. Wants to sit in on Wiltraud.'

'*Okay*,' said Yiannis.

'Look, we know they're all in on it, to a greater or lesser extent.'

'Not unless someone changes their story,' he objected. 'Prys and Jean-Yves were away, so that only leaves the main players – who're still swearing blind that Kruja left the commune months ago.'

'And we're supposed to believe that?'

'Well, I can't see them swearing the kids to silence, can you?'

Kyriaki dismissed this with a shrug, and stamped her cigarette out on the floor. Was it naive of him to suppose that asking the twins to lie wouldn't sit easily with their high and mighty principles? 'Let's see what Vasilakis gets out of Wiltraud. If you ask me, they're as tight as a vixen's arse, the lot of them.'

*

Vasilakis seemed not to notice the parlous state of the snacks that had been sent down by the canteen. Although the sandwiches were dry, their corners curling in the heat, his hand was an automaton which reached for one after another and stuffed them into his mouth while he talked on, oblivious.

The bad news was that the tests on Margrit and Wiltraud were not a match for the female DNA found on the body – which, as Vasilakis pointed out, put an entirely different complexion on things.

For a moment Yiannis was too crestfallen to speak. He'd been so sure the tests would prove that one or the other had been, at the very least, an accessory, that he felt he'd personally let Vasilakis down.

Vasilakis washed his last sandwich down with a gulp of coffee, and tapped the file with a fingernail. 'So let's try to separate fact from fiction, shall we? Fact: we've got a body stripped of all ID, covered in honey and bees – which may have been self-administered, or administered by others. Toxicology shows that he either drugged himself, or was drugged. We have unidentified female DNA which proves that the

355

victim had sex shortly beflore he died, so we have a third party. Wiltraud admitted that she followed Kruja and found his body at the Anemospilia archaeological site. Your Dutchman saw her in the vicinity of Panomeli early that morning, and trace evidence on an organic compost bag in Stavlakis' olive grove links it to the body.

'Then we're left with the fiction. We have an admixture of myth supplied by the ever-obliging Ms. Hourdaki, and also the writings of Kruja himself, which according to Yiannis's archaeologist contact appear to be flaky in the extreme. As for his literary forays into the prehistoric, well, they don't float my boat, I have to say, and they wouldn't cut much ice with a judge either. The long and the short of it is, too many man-hours spent on something that's going to be given as misadventure.' Vasilakis shrugged dolefully. 'I'm sorry, guys, I've done my best, but to be quite honest I'm being pressured to wind things up as soon as possible.'

'But sir,' Yiannis objected, 'we know someone, probably Wiltraud, moved the body. We're still waiting for trace on the jeep.'

'That's the crunch, certainly. I'll be very interested to hear what Wiltraud says about that now. It's not that I'm against ifs and buts *per se* – life's full of them, after all – but they don't belong on a charge sheet.' His eyes lingered on Yiannis, who wondered if he was being reproached. Was Vasilakis implying that he'd let his imagination run away with him?

'The lawyer, by the way – do we know who he is?'

'He's a she,' Kyriaki said pertly. 'Olympia Athanasiou.'

Vasilakis grimaced. 'Right. No pressure, then.' He brushed crumbs off his shirt-front and eased his bulk out of the seat. 'So I guess that's about as far as it goes.' He grinned wanly. 'Short of a signed confession of murder, of course!' He glanced at Yiannis, who had also got to his feet. 'Relax, Yianni. I can handle the English perfectly well.'

It took Yiannis a second to realise what he meant. 'But sir,' he protested.

Vasilakis waved aside the objection. 'Ioanna says you were at it till late last night. And frankly, *pedi-mou*, you look fucked.'

356

Pausing beside Yiannis, he laid a hand on his shoulder. '*You did good*,' he said in parodic American. 'So get some rest. That's an order. Ioanna will keep you in the picture.'

*

Yiannis knew in theory where the boat was, but as he paced the boardwalk between the moored dinghies he began to mistrust his memory.

On the deck of a yacht a tanned woman raised her sunglasses and eyed him with interest. She wore a lime green bikini and gold mules; her hair, bleached to the same gold as the mules, was scraped back from her face and clamped at the nape by a large artificial daisy. He greeted her politely, turned on his heel, and retreated to the shoreward end of the boardwalk. Pelicans waddled out of his way, hissing sullenly. At last he caught sight of it: a white dinghy with a scarlet stripe, the name *Dimitroula* in faded blue letters on the prow.

When he stepped down into the boat his nostrils were assailed by the nostalgic smell of pitch and salt-soaked wood. The oars lay in the bottom. Archaic, sun-bleached things roughly carved from olive boughs, they were as heavy as railway sleepers and suitable only for dire emergencies. Certainly he'd never seen them in use.

Since Irini and Tassos had taken the boat out only a day or two ago, there was petrol in the engine. He cast off, gave the throttle chain a sharp tug, and heard it splutter into life. The sky above was a steady blue, the swell gentle. He chugged sedately past the harbour arm and headed due north, towards nothing in particular, except perhaps the brink of the known world.

Farther out, the Filips Marina taxi-boat laboured eastwards on its way to Agios Nikolas. It was a large open dinghy with a canvas sun-shade, maximum load 28, and far too low in the water. Some of the passengers were standing up, clinging to the poles that supported the awning. Although even from here Yiannis could see there were at least 40 aboard, well over the

357

limit, he didn't feel like intervening – just as, earlier, he'd driven past Katomeli station without the slightest desire to call in. Evidently his secondment to Heraklion had spoiled his appetite for tackling minor infringements of the law: the break-ins, the domestic quarrels, the beer-fuelled blood-lettings of British youth.

When someone waved at him from the taxi-boat he waved back and watched it go, content on this occasion to leave the safety of the passengers in the purview of the gods.

Snug in the stern with his hand resting lightly on the tiller, he watched the *Dimitroula*'s prow cutting through the wake, heading for the rise and fall of the horizon. Its intentful motion absolved him of responsibility – for finding a purpose, perhaps, for charting a life's course? – and at least for a little while kept self-castigation at bay.

Once he'd cleared the coastal traffic he killed the engine and stretched out in the bottom of the boat, cradling his head on his arms. No longer trying to argue with the voice which told him he was a two time loser, he closed his eyes and with a kind of mournful relief surrendered himself to the sensation of being doubly cast adrift.

He woke from his doze with his heart ticking loudly in his ears. The sun was high and brassy overhead, scorching down on his forehead. He had been dreaming of a clock, one that operated on the same principle as a cuckoo clock, except that when the hand reached the hour it was a dolphin, not a cuckoo, which leapt out from a fretwork of wooden waves. His father had made it for Irini's fifth birthday – even as a little girl she'd been fascinated by the tiny ratchets and cogs, how they moved against one another. He remembered how she'd shrieked with delight when the dolphin jumped out and waved its flippers at her. And how his father had laughed, his face lit up by what he could now see had been absolute, unconditional love.

As a boy he'd been accustomed to thinking of himself as the centre of attention, and because to this day he'd been unable

358

to get Irini to say what effect their mother's unconcealed preference had had on her, the guilt of it had lingered. So if their father's love had somehow balanced the deficit and salved his sister's wounds, surely that was all well and good. But why did he suddenly feel so jealous, and so bereft?

Yiannis felt overheated and headachey. The tick of the clock still echoed in his ears. He stripped to his shorts, dived overboard, and paddled in ever-increasing circles round the boat, treading water from time to time, and trying not to think of the empty house that awaited him.

Suddenly his cellphone rang. Cursing, he took a breath, shoved his head under, and did his fastest crawl back to the boat. Just as he heaved himself over the gunwale the ringing stopped.

Kyriaki had left a message to call her. He dried his hands on his shirt and scrolled through in the vain hope that something from Ingrid might be lurking there unread. It was too early, he knew: she probably wasn't even in Glasgow yet. When he pressed callback Kyriaki answered immediately.

'Yianni! Are you okay?'

'*Etsi-ketsi*' he snapped. 'What do you think?'

Kyriaki hesitated. 'Look, I'm sorry about the DNA too. It's a real downer. Guess what, though . . .' Her voice was taut with excitement. 'Wiltraud made a statement. It was Manoli Dimeros who helped her!'

'You're kidding.'

'Seems they were an item. Or had been. Were you aware of that?'

'No I was not.' Yiannis cast his mind back to the Medusa: had he seen the two of them exchanging heedful glances? Or was it simply Ingrid's presence that cast a retrospective fog of eroticism over the entire evening? 'And I bet the family weren't aware of it either.' Aglaia, he imagined, would have had a thing or two to say about that particular liaison. 'So you've pulled Manoli in?'

'On his way as we speak. Seems she panicked when she found the body, and called him.'

'She didn't call Wolfgang?'

'He wouldn't have been able to get there. Prys and Jean-Yves had the truck that night. She says they wrapped the body in the compost bag, drove to the Panomeli road, and dragged it down through the olive grove . . . all because she was terrified suspicion would fall on the commune!'

'But why Stavlakis' patch, for God's sake?'

'She said Dimeros told her no one went there, it was a wilderness.'

'And that's all Manoli helped her with?' Yiannis asked suspiciously.

'According to her statement, yes. Of course Dimeros could deny the lot, if we don't get prints off the compost bag. Why do you ask?'

'I just can't see him as a knight in shining armour, that's all,' said Yiannis. Then he had a thought. Wiltraud's phone had been conveniently disposed of in the eco-cull, but Manoli's had not. 'His mobile!' he said. 'Did they get their hands on that?'

'I expect so.' Kyriaki sounded doubtful. 'I'll call now and check.'

'Right,' said Yiannis, savouring the minor satisfaction of having scored a point. 'So that's it?' he demanded after a moment, tired of waiting for her to tell him whether he was in or out.

'Well, Vasilakis is sure she'll go down, although with no previous it could be a suspended. Dimeros too, you'd think.'

'Depending,' Yiannis said.

There was a heavy silence which Kyriaki broke with a fruity cough – clearly she'd gone back to inhaling. 'Look Yianni, I'd feel exactly the same . . .'

'Would you?' Immediately he was embarrassed by his own pettiness: he sounded like a five-year-old kid with the hump.

'Where are you, anyway?'

Standing in the boat, he surveyed the empty horizon. 'Lost at sea. Does it matter?'

Kyriaki let out a sigh of exasperation. 'Yianni, he's busy singing your praises! The boss. Think you could feed that into the loop?'

57

Ingrid wakes sweating in a tight girdle of blankets. The slithery pink quilt, which has fallen off the single bed during the night, lies in a heap on the floor. For a moment she wonders who and where she is: transported back to childhood, maybe, consigned to celibacy. Crammed into the alcove of the dormer window is a small table on which sit her laptop and files; she might be Alice Kober herself, waking in her lone eyrie, facing yet another day in a life of contemplation.

In the spare room little has changed since she was a girl – the tongue-and-groove boarding on the slanted ceiling, the ornithological prints of Scottish birds on the walls: the curlew and the grouse, the golden eagle and the garishly plumaged capercailzie. In the centre of the floor lies the same white sheepskin rug, the long-haired kind that fleas adore. The shabby veneer bookcase still stands by the door, groaning with Elsa's walking maps, box-games, and old Penguin editions of Agatha Christie.

After a delay at Athens, there were cancellations at Heathrow. By the time she landed at Glasgow it was too late to get to Buncranna House.

'They have the poor blighters in their beds by 9,' Elsa complained. 'As if they needed any more sleep!'

Instead they'd driven straight to Calderbank, through squally weather and occasional flashes of a sun that seemed puzzlingly reluctant to set, until she remembered how far north they were, how in summer you could fish up here as late as midnight.

Cooking smells rise from the kitchen below. A bluish haze of bacon fat percolates up the stairwell. She puts on the old candlewick dressing gown that hangs on the back of the door and goes downstairs. The kitchen door is open to the garden to let out the fumes.

'Do you want your breakfast outside?' Elsa asks, bending to take a plate from the oven. 'It's nice enough.' She sets the plate on a tray and takes off her oven gloves. As well as bacon there's black pudding, egg, mushrooms, fried potato scone. The Full Scottish. 'Mind out, the plate's hot.'

'Aren't you having any?'

Elsa grimaces. 'Nah. Rabbit food for me these days. Cholesterol, you know?'

Ingrid is startled. Elsa slaves in the garden all summer, tramps the hills with the Ramblers all year round. 'That's hard to believe!'

Elsa's shrug suggests that she isn't inclined to believe it either. 'Bloody doctors. Once you're past sixty they just won't leave you be. Tests for this, tests for that. I'd rather be kept in the dark about my 'risk factors', thank you very much!' Parking a mug of coffee on the tray, she lights a cigarette and inhales with gusto. 'I mean, it's not as if you expect to live for ever, is it?'

'Well, you look in great shape to me,' she says loyally. Elsa's skin, although weathered by outdoor work, stretches tautly over strong cheekbones, and her blue eyes are quick and bright. Her grey hair, cropped close at the back, falls in dashing long wings to her jawline. She looks trim and vigorous in her jeans and checked shirt – for a seventy-year-old, Ingrid reminds herself. If she's always pooh-poohed any possibility of frailty in her aunt, perhaps that's because she can't afford to recognise it.

Soon after Greta went into Buncranna, Elsa revised her will, bequeathing the Calderbank cottage, as well as the nursery, to Ingrid. Elsa told her that the will included instructions for her funeral, and the funds to pay for it, so that Ingrid wouldn't be left to foot the bill. Appalled by this new morbid Elsa, she'd tried to laugh her out of it. Although she still has the copy of the will her aunt insisted on giving her, to this day she hasn't been able to bring herself to read it.

Elsa is her rock, after all; she simply isn't allowed to crumble.

She carries the laden tray out to the garden, where the morning air has a cool dewy edge to it. She pulls the table into the triangle of sun at the outer edge of the patio, and fetches a garden chair.

From here she has a view past the greenhouses – one large one, abutted by a smaller low-span shed for grafting and propagation – to the hazel thicket at the bottom of the garden, and thence to the fields and hills of Breadalbane beyond. Before the glasshouses were built the lawn had sloped all the way down to the burn, but now what's left of it is largely taken up by the spreading foliage of the old magnolia tree – a Globosa, summer-flowering, with creamy white petals.

To her right, against the high south-facing wall, grows an espaliered greengage which has been here since she was a child – she'd always found it marvellous that three dimensions could be flattened into two, and branches trained to grow first horizontally, then angled up, like the hieratic arms of Kali – and, underneath, a border of old-fashioned perennials: stocks and delphiniums and sweet william.

The gravel drive which leads past the white pebble-dash wall of the garage has been tarmacked and widened to provide parking space for customers, and a smart new shed has been built of wood the colour of preserved ginger; this is Elsa's office, where she does the books and conducts the online part of the business.

Elsa comes out with a plate of buttered toast and sets it in front of Ingrid; in her other hand she's carrying a pail full of eggshells and vegetable peelings.

'Have you still got the kitchen garden, then?' Ingrid indicates the compost pail.

'Oh aye, you just can't see it from here, not any more. The rasps are no great shakes this year, too much rain for them.

There'll be enough for your tea, though. And we should have a good crop of gooseberries, they don't mind a soaking.' She smiles at Ingrid, whose love of home-grown berries is legendary. 'Look at the colour of you, though! Greece must have done you good, eh?'

Ingrid surveys her arms: in the morning sun they look brown and smooth, undeniably well-holidayed. 'I was working too, you know.' Even though it's the honest truth it sounds like a cover-up. She squints a smile up at her aunt. Now's the time to say, I've met someone, Elsa, but she can't bring herself to say it. The feeling that binds her to Yiannis exists in some other, wordless element; like the baby hedgehog on the terrace of the Minimarket, it's too young and frail to walk into the world unaided.

She watches her aunt stride off in the direction of the compost heap, swinging the plastic pail. She's also afraid Elsa will worry about her, give her the kind of careful forbearing glance which reminds you that passion is a dangerous, unstable force, one which can make a goat walk on its hind legs or strike sparks fom a belt-buckle at a hundred paces.

A nice, stable, boring relationship. That's what Tim thinks she needs: the sort of thing you can rely on. She can just see it. Give her a month and she'd be tearing it limb from limb.

When she bites into the black pudding her eyes fill with tears of grief and pleasure.

A taste for blood, is it? Your Aunt Elsa's been turning you into a wee barbarian!

What surprises her is the glow, as if something bright is trying to surface from a meagre bank of memories. She remembers the photographs laid out across Elsa's kitchen table: holiday snaps of wherever it was her parents had been – Corfu, perhaps, or Amalfi. Greta in a spotted bikini, tanned as a movie star. Greta at cocktail time, Greta smiling in sunglasses on an open boat.

Ingrid's father had said he was taking her away for a rest

but he didn't say what from. Greta had always loved the sun, and complained bitterly about the miserly ration she had to be content with. But now it was as if two whole weeks of it spilled out of her and shone, for once, on Ingrid. She remembers sitting at her breakfast in Elsa's kitchen, and her mother hugging her, sparkling with high spirits, as if nothing could delight her more than the sight of a daughter's healthy appetite.

Pride, perhaps, is the word she's looking for. Perhaps it was as simple as that – the shock of feeling, just for once, that she had the power to give her mother pleasure.

A van noses round the side of the house with *Calderbank Nurseries* painted on the door above a stencilled pink magnolia. The driver parks in front of the office and nods to her as he gets out. He's only a youth, with a square red-cheeked face and a tuft of bleached hair, wearing a white T shirt with the magnolia logo, khaki shorts, and stout work boots. Just then Elsa reappears with her empty pail and stops to talk to him. As they go through the gate into the bamboo-fenced enclosure Ingrid hears the murmur of Scottish voices, low-pitched, like the sound of bees in lavender.

She'd forgotten how quiet the place is: no traffic noise, just invisible larks, and somewhere in the distance the faint thud of a farmer knocking in a fence post. When the youth emerges from the enclosure he's carrying a sizeable bush with deep crimson flowers. Elsa opens the boot of her car and watches as he manoeuvers it inside.

'I'll leave you holding the fort, then.'

'Right you are, Miss Henderson.'

Elsa comes towards the patio, bending to dead-head a rose on the way. 'Alastair,' she explains, 'My right hand man. He does the local deliveries.'

Ingrid jumps up and begins to load the crockery on to the tray. 'I'd better get dressed.'

'Don't hurry yourself, pet. Finish your cigarette. It's not as if she's going anywhere.' She rinses the pail at a faucet under the kitchen window and sets it down on the step.' I got her a couple more nighties at Marks. Doesn't matter how many name-tapes I sew on, that laundry woman just keeps losing them!' Picking a bacon rind off the plate she hurls it into the pristine centre of the lawn. 'I'm taking in a rhododendron for that blasted prison yard. Give the poor buggers something to look at, for God's sake'

In the silence Ingrid watches two sparrows swoop down from the globosa and peck at the rind until it jumps and wriggles like a worm.

Elsa lets out a sigh and stands back, shaking her head at herself. 'Och, I'm sorry, dear. You know me. Madam Big-mouth!'

At Dunkeld they pick up the A9 and head down the dual carriageway to Perth. On either side of the road the Tay valley and its tractors lie under a Mediterranean sheen. Jet-lagged, her mind harks back to the frame of outing, holidays, the passive pleasure of being driven. She remembers hot air buffetting in though the open window, Yiannis's hand on her knee – not pinning her down this time, but holding her steady.

Elsa nods towards a field of barley which is tufted and flattened, like hair after a sleepless night. 'Aye, we need a few more days like this. Then they'll be able to get the harvest in.'

Ingrid watches the passing landscape in a daze: rhododendrons have become oleanders, a myrtle tree transmutes into an olive. Higher up, the white granite outcrops have a fictional glitter. She's unnerved by the traffic hammering along on the left. Ever since she arrived she's been trying to get in at the wrong side of Elsa's car.

From Bridgend they take the back road through the forest to Glencarse. Elsa accelerates up a short but steep hill and turns into the drive. 'Here we go, then. Gird your loins, eh?'

Buncranna House comes into view through the beech trees, white and ornate as a wedding cake. Urns full of geraniums and petunias flank the Doric portico. The clipped lawns are deserted; apart from two nurses smoking on the steps, no one is out enjoying the sun. Elsa parks on the gravel forecourt and pauses with one hand on the door. The face she turns to Ingrid is neutral and composed. 'I'm just warning you, dear. Don't be too upset if she doesn't recognise you straight away. It sometimes takes her a minute.'

She follows Elsa along a ground floor corridor, across the patio, and through the sliding doors of an empty conservatory. Another corridor with open doors which give on to single-bedded units leads to a carpeted lounge area, marked off by trellises decorated with artificial ivy trailers.

A TV at the far end blares out a children's programme; either the reception is terrible or no one has got around to tuning it, for the images on the screen are raw neon, pixillating. Of the half-dozen inmates strapped into armchairs, or lolling back in the abominable hip-bath contraptions, not one is watching it.

The only man in evidence – an old fellow so chronically hunched that his head has retracted, tortoise-like, into his chest – shuffles his walking-frame determinedly along the corridor that borders the lounge. She can see no sign of Greta.

Taking her cue from Elsa, she pastes an inclusive smile on her face and hurries on by. They give way briefly to let the tortoise man speed past, then turn into a transverse corridor, at the end of which a window overlooks the staff car-park, and beyond it the dark ramparts of a fir forest. When Elsa stops at the last unit on the left Ingrid reads the sign on the door. *Mrs Greta Laurie.* At least it's got her name on it.

Greta is lying on the single bed, dressed in a powder-blue fleece and navy jogging pants that are too short for her, revealing inches of puffy ankle above the tight ribbing of her popsocks. A nurse turns from the bedside locker, holding a plastic water jug. She's small and stout, her short brown hair striped with highlights as blonde and thick as kindling-sticks. She eyes Ingrid appraisingly.

'So you'll be her daughter? Miss Henderson said you'd be

coming.' The accent is Antipodean, Australian probably; the badge on her tunic says *Elaine*. 'Look, Greta!' she cries, beating up a pillow and thrusting it under Greta's shoulders, 'It's your daughter come to visit!'

Elsa marches round the bed and kisses her sister smartly on the forehead. 'It's Ingrid, Greta!'

Greta licks her lips, ignoring both of them; her eyes are fixed on Ingrid. Her hair is long and unkempt, pink scalp showing through on the crown; even her eyebrows are overgrown, white wires that curl fiercely up towards her forehead. The skin on her face is rough and dry and her eyes, redrimmed, look girlishly tiny. She looks not blank, exactly, but politely puzzled.

Ingrid forces herself to sit down on the bed and take her hand. 'It's me, Mum!' It strikes her that they're all talking in exclamation points. Is this because there's no vocative case in English, no salutary mode?

She realises that she can't remember ever having seen her mother without makeup.

Elsa produces the two nighties from their M&S bag, flaps them in front of Greta, and lays them on the bed. 'So what kind of sleep did she have?' she asks Elaine.

'Well, not so good again. We've settled her now, but she had us up all night.' Planting a hand on Greta's shoulder, Elaine shouts, 'Didn't you, dear?'

Ingrid wants to tell her that her mother is not, never has been, deaf.

Greta flinches away, scowling vigorously.Her eyes haven't moved from Ingrid's face. Her gaze is eerily disinterested, like that of a cat. Ingrid feels like stroking the furry fleece, establishing some definite principle of friendship.

Raising a finger, her mother tries to point. 'You?' Something is dawning on her face: suspicion, maybe, or a faltering surprise, followed suddenly by an almost theatrical expression of delight. She might be the Virgin Mary in a nativity play, bowled over by her first encounter with the angel. Her grip tightens on Ingrid's hand. *'Bow one truffle soup iyu!'* She shakes her head angrily, tears filling her eyes as she struggles to speak. Her lower lip juts. Clenching her hands into fists, she spits, *'Fought cupid!'*

Ingrid makes a wild guess.'You're not stupid at all, Mum.'

'Yesh.' Greta nods emphatically. *'Tall rong!'*

'It's the stroke, Mum. They'll come back, the words. You'll see. You just have to be patient.'

'Now now, Greta, don't go upsetting yourself . . .' Elaine gives Ingrid a warning look as she bustles up to the bed. 'I'll just get her toiletted, shall I? Then you can take her through to the conservatory.' Brooking no objection, she hoists Greta into a sitting position and scoops her legs sideways so that they dangle over the edge of the bed. 'Oops-a-daisy!' Greta sits there while Elaine moves the walking frame into range, observing her slippered feet with bewilderment.

Like a conjuror producing a rabbit from a hat, Elsa whips out a bag of Juicy Fruits and dangles it from her fingers. 'Your favourite, Greta!'

Distracted, Greta twists her head round, trying to see. When Elsa tears open the packet and shakes out a sugar-crusted pastille her face crumples with impatience. Her mouth opens urgently, like a fledgling's beak, so that Elsa the mother-bird can pop it in. Eyes closed, she chews with utter absorption.

The sight makes Ingrid feel bereft, as if the one glimpse of conscious awareness granted to her has been suddenly snatched away. It's like watching someone surf the TV channnels, flicking through a series of discrete realities, none of which bears any relation to the one before. In the gaps between, nothing but white noise and static.

Amnesia, she thinks. From *amnemon*: forgetful. *Amnemosini*: forgetfulness.

Once she's positioned Greta's hands on the rubber grip of the walking frame, Elaine hooks an arm round her waist and coaxes her across the room. When the toilet door slides shut Ingrid rounds on Elsa. 'Where on earth's her makeup?'

'Don't ask me,' Elsa says defensively. 'Try the bedside locker. Or under the bed – I found her false teeth there the other day.' Whisking the nighties off the bed, she folds them up and stows them in the bottom drawer of the dresser. On top there's a vase of irises, their leaves yellowing in the oppressive heat of the room, their blue petals pale and papery.

In the locker she finds a handbag which contains only a purse, a comb, and an unopened packet of Rolos. Under the bed there's nothing but a couple of sweet wrappers and a worrying residue of dust and fluff. She's still furious, a free-floating turbulence that's looking for someone to blame. The cleaners clearly aren't up to scratch, and if it comes to that, why has no one bothered to comb her mother's hair? Even if Elsa doesn't pay much regard to such things, Greta certainly does. Is what seems like an oversight rather more than that? Unconscious jealousy? The plain sister's revenge on the pretty one?

Tutting, Elsa snatches the irises out of the vase and dumps them into a swing-bin. The toilet flushes, and as the door begins to slide open she looks at Ingrid and hisses, 'Don't cry, whatever you do. You'll only start me off.'

Emerging, Greta looks at them with surprise, as though she's already forgotten who they are. After a few steps she stops dead and stares mutinously at the nurse.

'Doesn't want to walk today, does she?' Elaine chirps. Elsa is already unfolding the collapsible wheelchair. Greta allows herself to be lowered into the seat, her feet lined up on the metal foot-rest. Elaine tucks a blue cellular blanket around her knees, which at least conceals the popsocks.

'All set?'

The Unit is laid out on some kind of grid system. This time Elsa the expert turns right and whizzes Greta down another corridor, on either side of which open doors reveal more single beds, and frozen-faced relatives holding flowers. While Ingrid tries not to look in, Greta is uninhibited, and twists her head from side to side, her eyes darting curiously. Back straight, handbag clutched in her lap, she gives every evidence of enjoying the outing.

The Conservatory is full of plump sofas and armchairs; in the corner a music-centre stands on a trolley scattered with CDs. When Ingrid opens the sliding glass door to let in the air birdsong bursts into the room, a chorus of six sparrows perched on the veranda roof of the wing opposite. The porter is unloading Elsa's plant from a wheelbarrow. It looks small and stranded in the centre of the patio. A man is smoking on a bench in the shade of the veranda, hunched over, cigarette cosied inside his fist. There's no mistaking the catastrophic cough of emphysema.

Elsa has positioned the wheelchair between two cretonne-covered armchairs. She produces a pot of vanilla yoghurt from her bag and peels off the top, handing Greta a plastic spoon. Greta sups it avidly, hardly waiting to swallow one spoonful before shovelling in another.

'Honestly,' Elsa says, 'Look at her, she's starving hungry!'

Perched on the edge of the armchair, Ingrid nods encouragement. 'Is that good, Mum?' Greta's eyes meet hers for a second. She wonders if she's imagined the glimmer of gratitude.

As soon as she's finished the yoghourt Greta closes her eyes and lets the pot loll stickily on the cellular blanket. '*Ryre tout*,' she mutters, letting her chin sink on to her chest.

Ingrid smooths the hair back from her forehead. 'Tired out?' she ventures, and Greta's head nods under her hand.

'She probably had no sleep worth the mention,' Elsa says, wiping milky smears from her sister's upper lip.

Ingrid retrieves the handbag from Greta's lap, takes out the comb, and begins to tease out the snarls in her hair. 'You used to like this, didn't you?' Greta nods again; although her eyes are still closed, a smile flits across her face, as if she does in fact remember.

Once the tugs are out she begins to ease the comb through rhythmically from root to tip. The fine white hairs, crackling with static, reach up to welcome the comb. She sees herself at 6

371

or 7, brushing out the long gold waves, plaiting and coiling, twisting the hair up into what Greta called a French Pleat. *I love my hair combed*, she'd sigh, luxuriating, *I could just sit here for ever.*

An expression of bliss has settled on Greta's face. 'You used to purr like a cat,' Ingrid says, remembering how proud she used to feel, playing handmaiden, being allowed to perform the soothing rituals of beauty.

She digs out her makeup bag, squeezes Nivea on to her fingertips, and smoothes the cream into the dry skin on her mother's face. Opening her eyes, Greta spots the bag and reaches for it. When Ingrid brings out her compact she grabs it, snaps it open, and glares at herself in the mirror. '*Mesh!*' she accuses, seizing the powder puff and punishing her cheeks with it.

This time there's no problem translating. Ingrid offers her own lipstick, although it's too pale, not Greta's habitual crimson. She'll have to stop off at Boots, get her a new one. Greta winds the lipstick up dexterously, applies it to her lower lip, rolls the bottom lip over the top one to spread the colour, and finishes off with an expert cupid's bow.

'Well then!' says Ingrid, smiling at the face that's coming to light, the face that's beginning to resemble her mother's.

Eyebrows raised at her reflection, Greta pats her hair, touches the outer corners of her lips with a fingertip. Then she says something that might be 'better', and looks around with the bright questing expression of a Minister's wife at a coffee mornng.

The emphysemic smoker has appeared in the doorway. A tall, stooping man, with a full head of greying hair, his eyes are grey and kind; he looks, Ingrid thinks, a good deal younger than any of the other inmates. He wheezes across the room and stops to lean on the back of a sofa and catch his breath.

'All right, Greta?' he says, but Greta sniffs, eyeing him as if he has committed some serious breach of protocol. 'I'm Donny,' he says, nodding to Ingrid.

'Greta's daughter,' she explains quickly.

Her mother's scowl is regal. '*By tochter!*' she announces, with boastful scorn. Ingrid is embarrassed for her. It's hardly the way to win friends and influence people, when you need all the friends you can get.

Donny catches Ingrid's eye. 'Aye well, we all have our good days and our bad, right enough.' His voice is low-pitched, his smile rueful. He eases himself up straight and turns to go. 'Better get across for my lunch, then. Awful slop they give you here, isn't that right, Greta?'

'Nice man,' Ingrid observes when he's out of earshot.

Elsa nods in agreement. 'Used to work in the forestry. A widower, from up Blairgowrie way.'

Ingrid raises her eyebrows. 'You've been chatting him up, then?'

Elsa gives her a look. 'We've had a smoke now and then,' she concedes, jerking her head at the patio. 'His son and daughter are having to sell his house now, to pay the fees. Who makes these kinds of laws, eh?'

Greta sighs loudly, as if to remind them that she's the rightful centre of attention. Her gaze is fixed on Ingrid's small backpack, which is propped against the cretonne skirt of her armchair.

'*Duckflap,*' she says conversationally, wagging a finger at it.

Ingrid makes a deduction. 'Yes, it's my rucksack, Mum.'

'*Rucksnap,*' Greta agrees with a nod of satisfaction.

Ingrid brings out the contents and shows them to her. Sunglasses, cigarettes. Hutchinson, stained with suntan oil and still gritty with Aegean sand. 'Nothing much interesting , I'm afraid!'

With a dismissive shrug Greta turns her attention to Ingrid's face, studying her with a critical frown that's all too familar. 'I don't like your hair like that,' she announces, her enunciation perfect. 'Too short!'

Elsa mutters 'Would you credit it?' and Ingrid has to laugh. For once she'd forgotten to steel herself, to remind herself that just when you think love has soothed it, the savage breast will bite right back at you. But at least spite is something she recognises, and the relief is so great that she hardly feels the sting.

'Well, Mum, *now* you're sounding more like yourself!'

58

When his confusion lifts, the way ahead is open like a road. But Pericles knows the rule: you can no more go inside a shop without money than turn up at a wedding without gifts: sugared almonds, rice to throw. On the steps of the grocery he agonises: there's a right way and a wrong way to do things, his mother says; say thank-you, Pericles, do you say thank-you?

Inside the goods wait for him on shelves taller than a man, leaning towards each other across the narrow aisles. Markos the shopkeeper is nowhere to be seen. Away from the heat-shimmer and its floating insects Pericles blinks in the gloom. He peers, edging his way along an aisle. There's no method in the stacking, no logic in the grouping of categories. Cereals jostle soap-powder, jars of olives sit next to toilet rolls. Hypnotised by the disorder, he becomes more agitated. Rice could be any-where, with beer or baked beans or honey. There's no time to waste, but where is a man in a hurry to look?

Someone enters the shop with a bright cry of *Kalimera* – Kyria Dora, there's no mistaking the voice – and Markos answers faintly from the inner regions. Pericles' eye falls on a display of small netting bags, each one tied with a pink silk ribbon. Inside are pink and white sugared almonds. After a struggle with the elastic fastening he manages to detach one bag from the display card. Shivering in the cold draught of air from the cheese cabinet, he weighs it in his palm. At last he spots the rice, a whole shelf of it in 250 gram boxes. He picks one out and hides it inside his jacket.

Markos is calling his name, his voice loud with irritation. He advances on Pericles, wiping his hands on his apron. His bulk looms in the narrow aisle.

'Okay, old man. Now put these back where they came from, eh?'

Pericles shakes his head and stares stubbornly at the ground.

'Are you going to a wedding, Pericles?' A kind voice, tinkling like goat bells. It's Kyria Dora, smiling, in a white dress, with loaves in her basket.

He nods in a fury of relief. When Markos tries to grab the gifts from him he clutches them tightly to his chest. Now that he has what he needs, the very thought of leaving empty-handed is enough to shut off the light in his head and fill it with blackness. Red-faced with anger, the shopkeeper shouts out a bad word with apologies to the lady. Putting a restraining hand on his arm, Kyria Dora whispers in his ear. Markos shakes his head roughly and slaps the cheese cabinet with his hand, like a man whose pride is offended.

'Keep your money, Kyria! I've just had it with him. Finish! *Kaput*, you hear?' He glares at Pericles. 'He's scaring my customers away, that's what, and I've had enough of it!'

Pericles feels the wind go out of him. His knees are sinking under him like baggy sails. He wants to explain the urgency, but what good is it trying to explain to people who don't know what's what? He can see in Markos' eyes that he'll never understand – that it's nothing to do with taking or stealing. That the world is a void which only tribute will fill.

Markos takes a phone from his apron pocket and hits the buttons, and the darkness closes in. Above his head the shelves teeter, sharp-edged and vengeful. The aisle is a dark space, narrow like a cell. Outside, the clear air, the sky like a bowl held out for offerings.

He tries a step towards the door but his knees refuse

'He's not well!' Kyria Dora exclaims, reaching out her arm to steady him. 'Come and sit down.' She steers him to a chair beside the checkout and makes him sit, pushing his head gently down between his knees. Pericles holds on to the gifts, the almonds in their netting bag heavy and hard as marbles. When the blackness eases he lifts his head cautiously.

'Better?' she says, with worry on her face. Pericles gestures at the door and the bright square of sunlight that falls between the patio awnings.

'You want to go outside?'

'First he wants to come in,' Markos snorts, 'then he wants to go out!'

'I'll take him,' she says. 'Can you walk now, Pericles?' Putting her arm around his waist, she helps him out and sits down beside him on the step where he belongs.

He is eating the cheese pie Kyria Dora has bought him when the police car stops at the kerb. Inside he spots his friend the Sergeant. With the police car is a white van with seats and two people in it.

'Now then, my friend,' says the Sergeant. 'Maybe you should just give Markos the stuff, eh?'

'Let him keep the damn things,' Markos growls, 'What do I care?' He kicks at a box of tomatoes so that they jump out, and stamps back into the shop. Pericles watches the tomatoes spin across the patio and roll down the steps and into the road. He's afraid to look at the Sergeant.

'You'll put me in jail?'

'Not at all! But I'll be frank with you, Pericles. We're worried about you. Isn't that right, Dora?' He glances at Kyria Dora, who nods emphatically. 'The truth is that you've not been doing so well lately, have you. At your age you deserve to put your feet up a bit, get some looking after.'

The van people have got out, a man and a woman in blue tabards. They have bare arms and wristwatches, but they don't look like police. The woman comes towards him, smiling; she has short black hair and round dimpled cheeks.

'Going to take a trip with us, then, Pericles?'

'Up you get,' says the Sergeant, supporting him under the armpits and heaving him to his feet.

The young woman lends a hand. 'Gently does it.'

'Wait!' says Kyria Dora, going to rescue the sandal that has fallen off his foot and been left behind. She grasps his ankle and braces his foot in the lap of her white skirt, so that he

377

worries about thr mark it will leave there, like a footprint on a perfectly empty white beach. When she slips the sandal on her fingers are soft and cool, with bright pink nails. 'There you are, Pericles.'

One of the runaway tomatoes has burst under the wheels of a car, while several others loll perilously in the road. Knowing that it's a crime to waste food, for waste makes an empty larder, he cranes his neck, fretting, as they steer him towards the van. He was the one who made Markos so angry, wasn't he, so shouldn't he be the one to pick them up?

'He likes to sit up front,' the Sergeant says. There are three seats, one for the driver and a double one next to it. The young woman climbs in first and waits for the Sergeant to help Pericles up the step. He clasps the gifts tightly to him while she struggles with his seatbelt, pinning them under his right arm while they get the belt under his left and buckle him him.

Then Kyria Dora comes running and thrusts a plastic bag through the open window. Inside are two cans of 7up, Swiss chocolate, and twenty cigarettes.

'For the wedding?' he asks, and she covers her mouth with her hand.

'Good luck, old friend. Behave yourself!' The Sergeant slaps the wing of the van and, stepping back, gives him a smart salute. As the van drives off Pericles sees them in the wing-mirror: Kyria Dora with her face in a handkerchief, his friend the Sergeant with his hand steady on her shoulder.

'All right?' the young woman says, patting his knee. 'Don't worry, you're in safe hands now. Just you sit back and enjoy the ride.' Her hands are plump and dimpled like her cheeks, her bosoms like warm loaves. Her shoulder so near his own he could lean his head on it.

Katomeli shrinks in the mirror. Pericles watches signposts, cars zipping by in the fast lane. Buses too, like the one he took to Knossos. The young woman taps his arm and tells him that her name is Flora. Her pink tongue teases around the name.

378

The sight of it makes Pericles blush and look away. The driver lights a cigarette and turns on the radio: Greek tunes which make his foot jig, make him sorry he never learned to dance.

Flora grins at the driver. 'Ready for the clubbing scene, this one!'

Soon the city looms into view, a bowl of sugar-white buildings with huge boats in the bay and the harbour arm reaching out like a claw to clasp at the sea. The van slows down with the rest of the traffic, and the air is so heavy with exhaust fumes that Pericles wants to hold his breath. There are red lights, delivery vans, darting motorbikes. Also crossings where everything stops for pedestrians and makes you late.

'Oh for Christ's sake!' says the driver, sounding his horn. 'We'll be here all day!'

As the procession trails across, the lights turn from green to orange to red again.

'They certainly lay it on for the tourists these days, don't they?' Flora says.

Pericles shakes his head. He sees no tourists. Tourists have cameras; they wear trainers and shorts and sunglasses. The driver has leant out of his window to gesture rudely.

'Bloody re-enactors! Haven't you got honest jobs to go to?'

What is invisible to man is visible to the gods. On the 12th day of Hekatombaion, when the old year is over and grain fills the *pithoi* to the brim, the new Year King is inaugurated at the harvest festival of the *Kronia*.

At the head of the procession come the most beautiful children – for all who attend the festivities must be *kaloi k'agathoi*, good-looking and free of blemishes – some bearing boxes of incense to fill the *thumisteria*, while others carry small chairs and tables to accommodate the chthonic goddesses, and a larger chair for *Ge Kourotrophos*, the Great Nursing Mother, who receives the first offering of barley and honey-cakes.

Following the children come the four *Hydriaphoroi* – for four is the sacred unit – carrying their water jugs on their

379

shoulders, and four *Kitharodoi* strumming their lutes, and the four flute-players or *Auletes*, dressed in short chitons and mantles, leading four flawless ewes and four flawless heifers with necks garlanded for the sacrifice.

After the sacred animals come the purple-gowned *Skaphephoroi*, who carry bronze trays of cakes and honeycombs, followed by a crowd of the most handsome and distinguished elders, the *Thallophoroi* or sprig-bearers, waving their olive branches.

The first of the ox-carts is dedicated to Kronos himself, god of the Harvest and the Last Sheaf, he whose year has run its course. His presence requires no statue or graven image, and is symbolised only by the barley stooks and the sickle with which he castrated his father Unranos.

On the second cart, drawn by two oxen coloured uniformly white, and seated on a throne surmounted by bulls' horns, is the Priestess herself, she who incarnates Ge, as indicated by the milking-goat tethered at the foot of her throne. In her right hand she holds an olive-wood staff encircled by the holy snake. Her face and breasts are painted chalk-white, the nipples rouged red and ringed with the same black pigment that outlines her almond eyes. Like the yokes of the white oxen, her throne is wound around with honeysuckle, barley ears, and the scarlet poppies which bring both ecstasy and sleep.

The last cart is surrounded by a prancing, laughing throng of masked athletes of both sexes, who pelt the onlookers with cakes and flower petals. On this cart stands the triumphant *eniautos*, the Chosen One. Winner of the *agones* or contests, king of the *kali k'agathoi*, and bridegroom to the goddess. Slender and muscular, with long oiled locks curling over his shoulders, he wears a short saffron skirt in place of the athlete's bronze codpiece, the absence of which signals the successful consummation, and the concomitant change in his status. On his head the tall crown of white lilies and cascading peacock feathers symbolises fertility in the year to come. The sight of this beautiful youth occasions joy and awe in the hearts of the onlookers, who salute his bravery as they salute his coronation, knowing it is no mean feat to mate with the goddess.

The dance tunes on the car radio are drowned out by the tumultuous sounds of the procession: the rumble of wooden wheels on the tarmac, the shouts and whoops, the music of drums and lyres and flutes. Flower petals litter the car bonnets, and cow-shit has been trodden into the road.

Even from here Pericles can tell it's his friend up there, his peacock head-dress bobbing proudly above the crowd. Those oiled locks, and the smile he remembers: sidelong, insinuating. The sheaf of lilies he holds in his hand like some angel would.

Happiness makes him hold his breath; he laughs suddenly, full of light energy, the gifts burning their eager hole in his lap. This time he won't let him down. Even if he's afraid of crowds – the elbows and voices and strange shifting faces – Pericles knows that he has to go. Before the procession ends, before the lights turn green again, while the aura of his friend still infects him with the fever of youth.

The driver gives another blast on the horn. 'Get a bloody move on!'

The door opens easily but the seat-belt is harder to un-buckle. His old man's trousers stick sweatily to the plastic cover of the seat.

'Hey, steady on, *pedi-mou!*' Flora grabs at the back of his jacket and holds on. 'Where are you off to?' Pericles feels the weight of her as she leans over to slam the door, the strong arms pinning him down. 'You forgot to lock the damn thing!' she shouts at the driver, who pushes something on the dash-board, cursing. 'Fed up with us already?' she chides, as she fusses with the seat-belt. 'That's not very nice, is it?'

Pericles looks at her flushed face. One minute her presence is warm and kind and draws him like a thirsty horse to a water-trough, but the next minute he shies away from the angry shimmer in her eyes. The packet of rice has burst in the scuffle, scattering grains across the floor. See what a mess you've made, Pericles. He catches sight of himself in the mirror, his hands locked over his ears to blot out the scolding. A bald head dappled with brown sun-spots, grey hairs bristling out of his chin. His face has the haggard look of one of the pedlars his mother used to shoo away from the door: poor, foreign people who sold shoelaces, sharpened scissors. There's an aureole of blue sky around it, framed in silver.

He thinks of the Sergeant's girlfriend, Kyria Dora, her hands cool as water. If he did what he wasn't supposed to do it was only because he was *invited*. And even if he wanted to say Sorry the element that beckons him is so huge and speechlessly beautiful that it strangles the word in his throat.

What he's *supposed* to do is kick off his rotten flip-flops, dart barefoot across the pavements to catch up with the crowd, dodge like a Beckham through the defenders.

What he's *supposed* to be is shoeless, shadowless.

59

Yiannis felt he had taken a Great Leap Backwards. Every day at the Station he discharged the duties that were required of him, while inwardly shrinking from the dullness of routine. In the time since Ingrid left he'd dealt not only with the unhappy departure of Pericles, and the usual summer rash of thefts on Katomeli beach, but also with the recovery of the body of an old man who'd lain undetected in his farmhouse for 2 weeks, and an outbreak of food poisoning tracked down to a Turkish-owned café called *The Perfect Kebab* which had recently opened on the beachfront. The culprit turned out to be the 'Perfect Special' offer – a chickenburger with cheese, chips, and a Pepsi, all for 1 euro 95.

The Flagstaff group had flown safely back to England, after being personally escorted to the airport by Gaylene Evnochides, who was glad to see the back of them. 'There's always one group, isn't there,' she complained, as if the drama had been all their fault. At the last minute the Wilson-Wilsons had asked her to convey their thanks for his assistance, a display of gratitude Yiannis hadn't expected.

Every day Karen smiled her timeless smile from his desk, reminding him of the dead weight of the past and making him all too conscious that he had no photographs of Ingrid – nothing, in fact, that waved a promising flag from the future. At nights he came home to a house of ghosts. A house his father had built for his mother, in which he himself had lived as a child, an adolescent, and finally as a widower. Never as a husband, as a man with his own woman.

When he wandered through the rooms he saw only the traces of others: the heavy oak furniture which had been there since the 50s, the rugs, hand-woven by his grandother, the dowry chest in which his mother had kept her best embroidered linen. It was a family house, built for a family to live in: too big by far for a single man. He'd considered buying new furniture, skinny and Swedish, and painting the rooms in rainbow colours, like the refurbished city of Tirana. Or else simply selling up, building something smaller that would feel more like his own.

In his dreams Ingrid was a pale shape he clung to when the decrepit roof-joists fell in, crushing the washing-machine like a tin can and scattering broken tiles across the rooms. Their marriage bed, dust-shrouded, was afloat on a sea of terracotta rubble. Let loose by the earthquake, his little companions crawled out of their ruined crevices and cupboards and took up residence between the sheets. He would wake in a cold sweat with an erection, quivering with the shadow-memory of caresses, still half-believing that if he vibrated at the wrong pitch the bees, offended, would take revenge on him.

It had struck him that he ought to propose some sort of arrangement to Irini, perhaps raise the possibility of a move. But before that, he really ought to set the place to rights. Plane down the sides of the doors that kept sticking, for a start. Repair the subsidence damage to the terrace wall.

Within a month or so, Irini and Tassos would need more space. He'd gone to eat with them, sitting out on the tiny balcony, which floated on the gusts of traffic noise like a ship riding out a storm. Hands proudly clasped over a stomach that was still as flat as a washboard, his sister had announced that she was pregnant at long last. He'd been happy for her; his congratulations to both of them had been sincere. He felt obliged to accept their invitation to a celebration at the Medusa, even though he was fairly sure Dora, whose name hadn't been mentioned, would be there. The Pericles business seemed to have put things in perspective, at least while they'd been linked by circumstance. She'd been upset about the old man, and she'd accepted his comfort: did that amount, perhaps, to a *détente*?

384

Irini, who liked things to be cut and dried, had interrogated him about Ingrid. She was worried for him, she insisted. Had he thought about the future? A foreign woman, from a far-off country, and neither of them in the first flush of youth. Was he being realistic about their prospects?

Yiannis reminded her that Australia was even more foreign, and much farther away, but Irini persisted.

'You haven't even met her!' he protested, trying to deflect the onslaught, although, thinking about it, he couldn't honestly see them ever being bosom buddies.

All dark looks and pursed lips. Irini clattered the dishes on to a tray and carried it inside, returning with a dish of baked custard. She slammed a plate of melon down in front of Yiannis, glaring at him.

'What now?' he said tiredly.

'Oh, they seem friendly enough, the English! But they're a cold-blooded bunch, when you get right down to it.'

This gem of national prejudice was delivered with the authority of one who had spent six whole months in London. He laughed angrily. 'She's Scottish,' he objected.

'Even worse! Ice-water in the veins! Not like Dora. Your trouble is, you don't know when you're well-off!'

And your trouble is you're an idiot, thought Yiannis. Luckily Tassos had chosen that moment to step in. 'Give the guy a break, Irini,' he said, in the mild tone he saved for keeping the peace between the siblings.

*

Yiannis ate his supper in front of the television. The programme was a compilation of archive news clips, one of which featured George Bush delivering a laughably dyslexic tirade against Al Qaeda tourists in Iraq and fatter gunmen on the West Bank.

'*Ai gamisou!*' he shouted, changing the channel, although ever since George Dubya had been consigned to the dustbin of history he'd missed the mordant pleasures of jeering at him.

Last night his mother had phoned to say her left knee had

385

blown up like a football, and the doctor advised against flying. She could take the ferry, he'd pointed out, but although he didn't like to think of her sweltering out the summer in Athens while Crete enjoyed the benefits of clear air and cooling sea-breezes, his encouragement was half-hearted. When she insisted she couldn't come until well into the second half of August, and then only if the doctor permitted, he'd made the appropriate noises, but secretly he was relieved to be left alone with his depression.

He set his plate down on the coffee table and gazed critically around the room. The sideboard he should have thrown out years ago, with its glass cupboards full of terra-cotta cockerels and dreary key-patterned tureens. On top of it the silver-framed family photos were arranged on a crocheted runner: weddings, christenings, graduations, the gathering of clans at his grandfather's 90th birthday. All the marker-posts of life, at least those that were sanctioned by social ritual. Although death was the final, culminating stage, no one ever took photographs at funerals.

On impulse, he went to the sideboard and took down his wedding photograph. Wrapping it in tissue paper, he carried it through to the bedroom, opened the dowry chest, and tucked it inside the folds of a lace tablecloth.

The bed had a raddled look. Although the sheets had been on for a week he'd had no inclination to change them, part of him clinging on like a babe at the breast, nuzzling hopefully for some faint scent-memory of Ingrid. He stripped them off, carried them to the washing machine, and bundled them in.

Although he'd put up a spirited defence against Irini's sisterly outburst, she'd managed to activate some fundamental fright in him, for the qualities that initially attracted him to Ingrid – her autonomy, perhaps, her self-sufficiency, now appeared in their negative aspect. That coolness of hers could also be construed as the power to shut him out and hug her troubles jealously to herself.

Not a card, not a word. As if she had no notion that he

might want to know how she was, or, for that matter, her ailing mother. As if she didn't know how much that terrible reserve could hurt him.

He took fresh sheets from the airing cupboard, and grimly set about remaking the bed. His mobile rang in the sitting room, and he went through to answer it. Hoping against hope, he snatched up the receiver and said '*Embros*.'

It wasn't Ingrid, however, but Panos at the Station, apologising. 'There's some kind of domestic over at Panomeli, can you attend?'

Yiannis swore under his breath. Had they forgotten there were such things as duty rosters? Okay, Christos had finished his secondment and was currently earning his spurs at Agios Nikolas, but what about Sotiris? 'Isn't there anyone else you can send?

'I wouldn't be calling if there was, would I?' Panos said huffily.

Kore was poised on the coffee table, tail erect, nibbling at his leftovers. The sight enraged him, for it seemed to symbolise everything in his life that was, or could become, sordid. He scooped her up and threw her on to the sofa, furious at himself for letting the place go to rack and ruin.

Outside the shadows were long and low, the setting sun a dazzle in the driving mirror. By the time he reached Panomeli the sun had gone and the first bats were flitting about the rooftops. He stopped for a moment at the corner of main street, considered picking up some cigarettes at the Minimarket. There was a light on the balcony that had been Ingrid's, but was no longer. A tall, elbowy man was leaning on the railing while a woman in a sarong poured drinks. These new arrivals need never know about the tragedy that had happened in the village; seeing only the unsullied face of Panomeli, they'd be able to enjoy the peaceful idyll they'd paid for. From this distance he couldn't see what age or nationality they were, but the mere sight of them was like a slap in the face.

Only a masochist would hang about here, yearning after

shadows, gloating over what was gone. Abandoning the idea of cigarettes, he turned right up the track that led to the Zois smallholding. He parked where the track ended in a dusty turning-circle, and took the torch from the glove compartment. Up ahead every light in the house was burning, but as he climbed up the path he heard none of the usual night sounds, no cluckings or brayings, no clattering of crockery, nor threads of music from the radio. The silence had a dense quality that raised the hairs on the back of his neck.

When he rounded the end of the terrace he saw a squat, gnome-like figure silhouetted by the light from the open door. Old Androula sat on a small straw-seated stool, knees akimbo.

'Kyria Zois?' he called out 'Are you all right?'

Androula turned her head towards him but did not speak. She wore an old-lady print house dress and, with it, what appeared to be a pair of large leather riding-boots. 'It's Sergeant Stephanoudakis,' he said, approaching cautiously.

'I know you,' she said accusingly. 'Nikos's boy.'

He switched off his torch, so as not to dazzle her, and shielded his eyes from the light blazing from the door. It took him a moment to make out the object cradled in the lap of her dress. It looked like a cleaver, of the sort used for chopping up soup bones.

Taking a handkerchief from his pocket, he got hold of the knife and carefully lifted it out of her lap. She glanced dully at it, but made no move to resist. There was blood on the blade, dry and crusted. Crouching beside her, he said gently, 'Can you tell me what happened, Kyria?'

Androula made a clicking sound with her teeth, as if to say it was beneath her dignity to answer.

'Is your brother at home?'

'How should I know?' Even in the shadow he could have sworn the expression on her face was one of satisfaction.

A low whistle came from the tin-roofed woodshed attached to the side of the house. He switched on his torch and went over to try the door. Although the padlock was open, the door refused to budge. There was a tiny unglazed window in the wall.When he shone the torch through the beam fell on a figure squatting on a pile of logs.

'Open the door, Asterios!'

'No way! And you can stop shining that bloody thing in my eyes!'

Switching off the torch, Yiannis spoke into the cobwebbed gloom. 'Look, why don't you come out, and we can discuss things calmly.'

'I can't, can I.' Asterios' voice was sulky. 'She'll kill me.'

'Oh for God's sake!' Yiannis snorted. 'Don't be ridiculous.'

'Take a look at the chicken run if you don't believe me.'

A narrow path, overhung by foliage, led along the side of the house. Yiannis pushed his way through briars and vine tendrils and emerged at the back of the building, where the torch illuminated a kitchen garden with rows of neatly staked tomato and aubergine plants. Beyond it a cleared patch of ground was enclosed by a wire-netting fence. Inside all seemed quiet, the plywood coop exuding the silence of deep sleep.

The acrid smell of droppings made his eyes water. He saw that the gate hung open on its hinge. He stepped gingerly inside the pen, momentarily startled by what he took to be a plastic toy perched on top of the gatepost. His skin prickling with the sensation of being watched, he made himself go back and shine the beam on the post.

Had it been possible for a bird's features to show expression, Yiannis would have said it was one of deep insult. Supported by the ruff of neck-feathers, the cockerel's head sat atop the post, its eyes imperious, its scarlet crop proud as the plume on a hoplite's helmet.

A moth dive-bombed the torch beam, and he jumped back, stifling a gasp. If it was a joke it was a bad one. With a premonituon of what he would find, he re-entered the gate and began to patrol the inside of the fence, sweeping the beam ahead of him. As he'd feared, the cockerel wasn't the only sacrifice. Mounted along the ramparts like the victims of some medieval siege, the chickens' heads kept their eerie watch from every fencepost.

Stumbling on something, he stabbed the torch beam down into the darkness, where drifts of downy feathers foamed around his feet. What had appeared in the glancing torchlight to be a midden heap now revealed itself as a pile of headless corpses. He stepped back smartly, shaking his head in disbelief. For a moment he stood in the killing fields, asking himself what furies had possessed the old girl, had fuelled her with the energy required to carry out an organised massacre.

Round at the front of the house Androula was still ensconced, rocking slightly on her stool. Picking up her walking stick, he helped her inside and sat her down at the kitchen table. She looked down at her hands, shook her head at the crusted blood, and turned them over to examine the palms.

Yiannis put the kettle on and searched the cupboards for tea, chamomile if possible. He filled a cup, put it on the table, and sat down opposite her.

'Did you threaten your brother, Kyria?'

Androula gave him a look of pure derision. And of course it was derisory. Asterios might be getting on a bit but he was fit and sinewy, with the cunning eyes of a jackal. The role of cowering victim simply didn't suit him.

Feathers adhered to the blood spatters on Androula's once-handsome boots. Yiannis began to feel profoundly sorry for her. As she sipped her tea the colour returned to her face, and bit by bit he elicited a narrative that was interspersed by bitter outbursts.

'Who's looked after him for fifty years?' she cried. 'And he thinks he can just put me out on the street?'

He filled the washing-up bowl with water and found a towel. There was a sliver of carbolic in a plastic soap-dish. 'Why don't you clean yourself up, Kyria, while I have a word with him. Is there anyone you could stay with to-night?'

'Sofia,' she said petulantly, gesturing towards the telephone in the hall. 'I want to see Sofia!'

Yiannis went round to the woodshed and banged on the door until Asterios slid back the bolt. He felt for the light switch and flicked it. Asterios blinked and scowled in the glare of the naked bulb; moss and lichen clung to his trousers and his singlet was smeared with cobwebs, but there wasn't a bruise on him. He hardly looked like the victim of a serious assault.

'Your sister tells me you were planning to sell the house.'

'Don't listen to the mad old witch! It was the meadow, not the whole bloody house! Anyway, what does it matter now? Manoli's in jail, isn't he? It's all fallen through.' Although his jaw jutted pugnaciously, a whine had entered his voice. 'So she's got her own way, hasn't she? I was only thinking of the future, and see what thanks I get for it!'

Yiannis looked at him sternly. 'I'm taking your sister down to her niece's house. I suggest you stay up here and cool your heels.'

Asterios' mouth fell open. 'Up here?'

'Unless of course you'd feel safer in a police cell? I can always take you down to Katomeli.'

'What the fuck have I done? She's the one who ought to be locked up!' He spat on the floor and glared at Yiannis, hunched as a gnome, hostile and venal.

Choosing to ignore the provocation, Yiannis said coldly, 'And in the morning you can start thinking about how to clean up the mess.'

'Me? It's all her doing, not mine.'

'Don't tell me, tell the Magistrate,' Yiannis snapped, 'if that's the way you want it!'

Asterios shrank visibly: the threat of the courts had hit home. The old sod knew as well as he did that there were laws which regulated the disposal of property, but none that stopped you slaughtering your own chickens.

'It's a health hazard out there. See to it!'

Yiannis turned to go, railing inwardly against the moral depletion of the human race. Briefly he saw the world through

Wolfgang's spectacles, as a place bled of all goodness and terminally infected by fear, greed, and hypocrisy. Let Asterios stew in his own juice for a while, he thought, contemplate the rights and wrongs of the matter. In the doorway he added with sarcastic emphasis, 'I presume you won't be pressing charges.'

60

Throughout the spring of 1949 Alice Kober ploughed on, sending out flyers to announce the inauguration of the Center for Minoan Linguistic Research and visiting Philadelphia to confer with Rodney Young, who had replaced John Franklin Daniel as Curator of the Museum's Mediterranean section.

College continued to weigh on her, as evidenced by her complaints to Myres about 'silly chores' *like marking.* 'My, I am sorry for myself!' *the letter concludes,* 'Will stop weeping on your shoulder.'

By May she was clearly struggling, and wrote to Myres, 'This year has been a nightmare. More and more work at school, and no prospect of a let-up until the middle of June,' *finally confessing,* 'I am so worn out that for the first time in my life I am worrying about my health.'

With the end of the semester in sight, Kober resumed her technical correspondence with Johannes Sundwall. Perhaps the prospect of a respite from college brought some relief, for she writes of her hopes to visit him in Finland 'when I go to Crete, if I ever do. I am hoping that the Heraklion Museum will be ready by the summer of 1950, but I have been waiting so long that it seems more like a dream than something that will actually happen.'

Kober still hoped, with Myres' help, to obtain casts and photographs of the Heraklion inscriptions for the Minoan Research Centre, although it is not clear when or if these negotiations began. Her frustration with Evans' photographs of the Knossos inscriptions continued, and she suspected duplication in his drawings.

'I am coming to the conclusion that he often drew fragments, and later joined them to other fragments, so that I am suspicious of many of the smaller fragments which are identical with parts of other inscriptions, and am also beginning to suspect that even fragments which do not look identical in the drawing may be only different drawings of the same inscription. This sort of thing is dangerous, because one can so easily base theories on what seems to be cogent evidence, only to find that the evidence is wrong. As I now suspect, at least 100 of the fragments will have to be eliminated. Then too, as I continue my working, I am beginning to suspect that a larger number of the drawings than I first supposed are not Evans' at all, but Myres' – or those of somebody else. If my suspicions are true, the publication of SM11 before the originals are checked may do a great deal of harm.'

In mid June Kober wrote to Myres that she hoped to take a short break before plunging into Minoan again, as her health had not yet improved, adding wistfully, 'I want England, an ocean voyage . . . but this summer I shall stay home and rest.'

Rest, however, did not improve her condition, nor, apparently, did the 'rigorously self-imposed system of dieting' *later mentioned in an obituary by Kober's ex-Hunter College Professor E. Adelaide Hahn. By the end of August the news was worse. Kober reported to Myres that the doctor had ordered her to hospital on July 27th where, after three weeks observation, she had undergone an operation, and had only just returned home. She also sent a handwritten note to Sundwall, explaining why she had not written for so long, and might not be able to write for a while, confiding, with typical understatement,* 'I have not been feeling well for some time.' *This was the first Sundwall had heard of Kober's failing health, and one can imagine his shock at receiving the news that his indefatigable correspondent had been operated on, and was still* 'too weak to sit at a typewriter.'

While Alice Kober fought to regain her health, in London Michael Ventris, who had recently qualified in Town Planning, joined the Ministry of Education as part of a group of architects allocated to the design of new schools.

He had not given up on the Minoan scripts, however, and spent his lunch breaks looking for similarities between Linear B and Linear A signs, filling his architect's sketchbooks with lists of L.B signs and their possible Etruscan parallels. Later that autumn, conscious of the approach of 1950 – the 50 year anniversary of Evans' discovery of the scripts – Ventris circulated a questionnaire to scholars all over Europe and the USA, aiming to collate their responses into a 'progress report' – later to become known as The Mid-Century Report *– on the current position with the Minoan scripts.*

The questionnaire contained 21 questions, most of which invited the kind of naive speculation Kober had firmly resisted in her own practice.

Question 1 alone must have exasperated her beyond measure.

'What kind of language is represented in the Linear B inscriptions and to what other known languages is it related?

Is the relationship close enough to be a positive help in decipherment?

Is the language European? If so – what is its position within the present classification of IE languages?'

In the event, Kober replied flatly, 'I have no intention of answering the questionnaire. In my opinion it represents a step in the wrong direction and is a complete waste of time.'

Emmett L. Bennett Jnr., whose work method, like Kober's, focussed on internal structural patterns, was less curt but no more encouraging.

'I find that there are very few questions I can answer. I have so far assigned no values at all to the signs of Linear B, or A, and therefore cannot speak of the language, or answer the questions that presuppose that something of the language has been detected.'

Bennett goes on to reiterate Kober's principles of investigating the frequency and combination of signs and the principles of their formation and function – a position echoed in Johannes Sundwall's response.

'The most important task for the present seems to me to be

that of using Miss Kober's classification lists to draw up surveys of the Knossos inventory records and of their contents.' *Like Kober, Sundwall was all too aware of the inadequacy of the material available for research and goes on to stress that* 'It is not sufficient for Myres to publish Evans' drawings of the texts: they must be accompanied by photographic reproductions which make it possible to check the accuracy of the transcriptions. Otherwise the whole work remains, to a greater or lesser extent, unreliable.'

Sundwall adds that he has not heard from Miss Kober for some time, and is afraid that she may not yet have recovered from her operation.

'One has come to place a reliance on her painstaking work with the texts, and she is perhaps more than anyone familiar with them and with the formulae peculiar to the lists.'

Undeterred, Ventris collated the responses (translating most of them himself) and circulated the resulting report – albeit glossing Kober's refusal to contribute by referring readers to her resounding article in AJA 1948, The Minoan Scripts: Fact and Theory. *Although in fact the responses to the survey show little consensus, the tone of Ventris' 20 page conclusion is stubbornly upbeat, and shows his ability to cling to improbable hypotheses, restating his belief that Linear B and A were related to the other Pelasgian dialiects of the Bronze Age mainland and islands – a non-Indo-European Aegean group of languages of which Etruscan and Lemnian were the only survivals. He signed off by offering his best wishes to all scholars, and his hopes that a satisfactory solution would soon be found, adding that he was forced by pressure of other work* 'to make this my last small contribution to the problem.' *With that, Ventris declared his intention to return full-time to architecture.*

Through the autumn and winter Kober doggedly continued to plough her own furrow. If she had scaled down her college work to some extent, she continued resolutely with her research. There were proofs to correct for Scripta Minoa II, *and since Myres was keen to prepare Evans' Linear A finds for publication – a project he and Kober already referred to as* Scripta Minoa III *– she also had to deal with the batches of Linear A texts which arrived through the post.*

Her correspondence with Myres over this period shows mounting irritation about his inaccuracies, and the complaints she had voiced earlier to Sundwall now burst out at Myres himself.

'I mailed the B proofs of pages 17-32 to you at the beginning of the week. It took me a week to go through them, and I am still far from satisfied. You still list as separate signs with separate numeration, signs that probably do not exist. At the same time, in too many cases to make for accuracy, you list different signs together, as though they were simple variants of one another.'

By February, Kober is scathing. 'As you see, the number of errors – both of omission and commission – is enormous.' *In what is more or less a footnote she explained that she had been forced to take sick leave until September, adding,* 'My doctors are not encouraging about an early recovery.'

It is perhaps a mercy that the doctors told neither Kober nor, apparently, her family, that her illness was terminal. By now unable to leave the house, she penned a note to Sundwall explaining that although she found writing very hard, she would do her best to 'answer anything to do with Minoan as soon as possible, but please excuse me if I am slow.'

In April, debilitated by pain, her frustration with Myres boiled over.

'Finally, I finished going over this last batch. What a mess! Frankly, if anyone but you had sent it to me, I'd have sent it right back – I never saw so many inexcusable errors, both in numerals, and, what is infinitely worse, in signs. You were once furious at me for saying you *confuse* certain signs – but you do, over and over again!'

Myres replied immediately by telegram, followed by a letter. On May 8th, a week before she died, Kober responded in a tone that was only partly placatory.

'Yes, I am in a bad temper. I'm in considerable pain, and am writing under difficulties. Forgive me if I am less than tactful.'

She did not retract her criticisms, however – gravely ill though she was, Kober was not one to back away from intellectual fisticuffs. She concludes, 'I apologise if anything I say is offensive. Forgive it and impute it to my health. The success of SM II and your reputation mean a great deal to me – I'm a terrific sentimentalist about people I admire and I cannot bear to have any imperfections that I can correct. You've put up with my bluntness so long now, perhaps you can condone it.'

Alice Kober died a week later, on May 17th, without ever having known just how ill she was.

It's not, of course, the end. Ingrid can no more let Alice rest in such a barren grave than consign herself to the same fate. There will have to be a conclusion, a definitive summing up of how much the Ventris decipherment, two years later, owed to her groundwork. The tone, too, is wrong: Kober's bitter frustration with Myres' failings makes grim reading. Not to mention the final image of the invalid in bed with her Linear B jigsaws, still struggling to fit together the right pieces, still hoping against hope to come up with the unassailable solution.

61

Elsa has dug out the family albums, which as far as Ingrid can see go back to the birth of photography – none, noticeably, from the Laurie side, but generations of stiff Stewarts and Hendersons, poker-faced in sepia, as well as other antecedents Elsa hasn't yet managed to identify. Greta needed visual stimuli, they'd decided, and here was a regular dynasty to hone her memory.

While Ingrid turns the pages Greta peers at the photographs, but listlessly, as if she can't really see the point but has decided to play along. 'Who's that, then?' says Ingrid, pointing, but her mother seems impatient with crofting great-grannies and fresh-faced soldiers off to Flanders Field. Only the colour photos engage her – specifically, those she appears in: a Silver Wedding portrait, Greta in navy-blue satin cleavage with pearls. And of course the luminous Corfu snaps.

'Don't I look young, though?' she says mournfully, to no one in particular.

Ingrid's wedding pictures perturb her. Her finger hovers over the three tier wedding-cake, the young couple with hands clasped together on the hilt of the knife. There's a model of the Parthenon on the top tier, made of white icing, someone's bright idea at the time.

'That's you, is it?'

Ingrid cringes at the big 80s hair and shoulderpads. 'Oh, indeed it is. Twenty-two going on fifty, if you ask me!' She's touched, suddenly, by the youth of the couple, by the unguarded happiness in Tim's smile. 'And there's your favourite man.'

'Tim?' Greta runs an experimental finger over his face, like an archaeologist brushing the dust of millenia off a Bronze Age coin. She nods, beaming. 'Aye, so it is!' After a moment her face crumples with confusion. She glances agitatedly around the room, casing every corner. 'But he didn't come with you?'

'He's busy, Mum.' Quickly Ingrid turns the page. If Greta has trouble recalling the marriage, why bother reminding her about the divorce?

Day by day Greta is losing weight, metamorphosing into a quick, aerial creature. She's become sparrowlike, her blue eyes beady with alarm. Every morning, arriving at the Home, Ingrid and Elsa smoke on the front steps, procrastinating. Neither saying a word but both asking themselves the same question: what state will she be in today? Sometimes she'll be scooting around the corridors with her wheelie, pursued by nurses: she's taken to darting into the rooms of other inmates and swearing blue murder when admonished. Soothed by stroking, she slumps in her chair, earthbound again, drops off with the smile still on her face.

When was the last time she saw her mother well? Spring, it must have been. Daffodils dotted the lawn, and the azaleas were coming into bloom in the borders. Just before she flew off to the States. She remembers having to explain to Greta why it was necessary to go all that way for the sake of some old papers.

Greta wasn't convinced. *Well I can't see what's so interesting about this Kober woman,* she retorted. *Why can't you write my biography?*

It's the randomness that alarms her, the sudden frights and furies. The symptoms spring out from an invisible core, like radio signals that prove the existence of some far-off planet. She keeps trying to make sense of them, when perhaps there's no sense to be made. Yet the effort feels oddly familiar, as though the script was written for her years ago, and all she has to do is reprise the role.

What were Greta's interests? the Activities Leader had inquired.

400

Ingrid racked her brains. 'Crosswords,' she said at last. 'She was always a dab hand at crosswords. Weren't you, Mum?'

Greta's nod was apathetic. Fingers laced together in her lap, she was literally twiddling her thumbs, as if waiting for the real action to begin. Ingrid was struggling. Greta needed something to occupy her, certainly, but the word *rehabilitation* implied that once upon a time there was something substantial which could now be rebuilt, and it was years, really, since she'd shown much interest in anything. 'She used to go to whist-drives. And I think she liked country dancing when she was young. Didn't you, mum?'

It didn't sound much to be going on with, like trying to rebuild a house out of spun sugar, but it was enough to bring a beam of enthusiasm to Kelly's face. 'We'll have to have a wee game of cards, then, won't we, Greta.'

Although the weight of fat on Kelly's hips and thighs rather belied her optimism, at least she was energetic, and keen to do good. For that she was more than thankful, if it brought pleasure or order into the toxic disorganisation of her mother's days.

Every afternoon before they left, she and Elsa left notes for the nurses on Greta's locker.

Greta would like her brassière on in the morning.

The silk scarf Greta likes seems to have vanished.

We have brought in 10 pairs of labelled jog-pants so far – where are they?

' "Care Home"!' Elsa snorted, 'Careless Home's more like it! One night in that place would drive anybody round the bend.'

Thanks to Elsa's insider knowledge of State bureaucracies, an appointment with the hot-shot geriatrician at the Perth Royal had been brought forward. Dr. Fitzwilliam was a stocky, jovial thirty-something, with thick thighs and a pronounced limp which he was quick to dismiss as the after-effects of a tackle in the weekend rugby match. His hair was straw-blond, his prominent blue eyes framed by pale eyelashes.

Lipsticked and ladylike in her wheelchair, Greta assessed him coolly. 'You are pretty,' she said at last, pronouncing each word with care.

The consultant's laugh boomed out. 'Looks like we'll have to send you for an eye test as well, Greta!' His accent was Anglo-Scots. A top-notch public school, Ingrid thought: Fettes, Invergordon. 'Eye for the chaps, has she?'

'You could say that,' Ingrid agreed ruefully. 'She always did prefer the men.'

Fitzwilliam pulled Greta's wheelchair towards his own chair, spreading his thighs so that his knees flanked hers. 'Now then, Greta. Can you say "British Constitution" for me?'

Pursing her lips, Greta spat it out in one breath. '*Brishconstitution*!'

'Excellent.' He pulled a fountain pen from his top pocket and held it up. 'Can you tell me what this is?' Ingrid tensed, willing her to pass the test.

'Pen,' Greta replied. Her bemused look said that only an idiot would ask such a question. Her eyes hadn't left Fitzilliam's face; she appeared to be quite at ease, fascinated, even, by his professional glamour. Ingrid watched in silence, envying his expertise.

Picking up a stethoscope, he dangled it in front of her. 'And what's this, Greta?'

For the first time Greta seemed uncertain. 'Now I should know that, shouldn't I?' Her eyes appealed to Ingrid. 'Scope? Telescope?'

'Nearly there,' Fitwilliam encouraged. 'It's a stethoscope.' Greta tsked at herself. 'Och, of course it is!'

'Righty ho,' he said cheerily. 'So let's see if you can recite the alphabet for me.'

Greta could, sailing all the way through to O, getting muddled on the PQR. Prompted, she picked it up again and finished off with a flourish on the Z.

Fitzwilliam clapped, and Ingrid joined in; even Elsa tilted her eyebrows, impressed. 'Has she been geting any speech therapy?'

'None at all,' said Ingrid.

Her enquiries at Buncranna house had been met with blank looks. She'd conducted her own experiments with Elsa's old scrabble game, sorting out 7 counters for Greta and 7 for herself, laying out the word STRONG in the centre of the board.

At first Greta had looked dully at the letters in her tray, as though she'd forgotten the rules. Leaning over, Ingrid saw an O and a T. 'You can have GOT, Mum!'

Her mother had hesitated, frowning down at her counters. 'Can't I have INGOT, though?'

When Ingrid told Fitwilliam he slapped his thighs and laughed with what seemed like genuine pleasure. 'Well, you'd beat me at it, Greta, that's for sure!'

She'd felt vindicated then: intermittent her speech might be, but surely this was proof not only that sound and script were a world apart, but also that Greta was a woman who certainly hadn't lost her marbles.

Delirium after stroke was the diagnosis – exacerbated, Fitzwilliam suspected, by a urinary infection. The dysphasia was already improving, he informed them, riffling through the heap of forms and photocopies on his desk – but it could take another month or so.

He signed referral forms in rapid succession, like a tennis star autographing Wimbledon programmes. CT scan, urine test, speech support, endoscopy. He shook hands with Ingrid and Elsa and then, ceremoniously, with Greta, and limped ahead of them to open the door.

'To be perfectly honest, I'm surprised they didn't have her in hospital straight away!'

*

The walls of the shed insulate her from outside noises: although she can see Elsa wheeling pots around in the enclosure, she can't hear a thing. Her eyes are gritty with weariness; her mind stots about like a cricket in a belljar.

403

Rotating her jaw to loosen the tension, she forces herself to check her emails.

There are two from Maxine, and one from the Institute, warning of predictable snarl-ups in next semester's teaching timetable. There's also a surprise update from Pamela D., who appears to have been soliciting information from far-flung cousins. None of the Gruber relatives has any recollection whatsoever of a break-up between Franz and Katarina. The consensus is that, at a time when millions were out of work, people took what employment they could get, and, as a janitor, Franz would have had to reside at the building where he worked.

Are they closing ranks, perhaps: protecting the family reputation?

About his downward trajectory, however, there's no doubt. Before he married, Pamela says, Franz was a seminarist, in training for the priesthood. Education, she stresses, was always a priority for the Kober family.

This, surely, is a crucial clue. Or rather *clew*. The failed ambitions of the father forcing the daughter to carry the torch.

The bad news comes at the end of the email. Even as a relative, Pamela will not be given access to the cause of death. The confidential medical report filed with the Department of Health is unobtainable information 'under almost any circumstances', and only half a dozen times in the last few years has the regulation been overturned. Pamela reiterates that, at the time of Alice's death, cancer was never mentioned as a cause, at least not to the children, who were told that her health gave out due to over-work, stress, and lack of proper food and heating on her visits to post-war England.

Pamela has done her best, and no more can be asked of her. So, short of lengthy court cases on the part of the family, that, presumably, is that. The bureaucracy of the State has slammed its doors, and the mystery will remain unsolved.

While she waits for Pamela's email to print she stares at the words on the screen, trying not to dwell on the fact that there's been no word from Yiannis.

404

Elsa's shed smells of new paint and wood-glue. Like Dr.Who's Tardis, the interior is far bigger than it appears from the outside. Apart from the work-station and photo-copier, there's room for a sink, a fridge, even a toilet hidden behind a door at the far end. Shelves groan with shiny trowels, Miracle Gro, and aphid sprays, and on a carousel hang packets which contain an entire A-Z of British flora, from Antirrhinum to Zinnia: Elsa's time capsule holds enough seeds to colonise several unsuspecting planets with the offshoots of Mother Earth. If they survived the journey, that is – hasn't she read somewhere that seeds don't germinate in zero gravity?

Why can't she just accept that limbo is where she lives right now; it's no kind of time to be making decisions? She can take only one thing at a time; see no farther than the next day, the next visit to Buncranna.

Like strangers who meet on a plane, they made no pro-mises. If she hasn't emailed him herself, mustn't that mean she has nothing of substance to say?

62

Between call-outs, Yiannis laboured on his deposition. Wiltraud and Manoli Dimeros were both in custody, awaiting trial; the Magistrate had not granted bail. Wolfgang, Margrit and the others continued to maintain that Kruja had left the commune two months before, while Prys had expounded so persuasively on the ethical disposal of mobile phones that the Magistrate, no doubt thoroughly bamboozled, had dismissed them on the basis that there were insufficient grounds to proceed.

To pass muster with the Public Prosecutor the police case would have to be unassailable; anything less would be shot down in flames before it even reached the court.

Elena Lambrou, aka the scourge of ELAS, was old school, and followed the constitutional principle of objectivity to the letter. Rumour had it that, after treatment for cancer, the Prosecutor wore an auburn wig which she had a habit of removing at odd moments, a gesture guaranteed to intimidate obstructive witnesses or stop logorrheaic lawyers in mid-flow.

Lambrou would see it as her duty to investigate the clues and circumstances that favoured the accused, as well as those that went against them: to ferret out the truth, rather than secure a conviction at all costs.

Although he doubted that even Lambrou would be able to shed light on Ivo Kruja's fate, he couldn't help wishing her luck. Perhaps Ingrid, so far, had come closest to the truth. Perhaps mere theorising wasn't enough for Kruja: he'd wanted to experience prehistory for himself, plug into its ecstatic practices. For all Yiannis knew, the kid had seen himself as an explorer of unknown spiritual galaxies, like some cosmonaut sacrificing himself for the advancement of science.

Not that any of this mattered now. The facts were what mattered, not the extrapolations from the facts, nor the wild and wishful speculations which bore more relation to the beehives skulking in his own brain than to any demonstrable reality – sworn statements, forensic evidence, the damning call made to Manoli's cellphone.

As if by some tacit agreement not to dwell on procedural failures, the dispiriting question of the still-unidentified DNA had been dropped. Which didn't mean it had escaped the notice of a press determined to undermine police credibility, and spurred on, as usual, by Hourdaki the gadfly, who made it her business to sting at every opportunity.

*

Crossing the dancefloor to the table where the others were already seated, Yiannis felt Aglaia's eyes burning into his back. Understandably, her greeting had been less cordial than usual – a cool nod from the kitchen doorway which he had answered in kind – but Aglaia Dimeros was a businesswoman first and foremost, and clearly wasn't about to risk a spat with a long-term customer.

Theo spotted him first and hailed him with a wave. Everyone except Irini stood up for handshakes and kisses, scattering napkins to the floor. A beribboned bouquet of roses and tall scented lilies lay on the tablecloth, but somehow he didn't think Aglaia would be bringing a vase to put it in.

As he embraced Tassos, whose domed forehead already bore the proud sheen of paternity, he saw with relief that the seat saved for him wasn't the one beside Dora's. Dora herself gave him a tight smile and an awkward peck on the cheek; she looked handsome, he thought, in something modest and midnight blue.

Ouzo was poured for him, and toasts drunk to the mother-to-be, who glowed decorously as she sipped her sparkling

407

mineral water. He looked round the table, wondering if they were all thinking what he was thinking: this would be the last year of carefree get-togethers, and from now on there would be buggies and curfews, and smoking bans, as the focus shifted – quite rightly, he reminded himself – to the next generation.

Theo slid a video cassette across the tablecloth. It was Pasolini's *Theorem*. Yiannis couldn't even remember lending it.

'Sorry, *pedi-mou*, must have had it for ages. Not my cup of tea, as they say.'

'Not even the bit where the maid levitates?' Yiannis shook his head reproachfully. 'You're a barbarian.'

Theo's eyes were on a young couple Aglaia was showing to the next table. The girl was bronzed and bosomy in a tight scarlet dress, while the boy wore faintly nautical white. Both had wraparound shades pasted to the tops of their heads, which meant they could only be Italians. As they took their seats Yiannis noticed the logo RICH embossed in brilliants on the stem of the boy's sunglasses. He also registered that the girl's cleavage was nothing short of spectacular.

With a furtive glance at Livia, Theo ran his tongue over his lips.

'*Malaka!*' Yiannis muttered, remembering, this time, to look hard at the deformed thumb.

Livia, luckily, was deep in baby-gossip with Irini and Dora. Beaming at them, Tassos cracked another pistachio nut with his thumbnail. He was building a small mountain of shells on the table.

Yiannis could see Theo was bursting to tell him something. 'What?' he demanded, praying to be spared yet more baby surprises.

'In confidence?'

'That depends, doesn't it,' Yiannis said sourly.

'Well, I don't want to blind you with science, but I will say it's had the backroom boys scratching their heads.'

Yiannis sighed. 'So go on, blind me.'

408

Theo's eyes darted at him. 'You know about mitochondrial DNA, right?'

'I know it's maternally inherited, that's about it.'

'Well, the cool thing is, you can use mtDNA to trace the human phylogenetic tree back in time, by how many mutations there are from the nucleotide bases in the standard CRS genome – that's the Cambridge Reference Sequence,' he added unhelpfully. 'Basically it's the genome of a British woman in the 1980s.'

'You don't say!' Yiannis said sarcastically.

Just then a youngish man with stringy, colourless hair materialised at his elbow. He laid a cheap-looking cigarette-lighter beside Yiannis's plate, and a card which explained in Greek, English and German that he was a deaf mute. Yiannis dug some coins out of his pocket, but waved away the shoddy lighter.

Theo had spread out a paper napkin and was scribbling a kind of upside-down tree on it. Yiannis saw that the branches were labelled with different letters.

'These are the Haplogroups, see? L for the original African group, then subdivisions down to H and V – the main European ones.'

'What kind of timescale are we talking here?' asked Yiannis, who personally didn't need fancy diagrams to trace Theo back to the ape.

'Oh, about 170,000 years.' Theo waved an airy hand. 'But what concerns us in this case are the most recent mutations, maybe 35,000 years ago.'

'Your point being?'

'My point being, it's no wonder you couldn't get a match with your lady communards! A match would be impossible with any modern genome.'

As if alerted by some marauding insect, a small legion of hairs stood to attention on the back of his neck. 'Come off it, Theo! That sample could have been degraded. Contaminated in some way.'

'Degraded at exactly these locations in the nucleotide base? Huge odds against, *pedi-mou*. Huge.'

'So what are you saying? That Kruja was fucking some antique corpse?'

Theo shook his head. His grin was triumphant. 'Think bodily fluids, Yianni! We're not talking archaeology here. It's causing quite a stir in boffin-land, believe you me. I predict a rash of scholarly papers by Christmas.' He sat back smugly, one hand smoothing the hairs that protruded at the open neck of his shirt. 'The original European genetic profile. Awesome, huh?'

Yiannis shivered, a phylogenetic tremor that started at the base of his spine, where knowledge lives before it collides with refusal. Across from him Theo's face was flushed with smiles, his mouth jabbering, but Yiannis heard nothing. He stared past Theo, past the fairy lights to the strings of stars above the black horizon of the sea. Knowing it couldn't be so, but still hypnotised by the image.

A youth divesting himself of his clothes, a youth who'd fasted for days before filling his belly with Christ knows what archaic hallucinogens. A youth who anointed himself with honey and released the bees from their jar. Offering himself up on a plate.

And what if She, the Someone, manifesting herself in some high and blinding way, had sampled him and found him wanting? Or perhaps the bees, snacking peaceably enough, at first, on the sticky glaze of honey, had detected his deceit and turned on him? The bees he'd written of as the final arbiters. Poor Kruja with his blind mimesis, trying to replicate some sacred marriage. Who'd failed the last test of the *eniautos*, who could never be the Prince he wanted to be.

Who was no match for her.

'Stop him, Yianni!' Livia leaned over abruptly and clamped her hand over Theo's, her beaded earrings dancing against the coppery skin of her neck. 'No more shop talk!' Her mother was Chilean, and Livia had inherited the severe profile and bitumen-black hair of the Aztec. Yiannis had always been convinced she disliked him, perhaps because the two vertical lines etched in the skin between her brows gave her a permanently disapproving look. 'Help us get the happy couple on their feet!' Although her tone was playful, there was no mistaking the commanding edge.

Egged on by Dora and Livia, a bashful Tassos rose and led Irini out on to the floor, where a few couples were already dancing.

Aretha Franklin's 'Natural Woman' floated from the PA system, a voice like the night itself breathing in and out. Broad-beamed and paunchy, Tassos was well on his way to male-pattern baldness; Irini was taller, delicate as a deer in a slim black shift dress with diagonal metallic threads. Arms round each other's necks, they began a slow, swaying shuffle.

As he watched, Yiannis felt a tightness in his chest. He was aware of the light falling on his sister's face, her secret, custodial smile. For a moment he was overwhelmed by a rush of protectiveness, and looked away quickly, feeling like a tresspasser. Was this brotherly love, or brotherly envy of the way her energies were realigning, focussing on the perfect mystery within?

Theo nudged him sharply in the ribs. Evidently he wasn't finished yet. When Yiannis ignored him he leaned in closer, breathing aniseed and smoke. 'But hey, it's pretty cool, isn't it? Mixing it with the Great Mother Goddess? Talk about literally going out with a Bang, eh!'

'*Ai gamisou!*' Rage seized him by the throat. Within an inch of thumping Theo, he jerked back angrily, clenching his fists by his sides. Nothing was sacred to Theo, not love or death, no mystery so tender that it couldn't be despoiled. Show Theo your heart and he'd only take a scalpel to it, just to see what it was made of. Speechless, he watched melting ice-cubes slither across the tablecloth. His recoil had knocked Theo's glass over, but he wasn't about to apologise. What he himself held sacred he couldn't have put into words, but what he did know was that there was a bottom line, and Theo had crossed it.

Out on the dancefloor the couple swung briefly apart as Tassos steered Irini into a lazy pirouette.

Dora and Livia were on their feet, clapping. As Yiannis rose to swell the applause, tears pricked violently at the corners of his eyes. While he wasn't even aware that he was thinking of her, the realisation leapt into his mind that he could not, would not, let Ingrid go.

63

Down on the Firth the sun is struggling to penetrate a fine sea-mist. Under the portico Elsa and Ingrid nip out their half-smoked cigarettes and drop them in the sand box. They're already late, after detouring by the coast road to pick up fish and chips for Greta's lunch. The food served in the Unit is unidentifiable even by smell – a green puree might be cabbage or stewed apple, a red one beetroot or tinned plums; a brown one could be minced beef, or equally chocolate mousse. No wonder poor Greta can't stomach it.

Dr. Fitzwilliam, as it turns out, was right about the urinary tract infection. Since starting on the antibiotics Greta seemed more like her old self. Her speech, generally, was clearer, whole sentences tripping off her tongue without a blunder. There were fewer frights, fewer excursions into the cobwebby realms of dream. She seemed aware, at least sporadically, of her surroundings.

Once, looking around the TV lounge, she'd said with resignation, 'This is my life now, isn't it. With the gaga girls.'

Ingrid knew she ought to see this clearsightedness as a step forward. On the other hand, given the conditions, who could swear that reality, or the facing of it, was an absolute good? Surely it made as much sense to take refuge in the consolations of magic, be the star of your own strange firmament?

As they turn down the corridor that leads to the lounge the salt and vinegar smell goes ahead of them. Although no one has mentioned a ban on takeaways, Ingrid feels shifty, like a smuggler concealing his contraband. It's almost noon: her mother will be ravenous by now.

After a concerted campaign she and Elsa have established the principle that Greta should be dressed and ready when they arrive. Sometimes she's even resplendent in makeup, depending on which Care Assistant is on shift. She'll be waiting in the lounge, prinked up for visitors, but her equanimity won't last for long.

Ahead she spots the hunched back of tortoise-man, scuttling along with his zimmer frame. 'He's doing well, isn't he,' she remarks, struggling to look on the bright side. 'Really getting those laps in!'

'Oh aye,' says Elsa, poker-faced, 'Shame he's got no head, eh?'

It's neither the time nor the place but the laughter is all the more explosive for that. Ingrid stops dead and sags against the wall. Tears stream from her eyes. The man with no head has vanished round the corner but the image remains. Elsa joins in, shaking her head, laughter wheezing in her chest. 'Och, that's better, though! I don't like to see you wearing yourself to a thread.'

At the far end of the lounge Greta is strapped into her wheelchair, on her lap a large yellow teddy-bear with a prize-winning red rosette pinned to its breast. *World's Best Mum,* the legend proclaims.

'Oh for God's sake!' Elsa hisses. 'Where did that come from?'

'Not from me!' says Ingrid, suppressing another burst of hysteria.

'Well I hardly thought so, pet!'

Watching them approach, Greta frowns suspiciously. 'What's so funny, eh?'

Ingrid leans over to kiss her. 'Nothing, Mum. Just a silly joke.' If her mother is aware of the teddy-bear she gives no sign of it.

One of the nurses puts her head round the office door, twitches a distracted smile at Ingrid and Elsa, and retreats inside. There are half a dozen other inmates parked in the lounge but none of them has visitors. Where are the other nurses, she wonders. Having coffee? Smoking on the patio? She imagines them in a cosy huddle, clock-watching, gossiping heartlessly about boyfriends and husbands, about the bustling off-duty lives they leave behind to put in their ill-paid hours.

The TV on the wall blasts out a Tom and Jerry cartoon but no one's laughing. All around the patients are fidgetting and whimpering in their seatbelts, without the words to communicate what they need. Out of sight, out of mind, when anyone with an ounce of empathy could see that a hug or a word would mean the world to them.

Unzipping her backpack, she wafts it under Greta's nose. 'Get a sniff of that, then!'

Greta's mouth forms an excited Ooh. She glances around with furtive triumph: nothing she likes better than to be one up on the others. When she grabs for the backpack Ingrid passes it over to Elsa

'It'll be quieter in the Conservatory, Mum.' Releasing the brake, she backs the wheelchair out of the carpeted area, away from the lost upturned faces, the eyes that beg for rescue.

*

She sits on the bottom step of the portico, taking deep draughts of the fresh damp air. Inside the Unit she breathes shallowly, open-mouthed, trying to block out the miasma of air freshener and its undertone of disastrous smells.

Elsa takes two cigarettes from her packet and passes one over. 'She'll have forgotten all about it by now,' she says, bending to light it for her.

The sea-fog hasn't dispersed, but thickened; the Firth has vanished, and the tree-fringed lawns languish under a bright shadowless mist. In the urn on the balustrade a cobweb glitters dewily among the geraniums. A spider hunkers at its centre, waiting for insect weather. She blows smoke at it, unconvinced. 'Will she?'

Elsa exhales with an angry sigh. 'Well, the fish and chips hit the spot, at least.'

They'd brought napkins and a plastic fork and knife but Greta dug straight in with her fingers and didn't raise her head until she'd finished. She allowed her chin to be cleaned up with a napkin, belched contentedly, and subsided into a doze.

Flanking her like sentinels, they'd mulled over her progress. Appetite was a good sign, they agreed; they'd even talked of taking her for a run down the coast, now she seemed a bit better.

False optimism. Why is it so impossible to accept that every improvement is quickly followed by a downturn? Because she so wants to prove she can haul her mother back to health, to convince herself that unstinting effort is as good as love – and, like it, can conquer all?

When Elsa went out to the patio to check on her rhododendron the noise of the sliding door had woken Greta. Within seconds, her vague, dazed gaze turned to one of unseeing fright. As if of their own accord her hands jerked up in front of her face, fingers steepling rigidly together, like the spire of a Presbyterian kirk. In the high, piping voice of a young girl, she began to recite the alphabet.

Grasping her hands, Ingrid tried to massage away the rictus, but Greta resisted, chanting her mantra even faster, as though it was her one defence against inexpressible terrors. Panicked, Ingrid called out for her aunt.

It was Elsa who read the situation. Gripping Greta by the shoulders, she said loudly, 'Have you got a pain, Greta?' Indigestion, she explained: she'd seen it happen before – although, admittedly, not accompanied by the alphabet. She slipped the tablet on to Greta's tongue like a professional, patted her back until at last she stilled and cried quietly, holding on to Ingrid's hand.

If she'd always dreaded the moment of parting, this time her mother's grief was unrestrained. Clinging to her hand, Greta refused to let go. She remembers the strength of her grip, the stickiness of the chip-grease on her fingers. The teddy-bear she'd exiled earlier smirking at her from the sofa. Greta begged, she demanded, her face red with uncomprehending fury.

The wail still rings in her ears. *Why can't you stay?*

Greta like a dark star, sucking her in. The memory fills her with a kind of nausea, as if something in her is still straining to make from this magma a locus of sleep, trust, love. She knew she couldn't leave, had neither an excuse to leave nor the words to make it. The alternative didn't bear thinking about: Greta rejected, Greta abandoned to the gaga girls.

If your mother's needs are indivisible from your own, how can you deny her?

Elsa had tried to tug her away. 'Just go!' she hissed. As if it was as easy as that. Finally she dashed out of the room and returned with Belinda. Ingrid remembers their scolding and jollying, Belinda's white teeth bared in a forbidding smile. The sight of the wheelchair whizzing away down the corridor.

A deer steps out of the forest and stands in an eerie mist-halo, like a messenger from another world. Foreleg poised, it scents at the air, and leaps marvellously, vanishing into the trees. Sweat itches at the roots of Ingrid's hair. The skin on her arms, sleeked by two weeks of sun oil, looks old as Greta's now, desiccated. She looks helplessly at Elsa. 'Nothing's ever enough, though, is it?'

Elsa taps ash into the sandbox with exaggerated care. 'What you've got to understand, pet, is that old people are very selfish.'

Ingrid feels as if she's been slapped. It's her mother they're talking about, not some wilful, manipulative child. How can Elsa be so callous?

'She's sick!' she protests. 'She's frightened.'

'I know that.' Elsa stabs her key fob at the car, which leaps to attention like a willing gun-dog. 'All I'm saying is, you've got your own life to think about, too.'

Only a few miles inland the sea-fog lifts, and heat shimmers up from the tarmac. Elsa is staring straight ahead, her eyes narrowed against the bright road or her cigarette smoke.

'No one's omnipotent, pet,' she says emphatically. 'You can only do your best.'

On the left hand side of the road a low safety barrier masks a steep drop to the valley below. She looks down at the wide loop of the river, where cattle stand thigh-deep in the shallows, cooling their heels. She remembers the dream of shadow-boxing, the amorphous, unbeatable opponent. What she can't explain to Elsa is that it isn't a question of choice, nor even of the noble virtues like like duty or devotion. Rather it's a feeling of chronic compression, as if something's out to remind her there's absolutely no point trying to wrestle with your own destiny.

64

Like those dreams you forget on waking, the unsolved cases are the ones that haunt you the longest.

After the inquest the body had been released for burial. Since there were no State funds available for repatriation, nor next-of-kin to request it, Kruja's remains would be interred in one of the few city cemeteries that made provision for foreigners. A funeral without family. It was as bad a thing as Yiannis could think of.

Which left him, however, with the problem of the personal effects – the books, the clothes, the thesis Ingrid thought might even be worth publishing. That the burden was self-imposed seemed irrelevant; what mattered more was the certainty that he wouldn't feel easy with his conscience if the boy's last vestiges ended up in the incinerator.

Did the Roma have libraries? Some central archive, perhaps, from which a rich culture might eventually burst forth?

His Internet search had drawn a blank, and while the Sokadre lawyer had subjected him to a tirade of details he'd rather not have known about – that the camp of 500 Roma at Dyo Aorika, for instance, consisted of shanty houses without water supply, electricity, sanitation, or garbage collection, and that although they were permanent residents, the local authorities had refused to register the inhabitants on the municipal lists – the man had been unable to provide him with an answer, and had finally – grudgingly, Yiannis thought – referred him to *Elpis*.

He copied the address and telephone number off the monitor screen. Apparently *Elpis*, which meant 'hope', was the title used by the Cultural Association of *Athinganoi* in the Heraklion prefecture. *Athinganoi,* according to the Sokadre man, was the preferred appellation these days – *tsinganoi* -gypsies – being considered derogatory.

Behind him Sotiris was lurking far too close for comfort. Proprioceptively speaking, the guy was definitely challenged. If there was a doorway, his shoulder would collide with the jamb; if there was a table, Sotiris would set his plate perilously on the edge. Passing him in the narrow corridor that led to the gents was positively hazardous. He'd often thought that if the world were recalibrated six inches to the left, Sotiris wouldn't have a problem.

Sotiris peered over his shoulder at the screen. 'It means 'untouchables' he said complacently. Eyeing the coffee Sotiris seemed to be about to set down in the gap between the desks, Yiannis put him straight. Actually it meant the opposite, he told him, relaying the lecture he'd had from the horse's mouth, as it were – 'Touch-me-nots'. The original *Athinganoi* were a heretical sect in 14th century Byzantium whose members shunned physical contact with outsiders for fear of defilement. If Yiannis hadn't quite seen the connection, he didn't feel like arguing with the expert.

65

Like a child, stretched out in the summer of a child, she lies face down under the globosa tree, bare limbs spreadeagled, daisies tickling at her nose. Gravity presses on her, gluing her to the grass. In her mind's eye she sees her cartoon silhouette like Tom's, flattened by the steamroller, thin as a slice of processed cheese.

Elsa and Alastair are in the shed; she can hear them through the open door, totalling up orders, their voices interspersed by the chattering of the keyboard. As soon as they've finished she'll get up and check her emails, access what Elsa calls *Her Own Life*. What Elsa really means by this is Yiannis, who has been mentioned, but only in passing.

Last night, as they kept company with Elsa's best Glen Farclas, she'd prodded, 'But you haven't been in touch?'

'No,' Ingrid said, for that much was true, even if part of her mind has been keeping a furtive tally, like a prisoner scratching off the days on a cell wall. She knows, for instance, that they've already been apart longer than they were together. A statistic that seems to underline the inevitable. That and the silence.

'Well that's a pity,' Elsa persisted, the empty whisky glass dangling from her fingers. 'I got the feeling he was a bit special.'

A few sandwiches short of a picnic, she thought. Clearly her aunt wasn't up to speed on current parlance.

'Aye, well,' Elsa said mournfully. Pouring them both another nip, she raised her glass. '*Here's tae us, wha's like us, gey few and they're a' deid!*'

There's no beating the Scots when it comes to looking on the dark side.

Two inches from her outstretched arm a black slug slides into view, harbinger of rain. She feels the vibration of Elsa's feet before she sees her. When she lifts her head her aunt is standing over her, holding out a tumbler which clinks with ice.

'Thought you'd be needing your aperitif by now. I certainly am.'

On the patio table pretzels and olives are already laid out, as well as the ashtray she brought Elsa from Provence years ago: a Ricard one, made of Bakelite. Retro yellow with red lettering.

'Alastair caught us some trout. I was thinking of doing them cold, with a green mayonnaise, if you fancy that?'

While no domestic goddess, Elsa is a more than capable cook She's been making it her business to tempt Ingrid's listless appetite with burly flavours: mackerel with gooseberries, smoked eel from the upmarket deli in the village, rabbit stuffed with anchovies and capers.

'We should eat outside, don't you think?' Elsa says, surveying the western sky. 'Could be the last fine night.' Waving away offers of help, she goes indoors to put the fish in the oven.

Sparrows are gathering more or less politely on the edge of the patio. Ingrid puts her feet up on a chair and gives in gracefully to the gin and tonic. The computer, she decides, can wait for another day. As can *Her Own Life*. She crushes a pretzel and distributes the crumbs equally, surrendering it to the sparrows.

When Elsa reappears she's wearing a striped apron over her Bermudas. Her glass has been topped up, and her face is sweaty from the oven.

'Have you been in yet to see my Hendersonii?'

For a moment Ingrid envies Elsa her obsessiveness. Obsessions are what keep you going as you get older. Golf or gun-dogs or rock-gardens, consuming interests to keep you company. Although Elsa's been experimenting for years – pottering, she calls it, for she's in it more for love than money – she hasn't yet produced what she would deem a worthy cultivar: a cross reliable enough to be registered and marketed.

Ingrid follows her past the large greenhouse to the low-span house at the back. Inside, opaque polythene sheets have been stapled to the sash-bars. The benches for seedlings and grafts are shrouded by overlapping plastic strips which look rather like shower-curtains; pressurised pipes with nozzles for misting the young plants have been bolted along the ceiling.

A worktop by the sink holds the wherewithal for alchemy: clippers and surgical scalpels, tape, sable brushes, paraffin wax.

By all accounts, usurping the bees' business is a hit-and-miss affair. Out of a series of hand pollinations, Elsa says, only one may produce a viable seed cone, and of five plants grown from that seed – which may take years to flower – three could be pink, one white, and one striated. Ingrid can't help feeling a certain satisfaction that Nature doesn't capitulate too easily.

Elsa has rolled up two of the plastic strips and attached them to hooks on the sash bars. The plants, segregated by year of planting, show various stages of development. Plastic tags list their parentage: *Campbellii x heptopata, Campbellii x acuminata*, and so on. Some of the larger plants are in flower, and have been given provisional names. A saucer-sized ice-pink bloom with a lavender rim is called *May Queen*; a smaller bloom with a magenta stripe is *Greta*.

Elsa touches *Greta*'s petals with a fingertip. 'She's quite promising, her. But there's many a slip between cup and lip, as they say. Likely I'll be long gone by the time this lot are established.'

Ingrid looks warily at her aunt. That pensive expression on her face spells trouble. 'Aye, acts of faith.' Elsa takes a gulp of her G&T, eyeing Ingrid over the glass. 'By the way, I've been meaning to ask you a favour, pet.'

Her response is automatic. 'Of course.' She wonders if Elsa is a little bit tipsy.

'It's all in the will, of course . . . but well . . . afterwards, if you'd just tip the, you know, doings, in among these wee lassies here, then I'd rest content.'

Although she knows perfectly well what Elsa means, Ingrid can't quite bring herself to say the word 'ashes'. Her first instinct is to tease her out of it. 'As in, pushing up the magnolias?'

Elsa manages a half-hearted grin. 'Aye, that's about the size of it'

Remorseful, Ingrid says of course she will. It's a small enough favour to ask, and if it comes to that, who else is Elsa to ask it of?

Nodding briskly, as if to say that's that done and dusted, Elsa turns her attention to the bud-scales on one of the grafts. The rootstock and the cutting, which Ingrid remembers is called the scion, are joined at a 45 degree angle, the joint spiral-bound and sealed with wax. Scion, she recalls, also means descendant, heir, or young member of a family.

Campbellii are a reliable understock. If *Hendersonii* ever move from myth to reality, they'll be glossy-leaved, May-flowering, hardy enough for the severest northern climes.

Elsa is pricking the bud-scales with a scalpel. Ingrid leans against the sink, arms folded, watching her. The air in the greenhouse is humid, infused with fertility. She has a sense of sap rising; all around her, cells are transpiring, leaves busying away at their photosynthesis. The peaty compost gives off a dark, encouraging smell. She thinks of Kruja's Osiris Beds, with their rich Nile silt, their tender shoots of barley.

As she watches Elsa reach up to unhook the polythene strips it strikes her that Alice the barren woman, Alice of the 'frigid logic' was nothing of the sort. For a startled, spacious moment she can see Alice as the seed. The *sperma*. Not dead at all, but generously sown, so that those who came after her could reap the crop: Michael Ventris and Emmett Bennett,

424

and the Cambridge philologist John Chadwick – *the sleuths*, as Ventris cosily referred to them.

Wishful thinking, unfortunately, isn't going to help her write her conclusion, but even if all belief is suspect – in that it isn't supported by reason, can neither be proved nor disproved – the relief of it weakens her knees and loosens the warmth of tears in her throat. It could, of course, be the effects of the gin. Soothing, psychotropic. Really she ought to sprinkle some on the *Hendersonii*, grace Elsa's wee lassies with a libation.

Lathes have been tacked to the bottom of the strips to make them hang properly. Her aunt has crouched down to settle the overlaps into place, and as she straightens up Ingrid notices how she braces her hands on her thighs to support herself.

Elsa is nothing if not gallant. She'd like to think that one day she'll turn out to be as courageous.

66

Kruja's belongings were stored in the basement at Dikeosinas Street. On his way to sign them out he saw Constable Nina beckoning him from her desk in the Co Ops room. She swallowed a mouthful of the sandwich she'd been eating and dabbed her mouth with a tissue. 'I'm not sure if it's important, sir, but something came through from Scotland Yard you might want to see?'

'Scotland Yard?' said Yiannis, mystified.

'The passport check?'

'Christ, they certainly took their time!'

Nina had printed out the report: a brief item, about a 5 year old case. He read the details with astonishment. Zoe Shapcott had had a twin sister, Miranda by name. On her way home from school the girl had been sexually assaulted, before being stabbed to death. The body had been found two months after her disappearance, in a copse by Regent's Canal. Since the perpetrator had never been found, the case remained open.

Thanking Nina, he grabbed a coffee from the machine and escaped outside for some air. He sat down on a stone bench in the yard behind the Station and smoked a cigarette in the shade of an acacia tree, inhaling deeply and sighing the smoke out.

Was it important? Chilled to the bone, he revised the question. Of course it was important. Just because it had no bearing on the Kruja case didn't mean it wasn't tragic, devastating. The kind of blow you'd never recover from.

Who could ever tell what forces were at work beneath the surface of apparently normal lives? The jealous vigilance he'd sensed in Mr. Shapcott, and judged so casually to be unhealthy, even incestuous, took on a different complexion now. He stared blankly at the shadows the leaves cast on his bare arms, wishing he could apologise to the guy, whose fate, he could see now, was to suffer not only that agonising failure to keep one daughter safe from harm, but also constant fear for the safety of the other.

*

By now the raging heat of August was thoroughly entrenched; only a sporadic breeze from the Aegean mitigated the desperate temperatures. Tarmac melted, figs and pomegranates fell from the trees and split open to reveal their glistening scarlet seeds. Dogs panted in the shade, and Kore mewed resentfully when served milk that had soured in the fridge. Tourists wilted, clubbers collapsed from dehydration, and elderly locals expired.

It was as well, he thought, that his mother's visit, first postponed, had been definitively cancelled: Aegina, for once, was a good few degrees cooler than Katomeli. Although he had postponed his summer leave, he was beginning to regret it. It was weather for early morning swims, long shady lunches, and even longer siestas, not for enforcing bylaws, recording lost passports, or collaring pickpockets.

Tassos and Irini had jetted off to the mountain freshness of Lake Maggiore – their final holiday *à deux* before the baby – and had sent him enviable texts, as well as a postcard of the snow-capped Matterhorn.

Even at nights the temperature remained in the high 30s, and Yiannis, unable to sleep, soaked a sheet in the shower, wrapped it round himself, and went back to bed. Imagining the steam rising from the conjunction of wet cotton and red-hot body. Towards dawn, in fitful sleep, he would dream wistfully of thunderstorms and rain-swept Scottish mountains.

One night when nothing worked he got up in the small hours, refreshed his sheet, and sat down at the computer. On Yahoo Maps he called up Tayside, and zoomed in on Calderbank. The Satellite Function showed a river, patchwork fields of grass-green and corn-yellow, and heathery-shaded uplands; here and there were small settlements he supposed were crofts. He zoomed in closer and peered at a cluster of buildings, some of which looked like glass-houses. He could make out a cottage, sheds, a sizeable area of land. For a moment he hovered on the airwaves, Zeus-like in his chiton, spying with his lammergeier's eye. Although the scene below was frozen in time, obsession convinced him that at any moment he might see movement in a doorway, the tiny foreshortened figure of Ingrid crossing the yard, shielding her eyes from the sun as she glanced up to check some altered aspect of the sky.

He clicked on Terrain, Hybrid, then back to Satellite, zooming till he could zoom no closer, telling himself he was simply getting acquainted with her territory. From the sofa Kore's gaze disagreed, reminding him that he was embarrassingly old for geekish electronic reveries, not to mention virtual courtship.

Zeus the Stalker. If she had voicemail he'd be hacking it.

Abruptly he quit the file and shut down the machine. Breathless with agitation, he went out on to the terrace, trailing his sheet behind him, and wandered up and down, synapses still firing away, the low moon tracking him through the lemon trees. Clearly it was no longer possible to do nothing.

It was then he had what could even be called a brainwave. The idea that came to his mind – a light, graceful, unthreatening idea – demanded immediate action. He couldn't run the risk of it fading away with the dawn.

It would have to be a simpler, older model. No fancy Blackberrys or iPhones. A basic Nokia, perhaps – a 6300 if they still made them.

On a wave of relief he surged indoors, threw the damp and sweaty sheet into the washing machine, and stepped into the shower. The hot water coursing down his back was comforting, and sluiced away his doubts. So what if he was shaved and dressed and breakfasted a good three hours before the shops opened?

67

After days of heavy heat the rain begins, slapping at the roof slates in the night, roaring down the overflow pipes from the gutters. Clouds slide down the heathered planes of the hills and roil whitely in the valley. A wind has got up, as if pummelled into motion by the force of the rain; in the bamboo-fenced enclosure, Alastair rushes to cover the more vulnerable shrubs with plastic sheeting.

Grumbling about her newly-washed French doors, Elsa shuts all the windows before they set out for Buncranna, lugging vanilla yoghurts, a blue angora bedjacket, and videos of *The King and I* and *Brief Encounter*. Although Elsa has suggested going in only every second day – (Why? To wean the mother off the daughter, or vice versa?) – Ingrid knows she couldn't face the guilt. In any case the worry of staying away would be far worse, she suspects, than the ordinary torments of being there.

Down at the coast the squalls have passed over, and intermittent sunbeams glitter on the wet fir trees of Buncranna. On the patio of the High Care Unit Elsa's rhododendron is flourishing. The mountainous Kelly, her hair in two long plaits which frame her earnest face, is sharing a bench with Donny the forester. Greta's wheelchair has been pulled up to face them; on her lap is a tray with a padded base, on which cards are laid out. The three of them appear to be playing some kind of game.

Donny half-rises to greet them, cigarette in hand and wheezing manfully, his weathered face wreathed in smiles. When Greta swivels her head to check out the vistors, he leans over and peeks at her hand.

'Oh you!' she scolds, and there's a hint of the old flirtatiousness in the playful biff she gives him.

From the beginning Ingrid has sensed his interest in her mother, and now she wonders if it might even be reciprocated. After all, Donny is really quite a good-looking guy – if, she fears, a dying one. When he isn't smoking on the patio, he's watching TV in his room; she has glimpsed him through the open door, flat out on the bed, plugged into his oxygen cylinder. But at least he's a man, and it has to be said that men are in short supply in Buncranna.

Greta looks neither pleased nor displeased to see them; her expression shows the mild surprise of one whose mind is thoroughly occupied elsewhere.

'She likes her cards,' Kelly announces with more than a hint of pride. 'Isn't that right, Greta?'

'Don't let us interrupt!' Ingrid says hastily, kissing Greta's cheek. She's nicely powdered and lipsticked, her new short hair fluffed up flatteringly above her forehead; the scarf at her neck has been fastened with her best Cairngorm brooch: silver filigree set with smoky amethysts. When Ingrid tells her how pretty she looks, Greta receives the compliment as no more than her due.

Perhaps Kelly sees it as part of her brief to foster romance – although it's hard to imagine what form that might take – sitting together at lunch, bitching about the multi-coloured purees? Hand-holding in front of B*rief Encounter?* For a second she wonders if there's a ban on locking your door to entertain your boyfriend. Then she realises: no such ban is necessary, because there are no locks. Privacy is the prerogative of the healthy, for obvious reasons. She can just imagine what the nurses would say about it: *Give them locks and they'll only go and die behind them.*

With a whoop of triumph, Donny slaps down the Ace of Spades. Well and truly trumped, Greta favours him with a ferocious scowl. Elsa rolls her eyes heavenwards, while the forester chuckles delightedly, the phlegm cataclysmic in his chest. Ingrid

431

feels like hugging him. Maybe she should bring a bottle of sherry in with her tomorrow, see if that helps things along.

*

'Postie's been,' Elsa announces, putting down her Sainsbury's bags and sorting through the pile of mail on the hallstand. She hands Ingrid a padded envelope. 'This one's for you.'

The stamps are definitely Greek. She weighs the package in her hand. She'd forgotten there were still places in the country where no one bothered to lock their doors.

Elsa is shaking her head over a newsletter from the local Ramblers. 'Would you credit it? Miss one meeting and they put you down to lead the Lairig Ghru. Do they think I'm Superwoman or something?'

Inside the envelope there's a small oblong plastic box, but no message. She prises it open and finds herself staring at a remarkably tiny mobile phone.

'Well it won't bite, dear. Why don't you turn it on?' Taking the phone from her, Elsa pokes at the keyboard, and a screen begins to glow. She hands it back with a straight face. 'Better leave it on, eh, in case you get a call?'

Elsa is no fool: she knows better than to ask who it's from. Ingrid leaves the cellphone on the kitchen counter while they unpack the shopping, keeping it in her sight-line. Putting off the moment when she'll have to get her glasses out and read the instructions.

Since the terrace is still awash, they'll eat indoors for once: although dusk hasn't even fallen yet, the damp has brought the midges out with a vengeance.

Elsa mixes pastry for an onion tart while Ingrid rinses beans in the colander, ready for stringing. The presence of the cellphone seems to alter the quality of the silence, stretching and thinning it. From time to time she risks a glance at the thing, just in case it springs a surprise on her.

'He's got an eye for our Greta, wouldn't you say?' Strewing flour across the oilcloth, Elsa thumps down the ball of pastry and sets about it with a rolling pin.

'I noticed!' Elsa doesn't have to name him: Ingrid knows exactly who she means.

'You know, pet, as far as I'm concerned you can stay as long as you like. But you heard what Fitzwilliam said. She could go on, well, for ages really.'

But Donny won't, she thinks.

Light-headed, she leans against the sink. Images of the tall, stooped forester merge with memories of Yiannis – his hair powdered grey with flour, his chest sunken and decrepit at first . . . and then straightening, growing tall like a tree, magically rejuvenated by the dance.

Outside the lawn is strewn with rain-bludgeoned white petals and the mist rising from the valley is tinged with pink. She remembers his long fingers, his scrutiny. That quake in the stomach when someone reads you like a book.

A light burring sound makes her spin round and stare. The phone is vibrating, crawling across the formica counter like some alien insect.

'What does that mean?'

'Oh bless!' sighs Elsa. 'Someone's texting you, dear.' Wiping floury hands on her apron, she picks the phone up and flips it open with a wry smile. 'And you're supposed to be the brainy one?'

Ingrid finds her glasses and puts them on. Even so, it's hard to make out the message on the screen.

Me poli agapi
Yiannis

Although the words are easy enough to translate their exact import eludes her.

With much love.

She stares at the keypad, at the inscrutable icons and arrows. 'What do I press for reply?'

68

On the day after Ivo Kruja's funeral Yiannis cleared his in-tray, said his yassous, and headed home. The interment, in a parched stony plot amid stringy oleanders – an area reserved for waifs and strays – was a bleak affair, attended only by the priest, Yiannis, and Prys, sweating in sandals and what looked like a charity-shop suit. Dust fine as ashes hung above the heaped soil by the grave, and the priest's eulogy was interrupted by bursts of coughing. Prys had acknowledged Yiannis with a nod, but thereafter ignored him. He offered no explanation for the absence of his co-communards, and Yiannis didn't ask for one.

After several phone calls, he had secured an agreement with a reluctant-sounding *Elpis* woman to deposit Kruja's boxes at their premises in the western suburbs of the city, traffic permitting. That should leave him just about enough time to drop the cat off and get back across town to the airport.

On the bed, beside a pile of folded clothes, his suitcase lay open, ancient airline labels still looped around the handle. Kore was sitting on the linen chest, her paws precisely aligned and her eyes fixed on the case. She knew something was up, but what she didn't know yet – he was waiting till the last minute to bring the cat-box out of the cupboard – was that she was going to be boarding with her Aunt Irini.

Once he'd changed out of his uniform he took his coffee out to the veranda, dialled Ingrid, and gabbled sweet nothings into the phone.

'Have you got your passport?' she asked, sounding even more nervous than he was, which instantly filled him with a kind of fatuous joy.

'Of course,' he said serenely, and remembered with a thrill of shock that he hadn't. It struck him then that he hadn't actually been out of the country for years. What if the damned thing had expired? He rang off and rushed from room to room, opening cupboards and rummaging through files. Finally he discovered it in the drawer of the old telephone table in the hall; with immense relief, he saw that it was still valid.

He rang back to reassure Ingrid, hustled the growling Kore into her box, and ferried his luggage out to the car. Even in the shade of the fig tree the air on his bare arms was like warm velvet, scented lazily with mimosa.

The sight of the shuttered house made him feel queasy. For a second he quailed at the thought that the whole love affair had been a particularly lengthy and vivid dream from which, in a few hours, he would wake and find himself impaled on the horns of reality. Light-headed, his pulse racing, he fumbled for his sunglasses and put them on. Blinkered, he felt safer, his compass set squarely on the future. It was a mistake to look back, he knew: the fates, pissed off, would always make you pay for it.

Throwing his case into the boot, he told himself, as he had once told Ingrid, that it wasn't so very far to go – not half as far, certainly, as Australia.

Out on the dual carriageway he put his foot down, ignoring the protests from the back seat. Just past the Amnisos turn-off roadworks signs had sprouted like mushrooms overnight; temporary traffic lights had been erected, but – no doubt by some eldritch trick of the Highways Department – men and machines were operating under a cloak of invisibility.

Although the road ahead was clear the lights stayed stolidly red. Yiannis sat there, seething. On the dashboard clock the sweaty seconds ticked by. As he watched an Olympic Airbus lumbering down from the blue Aegean sky, he realised that he'd forgotten to pack his raincoat.

435

69

What is invisible to men, is visible to the gods.

In her dream the classroom door has been wedged open and the blinds lowered to keep out the Cretan sun. Yiannis is wearing cowboy boots, tapping the blackboard with a long wooden pointer.

There are signs chalked on the board, Linear A signs, untranslateable.

Ja-sa-sa-ra, Yiannis recites, smiling expectantly, and her mind, spurred to work at scintillating speed, not only marries sound and script but solves, once and for all, the riddle of the unknown language.

At last the meaning is clear as day. Her eager hand is in the air, her face lit up by the answer.